THE BLACK RAVEN

Katharine Kerr was born in Ohio in 1944. Her fascination for all things Celtic and her extensive reading of mediaeval and Dark Ages history have all had a direct influence on the direction of her fantasy writing. Her novels have been published around the world and she is a bestseller on both sides of the Atlantic.

Also by Katharine Kerr

KATHARINE KERR

THE BLACK RAVEN

Book Two of the Dragon Mage

HARPER
Voyager

Voyager
An Imprint of HarperCollins*Publishers*,
77–85 Fulham Palace Road,
Hammersmith, London w6 8jb

www.voyager-books.com

This paperback edition 2000
8

First published in Great Britain by *Voyager* 1999

ISBN 13: 978-0-00-648260-4
ISBN 10: -0-00-648260-0

Typeset in Fairfield Light by
Palimpsest Book Production Limited,
Polmont, Stirlingshire

Printed and bound in Great Britain by
Clays Ltd, St Ives plc

For my grandmother,
Elsa Petersen Brahtin
1899–1985

The courage in her life amazed me

ACKNOWLEDGEMENTS

Many thanks again to Barbara Denz,
master of ferret lore.

A NOTE ON THE DEVERRY SEQUENCE

It occurs to me that readers might find it helpful to know something about the overall structure of the Deverry series. From the beginning of this rather large enterprise, I have had an actual ending in mind, a set of events that should wrap up all the books in dramatic conclusion. It's merely taken me much longer to get there than I ever thought it would.

If you think of Deverry as a stage play, the sets of books make up its acts. Act One consists of the Deverry books proper, that is, *Daggerspell*, *Darkspell*, *Dawnspell*, and *Dragonspell*. The 'Westlands' books, *A Time of Exile*, *A Time of Omens*, *A Time of War*, and *A Time of Justice*, make up Act Two, while Act Three will unfold in the current quintet, 'The Dragon Mage,' that is, *The Red Wyvern*, *The Black Raven*, the volume you now have in hand, and its 'sister', *The Fire Dragon*. *The Gold Falcon* and *The Silver Wyrm* will bring the sequence to its end at last.

As for the way that the series alternates between past and present lives, think of the structure of a line of Celtic interlace, some examples of which have decorated the various books in this set. Although each knot appears to be a separate figure, when you look closely you can see that they are actually formed from one continuous line. Similarly, this line weaves over and under itself to form the figures. A small section of line seems to run over or under another line to form a knot.

The past incarnations of the characters in this book and their present tense story really are one continuous line, but this line interweaves to form the individual volumes. Eventually – soon, I hope – the pattern will complete itself, and you will be able to see that the set of books forms a circle of knots.

Katharine Kerr

PROLOGUE

Winter, 1117
Bardek

Always the sorcerer must prepare for hindrances and set-backs. Before any working of great length and import, he must spend long nights in study of the omens, for if the Macrocosm can find a way to defeat him, it will, preferring in its laziness the natural order over any change wrought by our arts, no matter how greatly that change will be to its benefit.

The Pseudo-Iamblichus Scroll

'Marka, dearest?' Keeta said. 'I'm sorry. There's something wrong with him.'

Marka tried to answer, but her throat filled with tears. Her youngest son, not yet two years old, sat on a red and blue carpet in a patch of sunlight that spilled through the tent door. He was frowning at the edge of the brightness; over and over again he would reach out a pale brown hand and touch the shadow next to it, then draw his hand back and frown the harder. Tight brown curls hung over his forehead; now and then he would bat at them as if they bothered him, only to forget them again in an instant.

'He does know his name,' Marka said. 'He may not have any other words, but he does know his name.'

Keeta sighed and sat down next to the boy, who ignored her. They made an odd pair, Keeta so massive and dark, Zandro so slender and pale. Even though she had taken over the business end of managing their travelling show, Keeta still juggled, and her long arms sported muscles many a man had envied over the years. In her curly black hair, which she wore cropped close to her skull, grey sprouted at the temples.

'I've been afraid for months,' Marka said at last. 'He still can't use a spoon.'

'Is it that he can't use one?' Keeta held out her hand to Zandro. 'Or that he simply won't?'

Zandro whipped his head around and bit her on the thumb. Calmly, without speaking, Keeta put her other hand under his chin, spread her fingers and thumb, and pressed on both points of his jaw. With a squeal he opened his mouth and let her go.

'That's better,' Keeta said to him. 'No biting.'

His head tilted to one side, he considered her. She pointed to the teeth marks on her thumb.

'No! No biting!'

All at once he smiled and nodded.

'Very good,' Keeta said. 'You understood me.'

This he ignored; with a yawn he returned to his study of the edge between light and shadow.

'Ah ye gods!' Marka said. 'Just when I think it's hopeless, he'll do something like that. Understand a word, I mean, or even do something kind. When Kivva fell and cut herself yesterday? He came running and kissed her and tried to help.'

'I saw that, yes. At times he's really very sweet.'

Marka nodded. In the twenty years since her marriage, she'd borne nine pregnancies, not counting the miscarriages. Six of the children had lived past infancy – Kwinto, their first-born son; Tillya, the eldest daughter; Terrenz, born so soon after Tillya that they loved each other like twins; their sisters Kivva and Delya, named after Keeta's long-time companion, who had died in the same fever that had killed another infant son. Zandro would, she hoped, be the last. She wondered how she was going to find the love and strength to deal with him, who would demand more of both than all the rest of them put together. Keeta must have been thinking along the same lines.

'It's not like you don't have enough troubles on your mind already. What with Ebañy's' – a long pause – 'illness.'

'Oh, come right out and say it!' Marka snapped. 'He's gone mad. We all know it. And now his youngest son is obviously mad, too. Why are we all being so coy? How would Ebañy put it? He's demented, lunatic, deranged, insane –' Tears overwhelmed her.

Marka was aware of Keeta getting up, then kneeling again next to her. She turned into her friend's embrace and sobbed. Keeta stroked her hair with a huge hand.

'There, there, little one. We'll find a way to heal your husband yet. We'll be playing in Myleton next. They have physicians and priests and the gods only know who else, and one of them will know what to do.'

'Do you think so?' Marka raised a tear-stained face. 'Do you really think so?'

'I have to. And so do you.'

The tears stopped. Marka sat back on her heels and wiped her face on the sleeve of her tunic. A sudden thought turned her cold.

'Wait – where *is* Ebañy?' Marka scrambled to her feet. 'Here we are, on the coast, with the cliffs –'

'I'll stay here with the child.'

Marka ducked out of the tent, then stood blinking for a moment in the bright sunlight. Around her the camp spread out, a grand thing of white tents and painted wagons, the biggest travelling show that Bardek had ever seen. At the moment, however, the camp seemed curiously empty. Most of the performers had retired to their tents to sleep away the noon heat. Since she could see none of their animals, some of the men must have led them to the water trough by the public fountain, hidden from her sight by trees. Nowhere did Marka find Ebañy, but in the far view, at the edge of the caravanserai, between the palms and the plane trees, she could see the cliffs and distantly hear the sea, pounding on rocks below.

Marka trotted off, panting a little for breath in the hot sun. All those pregnancies had buried the slender girl acrobat somewhere deep inside a thick-waisted matron who had to bind up her heavy breasts for comfort's sake. At those moments when she had the leisure to remember her younger self, Marka hated what she had become. Especially when she looked at her husband – as she hurried along the cliffs, she saw him at last, strolling along and singing to himself a good safe distance back from the edge. Her relief mingled with anger, that he could still look so young and so handsome, with his pale blond hair and his pale grey eyes, his pinkish-white skin just glazed with tan and as smooth as a young lad's. When he saw her, he smiled and waved.

'There you are, my love,' he called out. 'Do you have need of me for something?'

'Oh, I was just wondering where you were.'

'Enjoying this glorious day under the dome of the sky. The sea's full of spirits, and so is the wind, and they're all enjoying it with me.'

'Ah. I see.'

Not of course that she did see the spirits teeming. He often spoke of spirits, as well as demons, portents, and visions, all of them invisible to everyone else. Still, she had to agree about the glory of this particular day, with the sea a winter-dark blue, scoured into white caps by the fresh wind.

'I've been thinking about the show,' Ebañy said. 'I want to add something new to my displays, in the parts with the coloured lights. I'm just not sure what yet.'

'It'll come to you. I have faith.'

'Well, so do I.'

They shared a smile. Hand in hand they walked back to the camp while he sang in the language of far-off Deverry.

'A love song,' he said abruptly. 'For you, my beautiful darling.'

And he did love her, of that she was sure. Never in their years together had he spurned her, never had he amused himself with the young women who performed in the troupe, not even once, no matter how old and thick and worn she'd become. For that alone she would always love him, even though at times, such as now, when he studied her face with a strange intensity, she wondered what he was seeing when he looked at her.

With a squeal of delight Zandro came trotting to meet them. Keeta strolled after, shaking her head, as if to say that he was beyond her control. It was one of the strangest things about the boy, that he could walk as well as a much older child, yet not be able to form a single word.

'Well!' Marka pointed them out. 'Look who's coming.'

'I see him, and a fine sight he is.'

When Marka said nothing, Ebañy paused to look at her.

'You're frowning,' he said. 'Why?'

'I'm just so worried about our Zan. He's just not right. We

can't go on hiding it from ourselves. I mean, he should be talking more, and then –'

'What? No, he's fine for what he is. He's a very young soul, just born for the first time. And he's not human, truly. You can see it in his aura.'

He bent down and scooped the boy up. Laughing, Zandro buried his face in his father's shoulder.

'What do you mean, aura?' Marka said.

'Look for yourself.' Ebañy waved his free hand around the boy's head. 'All the colours are wrong. What are you, my son? One of the Wildfolk, seeing what flesh feels like? Did you choose this, or did we trap you, my wife and I, when we were making a body for someone to wear?'

Marka felt her hands clenching into fists as if she could pummel his madness into silence. When Ebañy looked into Zandro's eyes, the boy stared steadily back.

'Not one of the Wildfolk,' Ebañy said at last. 'But some spirit whose time has come to be born. You've a lot to learn, my darling, but now the world is yours and all its marvels too.'

Carrying Zandro, Ebañy walked back toward their tent. Marka lingered, fighting back tears, until Keeta laid an enormous hand on her shoulder.

'I'm so sorry,' she murmured. 'It's so sad.'

'Yes.' Marka wiped her eyes on her sleeve. 'It came on so slowly, didn't it? I wonder now how long he's been this way, and I never would let myself notice.'

'None of us wanted to notice. Don't berate yourself.'

'Thank you. When he's not – well, when he's not saying peculiar things, I can pretend that we still have our wonderful life. But then he'll come out with something, like just now, and I don't know what to say.'

'There probably isn't anything to say. Ah well, we'll see what Myleton brings us.'

*   *   *

Wherever Ebañy walked, the Wildfolk went with him, sylph, sprite, and gnome, and in the water undines, rising up to beckon him into the waves. In the fires the salamanders played, rubbing their backs on the logs like cats, leaping up with the flames. At one time in his life he'd called himself Salamander, back in the land of his birth. That he did remember, though a great many other memories escaped him. The world teemed with visions that drove out the ordinary details, such as the names of the cities they visited and at times even the names of his wife and children. That they were his wife and children he never forgot.

At night when he slept, his dreams took him to strange worlds filled with stranger spirits. On purple seas he travelled in a barge while a sun of poison green hung at zenith. Enormous undines followed and held out long grey hands while they asked him questions in a language he'd never heard. Other nights he climbed mountains of crystal where the rivers ran with blood, or he would ride six-legged beasts like emerald insects across sand dunes to the ruins of cities.

Every dream ended the same way. He would reach his destination, whether a city of gold by a harbour or a cavern glittering with sapphires and emeralds, and walk into a building – a temple, perhaps, to unknown gods or a tavern filled with incense smoke and plangent music. The room would annoy him, and he would leave it, going from chamber to chamber or down long halls until at last he would see the door. It was always the same, this door, a solid thing of dark wood bound with iron. He would remember that in the room behind this door lay a magical book. If he could read that book, he would once again know who he was.

When he pushed on it, the door opened easily, but instead of a room, he would find himself in a large canvas tent, lying on a sleeping mat. Usually sunlight would glow through the walls, and he would see wealth around him: brightly-coloured tent bags and carpets, rolled mats, wooden stools, big pottery jars. Sometimes people with dark skins and black hair would be sitting nearby. He would find his clothes lying beside him on the floor cloth, and he would dress, looking round at the objects in the tent and trying to remember their names while the Wildfolk flocked around him or chased each other back and forth.

Some while later, he would realize that he was awake.

A city of trees and broad avenues, Myleton lay on the northern seacoast of Bardektinna, the biggest island in the vast and complex archipelago that Deverry men call Bardek, lumping all the islands together with a fine disregard for their inhabitants' politics and geography both. It was a rich city, too, where the public buildings gleamed with pale marble and the homes of the prosperous aped them with white stucco walls. Just to the south stood a public caravanserai with good deep wells and shade trees. After Keeta bargained with the archon's men – public servants in charge of the campground – the troupe pulled in and got itself settled. Since the rainy season had begun, they had the caravanserai to themselves.

'At least there won't be strangers,' Marka said. 'Sometimes when Ebañy's babbling, and there are strangers listening, I just want to die.'

'Now, now, little one,' Keeta said. 'It's no fault of yours, and who cares what strangers think? I'm more worried about the children, myself. Their father's madness – it can't be good for them to see him like this.'

'It's not, no. I try to talk with Kwinto, but he just shrugs me off. After all, he's almost a man now, he keeps things to himself. But Tillya – she's truly upset. She loves her father so much, and she's old enough to understand.'

Marka and Keeta were walking through the public bazaar, which, here in winter, stayed open through the midday. In the centre of the white plaza, public fountains gushed and glittered in the cool sunlight. Around them a sea of brightly-coloured sunshades rippled in the wind over the hundreds of booths. Close to the fountains lay luxury goods such as silver work and brass ware, oil lamps, silks, perfumes, jewellery, strangely shaped knives, and decorative leather work, while the practical vegetable and fish stands stood at the downwind edge of the market. Here and there a few performers struggled to get the crowd's attention – inept tumblers, a clumsy juggler, a pair of musicians who showed talent but needed practice.

'There's nothing here to compete with us,' Marka said. 'Good. And Myleton knows us. Everyone will come running to see us. Particularly Ebañy's act.'

'And so they should,' Keeta said. 'It's spectacular. I'm not prying into his trade secrets, mind, but you can't help wondering how he gets those effects. I've never seen him mixing chemicals or anything like that.'

'Do you want to know what's really strange? I don't know how he does it, either.'

'Really?' Keeta stared for a moment. 'Well, by the Wave Father! Your man's a tight-lipped fellow, that's for sure. I hope he's at least teaching Kwinto.'

'No, he's not. He keeps saying it's all real magic, just like they have in Deverry. There's a funny name for it. Dwimmer or something. But Ebañy said Kwinto doesn't have the talent for it. That's why we have him juggling instead.'

They walked a ways in silence, then paused by the fountains, where clean water bubbled up into white marble basins.

'I know it sounds like I've gone mad myself,' Marka said at last. 'Talking of magic, real magic I mean.'

'Well, yes, but what if it isn't mad? What if your husband's telling the plain and simple truth? They always say that studying sorcery drives men insane, don't they?'

'But it can't be true!'

'Why not? The sun rises and sets again on many a strange thing. If Ebañy says he calls fire out of the sky with magic – well, do we have a better explanation?'

Marka merely shook her head.

'I keep thinking about Jill,' Keeta went on. 'You remember her – she was travelling with Ebañy when we first met him, all

those years ago now, but I can still see her in my mind quite
clearly. A wandering scholar, she called herself. Huh. She was
a lot more impressive than that.'

'Well, that's true,' Marka said. 'And Ebañy was always trying
to get her approval for things, but he was afraid of her, too. I
never knew why. Ye gods, I was so young then! I don't suppose
I really cared.'

'Well yes, it was a long time ago, all right. My memory could
be playing tricks on me, but you know, looking back, I really
do wonder if Jill was a sorcerer, and if your husband knew a
great deal more about such things than we would ever have
believed.'

Marka could think of nothing to say. The idea made a certain
bitter sense.

'Ah well,' Keeta went on. 'After the show tonight, when we
know how much coin we have to spend, I'll come back into
town and start asking about the priests. If one of them can
drive out demons, everyone will know about it, and maybe it's
only a demon that's troubling Ebañy so.'

Since in winter the Bardekian days ended early and lacked a
proper twilight, the troupe of performers went into Myleton
well before sunset. At nightfall the western sea swallowed
the sun in one gulp to leave only a faint greenish glow at
the horizon. As oil lamps began to flicker into life in the
bazaar, the troupe set up for a show. Although they carried
a portable stage of planks in their caravan, Myleton supplied
– for a suitable bribe to the archon's men – a better stage than
that, the long marble terrace running alongside the Customs
House at the edge of the bazaar. While some of the acrobats
set up brass poles for the standing torches, the musicians, led
by Kwinto and Tillya, paraded through the crowd and cried
the show with a loud banging of drums. Below an audience
gathered, small at first, then suddenly swelling as the word
went round the bazaar: the Great Krysello is here! He's going

to perform! By the time the parade returned, there were too many spectators to count.

The Great Krysello, or Salamander, as Ebañy thought of himself, because on that particular night Salamander was the only name he could remember, waited in the darkness at the far side of the stage while the dancers performed, swirling with scarves to a flute and drum accompaniment. While he watched, he sang along to the music and laughed. Once he stepped onto the stage, he felt in command of himself again, sure of where he was and what exactly he should do there.

Many years ago he'd been a juggler, and juggler only, and to warm up the crowd he still tossed scarves and juggled eggs and such, talking and singing all the while. But somewhere along the years he'd discovered he could do much more to entertain. Or had he perhaps always known he could summon the Wildfolk of Fire and Aethyr to fill the sky with fire in lurid colours? Dimly he could remember being warned against such things. An old man had spoken to him harshly about it, once a long time ago. Somewhere in his mind, however, he also remembered that this fellow was no one. Since nothing was left of the memory but those words, 'he's no one,' Salamander could assume the memory image of a tall old man with ice-blue eyes and white hair was just another dream come to walk the day.

And on nights like this one, when he walked onto the stage and looked out at the dark swelling shape of the audience, a single animal it seemed, lying just beyond the glare of oil lamps and the torchlight, he forgot any strictures he might have once heard. When the crowd roared and clapped, he felt its love pour over him, and he laughed, throwing his arms into the air.

'Greetings!' he called out. 'The Great Krysello gives you his humble thanks!'

From his sleeves he flicked scarves and began to circle them from hand to hand, but always he was aware of the Wildfolk, sylphs and sprites, gnomes and salamanders, gathering on the stage, forming above the incense braziers, flocking around him and flitting this way and that, grinning and pointing at the crowd. In a flood of Elvish words he called out orders, and for the sheer love of play they obeyed him. Suddenly, far above the crowd, red and blue lightning crackled. With each boom of false thunder, sheets of colour fell and twisted in every rainbow the Wildfolk knew. The crowd roared its approval as the sheets broke into glowing drops and vanished just above their heads.

A green and purple mist burst into being around the stage, and deep within it voices sang alien songs. Once the crowd fell silent to listen, Salamander added explosions and bursts of gold and silver. Then back to the colours sheeting the sky – on and on he went until sweat soaked his costume and plastered his hair to his head. He let the colours fade and the music die away, then bowed deeply to the crowd.

'The Great Krysello is weary! But lo! we have other wonders to show you.'

At the signal Vinto's acrobats, all dressed in gaudy silks, rushed onto the stage. The crowd roared and threw coins in a copper and silver rain. As they tumbled around the stage, the acrobats scooped them up. Salamander stepped back to the shadows at the rear. While he mopped the sweat from his face and hair with a scarf, he looked out over the crowd.

One man caught his attention immediately, a tall fellow, standing right in front. His body seemed to waver like a reflection on moving water, and his clothes looked more like wisps of fog or smoke hung around him, or maybe just placed in his general vicinity, than solid cloth. Yet no one standing near him seemed to notice the least thing unusual. When the acrobats arranged themselves into a human pyramid, he clapped and smiled like anyone else. The flute and drums began their music; applause rippled, then died. The flickering stranger crossed his arms over his chest and stood reasonably still.

But always his eyes searched through the shadows. Salamander knew at once that the man – no, the being, some strange non-human thing – was looking for him. He could feel a gaze probing, feel alien sight run down his body like clammy hands. With a shriek lost in the music, he turned and leapt down from the stage, then took out running through the night. Down long streets he raced, panting for breath; in alleyways he stopped and looked around him. The door. He had to find the dark wood door bound in iron.

Past taverns, past craftsmen's shops he jogged, looking at each door, peering into shadows while cold sweat ran down his back and his chest ached – nowhere did he find it. He ran again, then slowed to a stumbling walk. Around him the city lay dark and silent. The night hung over the river, an oily rush of dark water against a darker sky. Salamander stopped, listening. Water slapped against wooden docks. Footsteps rustled on stone. With a roar to the Lords of Fire, he spun around and flung up both hands. A gust of silver flame towered up and lit the alley in a cold glare. Black shadow outlined every stone on wall and street and seemed to carve some incomprehensible meaning into them. Thieves shrieked and ran, dashing away down the alley – two small men, carrying knives. In the dying light from the silver flare he watched them till they skittered around a corner and disappeared. Salamander laughed, then headed to the river bank. He could follow it upstream to the caravanserai.

He arrived to find the troupe clustering around a fire and talking. Marka paced back and forth at the edge of the pool of light, and every now and then she raised her hands to her face as if she wept.

'Here!' Salamander called out. 'What's so wrong?'

The troupe froze, then burst out laughing and cheering all at once. Marka ran to him and flung her arms around him.

'My thanks to every god!' Her voice quavered on the edge of sobs. 'I was so worried.'

Salamander slipped his arms around her waist and held her while he murmured small soothing noises. At last her trembling quieted.

'Have I been gone so long?' he said.

'Well past the midnight bells, yes.' She looked up at him. 'Why did you run like that?'

'I don't remember.' He felt himself yawn and shook his head. 'I'm exhausted, my love. I've got to go lie down.'

That morning Marka gave up on sleep early. When the sun was rising in a pink blaze of distant fog, and the sea wind was making the tents flap and rustle, she put on a short dress and went outside, yawning and stretching in the cool air. As she glanced around, she saw a stranger, dressed in Bardekian tunic and sandals, leading his horse through the camp. He saw her, waved, and strolled over. His skin was as pale as Ebañy's, and his eyes a strange turquoise colour, as vivid as the stones, but since he wore a leather riding hat pulled down over his ears, she could see nothing of his hair.

'Good morning,' Marka said. 'Are you looking for someone?'

'Yes, actually. The magician who performed in the market place last night.'

'Indeed? Well, I happen to be his wife.'

'Ah. How do you do?' The stranger swept off his hat and bowed to her. 'I'm a friend of his father's.'

Marka stared like a rude child, then pulled her gaze away. His ears were impossibly long, impossibly furled, and pointed.

'Well, then, good sir.' She found her voice with a little gulp. 'You're certainly welcome in our humble camp.'

'Thank you. My name is Evandar.'

'My husband's still asleep.' Marka glanced back at the tent and saw the flap moving. 'Or no, here he is.'

Salamander stepped outside, saw Evandar, and screamed aloud.

'No, no, no!' Evandar said. 'I'm here to help you, truly I am. What's so wrong?'

'There's nothing to you,' Salamander said, and he was shaking so badly his hands knocked together. 'You're not really here.'

'Well, I'm here as much I can be anywhere.' Evandar looked down at himself and frowned. 'Everyone else always thinks I look solid enough. Your charming wife, for instance, didn't shriek at the sight of me.'

'Indeed?' Ebañy turned to her. 'What do you see, when you look at him?'

'Just a man like any other, as pale as you are, and so I guess he must be from your homeland. But I don't understand what you're saying. His ears are – well, forgive me, sir – but they're awfully strange, but otherwise, he looks ordinary enough.'

For a long moment Ebañy stood unspeaking, glancing back and forth between the two of them. Behind him Kivva, their second daughter, flung open the tent flap and stared out, a tall girl, dark like her mother, with tight black curls cut close to her head. Zandro wiggled out between his sister's legs, saw Evandar, and squealed one high-pitched note. He laughed, stuck out his tongue, then threw his head back and pranced around in a tight circle whilst waggling his fingers in Evandar's general direction. Everyone stared, speechless, until Marka found her voice.

'Zan! What are you doing? Stop that!' Marka stepped forward and grabbed. 'This man is our guest, and taunting him is very rude.'

Giggling, Zandro raced back into the tent. When Marka pointed, Kivva obligingly went in after him. Marka turned back to find Evandar considering her with a smile as sly as any merchant closing a deal.

'Please, let me apologize for my son,' Marka said.

'Oh, no apologies needed,' Evandar said. 'He must be an unusual child, yes? Difficult to handle, perhaps?'

'Well, yes.'

'I'm not surprised. He's not really human, you see.'

'That's what my husband says!' Marka turned to Ebañy. 'I don't understand any of this!'

'No doubt.' Evandar bowed to her. 'But I see this interests you. Perhaps we can discuss it?'

Ebañy merely glared at him, trembling on the edge of rage.
'The Guardians,' Evandar hissed. 'Does that name mean
anything to you?'

All at once Ebañy laughed, relaxed, and began speaking to
him in an incomprehensible language. For a moment Marka
felt like screaming herself, but the stranger seemed to understand the words; he answered in the same tongue. When she
started to ask them what it was, Ebañy silenced her with
a wave.

'I'm sorry, my love, and truly, I'm forgetting all my manners.'
Ebañy laid a soft hand on her arm. 'We have a guest, a stranger
in our camp!'

'So we do.' She saw her chance for escape and took it. 'We'll
all have a lovely breakfast. I'll go attend to it.'

'None for me!' Evandar broke in. 'I don't exactly eat, you
see.'

There seemed to be nothing to say to this announcement.
Marka hurried away, calling to her daughters to come help
with the meal.

Inside the tent Salamander offered his guest cushions, and they
sat across from each other on a flat-woven carpet of green and
blue. Kwinto, dark and graceful with his father's long fingers
and slight build, sat cross-legged on the floor cloth nearby.
When Salamander glanced his way he found the boy's face a
tightly-controlled mask.

'Did I ever tell you about the Guardians?' Salamander said.
Kwinto shook his head.

'They're a race of spirits, like the Elementals, but far far
more advanced and more powerful than that. This fellow,
sitting here? The man you see is just an illusion.'

'A bit more than that, please,' Evandar said. 'I don't know
what I make myself out of, exactly, but it suffices.' He picked
up a silk scarf, flicked it, then tossed it to Kwinto. 'Illusions
don't have hands that hold and touch.'

Kwinto smiled briefly, then ducked his head to study the scarf as if perhaps he could read the secrets of the universe from the pale gold silk. Marka and the girls came in, set down plates of bread and fruit, cups, and a pitcher of water laced with wine. When they started out, Salamander called Marka back but let the girls run off.

'Come sit with me, my love,' he said. 'I think this news concerns you, too.'

'Where's Zandro?' Marka said. 'I should go see –'

'Terrenz has him.' Kwinto spoke up, his boy's voice cracking. 'They went out the back when we came in.'

'Leave him be, my love,' Salamander said. 'Sit down.'

When he shoved a cushion her way she sank onto it. For a long moment an awkward silence held, as Evandar studied her and Kwinto both, but neither would look his way. Salamander poured himself a cup of water.

'I should tell you why I'm here,' Evandar said at last. 'Your father is worried about you. He wants you to come home.'

'My life lies here.'

'And it seems to be a busy one, I must say.' Evandar glanced around the tent. 'And prosperous. Your tents are much richer than your father's.'

'Bardek's a richer country than the Westlands.'

'Just so, but your father's getting on in years. He desperately wants to see you. He worries about you, too, off in this far country. And now I see that he has grandchildren, and here he doesn't even know it.'

At that Marka made a little whimpering sound, quickly stifled. Salamander glanced her way.

'If he dies without seeing you,' Marka started, then let her voice fade away.

'And then there's your brother.' Evandar leaned forward, smiling at Kwinto, to press his advantage. 'Did you know you have an uncle, boy? In far-off Deverry? His name is Rhodry Maelwaedd, and he's a great warrior, one that poets make songs about.'

Kwinto's eyes widened. Salamander held up a hand to keep him silent.

'My father's concern,' Salamander said, and he could hear the bitterness in his own voice, 'my father's concern comes a bit late. When I rode with him at home all he ever felt for me was contempt.'

His voice drained all the colour from the tent and the people in it. He saw them all turn grey and as stiff as those little drawings a scribe makes in the margins of a scroll. The wind lifted the tent flap, and Devaberiel walked in to stand with his thumbs hooked in his belt. Salamander got to his feet.

'What are you doing here?' he snapped. 'Evandar just said you were back in Deverry.'

His father ignored the question and stood looking around the tent with a little twisted smile. He was a handsome man, Devaberiel, in the elvish manner, with moon-beam pale hair, and tall, walking round with a warrior's swagger as he looked over the tent and its contents.

'You could at least talk to me!' Salamander took one step toward him.

Devaberiel yawned in complete indifference.

'Curse you!'

'Oh please!' Marka rose to her knees and grabbed the edge of his tunic. 'Ebañy, stop it! There's no one there!'

She was right. His father had disappeared. No – he'd never really been there, had he? Salamander turned toward Marka and found her weeping. He could think of nothing to say, nothing at all, but he sat down next to her and reached out a hand. She clasped it in both of hers while the tears ran down her face. In a rustle of wind the Wildfolk crept into the tent and stood round the edge like a circle of mourners. Am I dead then? he thought.

At the thought he felt his consciousness rise and drift free of his body. Although the light turned bluish and dim, he could see his body slump and fall forward, spilling plates and cups alike. He could also see that he now occupied a strange silver flame-like shape, joined to that body by a mist of silver cord. Marka clasped her hands to her mouth to stifle a scream; Kwinto leapt to his feet. Evandar got up more slowly.

'Follow the cord,' he said. 'Follow the cord back.'

With a rush of dizzy fall Salamander felt himself descend and slam back into the flesh so hard he groaned aloud. He lay on his back amid spilled food and stared at the peak of the tent's roof, which seemed to be slowly turning.

'This is terrible,' Evandar was saying. 'What's happened to him?'

'He's gone mad,' Marka said. 'It's been coming on for a long time, but now – it's – it's taken him over.'

Salamander watched the roof spin and tried to think. He could hear Marka and Evandar talking, but their words made no sense. Was he mad, then? Were the marvels he'd been seeing signs of madness and naught more?

'It's the curse,' he whispered. 'When Jill left us she cursed me. That much I can remember.'

Evandar dropped to one knee next to him and caught his hand.

'Try to remember. Why would Jill –'

'I don't know. Something about dweomer.'

The tent spun to match the roof and dropped him into darkness.

With Kwinto's help Marka got Ebañy settled, then left the boy there to watch his father and followed Evandar out of the tent. Sun and air had never seemed so wholesome, nor a breeze so clean. Together they walked to the edge of the caravanserai and stood in the shade of the rustling trees. Far below them on its rocks the ocean boomed and hissed.

'Good sir,' Marka said. 'You seem to know a lot about all these strange things. Is Jill really working a curse against my husband?'

'Hardly.' Evandar paused for a short bark of a laugh. 'She's dead.'

Marka felt hot blood rush into her face. She could think of no apology that would matter.

'I'm very very sorry to see your husband in this state,' Evandar said after a moment. 'I'll have to do something about this.'

'Can you help him? Oh, if you only could, I'd – well, I don't know how we'd repay you, but we do have coin.'

'Hush! No payment needed. I made his father a promise, and I intend to keep it. I can't cure your husband, no. But I might know someone who can.'

Marka wept in sheer relief.

'But it's not going to be such an easy thing,' Evandar went on. 'This person is far away in your husband's homeland. The kingdom of Deverry. Do you know about it?'

'Well, a little. It's supposed to be a horrible place where everyone's a barbarian, and all the men carry swords and get drunk and chop each other to pieces.'

'A slight exaggeration.' Evandar grinned at her. 'Be that as it may, Deverry's also a wretchedly long way away, across a mighty ocean and all that, and I'm not truly sure of how we'll get there, or if she – the person I'm thinking of – can truly heal him once we do.'

Hope sank and left her exhausted. She rubbed her face with both hands and tried to think.

'My apologies,' Evandar said. 'I wish I could offer you a certainty. Although, don't lose heart! If the person I'm thinking of can't help, there may be others.'

'If anyone could do something – I'm just so frightened.'

'No doubt. Well, I'll be off then to see what I can find.'

Evandar bowed to her, then turned and began to walk toward the cliff's edge. He stopped and glanced back.

'Take care of my horse, will you?' he called out. 'I won't be needing him.'

He walked two paces more, then set one foot on the air as if it were as solid as a step, hauled himself up, and disappeared.

PART ONE

Winter, 1117
Deverry

Kings in their arrogance say, 'We were born to rule any land we can conquer.' I say to you, 'The universe holds lands beyond our imagining and peoples beyond our conquering.' Be ye always mindful that your sight is short and the universe, long.

The Secret Book of Cadwallon the Druid

I n Dun Cengarn, up in the far northlands of Deverry, snow
lay thick on field and thatch. The lazy sun stayed above the
horizon a little longer each day, but still it seemed that the
servants had barely cleared away the midday meal before the
darkness closed in again. On these frozen days the life of the
dun moved into the great hall. Servants, the nobleborn, the men
of the warband, the dogs – they all clustered at one or the other
of the two enormous hearths. On the coldest days, when the
wind howled around the towers of the dun and banged at the
doors and gates, everyone stayed in bed as long as possible and
crawled back into their blankets again as soon as they could.

At night, up in her tower room, Dallandra and Rhodry
huddled together under all the blankets they owned between
them. They slept in their clothes for the warmth, then stayed
late a-bed as well.

'You're much nicer than a pair of dogs,' she remarked one
morning. 'Warmer, too.'

'I'm glad I please my lady,' Rhodry said, yawning. 'I was
thinking much the same about you, actually. And no fleas.'

She laughed and kissed him, then rested her head on his
chest with the blanket drawn up around her ears.

'Is it snowing out?' Rhodry said. 'With the leather over the
shutters, I can't tell.'

'How would I know? Dweomer doesn't let you see through
stone walls.'

'That's a cursed pity. I don't care enough to get up and see.
I –' He paused, listening. 'Someone's at the door?'

Dalla poked her head out of the blankets. Sure enough, she
could hear someone shuffling on the landing outside, with the
occasional deep sigh, as if whoever it was feared to knock.

'Who's there?' she called out.

'Jahdo, my lady.' The boy's voice sounded of tears. 'I were wondering if you or my lord should be needing somewhat.'

'Come in, lad. I think me you're the one who needs a bit of company.'

Bundled up in a cloak, Jahdo opened the door and slipped in, ducking his head and rubbing his eyes with the back of one hand.

'Sit down at the end of the bed,' Dallandra said. 'There's enough room to get most of you under the blankets.'

Jahdo did as he was told, sitting crosswise with the cloak around his back and the blankets over his legs. Dalla could see the streaks of tears down his dirty face.

'What's so wrong?' she said.

'I be bereft, my lady, a-missing my Mam and Da and my sister and my brother and all our weasels.' Jahdo paused for a moist gulp. 'There be a longing on my heart for home.'

'Well, I understand. I miss my homeland, too, and Evandar,' Dallandra said. 'My heart aches for you, but soon with the spring, we'll be riding west.'

'So I do hope.'

'Oh come now, lad,' Rhodry said. 'I made you a promise, didn't I?'

'You did, but so did Jill, and then she –' His voice cracked. 'And then she died.'

'True spoken, but I'm too daft and mean and ugly to die.' Rhodry sat up, grinning. 'At least when there's no war to ride, and truly, my lady Death seems to be spurning my suit even then. When Arzosah flies back to Cerr Cawnen, we'll be on our way. She knows the weather and the seasons better than any sage or bard.'

Jahdo nodded, considering this. Privately Dallandra wondered if they'd ever see the dragon again. Wyrmkind was not known for its faithfulness.

'It won't be so long till spring,' she said to the boy. 'We're well past the shortest day.'

'I know, my lady. And truly do I think I could wait with good

heart but for my worrying about my kin. My Mam, she be frail
in the winter, and then my sister, she were to be married, and
here I don't even know which man they picked for her.' Jahdo
paused and took a deep breath. 'Uh, my lady, I did wonder
somewhat, you see.'

'Could I scry your family out, you mean?'

'Just that.' He was looking at her with begging eyes.

'Jahdo, I'm so sorry, but I can't. I can only scry someone out
if I've seen them in the flesh first.'

'Oh.' He gulped back tears. 'Why?'

'It's just the way dweomer works. I don't truly know why.
I'm sorry. It's a hard thing to be missing your kin and have no
way to get news of them.'

'That be true, sure enough. At least Evandar comes and goes,
and you do see him now and again.' Jahdo paused to wipe his
eyes with the back of a grubby hand. 'I did wake so cold this
morning, and I did think on how warm it be at home.'

'Oh come now!' Dallandra said with a laugh. 'Cerr Cawnen's
a good bit farther north than we are. It must be even colder.'

'Ah, you know not about the lake. Our lake, it be warm, my
lady, even in winter. My Da did tell me once that way down
in the deeps of the lake lie springs, where water bubbles up
from the fire mountain, and it be as hot as you'd heat for a
bath, hotter even.'

'Fire mountain?' Rhodry said. 'Does your town lie near a fire
mountain?'

'Too near, some say. I mean, we sit not in its shadow, but
it be close enough. One of our gods does live in it, you see.
As long as we do honour him and bring him gifts, he'll not
harm us.'

Dallandra had grave doubts, but she saw no use in worrying
the lad when there was naught to be done about it.

'So,' she said instead. 'Your town stands on the shores of
this warm lake?'

'On them and in them, my lady. You'll see, or so I do hope.
But truly, I might not shiver so badly now if my kin were here

with me. Rori, and what of your kin? Never have I heard you speak of them, not once.'

'Probably you never will,' Rhodry said. 'I've no idea if they ride above the earth or under it, and I care even less.'

Jahdo stared open-mouthed.

'A silver dagger can't afford a warm heart,' Rhodry went on. 'Think on Yraen, as much a friend as I've ever had, and ye gods, I don't even know where he lies buried, do I? You learn, lad, after a while and all, to keep your heart shut as tight as a miser's moneybox.'

'Mayhap so,' Jahdo said. 'But never could I be a silver dagger.'

'Good,' Rhodry said, smiling. 'You're a lucky man, then. Although, truly, there's one kinsman I do wonder over, just at times, and that's my brother Salamander, as his name goes in this country.' He glanced at Dallandra. 'Did you ever meet him? In our father's country he's called Ebañy Salomanderiel tran Devaberiel.'

'I've not,' Dallandra said. 'Although Jill told me a lot about him. He seemed to irritate her beyond belief.'

'He takes some people that way. What's so wrong, Jahdo? You look like you've just heard one of Evandar's riddles.'

'That be the longest name that ever I've heard in my life,' Jahdo said. 'How do you remember such?'

'Practice.' Rhodry suddenly laughed. 'Let's get up, shall we? I'm hungry enough to eat a wolf, pelt and all.'

'So am I,' Dallandra said. 'And speaking of Evandar, I dreamt about him last night, and I have an errand to run.'

Since the presence of iron caused him agony, and the dun held an enormous amount of the stuff, Evandar had taken to finding Dallandra in the Gatelands of Sleep. They would then arrange a meeting somewhere free of the demon metal, as he called it. In the brief afternoon, when the air felt not warm but certainly less cold, Dalla wrapped herself in a heavy cloak and trudged through Cengarn to the market hill. At its crest the open commons lay thick with snow, crusted black with soot and ash from household fires. A group of children ran and played, their young voices sharp as the wind as they dug under the crust to find clean snow. Dallandra suppressed the urge to make a few snowballs herself and slogged across to a small copse of trees, where in the streaky shade of bare branches Evandar waited, wrapped in his blue cloak.

'There you are, my love,' he said.

'I am indeed,' Dallandra said. 'Now what's this urgent matter?'

'Rhodry's brother. Ebañy, as his name goes in Bardek.'

'How very odd! We were just speaking of him, Rhodry and I.'

'Not odd at all. You were feeling his approach, my love, through the mists of the future.'

'His approach?'

'That's what I've come to ask you about. You see, he's gone quite mad, and I don't have the slightest idea of what to do about it.'

'Ah. And I suppose you think I do.'

'Don't you?'

Dalla considered for a long moment.

'Perhaps,' she said at last. 'I'm remembering some of the things Jill told me about him. He had a great talent for dweomer, so she said. He studied it for many years, but then he just walked away from it.'

'Will that drive someone mad?'

'Indeed it will. You can't just stop your studies once you've reached a certain point.'

'Imph.' Evandar rubbed his chin with one hand. 'This world of yours, my love. Everything here seems so – so wretchedly irrevocable.'

'Not exactly.' Dallandra paused for a laugh. 'He could have left the dweomer, certainly, if he'd wished. But he needed to go back to his teacher and have her help him. How to explain this – let me think – well, I can't, really, but there are rituals that seal things off properly, that stop certain processes which studying dweomer starts in motion.'

Evandar blinked rapidly several times.

'Oh well,' Dallandra went on. 'It doesn't particularly matter. I suppose you want me to try to cure Ebañy for you.'

'Not so much for me, but for his own self and his father. You see, I promised Devaberiel that I'd bring his son home. And so I went looking for him in Bardek, and I found him quite deranged. His wife's frantic about it.'

'He has a wife, then.'

'And children. A lot of children, actually. I didn't get a chance to count them.'

'Well, you can't just snatch him away from his family.'

'Here's a great marvel. I realized that all on my own.' Evandar smiled and leaned over to kiss her. 'So I thought I'd bring them all over.'

'Over where?' Dallandra grabbed his shoulders and pushed him to arm's length. 'And when? There's not enough food in the dun for everyone who's already in it. You'll have to wait until the first harvest – early summer, that will be.'

'Well, then, you see? It's a grand thing that I thought to consult with you first. Especially since there's also the little matter of his travelling show.'

'Travelling show?'

'His eldest son juggles. His eldest daughter and her brother walk the slack wire.' Evandar held up one hand and began counting things off on his fingers. 'Then he's got friends who are jugglers and acrobats. Rather a lot of those, actually. Some lasses rescued from slavery who dance with scarves. Servants. Horse handlers, and of course, the horses and wagons. And then –'

'That's quite enough.'

'And then,' Evandar went inexorably on, 'the elephant.'

Dallandra goggled at him.

'An elephant, my love,' Evandar said, grinning, 'is an enormous beast. Not quite so big as a dragon, but large enough. It has a thick grey hide, a pair of huge ears, and then a long nose that acts like a hand. It picks things up.'

'I don't care about its nose. You can't bring it here.'

'I did come to that conclusion.' He went on grinning. 'So where, my love, shall I bring it and all the rest of them?'

'I haven't the slightest idea. Let me think on it.' Dallandra paused for a sigh that came out more like a growl. 'I'm beginning to understand why the very mention of Salamander made Jill furious.'

'Indeed? Here, Salamander claims that Jill cursed him when they parted, but frankly, I can't believe it of her.'

'No more can I. How very very odd! I'll ask Rhodry what he thinks.'

'Do that, if you'd be so kind.' Evandar frowned down at the filthy snow. 'And now I'd best be off again. I've a great many concerns these days, and they seem to have got themselves all tangled in my mind.'

From Cengarn Evandar took to the mothers of all roads. It seemed to him that he walked on the north wind like a long grey path in the sky. When he travelled between worlds, he heard now and again scattered words and snatches of conversations, and at other times he saw visions in brief glimpses, as if he looked through windows into the future, a vast shadowed room. Today, however, the omens shunned him. The silence irked; he found himself pausing to listen, but all he ever heard was the whistle and churn of the air, and all he saw were clouds.

When he left the north wind's road, he found himself at the edge of the forest that marked the border of his own true country. Instead of crossing it, he turned to his right and found a path that led into a scatter of boulders. As he strode along, the air grew colder; suddenly the sky turned grey, and snow fell in a scatter of flakes. It seemed that he was walking downhill; below him in the sunset light Loc Vaedd gleamed, a green jewel set in snow. Evandar took another step and found himself standing on Citadel's peak among the wind-twisted trees, the highest point of Cerr Cawnen, a city of circles. In the middle stood the rocky peak of Citadel Island. Around it stretched the blue-green lake, fed by hot springs and thus free of ice even in the dead of winter. At the edge of the lake on crannogs and shore stood the tangled houses of the city proper, while around them ran a huge circle of stone walls, where the town militia guarded shut gates. Just the summer before, Cerr Cawnen had received a warning that the savage Horsekin tribes of the far north were on the move, and such warnings were best attended to.

In fact, even though the town drowsed in blessed ignorance, a human being lived among them who spied for the Horsekin. Some twenty feet below Evandar's perch, on the east side of Citadel's peak a tunnel mouth gaped among tumbled chunks of stone and broken masonry. It led to an ancient temple, cracked and half-buried by an earthquake a long while previous. Evandar started to go down, but he saw the spy – Raena, her name was – climbing up the path from the town below. He stepped back into the trees to avoid her. Even though she was young and pretty in a fleshy sort of way, she walked bent over like an old woman as she struggled up the slope in her long cloak. When at the tunnel mouth she paused to pull her dark hair back from her face, Evandar could see the livid marks like bruises under her eyes and the pallor of her skin. Quite possibly Shaetano was using her as wood to fuel his fires even as she thought she was using him to serve her Horsekin masters.

Raena climbed down into the tunnel. Evandar waited a long moment, then shrank his form and turned himself into a large black dog. His nails clicked on stone as he followed her in. After a few yards the tunnel turned dark enough to hide him, but ahead, through the big split in the wall that formed the entrance to the temple room, he could see the silver glow of Raena's dweomer light. He stopped to one side of the narrow entrance and listened, head cocked to one side, ears pricked, long tongue lolling. At first he heard nothing but Raena's voice, chanting in a long wail and rise; then Shaetano joined her, speaking in the dialect of the Rhiddaer.

'What would you have of me, O my priestess?'

'To worship thee, Lord Havoc, O great one, and beg for knowledge.'

Evandar growled, then let himself expand until he could take back his normal elven form.

'All my knowledge shall be yours,' Shaetano was saying. 'What wouldst thou learn?'

'One riddle does make my heart burn within me. Where does she dwell now, my Alshandra? Why will she not come to me again? Why has she deserted me, my own true goddess, she whom I worship above all other gods?'

'Ah, this be a matter most recondite and admirable. Far far beyond what you would call the world does she dwell, in an ineffable refulgence.'

Evandar stepped through the opening. Dressed all in black, one arm raised in a dramatic flourish, Shaetano stood before a kneeling Raena.

'You might at least speak clearly,' Evandar remarked. 'How is the poor woman supposed to understand nonsense like that?'

Raena screamed. Shaetano's form wavered, as if he were about to step onto a Mother-road and disappear, then held steady as he held his ground. Evandar turned to Raena with a sigh.

'She never was a goddess, woman!' Evandar snapped. 'And now she's dead. You were there, you saw her die.'

'I saw naught of the sort!' Raena scrambled to her feet. 'She did but return to her own country. And she be a goddess. I do ken this deep in my heart, you stinking blasphemer! And she lives, I do ken that she lives still. Who are you, that lies like maggots fall from your lips?'

'I am Lord Harmony,' Evandar said to her. 'And your Lord Havoc is my brother. Flee this place! Leave us!'

Raena hesitated. Evandar raised a hand and called down the blue etheric fire, leaping and flashing at his fingertips. Raena squealed, then edged past him to squeeze through the entrance. He could hear her footsteps as she dashed down the tunnel. When he turned back, Shaetano was leaning insolently against the wall, arms crossed over his chest. In the shifting silver light he looked very like a fox in man's clothing. Russet hair sprouted from his face; his ears stood up sharply on the top of his head; his nose was black and shiny. Only his eyes were fully elven, a shifting gold and green.

'More and more you become your avatar, brother,' Evandar said.

Shaetano swore. For a moment his image wavered; when it stabilized, his ears had migrated back to the sides of his head, and his skin was smooth, with only a roach of red hair pluming on his skull. His shiny black nose, however, seemed permanently fox, twitching a little in the cold damp air.

'That's better,' Evandar said. 'Now then, I want a word with you. Though I'll admit to being surprised you'll stay and listen to it.'

'You can't kill me. Don't you remember what you said, that day upon the battle plain? You and I were born joined. You were the candle flame and I the shadow it cast? Well, elder brother,' Shaetano paused for a smile, 'if you kill me, who knows what will happen to you?'

'Here! How do you know that? I was talking with Dalla, and you were long gone by then.'

'I have my ways.' He curled a hand that was more like a paw and smiled at his black claws. 'And my allies.'

'Ah, I see. Your little raven was spying even then, was she? Very well. Say it I did. You learn your lessons well.'

'And haven't you been my most excellent teacher?' Again that smug smile. 'So talk away. What is it that you want with me now? I'll listen, though I may not answer.'

Evandar restrained the impulse to strangle him there and then, even if his own neck twisted.

'Ask I shall,' Evandar said aloud. 'What are you doing to this woman, pretending to be a god and filling her head with portentous words?'

'Doing to her? She's grateful. She begs me for knowledge.'

'And did she beg you to kill young Demet the weaver's son?'

Shaetano winced and looked down at the floor.

'I didn't mean to do that. Truly! He came bursting in here with a sword in his hand and iron cloth all over his chest. It stung me like fire. I was half-mad from it.'

'And you did what?'

'I just wanted to make him go away.' Shaetano's voice slipped and wavered. 'I shoved him, and the iron stung me, and so I threw him back against the wall.' He looked up, and his eyes gleamed green in the silver witch-light. 'I didn't know how hard. His head – it hit the stone.'

'Why wasn't there a mark on him then, where his skull got smashed?'

Caught in his lie Shaetano snarled and flung up both hands. Evandar crossed his arms over his chest and merely looked at him. In a moment Shaetano looked down.

'I don't know how I killed him. I did somewhat, I waved my hands at him because of the stinking iron. And rage flew out, and somehow his life – it spilled away.'

'What did this rage look like?'

'Naught. I mean, it wasn't a thing you could see. But he screamed and flung himself back and – and died.'

'You truly don't know what killed him?'

'I don't.' Shaetano looked up, and suddenly he snarled again. 'Oh, and what's it to you?'

'My heart aches for his young widow. Little Niffa. She mourns him every day still.'

Shaetano stared at him, his mouth half-open. White fangs gleamed.

'What's this, younger brother?' Evandar said with a grin. 'I see the word grief means naught to you. Let me tell you an interesting thing. I now know a great many things that you don't. I learn more daily, and soon one of them will be how I may dispose of you.'

With one last snarl, Shaetano vanished. Evandar stood in the empty temple and laughed.

*   *   *

Councilman Verrarc was sitting at a table in his great room when Raena came home. As a merchant's son, Verrarc had learned to read, but books to practise upon, as opposed to merchants' agreements and city laws, were scarce in Cerr Cawnen. He still read slowly, sounding words out one at a time, pausing often to look terms up in the home-made word list at his elbow. He was glad enough to lay his scroll aside at the distraction when, shivering in her thick green cloak, Raena hurried in. Without a word to him she rushed to the fire burning in the hearth and held her hands out to the warmth.

'What be wrong, my sweet?' he said.

'Naught.' Raena busied herself in taking off the cloak.

'Somewhat did turn you all pale and shivering.'

'It be cold out there, Verro.'

'Not as cold as all that.'

With a toss of her long black hair, Raena turned her back on him. She hung the cloak on a peg on the wall, then walked over to look at his work.

'What be those squiggly things?' she said.

'Words.' He paused, smiling at her. 'Here, look! To read these out, you do start here at the top on the right, and you do read straight across. At the end of the row you do drop down and read back the other way.'

'Ah.' She nodded as if in understanding, but he knew that she could read none of it. 'What does that scroll be saying, then?'

'I'll not tell you unless you do tell me where you've been this long while.'

'Oh, be not a beast, Verro!'

Verrarc shoved his chair back and stood up.

'Rae, it be time we had a talk. I do be sick to my heart of all your secrets. You do come and go at whim and never will you tell me where you've been.'

'Oh here, you don't think I have another man or suchlike, do you?' Raena laughed, and easily. 'I do swear to you, my love, that such be not true.'

'I believe you, but your secrets still vex me. How can I but wonder where you go?'

Raena considered him for a moment, then shrugged.

'To the temple in the ruins,' she said. 'I do go there to summon Lord Havoc.'

'Ah. So I thought. The fox spirit.'

'He be more than that. He does ken lore that I would have.'

When Verrarc said nothing, Raena sat down in a cushioned chair in front of the fire.

'Well,' she said, 'and what about your half of our bargain? What be this thing you read?'

'Some small part of a book of the witch lore.'

At that she twisted round in her chair to look up at him. Smiling, he rolled up the scroll and tied it with a thong.

'What sort of lore?' Raena said at last.

'Tell me what sort of lore you do seek from your Lord Havoc, and I'll tell you what this be.'

'I be not so curious as all that.' She turned back round to face the fire.

With a sigh that was near a snarl, Verrarc sat down in the matching chair opposite hers. For a long moment the only sound in the room was the roar and crackle of the fire.

'Soon, my love.' Raena spoke abruptly. 'Soon, I promise you, you shall hear the secret I do guard so carefully. It be a grand thing, I promise you, with naught of harm in it. But there be one last thing that escapes me, and it truly is needful for me to learn it before I may speak.'

'Well and good, then. But I'll hold you to that "soon", Rae, I truly will.'

'Fair enough. Tell me somewhat, if you can. What does this word mean: refulgence, I think it were?'

'I've not the slightest idea.'

'I were afraid of that. And if you ken it not, I doubt me if anyone in this town does. A nuisance, but not more.' She turned to him and gave him a slow, soft smile that warmed him more than the fire. 'It be a good day to spend a-bed, my love.'

'Just so.'

Verrarc rose, caught her hand, and as she got up pulled her into his arms. She kissed him, let him take another, and giggled like a lass as she squirmed free. As he followed her, he knocked against the little table and swept the scroll to the floor. With a soft curse he stooped and retrieved it, dusting a bit of soot from the roll.

'That be a valuable thing?' Raena remarked.

'It is. I did pick it up in trade, this summer past. It has no proper beginning nor an end, so I do think it were torn apart some while past, but still, the man who owned it did drive a hard bargain.'

'You did find it in a border village or suchlike?'

'I didn't, but in a dwarven holt. It be about the telling of omens in the signs of Earth.'

Raena tossed up her head and took a quick step back. Verrarc laid the scroll onto the table.

'What be so wrong?' he said.

'Oh, naught, naught.' Yet she laid a hand on her throat, and her face had turned a bit pale. 'I did forget that you trade among the Mountain Folk.'

'Every summer, truly.' Verrarc caught her hand and drew her close. 'You look frightened.'

'Be not so foolish!' Raena laughed, but it was forced. 'Come, my love, kiss me.'

It was an order he followed gladly, but later, when he had time to think, he wondered why she'd looked so afraid of his going among the Mountain People. Was there something there she didn't want him to find? Or could it be that she'd sheltered among them during one of her strange disappearances? Her secrets again, her cursed wretched secrets!

All his life Verrarc had craved the witch-knowledge and magical power. When he thought back, it seemed to him that he'd always known that such things existed, even though logically there was no way he could have known. As a child, he'd sought out the tales told in the market place or in the ancient songs, passed down from one scop to another, that told of sorcery and the strange powers of the witch road. When, as an older boy, he'd travelled with his father to Dwarveholt, he'd heard more and learned more in the strange little human villages on the borders of that country. Here and there he asked questions; once he grew into a man, he'd been given a few cautious answers.

The men of Dwarveholt proper professed to know nothing about such things, but the odd folk in the villages always had some tale or bit of lore to pass on. Finally his persistence brought success. On one journey a half-human trader had offered him a leather-bound book, written in the language of the Slavers. It was old, very old, or so the trader said, written by a priest named Cadwallon when the Slavers had first invaded the western lands. The price was steep, the writing faded and hard on the eyes – he'd paid over the jewels demanded without hesitating.

Together he and Raena had studied that book. He would read a passage aloud; they would puzzle over it until they forced some sense out of the lines. Both of them showed a gift for the witch road, as Rhiddaer folk called the dweomer, and together they learned a few tricks and a fair bit of lore. The marriage her parents arranged for her had interrupted them – for a while. On the pretext of visiting her husband, Chief Speaker in the town of Penli, he'd ridden her way often and spent time with her, until their studies revived their love-affair one drowsy summer afternoon. Her husband had discovered the truth and cast her out, setting her free to disappear from the Rhiddaer for two years.

Where had she gone? Verrarc could only wonder. She had never told him. Now and then she would visit him, turning up suddenly from nowhere, it seemed, as on that morning when he'd ensorcelled young Jahdo. She would drop a few hints about strange gods and stranger magicks, then be off once more. Certainly she'd learned more about witchery than he had thought possible. But this knowledge she refused to share.

In the middle of the night Verrarc woke to find Raena gone. On the hearthstone a candle stood burning in a punched tin lantern. He lay awake in their bed, watching the candle-thrown shadows dance on the ceiling. She had gone back to the temple, he supposed, and left the candle burning against her return. She might take all night for her scrying, but try as he might, he could not fall asleep with her gone. Although he tried to convince himself that he worried about her, he knew that in truth he was jealous.

Verrarc got up and dressed. From the stub of the dying candle he lit a fresh taper and placed it in the lantern. Just what was she doing with that Lord Havoc? If he wasn't truly a god, and Verrarc tended to believe his brother, Lord Harmony, on that point, then he was some sort of powerful spirit, and everyone knew that spirits took a fancy to flesh and blood women on occasion. The thought made Verrarc's fists clench. He grabbed the lantern and left the house by the back door.

Outside, the winter night lay damp around him. One of his watchdogs roused in its kennel, but he whispered, 'Good dog, Grey, good dog,' and the big hound lay back down. He unlatched the gate and left the courtyard, then turned uphill. By lantern light he picked his way across snow-slick cobblestones till he reached the frozen path that led to the ruined temple, directly above his compound on the east side of Citadel. Where the path levelled out, he paused in the shelter of a pair of huge boulders. If Raena should be leaving and see his light, she would throw a raging fit that he'd come spying on her. Let her! He walked on.

At the entrance to the tunnel he hesitated. Although he could hear nothing, he could see a faint silver glow down at the far end. She was working witchery, all right, and hiding it from him yet again. With a soft curse under his breath, he climbed through the narrow entrance. On the packed dry earth inside, his leather boots made no sound. Slowly, a few steps at a time, stopping often to listen, Verrarc crept toward the silver glow, which spilled out of the door to the inner chamber. Although he considered blowing out the candle, he had no way of lighting it again. He set the lantern down and edged forward until he could peer round the broken doorway into the chamber.

Naked to the cold Raena was kneeling on the cold dirt floor and staring at a pool of silver light that seemed to drip from the stone wall like water. All at once she flung her head back and began to chant in some language that he didn't know. She raised her arms and let her body sway back and forth as her voice sobbed and growled in a long sprung melody. Despite the cold she was sweating; he could see her face glistening in the silver light. Her black hair hung in thick damp strands like snakes. Even though he couldn't understand her words, he could recognize her tone of voice. She was begging someone or something; now and again she wailed on the edge of tears as if she keened at a wake.

The silver glare filled the corners of the chamber with night-dark shadows, and as Raena's swaying body blocked the light, her own shadow swayed and flickered on the far wall. Out of the corner of his eye Verrarc saw creatures standing in the dark, small things, half-human and half-beast, all blurred and faint as if they were but shadows themselves. One stepped far enough forward that he saw it clearly: the body of a wizened old woman, all bone and flabby skin, topped with the head of a drooling hound. It knelt down beside Raena's piled clothing and fingered the edge of her cloak while it watched Raena sway and sob. Involuntarily Verrarc shuddered in disgust. It looked up, saw him, and disappeared. Locked in her chant, Raena never noticed either of them.

Slowly, silently, Verrarc made his way out of the ruins. The air outside had never smelled so sweet, despite its biting cold, and he realized that he had felt close to vomiting, watching Raena plead with her spirits. For some while he stood among the tangled blocks of stone and looked down at the mists rising from the warm lake. Why was he waiting for her, he wondered? She would find her own way home easily enough. With a shrug he picked his way back to the path. By the time he got back to the house, he was tired enough to go back to bed, and this time he slept through till morning.

When he woke, Raena lay next to him, curled up on her side and breathing softly. Around the shutters a gleam of grey light announced dawn. In her sleep she smiled, a curve of her mouth that seemed to hint of secrets. He left their bed without waking her, and when some while later she joined him for breakfast, he said nothing about the night just past.

Dressed in green she sat down across from him at the little table near the fire. For a while they ate porridge in silence.

'My love?' Raena said at last. 'Is it that you must be about council business this afternoon?'

'It's not, truly, unless some sort of messenger does come from the Chief Speaker.'

'That gladdens my heart.'

'Indeed? Why?'

She shrugged, ate a few more mouthfuls, then laid her spoon down in the bowl.

'I did wish to walk about the town, tis all,' Raena said, 'and I fear to do it alone. The citizens, they do stare at me so, and I know they do whisper about me, too, behind my back.'

'Well, curse them all! One day soon, Rae, I do promise you, you'll be my wife, and none will dare say one word.'

'But till then –'

'True spoken. It would do me good to get out of this house, too. We'll have our stroll.'

In winter air Loc Vaedd steamed. From Citadel, the town below round its shore lay hidden in white mists. On the public plaza that graced the peak of the island, the cobbles lay slick and treacherous. Bundled in their winter cloaks, Verrarc and Raena walked slowly, side by side. In the brief daylight a number of other people were about, mostly servants of the wealthy and important souls who lived on Citadel. Some hurried past with buckets of water, drawn from the public well across from the Council House; others had been down in town, judging from the market baskets and bundles they carried.

About halfway through their slow circuit, however, they met Chief Speaker Admi, waddling along wrapped in a streaky scarlet cloak much like Verrarc's own – a mark of their position on the town council. Admi bobbed his head in Raena's direction with a pleasant enough smile, but when he spoke, he spoke only to Verrarc.

'And a good morrow to you, Councilman,' Admi said. 'There be luck upon me this morn, to meet up with you like this.'

'Indeed?' Verrarc said. 'Here, if you wish to speak with me, you be most welcome at my house.'

'Ah well, my thanks, but truly, just a word with you will do. I did speak last night with some of the townsfolk, and they be sore afraid still, due to young Demet's death. I did wonder if you might have some new understanding of the matter?'

'Not yet, truly.' Verrarc licked nervous lips. 'I did talk most carefully with Sergeant Gart and the men who were on watch that night. Many a time have I returned to the ruins where he were slain, as well, but never have I found a trace that might lead us to his killer. To hear the men talk, Demet had not an enemy in the world, much less in the town. Truly, I do wonder if the townsfolk have the truth of it, when they whisper of evil spirits.'

Admi shuddered, drawing his cloak tighter around his enormous belly. Still, Verrarc was aware of how shrewdly Admi studied him behind this little gesture of fear. Verrarc glanced away, but he made sure he didn't look at Raena.

'Tomorrow,' Admi said finally, 'I think me we should call a meeting of the council. Tomorrow, say?'

'Uh well, I'll not be ready by then. The day after?'

'Very well. When the sun's at its highest. There's a need on the full five of us to go over this matter and see what may be done to lay it to rest.'

'Well and good, then. Shall I go round to the others and tell them about the meeting?'

'Oh, I be out for a stroll alone, and it be no trouble for me to stop by their houses.' Admi patted his belly. 'My wife, she does say I grow too stout, and so she does turn me out into the cold like a horse into pasture to trot some of the flesh away.'

Admi laughed, but Verrarc found merriment beyond him. Raena stood watching the pair of them with eyes that revealed nothing. Admi nodded her way with another smile.

'My farewell to you both,' Admi said. 'I'll be off, then.'

For a moment they stood watching him waddle across the plaza, stepping carefully on the slick cobblestones. He turned down the narrow path that led to the western flank of Citadel, where the temple of the local gods and the cottage belonging to Werda, the town's Spirit Talker, stood close together.

'My curse upon him!' Raena snarled. 'Will no one in this stinking town even speak my name?'

'Here, he did give you a greeting of a sort. Some weeks past he'd not have done that much. Patience, my love.'

Raena tossed her head in such anger that the hood of her cloak fell back. With a muffled oath she pulled it back up again.

'Patience!' she snarled. 'I be sick of that as well.'

'Well, no doubt, and I can't hold it to your blame. I did speak with some of the townswomen and did ask them to intercede for us with the Spirit Talker. If only she'd bless our marriage –'

Raena jerked her head around and spat on the cobbles. Two of the passing servants stopped to consider her, and Verrarc could see the twist of contempt on their faces.

'Shall we go home?' Verrarc grabbed Raena's arm through the muffling cloak.

'I'd rather not!' She pulled away and strode off fast across the plaza, though in but a few steps she nearly slipped. With another curse she slowed down to let Verrarc catch up with her. When he touched her arm she turned and suddenly smiled at him.

'My apologies, my love,' she said. 'It does gripe my heart, is all, to see your fellow citizens look down long noses at me.'

'It does gripe mine, too.'

They walked on, past the stone council house that graced the side of the plaza opposite the temple. At the stone well Verrarc paused. Wrapped in her shabby cloak Dera was hauling up a bucket of water. He'd not heard that she'd mended from her latest bout of winter rheum, and her face seemed thinner than ever, framed by wisps of grey hair.

'Here!' Verrarc called out. 'Let me take that for you.'

He hurried over, leaving Raena to follow after, and grabbed the heavy bucket's handle in both hands. Dera let it go with a sigh of thanks. Her face was pale, as well as thin, and scored with deep wrinkles across her cheeks.

'You'll not be carrying such when I'm about,' Verrarc said, smiling. 'I do ken that Kiel be on watch, but surely your man or your daughter could have fetched this.'

'Lael be off setting traps in the granary.' Dera's voice rasped, all parched. 'And Niffa? Well, the poor little thing be wrapped in her grief. Sometimes she does stay abed all through the daylight, only to sit up weeping in the night.'

'Ai!' Verrarc shook his head and sighed. 'That be a sad thing, truly, and her so young.'

'It is. Well, good morrow, Mistress Raena! Taking a bit of air with your man?'

'I am indeed.' Raena had come up beside him. 'And a good morrow to you, Mistress Dera.' She smiled, nearly radiant. 'It does gladden my heart to see you well.'

'My thanks,' Dera said. 'But I'd best not stay out in this cold, alas.'

'Indeed you shouldn't,' Verrarc said. 'I'll just be carrying this down for you.'

'I'll be going back home, then.' Raena glanced his way. 'This winter air, it does cut like ice. But Mistress Dera, might I come pay a call on your daughter? Mayhap I could help cheer her.'

'Why, now, that would be most kind of you!'

Dera smiled, Raena smiled, but Verrarc found himself suddenly wondering if Raena would harm the lass. His fear shamed him; it seemed such a foreign thought, dropped into his mind by some other person or perhaps even a spirit. He carried the water bucket down the twisting path to Dera's rooms behind the public granary and saw her safely inside, then hurried back to the house. By then the sun hung close to the horizon, and the winter night loomed.

When he came in, Raena was sitting in her chair near the roaring fire. He hung his cloak on the peg next to hers and joined her, stretching out grateful hands to the warmth.

'Dera, she be a decent soul indeed,' Raena said.

'She is,' Verrarc said, 'and I trust you'll remember how highly I honour her and hers. No harm to her kin, Rae. I mean it.'

'Of course not! What do you think I might do?'

'I did wonder why you showed such interest in Niffa, naught more.'

They considered each other, and once again Verrarc felt his old suspicion rise. Had Raena somehow murdered Niffa's husband? She'd been worshipping her wretched Lord Havoc in the ruins when Demet had been slain, after all. Don't be a fool, he told himself. How could she possible have harmed a strong young lad such as he? Lord Havoc, now – him he could believe a murderer.

'Oh come now, Verro.' Raena lowered her voice. 'Remember you not the omen I did see, that Niffa does have the gifts of the witch road? Twere a grand thing if I did enlist her in our studies.'

'Ah. True spoken.'

Yet the fear returned from its hiding place, somewhere deep in his mind beyond his rational understanding. He felt as if he were remembering some incident, some time when she'd done something to earn this distrust, but no matter how hard he tried, the memory stayed stubbornly beyond his conscious mind.

*   *   *

A bowl of dried apples preserved in honey made a generous gift, here in winter when food was scarce, but Niffa felt like knocking it out of Raena's hands. Dera, however, smiled as she took it from their guest. She set it on the table, then bent her knees in an awkward curtsey.

'This be so generous of you, Mistress Raena,' Dera said. 'It will do my poor raw throat good.'

If it doesn't poison you, Niffa thought. She wanted to snatch the bowl and hurl it to the floor so badly that her hands shook. She clasped them tightly behind her and wondered if she were going daft, to believe that Verrarc's woman meant them harm, when she knew with equal certainty that the councilman would never allow anyone to injure Dera.

'My poor child!' Raena said. 'You do look so wan. You'd best sit down and close to your hearth too.'

Niffa managed to mumble a pleasantry and sat on the floor, leaving their only chair for the visitor and the bench for her mother. Raena sat down, opened her cloak, and pulled it back, but she left it draped over her shoulders to ward off the chill. Around her neck hung a silver pomander; she raised it to her nose and breathed deeply.

'I do apologize,' Dera said. 'The ferrets, they have a strong stench about them in winter. It be too cold, you see, to risk giving them a good wash.'

'Ah well, I mean not to be rude.' Raena sounded a bit faint. She raised the pomander again.

'It be kind of you to visit the likes of us,' Dera said. 'It be a long while since we've had a treat such as this.'

'Most welcome, I'm sure. Verrarc did think the honey might ease your throat.'

There, you see? Niffa told herself. If Verrarc sent it, then it must be harmless.

'It might at that,' Dera said. 'The herbwoman did suggest the same, but my man couldn't find any honey to be had in town, not for trade or coin.'

'Ah, then it be a good thing that we did have some laid by.'

Raena glanced at Niffa and gave her a sad-eyed look that was doubtless meant to be sympathetic. 'It be a great pity that there be no herb or simple that might ease your grief.'

Niffa rose, staring at her all the while. Abruptly Raena looked down at the floor.

'Er, well,' Raena went on, 'I mean not to press upon a wound or suchlike.'

'I be but sore surprised, is all,' Niffa felt her voice turn to a snarl, 'that you of all people would say such a thing.'

Raena went dead-white and crouched back in her chair.

'Now here!' Dera snapped. 'Mind your manners!'

Niffa turned and ran into the far chamber. She slammed the door behind her and leaned against it, her shoulders shaking. She could hear her mother's startled voice, and Raena murmuring a frightened goodbye. In a moment the voices stopped, and Dera came knocking on the door.

'Niffa! You come out of there!'

Niffa did. Her mother was standing with her arms crossed over her chest.

'Never did I raise my children to be as nasty as wild weasels,' Dera said. 'What meant you by –'

'She were there when my Demet died, and I wager she did kill him herself. I be as sure as I can be of that, and here she was, the filthy murderess, as bold as brass in our own house.'

Dera stared, open-mouthed.

'I did see it in vision,' Niffa went on. 'The night he were slain, that was, and I did see her, gloating and laughing as he did lie there dead. Think, Mam! Why else does Verrarc drag his feet and refuse to look into the murder? Kiel does agree with me. Ask him if you believe me not!'

With a long sigh Dera sat down on the bench by the fire.

'Well, now,' Dera said. 'Your visions, they be true things, by and large, but –'

'But what?'

'This be too grave a charge to trust to vision, lass. I do believe you saw what you say you saw, mind. Never would I call you a liar. But I do wonder if you did see the truth or only some part of it. Here, you've not told anyone else this but Kiel, have you?'

'I've not. There be fear in my heart, Mam. What if the townsfolk, they do think me the sort of witch who dabbles in evil things? Would they not drive me out of town into the snows?'

'That be my worst fear too.' Dera sat for a long while, staring silently into the fire. 'Ah ye gods! Well, if Kiel does come home before your father, I'll be asking him about all of this. Say naught to your father, lass, till I've had a chance to speak with him.'

'I shan't. But you saw that Raena. She went as pale as milk, didn't she? It were her guilt taking the blood from her face.'

'If that be true, then it's a dangerous thing you've done.'

Niffa felt herself turn cold. She sat down next to her mother and held trembling hands out to the fire.

'So it was,' Niffa said. 'I do wish I'd thought of that before I spoke, but truly, the words wouldn't stay in my mouth.'

'Well, there be little Raena could do to us, whether your charge be true or false.' Dera turned, looking at the bowl of honeyed apples. 'I did think she meant us well.'

'That be safe enough to eat, coming from our Verro,' Niffa said. 'But I'd not eat of any dish the bitch sends us from now on.'

'Hush! Don't you be calling anyone names such as that! We ken it not if Raena be guilty, and until we do, well then, let's not speak ill of her or anyone.'

Niffa merely nodded a hypocritical agreement. She had learned young that it was futile to argue with her mother's relentless desire to think the best of everyone.

Verrarc was puzzling over a strange passage in his dweomer scroll when Raena ran in, slamming the door behind her. She threw off her cloak and sank into her chair by the fire, then covered her face with trembling hands. For what seemed a long while she merely sat and shook.

'What be so wrong?' Verrarc said at last. 'My love –'

'That lass.' Raena let her hands fall into her lap and turned a dead-white face his way. 'Niffa. She did come as close as close can be to saying I murdered her man.'

'What? How would –'

'I ken it not! But she did let me see, oh and so full of hate she were as well, she did let me see that she thinks this ill lies at my door.'

Verrarc hesitated. All her life Raena had been prone to embroidering her truths to present them in the most exciting possible light, but this time there was no denying her terror. He stood and took a few steps toward her.

'Listen to me, Rae. The time be here for the truth. There be naught I can do to keep you safe without the truth.'

She leaned back in her chair and looked up at him, her lips trembling.

'Well, did you slay him?' Verrarc said. 'You do have strong witchery, Rae, and I ken not its limits. Did you slay Demet?'

'Never!' Her eyes glazed with tears. 'I swear it to you, Verro. Never would I do such a thing.'

'Then who did? Your Lord Havoc?'

'He were the one.' Raena started to get up, but she was shaking too hard. 'Demet did come blundering in. The silver light, it were so strong I never did see nor hear him till there he was. And Havoc – I ken not what he did. But the lad screamed and fell back dead.'

Verrarc realized that he'd been holding his breath and let it out in a long sigh. Raena raised one hand as if she feared he would strike her. Sweat was beading on her upper lip and forehead.

'I do believe you,' Verrarc said. 'But do you see what this means? Your Lord Havoc. He be no god, Rae, but an evil spirit indeed. It were best if never you invoked him again.'

'I must! You don't understand! There be a need on me to find out what he does ken about –' Her voice caught and stumbled. 'About a certain matter.'

'Rae! These cursed secrets!'

She moaned and let her head flop back, then forward. For a moment he stood staring at her until he at last realized that she had fainted. He ran to the door that led to the back of the house and called for his manservant.

'Harl! Come here!' Verrarc shouted. 'Your aid!'

Verrarc ran back to Raena, who lay sprawled in the chair. He knelt beside her and caught her cold hand between both of his. All at once her head jerked up, and she seemed to be looking about her.

'Rae?' he whispered.

Her head turned toward the sound, but her eyes – he'd never seen eyes so blank and dead. It seemed to him that her soul had fled, yet left her body still alive to move about and breathe like some mindless animal.

'Master!' Young Harl came running into the room. 'What – Ye gods! Your lady!'

Raena's head turned toward the sound of his voice, but her eyes stayed dead-seeming. Her mouth flopped open, and she began to make noises, first a sputter, then a gurgling ugly rumble in her throat that nonetheless had the cadence of words. Harl gasped and stepped back fast.

'Run get the herbwoman!' Verrarc snapped. 'I'll tend my lady.'

Harl nodded and raced out of the room. Verrarc squeezed Raena's hand hard.

'Rae, Rae,' he whispered. 'Come back!'

Her head flopped back with a long moist sigh. Verrarc stood, then picked her up, settling her head against his shoulder. Once she'd been a solid young woman, but now – he was shocked at how light she seemed. Without much difficulty he carried her into their bed chamber and laid her down on the bed. In the small hearth, wood and kindling stood stacked and ready.

Verrarc hurried back into the reception chamber and grabbed a long splint from the woodpile.

'Master?' Old Korla came shuffling in. 'Has Harl gone daft? He did come into my kitchen babbling of evil spirits.'

'Not daft in the least,' Verrarc heard his voice shaking. 'Did he go fetch Gwira as I asked him?'

'He did, truly.'

'Good. My lady does lie in our chamber. Go sit with her whilst I take some of this fire.'

When Verrarc came in with the blazing splint, he saw that Korla had spread a blanket over Raena, who lay unmoving, her open eyes staring at the ceiling. For a horrible moment he thought her dead, but she moaned and stirred. He knelt down by the hearth and touched the splint to the kindling, blew on the tentative flames, and tossed the splint into the fire as it blazed up.

'Well, Korla?' Verrarc got up and walked over to the bedside. 'What might this be but evil spirits?'

'Ah, gods protect!' She crossed her fingers in the sign of warding off witchcraft and stepped back from the bedside. 'I fear me you be right, unless Gwira does ken some other thing it might be.'

But the herbwoman had no other explanation to offer when she at last arrived. With Harl right behind, Gwira bustled in, carrying a big market basket crammed with little packets of medicaments. She took off her cloak and tossed it over a chair.

'Does she live?' Gwira snapped.

'She does,' Verrarc said. 'I did hold my hand in front of her mouth, and I did feel her breath.'

Gwira set the basket down on the floor, then wrapped one hand around her chin and considered Raena, who lay unmoving, her pale face and her hair soaked in sweat. After a moment she walked over to the side of the bed.

'Harl did tell me that this came on all of a sudden, like.' Gwira laid a hand on Raena's face. 'Huh, I like not how cold she be.'

She leaned over and pried open the lids of Raena's right eye.
For a moment more Raena lay wrapped in her faint, but the fire
crackled, a log burned through and dropped, and a brief flood of
light leapt up and washed the room. Raena suddenly moaned.
Gwira let her go and stepped back just as she woke, twisting
under the blanket and moaning again. When she opened her
eyes, Verrarc nearly wept with relief at seeing her soul look
out of them. When he held out his hand, she worked hers free
of the blanket and laid it in his grasp. It felt as cold and wet
as if she'd grasped snow.

'The light upon the eye, it do work wonders,' Gwira said.
'It does drive the spirit away.'

'Here!' Verrarc said. 'You too think her possessed!'

'I ken naught else that it might be.' Gwira glanced at Korla.
'Fetch me water, if you please. I can brew her up somewhat
with a bit of strength in it, but after that, this be a matter for
our Spirit Talker, not me.'

Korla shuddered and crossed her fingers again.

'So,' Verrarc whispered. 'So! I wonder, then, if it truly were
a spirit who did kill our Demet.'

'It may be,' Gwira said. 'And if so, then it does threaten the
town still.'

'Harl?' Verrarc turned to find him trembling in the doorway.
'Go fetch Mistress Werda. It were best she knew of this
and now.'

'Evil spirits,' Kiel said. 'Councilman Verrarc did say that he be
as sure as sure that evil spirits murdered your man. They did
try to possess his lady last night, says he.'

Niffa snorted and rolled her eyes heavenward.

'Gwira does say it be true,' Kiel went on, 'and Harl and Korla,
too. You see, the councilman came to my squad on the wall
this dawn, and he did tell us all about it.'

'That be hogwash!' Niffa snarled. 'I did see her, I tell you,
laughing and prancing over Demet's body.'

'Ah, but did you see her slay him? Mayhap she did call up these spirits, but they did the murdering, not her. Or even, what if they did possess her that night, so she kenned not what she did?'

Niffa felt like slapping him. The whole family had gathered round the table in their main room, Dera in the chair at the head, Lael on one bench, Niffa and Kiel on the other. Dera sat twisting and untwisting a bit of rag with both hands. Lael leaned forward, elbows on the table. The fire in the hearth crackled and flared, sending a wash of light over Lael's worn face. Niffa realized that she and Kiel both were waiting for their father to speak.

'Did the Council of Five believe Verrarc?' Lael said at last.

'They did. Gwira did speak before them, but truly, what did make up their minds, it were the silver light that Gart and the watch saw that night. I mean, who but a spirit could have made that light glow on Citadel? The sergeant, he did see it clear as clear, and he be not a fanciful man.'

'That be true a thousand times.' Lael glanced her way. 'Niffa, you do look as angry as a balked weasel!'

'Well, if they think it were a murdering spirit, never will they try Raena under our laws. Huh, if I did speak of visions and such, who would believe me?'

'No one,' Lael said. 'And so you'd best not say one word.'

'Da! How can you –'

'Hush!' Lael held up a broad hand for silence. 'Think you I be happy with this whole thing? Demet's mother and I, we did speak together but the other morn, and both of our hearts ache to see Demet's death lawfully avenged. Yet would it gladden our hearts to lose you too? I've no heart to see you turned out of the town because the citizens, they do think you the worst sort of witch.'

Niffa opened her mouth and shut it again. When Dera made a little sound, the family turned toward her.

'Your father be right.' Dera wiped her eyes on the rag.

'Of course I be so,' Lael snapped. 'Niffa, think! You be sure as sure the woman's a murderer, when the whole town, it does think the opposite. Why?'

Niffa opened her mouth to answer only to have her words desert her. But a moment before she had known deep in her soul that Raena had murdered Demet and a host of other persons as well. She poisoned them. The words rang in her mind, but faced with Lael's rational question, her mind refused to say more.

'I know not,' Niffa stammered. 'I just do.'

'Here, lass.' Lael made his voice gentle. 'Grief does put strange fancies in our minds. We all ken how well you loved your Demet. To lose him with not even a soul to blame – well, now.'

Niffa felt tears burn her eyes. She tried to wipe them away, but they spilled over and ran. Kiel flung one arm around her shoulders and pulled her close.

'Hush, hush!' he said. 'Even if Raena did hang in the market square, would it bring our Demet back? Here, here, little sister! It aches my heart to see you so sad.'

Slowly the tears stopped. Niffa wiped her face on her sleeve and grabbed a twist of straw from the floor to blow her nose. She tossed the twist into the fire and watched it flare. May Raena burn with shame just as the straw burns! She looked up to find Lael watching her, one eyebrow raised, as if he knew she worked a wishing charm.

'I do wonder one thing,' Dera said. 'What does Werda think of all this talk of spirits?'

'I know not,' Kiel said. 'A fair bit, I should think.'

Later that same day Niffa learned Werda's opinions on the matter. Lael and Niffa were sitting by their fire, while Dera lay tucked up in the big bed across the room to rest. Kiel had already gone to sleep in the other room, since he would be standing watch on the town walls again that night. At the door someone knocked in a loud quick drumming. Niffa ran to open it and found Werda, followed by her apprentice. She was a tall woman, Werda, and lean as well, all long bones and sharp angles, muffled up that morning in her white ceremonial cloak. Athra, her apprentice, wore an ordinary grey cloak, splashed here and there with whitewash, doubtless from the large bucket of the stuff that she was carrying. Athra's face gleamed with ointment, thick smears of lard flecked with some sort of herb from the smell of it. Blonde and round, Athra had the sort of rosy skin that chaps from a wrong look.

'Come in quick,' Niffa said. 'Do take of the warmth of our fire.'

'My thanks,' Werda said. 'It be powerful cold still.'

All three of them trooped in. Athra set herself and her bucket down by the fire, but Lael insisted that Werda take their only chair. She sat and for a moment busied herself with untying the hood of her cloak and pulling it back.

'How do you all fare?' Werda said finally.

'We all be well at long last,' Lael said, glancing Dera's way. 'Thanks to the gods and to Gwira's herbs.'

Werda nodded unsmiling. For a moment the silence held as she sat looking back and forth twixt Lael and Niffa.

'There be no use in polite chatter,' Werda said finally. 'I did come to see you, young Niffa. No doubt you've heard of the evil spirit loose in town?'

'I have,' Niffa said. 'They say it did kill my Demet.'

'Is it that you believe this?'

Niffa hesitated, gauging the black look on her father's face. She was aware of Athra watching her from one side and Werda from the other.

'I know not if I believe or disbelieve,' Niffa said. 'Think you it be the case?'

'I do. I did see that woman of the councilman's with my own eyes, and I talked a long time with Gwira and Korla about her faint. Truly, naught else could have caused her trouble but spirit possession. And then I did walk about the councilman's house and compound, and there be spirits there, sure enough. I did feel them like a tingling in the air round the walls. With the witch-vision the gods give me, I did see an evil thing:

a creature much like a stork, but it had the arms and face of a man.'

Lael swore under his breath. Niffa clasped her hands together so hard they ached.

'Huh!' Werda said. 'You've gone pale, lass, and I blame you not, quite frankly. I did come to ask if these spirits, they've been a-troubling you.'

'They've not.'

'Good.' Werda rose, gathering her cloak around her. 'If you do feel the slightest alarm, then come to me straightaway. I care not if it be in the middle of the night, young Niffa. You find yourself a lantern, Lael, and bring your daughter to my house. Do you understand me?'

'I do,' Lael said.

'But I don't understand,' Niffa said. 'Why would they come plaguing me?'

Werda merely looked at her with a twist to her mouth, as if she were wondering how Niffa could be so stupid. Lael sat like stone, but Niffa knew he was watching her. Her mouth went so dry she couldn't force out one word.

'Ah well,' Werda said at last. 'The time will come when you'll not be able to deny the truth. When it does, you come to me, and we shall talk.' She turned to Lael. 'Master Lael, I wish to paint a warding on the outside of your door. I do trust you'll not object.'

'Of course not.' Lael got up and bowed to her. 'If there be aught I can do –'

'Nah, nah, nah. Today we'll do naught but prepare the door.' Werda nodded at Athra and the bucket. 'On the morrow we'll be back to work the charm, once the whitewash does dry.'

'Well and good, then. Will you be painting such on the entire town?'

'We won't.' Werda paused for a significant look Niffa's way. 'Only on the public places, the council house and suchlike, and then on those few homes that I do deem vulnerable.'

They went out, and Lael closed the door and latched it

against the wind while Niffa mended up the fire again. They could hear Werda through the door, instructing Athra, and the soft whisk of the brush. Until the holy woman and her apprentice had finished, no one said a word. At the sound of their leaving, Dera sat up in bed and ran her hands through her hair to push it back from her face.

'You did well, lass,' Lael said to Niffa.

Dera nodded her agreement. Niffa managed a brief smile and stood up.

'I be weary again,' Niffa said. 'I'd best go lie down.'

'Ai, my poor lass!' Dera said. 'It does seem that all you do is sleep.'

'Mayhap. But this news – whose heart wouldn't it weary?'

In the long weeks since Demet's death, Niffa had indeed been hiding from her grief in the refuge of her dreams. Since childhood she had spent her nights in many-coloured kingdoms of sleep, had longed for sleep and dreams and treasured those she remembered upon waking. Now, however, the dreams had become more urgent than the doings of the day. While her parents talked in the great room, she crawled into her blankets, across the room from Kiel, who was snoring worse than the wind in the chimney. In their wooden pen the weasels chirped to her, but she lacked the strength to say a word to them.

As soon as she lay down, she felt as if she'd stepped into a boat and glided effortlessly out into a strange lake, huge and rippled with waves. She dreamt, as she often had, of Demet. Tonight she saw him standing on the far shore of the pale turquoise water. Her boat sailed steadily forward, but the shore just as steadily receded. At last she saw him turn and walk away into the white mists, and her dream faded.

In the middle of the night she suddenly woke. Kiel's bed lay empty. She could guess that the noise he'd made leaving to go on watch had wakened her. She got up, went to the tiny window, and pulled back the thick hide that kept the wind out. By craning her neck she could just see over the rooftops of Citadel, falling away down to the lake. A sliver of moon hung over the town, and she realized that soon the moon would go into its dark time. It had been full when they'd laid Demet's dead body out in the forest for the wild things. A half turn of the moon gone, she thought, and my grief rules me still.

All at once she heard someone come into the room. She turned, smiling, expecting to see Kiel, returned for some forgotten bit of his gear. No one was there. The cold draught from the window ran down her back and made her gasp, but she held the hide up nonetheless for the little light the moon gave her. In their pens the ferrets suddenly began rustling the straw. She could recognize Ambo's chuckle of warning; as their hob he would defend his pack. Someone, something stood in the doorway across the room. She was sure of it, could see nothing – but Ambo must have smelled it, whatever it was. He began to hiss in little moist bursts of sound like a sucked-in breath. Her danger-warning grew stronger. His hissing turned into one long threat. She could hear him rushing around the pen and scattering straw as he searched for this unseen intruder.

Suddenly the presence vanished. Ambo stopped hissing. The other ferrets chuckled, then fell silent; she could hear them all moving in the straw again. The icy air from the window was making her shiver so badly that she let the oxhide fall. In the dark she made her way back to bed and lay down, huddling and shivering under the blankets. She knew that she should wake the house and run to Werda, but the cold had got into her bones, or so she felt, and she couldn't make herself get out of the warm wrap of her bed.

'The jeopard, it be gone.' The voice was Werda's, but Niffa heard it only in her mind. 'You may sleep, child.'

Niffa sobbed once. Slowly the ferrets quieted. For a long while she lay shivering, sure that she would stay awake the entire night.

But suddenly she woke to morning and the sound of her mother and father talking in the room just beyond her door. She sat up and looked around. The ferrets lay piled on top of each other, asleep in the straw. Had she dreamt their ghostly visitor and Ambo's hiss?

'I do dream so many strange things,' she muttered to herself.

But Werda's voice, she knew, had been real, no matter how hard she tried to explain it away. She said nothing to her kinsfolk, but all that morning she noticed them watching her as she sat in her corner by the hearth with one or another of the ferrets in her lap.

Werda returned near mid-day, her arms full of bundles wrapped in rough sacking. Athra trailed after, carrying a big covered kettle. The kettle went by the fire to warm, whilst the bundles got set down carefully on the plank table.

'The warding black, it does contain pitch,' Werda said, pointing at the kettle. 'In this cold weather, it does grow too stiff to use after a bit.' She considered the bundles for a moment, then picked one up and handed it to Niffa. 'This be for you. Set it at the head of your bed.'

The bundle contained what at first glance seemed to be an ordinary pottery bowl. When Niffa took it, she could see that in truth it was a pair of bowls, the outer stuck to the inner with more pitch. A thin black line of squiggly decoration covered the inner bowl, starting at the middle of the flat bottom, then winding in a tight spiral out to the rim.

'It does confuse the spirits,' Werda said. 'That line of writing be a spell, and their curiosity does drive them into the bowl to read it, and then they slip between the bowls and cannot find their way out again. Once every some days Athra will fetch the trap away and leave another, that we may deal with the spirits in it once and for all.'

'My thanks,' Niffa said, stammering a little. 'I do ken that I need such.'

'Indeed?' Werda looked at her with a twist to her mouth. 'It gladdens my heart that you do.'

*   *   *

When the sun hung at the peak of the sky, Verrarc went to the stone council house, which stood on the north side of Citadel's plaza. In front of it rose a line of stone columns, a reminder of the trees that had surrounded the meeting places of the Ancestors, back before any of the Rhiddaer folk lived in cities. With him Verrarc carried a lit candle in a tin lantern, though the day was bright through thin clouds. At the door he paused to examine the wardings painted on its white-washed surface. Against the fresh whitewash the thick black lines of Werda's pitch and lampblack concoction stood out sharp and shiny. She had painted a design of two spiral mazes, one above the other, both amazingly intricate, to fascinate the spirits and keep them outside.

When Verrarc went inside, he closed the door carefully behind him. The stone room, with its high ceiling and rank of windows covered only by wooden shutters, was as cold as the open plaza. Earlier, Harl had on his orders laid a fire in the hearth and arranged the council's round table and chairs in front of it. Verrarc knelt down and used his candle to get the tinder started. A few quick breaths and the kindling caught as well, but Verrarc kept his cloak wrapped around him. The fire would do little but take off the chill.

Chief Speaker Admi joined him in but a few moments, still wheezing from his climb up the steep path to the plaza. He waddled across the room and stood in front of the crackling fire.

'Good morrow,' Verrarc said.

Admi nodded and fumbled inside his cloak for a rag to mop his face. When Verrarc pulled out a chair, Admi sank into it with a little nod of thanks in his direction. Verrarc took a chair next to his.

'Ah, there, my breath returns,' Admi said finally. 'Which does remind me. How fares your poor woman?'

'Better, my thanks.' Verrarc shuddered as the memory rose of Raena's dead gaze. 'Gwira did fear that fever would set in, but Raena, she's been naught but sleepy. This sort of possession, Gwira did tell me, exhausts the poor soul who suffers it.'

'No doubt.' Admi's fingers twitched in the warding sign. 'It gladdens my heart that she came to no harm.'

'My thanks. I do appreciate your nicety of feeling.'

'Welcome, I'm sure.'

'If only –' Verrarc hesitated, but Admi's eyes were all sympathy. 'If only my cursed father had let me marry Raena, back before her father did betroth her elsewhere, none of this trouble would have fallen upon us.'

Admi nodded, considering.

'True spoken,' Admi said at last. 'He did think her beneath you – ah. Here be Frie.'

The stocky blacksmith opened the door, then stood half in and half out while he looked over the warding.

'No use in discussing your woman in front of him,' Admi whispered.

'I know,' Verrarc said, and as softly. 'It be his wife, she did always hate my Raena.'

Admi raised one eyebrow, then forced out a bland smile. Frie had shut the door; he strolled over, wrapped in a thick grey cloak with his ceremonial scarlet draped on top. His thick dark moustache glittered with frozen breath.

'Good morrow, Frie,' Admi said.

'And to you both.' Frie sat down across the table. 'I did stop at old Hennis's house, and he be too ill to come out in this cold, or so his servants did tell me.'

'Huh!' Admi snorted. 'I'll wager I know what does sicken him. He does hate to hold his tongue and smile when Werda talks of the gods and spirits.'

'Can't understand the man,' Frie said. 'Cursed obvious, it is, that the world be full of gods and spirits. Makes you wonder, it does, if his long years be muddling his mind.'

'Well, now,' Verrarc put in, 'he does know the city laws off by heart still. His mind be sound enough on those matters.'

'True enough,' Admi said. 'Now, where be Burra? Late, no doubt, as always.'

Frie grunted his agreement and wiped the melting frost from his moustache with the back of a soot-stained hand.

'I'd hoped for a little chat among us before the Spirit Talker arrived,' Admi went on. 'Which we'll not have if he doesn't get himself here soon. I'd best have a private word with him. If he takes not his duty to the town seriously, well, then, there are others who long for a council seat.'

Not long after Burra did arrive, a skinny man with yellow hair, not much older than Verrarc and like him, a merchant who traded in the east. The councilmen barely had a chance at two private words, however, before Werda opened the door and strode in. Her apprentice followed with her arms full of bundled things. The Spirit Talker had bound her grey hair up into braids coiled round her head, and she wore the white cloak that normally she kept for ceremonial occasions. Without waiting to be asked, she pulled out a chair and sat down with her back to the fire. Athra laid her bundles down on the table, then stood behind her master's chair.

'I see that Hennis, he deigns not to join us,' Werda said.

'Er, just so,' Admi said. 'His servants did say that he be somewhat ill.'

'Huh.' Werda rolled her eyes. 'It be a foolish thing to deny the power of the gods. He does get his blasphemies from the Mountain Folk, no doubt. They do mock the spirits, calling them but idle fancies.'

'Er, mayhap,' Admi said, 'but no matter. There be four of us here in attendance upon the council, enough to make our decidings official.' He paused, glancing around the table. 'Now, then, by the power invested in me as Chief Speaker, I do open this meeting, come together to discuss the death of Demet, the weaver's second son. Yesterday morn Verrarc, chief officer of the town militia, did venture that evil spirits did slay the lad. Does any here dispute this finding?'

Frie and Burra shook their heads in a no. Admi turned to Werda.

'I too agree with Councilman Verrarc,' Werda said. 'This

night past have I walked round Citadel, and in many a place did I find spirits lurking. These were all weak little things, and I did invoke the gods upon them, and they did flee. No one of them could have slain Demet, but together, in a pack, they would be dangerous.'

'You have the thanks of the council,' Admi said, 'for sending them on their way.'

'But will they come right back again?' Frie broke in. 'That's what I be wanting to know.'

'With spirits, it be a constant battle.' Werda gestured at the bundles on the table. 'I did bring spirit traps for each of you to take to your dwellings and one to stay here in the council house.'

'You have our thanks,' Admi said.

'Most welcome,' Werda continued. 'And now I do ken that I'd best stay on guard against the spirits, which kenning be a weapon in itself. I have my own ways of standing watch.'

The councilmen all nodded as if they understood. Verrarc felt his stomach clench cold. If Raena insisted upon invoking her Lord Havoc again, Werda would be sure to know.

Lael brought Niffa the news of the council's decision, when, late that afternoon, he carried home the wicker cage of ferrets from their day's ratting. Niffa took the cage into the other room and released the weasels into their pen; Lael had already taken off their hunting hoods. She came back out to the great room and found him ladling himself a tankard of flat ale from the barrel near the hearth. Dera sat at table, eating a few slices of honeyed apples.

'Do have some of this,' she was saying.

'I won't,' Lael said. 'It be your medicaments, and I'd have you eat the lot, my love.'

Niffa set the empty cage down by the hearth. She was aware of her father watching her with sad eyes.

'What be so wrong, Da?' Niffa said.

'Well, when I were down in town, I did hear the crier. The council, they do say that the matter of Demet's death be closed. Evil spirits, and Werda, she did sanction their decision.'

Niffa stared down at the straw on the floor and wondered if she were going to weep.

'Here now,' Lael said softly. 'Had they ruled different, he still would have been gone.'

'Oh, true spoken. But now I've naught left of him, but my memories. Not even vengeance – not so much as that for a keepsake.'

Still, she did have one thing more, of course: her dreams. That evening and in those that followed she turned to her childhood refuge, where she could see Demet and pretend that he lived again. In those dreams she would perhaps come into a room and find him sitting there, laughing at her while she reproached him for pretending to die, or perhaps they would walk together by the lake and talk of what they would do come spring. Yet she always knew that she was dreaming, no matter how urgently she wanted the dream to last forever. Other times she would dream they were making love in their bed back in his family's house, and from those dreams she woke in tears. Yet as time went on, those dreams faded, to be replaced by something far stranger.

Many-towered cities rose in her nights, where she wandered with a lantern in hand while she searched for something she'd lost, though she could put no name to it. At other times she had walked in the city during a summer's day and marvelled at the strange buildings and the people she saw among them. In the centre of this city rose a hill, circled at intervals by five stone walls. At the top, inside the highest wall, stood a fortress of some kind. In her dreams all she could see were squat towers clustering behind the stone. Sometimes she knew that she had to get into that fortress; in other dreams, she needed to escape it – though paradoxically, she never dreamt of being inside it.

When she woke of a morning, she would lie in bed and

marvel at how clearly she saw the dream city. Even though its central hill reminded her of Citadel, the rest of it – the buildings, the people's clothing – looked nothing like Cerr Cawnen, the only city she'd ever seen. By brooding over the dream images this way she reinforced them, so that the city took a permanent form. Whenever she went back, the same houses and shops would occupy the same locations; the same hill would loom over the familiar streets.

Finally Niffa turned bold. When in her dream she came to its gate, she walked through. All around the city lay meadows where the grass grew as high as her waist, but narrow paths ran through them. She followed one a little ways down the road, stopping often to look back at the towered hill to keep within its sight, but she woke before she'd gone far. Over the next few nights she would walk a little way through these meadows, then rush back to the city before it could disappear. She had learned, just lately, that things you loved could disappear without warning.

Eventually, as she walked through the grass she saw far off to one side something gleaming like fire in the green, but no smoke rose. She left the road and struggled through the grass under a sky growing dim with twilight. Off to her right a huge purple moon trembled on the horizon as night deepened. When she looked back, the city walls still rose nearby, with here and there a point of lantern light upon them. The sight gave her the courage to keep going toward the fire-gleam, a strange red glow like a beacon in the grass.

Two huge five-pointed stars, each taller than a man and twined of stranded red and gold light, hung in the air just above a stretch of beaten-down grass. Between them the earth opened into the mouth of a tunnel sloping down into some unseeable darkness. On the other side of the stars someone was standing in the grass – a woman, judging from her long ash-blonde hair, but she wore tight leather trousers and a tunic rather than dresses.

'Here!' the woman called out. 'You're not Raena.'

'And I do thank every god in my heart for that,' Niffa called back. 'Who be you?'

The woman walked around the stars and stood looking her over with her hands on her hips. Niffa had never seen anyone so beautiful, or so she thought at first glance. She had silver blonde hair with silver eyes that matched it. Her features were even and perfect – but her ears! They were long and strangely furled like a new fern in spring.

'My name is Dallandra,' the woman said at last. 'And I made these wards to keep Raena away from a thing she seeks. Who are you?'

'Niffa be my name.'

'Jahdo's sister!'

'And is it that you know our Jahdo?' In her joy Niffa forgot her fear. 'Fares he well? Oh please, do tell me.'

'Well and safe, truly, and you'll be seeing him in the spring.'

The joy rose like a wave of pure water. All at once Niffa lay awake, tucked into her blankets with a ferret asleep on her chest and grey dawn flooding the window.

'Tek-tek, whist!' She shook the ferret awake, then picked her up and put her down on the bed next to her. 'It's needful I tell Mam straightaway.'

She found Dera awake, kneeling by the hearth and laying twigs upon blazing tinder. In the big bed at the far side of the room Lael still slept, wrapped around a pillow and snoring. Dera was concentrating on the fire, but she'd apparently heard her daughter approach.

'Early for you to be up and about,' Dera said.

'Mam, I did have the most wonderful dream, and it be one of my true ones, I do know it deep my heart. I did meet a woman who does know our Jahdo. He be safe and well, she did tell me, and he'll be returning in the spring.'

At that Dera did look up, and the warmth of her smile glowed like the spreading fire.

'I'll look forward, then,' Dera said. 'It does my heart no good, all this looking back.'

'I've got somewhat else for you to look forward to, Mam. I've not had my monthly bleeding.'

Dera rose, studying Niffa's face.

'Now here, don't you be getting your hopes up, lass. Grief will do strange things to a woman; it well might dry her up for a while, like.'

Niffa felt tears rise, choked them back, and turned away. She felt her mother's gentle hand on her shoulders.

'I know how much you did love your Demet,' Dera said. 'Mayhap the goddesses will bless you after all. There be a need on us to wait and see.'

When Dallandra woke in the morning, she lay in bed for a while, considering Jahdo's sister. How had Niffa got into the Gatelands of Sleep, and why did she seem so at home there? Later in the day Dallandra tracked Jahdo down, finding him at the servants' hearth in the great hall with Cae, an orphan boy who worked in the kitchens. On the smooth stones in front of the fire, they were playing with little wooden tops. For a moment she watched as each boy set his top spinning with a flick that bumped it against another. She waited until Jahdo had lost a match, then called him away. They stood to one side where they wouldn't be overheard.

'I want to ask you somewhat about your sister,' Dallandra said. 'And it's a very odd question.'

'Very well, my lady,' Jahdo said. 'Niffa be a very odd lass, so fair's fair.'

'Odd? How do you mean, odd?'

'Oh, all the folk in Cerr Cawnen, that's what they did always say. Our Niffa, she be an odd little soul.' Jahdo thought for a moment. 'She did see things. And she had dreams.'

'Tell me a bit more about that.'

'We'd be sitting at our fire, and you'd look at Niffa, and her eyes – they'd be moving back and forth, and she'd smile, too, at whatever it was. Or in the lake, she'd be seeing things. And the clouds sometimes too. And then there be her dreams. Mam stopped her from telling them after a while, because when they did come true, our neighbours and townsfolk would be ever so scared by it.'

'No doubt! Well, my thanks, Jahdo.'

'But my lady, what be your question?'

'You just answered it, lad. Now run along, go back to your game. The other lads are waiting for you.'

Only later did Dallandra remember that Jahdo was desperate for news of his family. How selfish of me! she thought. I'd best see what I can find out from Niffa – well, if I ever see her again! A girl little older than a child, with a raw gift for dweomer, wandering unknowingly around the astral plane – she might never stumble upon Dallandra's vigil again. And yet, as she thought about it, Dallandra realized with an odd certainty that she would see Niffa again in the lands of sleep. The thought was so clear that she knew it must be a message from the Great Ones. Why they'd sent the message was a question of the sort they never answered directly, but Dallandra could venture a guess. No doubt Raena was continuing to work her evil magicks. And no doubt, Dallandra thought, it's fallen to me to stop her.

'And just where, pray tell, have you been?' Verrarc felt his voice catch and growl.

In the pool of lantern light Raena half-crouched against the wall. Her cloak dripped wet snow onto the floor.

'As if I knew not!' Verrarc went on. 'Up in the ruins, bain't, with that cursed Havoc creature?'

'And what's it to you?'

'What be it to me? Ye gods, have you gone daft? If the town should find out – you up there, consorting with evil spirits – ye gods! I could be ruined! And you – think, woman! They love you not as it is. If they thought you to bring evil among them –'

With a toss of her head Raena tried to push past him. Verrarc caught her wrist in one hand and pulled her round to face him. He held the lantern high and let the light shine down upon her. In the flickering glow her lips seemed bruised, her entire face swollen.

'And just what might be so cursed important, Rae, that you would risk so much to have it? I'll have the truth, and I'll have it now.'

'Let me go!' She tried to pull her hand free, but he held on. 'Oh very well! Truly, it were time. Let me go, and I'll tell you.'

When he released her she walked a few steps away, then took off the damp cloak. Except for the dancing gleam of his lantern, the great room lay dark around them, silent in the dead of night.

'Come into our chamber,' Verrarc said. 'I'd not have the servants waking to hear this.'

Raena threw the cloak onto the floor and stomped off into the bedchamber, where a small fire burned in the hearth. She flopped down on the edge of the bed like a sulky child and began to pull off her wet boots. He set the lantern down on the mantle and took a chair opposite her. Once the boots were off she calmed. She set them carefully to dry near the hearthstone, then perched on the bed again.

'Truly, I did promise that you should know,' Raena said. 'I were but angry that you did snap at me.'

'I be frightened, Rae. That's the sad truth of it.'

She stopped on the edge of speaking and considered him.

'Not of you,' Verrarc went on, 'nor truly of what witchery you might work, but of the town and for the town. I'd not have any more of my fellow citizens murdered by your treacherous little spirits.'

'Well, that be fair, and my heart does ache for poor Niffa.' Raena sounded surprisingly genuine. 'But there were a need on me, a desperate need, Verro, to learn a thing Havoc could tell me.'

'It must have been desperate, all right, to risk so much for it.'

'It is, truly it is.' Raena looked at the fire and frowned, thinking. 'It be such a hard tale to start, my love. Here – what would you say if I did tell you that there be a new goddess in the world?'

For a long moment Verrarc could only stare at her.

'A what?' he said at last. 'A goddess? This be the last thing I thought you'd –'

'No doubt.' All at once Raena smiled in gathered confidence. 'It came as a strike of lightning to me as well, such a strange and marvellous thing it were. But she did reveal herself to me, and she did mark me out to be her priestess, to serve her all my born days and to live with her ever after in her glorious country beyond death.' She paused, and never had he seen her smile this way, as if she looked through the dark snowy night around them to the warm light of a spring day. 'Her name, it be Alshandra.'

Verrarc felt like a sudden half-wit, stripped of words.

'What?' he managed to say. 'What do you mean? A new goddess? How can there be such a thing? The gods did make the world, and they've been in it always.'

'Mayhap I speak wrongly, then.' Raena considered the fire and frowned again. 'She were hidden before, you see. Always has she been in the world, off in her own true country, but she never did show herself to the world.'

'Ah.' He felt his mind turn to an ugly thought: had Raena gone utterly mad? 'But she did show herself to you. Somehow.'

'It be a simple tale. When I was still the wife of my pig of a husband I did spend long hours weeping. You do remember that, I'm sure. And I would leave Penli and go walk among the trees, and I would sit upon the ground and weep some more. One afternoon she did come to me and ask me why I wept.' Raena's voice dropped, heavy with awe. 'She were huge and tall, floating down from the sky to stand before me, and she were so beautiful, too, and so kind, I did fall to my knees before her. That pleased her. She did tell me how to call to her, and when I would call, she would come to me.'

'Wait! Why did you not tell me about her, back then?'

'I did think you'd mock and say that she were but my fancy, and truly, I see naught but doubt upon your face now.'

'How could I not doubt, since you did never so much as mention her before?'

Raena shrugged his objection away.

'She did call me her chosen one,' Raena continued. 'She did tell me that she had watched me always, long before I were born, even. Oh, she did tell me so many marvellous things, and she did take me to her beautiful country, where there were green meadows and a river like silver, and strange cities to walk within! Gone now, all of it but the meadows, because her enemies, and she does have many, all of them evil in their very hearts, but they did destroy it to spite her. But she has another country, she told me, where there be no Time and no Death, and those that worship her shall travel there with her, to live forever in joy.'

Her eyes seemed to glow from within, all silver. She spoke so warmly, so sincerely, that Verrarc found himself wondering if she could possibly be speaking the truth.

'It would be a grand thing,' he said, 'never to die.'

'And with her there shall be no death, Verro. I have seen her country, and I have seen her miracles. I do more than know these things, I ken them, I tell you. They be the deepest truth that ever a woman could see.'

'Here, think you that she'd show them to me?'

'Ah, that's the bitter thing. She has withdrawn to her own true country, and she shows herself not to men or –' She hesitated, stumbling on some word, 'or to women either.'

The doubt rose up strong. Daft! he told himself. What if she's gone daft?

'My love, ponder this.' Raena leaned forward, suddenly urgent. 'In the past, when we did study witchlore together, could I call down the silver light and invoke mighty spirits?'

'Truly, you couldn't. And I do wonder, Rae, just where you might have learned it.'

'No doubt! It was Alshandra. She did teach me, she did lay her hands upon me, and she did give me freely of her power, that I might work magicks in the world. And those that will see them, well, then, they will believe what I say, that Alshandra is a goddess who blesses her worshippers. Where else might I have learned these things, Verro? Do you know a teacher somewhere in the Rhiddaer where I might have studied?'

'I don't.'

'And would I lie to you, the man I love second only to her?'

Verrarc was tempted to say that after all, she'd lied to him often enough before. But this time she was looking him straight in the face, her eyes focused on his, as if she were wishing she could show him her goddess by forcing the image into his mind. What if, just what if this were true, that her goddess would give him magical power beyond any he'd hoped to have? And if there would be no death –

'If only I could take you to her,' Raena said, and her voice stumbled in sheer urgency, 'if only you could see her!'

'Truly, I do wish I could. Why has she –'

'I know not.' Raena's voice shook, and she looked away.

There she was indeed lying; he recognized all the signs from past experience. Paradoxically, however, this lie brought home the truth of what she'd said before, just by the contrast in her telling.

'It be the reason that forces me to summon Lord Havoc,' Raena went on, staring at the far wall. 'There be a need on me to find out. Never have I felt such a desperation, Verro! It be like – well, it be like I were an orphan child, starving on the streets, and she were the wife of a rich guildmaster. And she did take me up and bring me to her home. She did feed me, and she did teach me a craft so that never again would I

be poor and starving. But then, somewhat did anger her, and
she cast me out again.' Tears sprang up in her eyes. 'And here
I be, wailing and alone.' The tears ran, but silently, and she
made no move to wipe them away.

'Ah,' Verrarc said. 'Then it were somewhat you did that did
drive her away?'

'Somewhat I did not, that I should have done.' The truth
sprang out, as sudden as the tears. 'She did lay upon me a
sacred charge, and I did fail in it. Ah ye gods, that I should
have been so weak and unworthy of her love!'

Verrarc moved to sit down with her on the bed. She turned
into his arms and sobbed, while he stroked her hair and whispered 'there, there' over and over again. At last she quieted,
but she clung to him.

'Well, now,' Verrarc said, 'this charge be best done, then,
and mayhap she'll return to you.'

'So I do hope, though it be not such an easy task. It were
about a thing that had been stolen from her, you see, and it
does lie now in the midst of her enemies. She did ask me to
restore it to her.'

'What might this thing be?'

She looked up, and he could feel her trembling in his
arms.

'That I can never tell you, Verro,' she whispered. 'I beg you,
demand not that from me. My secrets you shall have, when the
time be ripe for the telling of them. But it were a blasphemy
were I to tell you her secrets.'

For a long moment he studied her face. Was she lying or
not? He simply couldn't tell.

'Well and good then,' Verrarc said at last. 'What lies between
you and your goddess be not mine to meddle in, anyway.'

Once, long ago, in some immeasurably ancient time, Evandar
and his people, Alshandra among them, had dwelt between
the stars as beings of pure energy and no form. Somehow,

when the Light birthed the vast panoply of worlds, they had been 'left behind', as Evandar put it to himself. How or why, he could no longer remember. Yet, since they had been born to follow the path that all souls must take into the physical plane and the world of matter, they had longed for a solid existence in the beauty of a world. To sate their hunger for life he had built that area of the etheric plane he called the Lands, a perfect illusion of the world of Annwn, with its grassy meadows and rivers, its forests and hills – a shadow world so lovely that they had spurned the real world waiting for them on the physical plane.

He had woven them bodies, too, out of the astral substance, modelling them on the elven race he had come to love. Over the aeons Evandar's dweomer had grown so immensely powerful that he had for a time thought himself as powerful as a god, until the destruction of the Seven Cities of the Far West had stripped him of his arrogance. No matter how much raw dweomer power he expended, no matter how hard he fought with every sort of weapon, in the end the Hordes had won and destroyed every beauty of the elven world. The lesson lived with him still, that as soon as he left his own lands, he too was a slave of change and death, even though his own being seemed immune to both.

And now Time was pursuing him, it seemed, determined to force the lesson home another time. After untold centuries of a perfect spring, the Lands lay besieged by winter. Evandar returned to find his meadows frosted white, his streams frozen, his trees stripped bare, and his people huddled miserably together by the bank of a silver river. When they saw him they cried out.

'Bring back the spring! Give us summer!'

'I did that before, and the winter returned to us anyway. Mayhap we'd best just ride the winter out.'

In a screaming pack they rushed forward and surrounded him, yelling, begging, weeping all at once. Evandar raised his arms and shouted for silence. Slowly the babble died.

'Well and good, then,' Evandar said. 'Spring you shall have.'

In his mind he visualized a gigantic silver horn, and in the Lands what Evandar saw appeared for all to see. His folk gasped and moved back to give him room as the horn floated into the air, an apparition the size of a horse and wagon. Through it Evandar called down the astral light. He saw it as a golden surge of raw power that flowed through the horn's tip and spread out across the meadowlands and into the river. Suddenly the air turned warm; the grass sprang up green; the trees burst into full leaf. On the river bank a cloth-of-gold pavilion sprang into existence.

'Let us feast,' Evandar cried out. 'Let us have music!'

The crowd laughed, calling out his name and cheering him. Yet once they were settled at their feasting, Evandar slipped out of the pavilion. He ran a few steps across the grass, let his elven form dissolve, and as a red hawk he sprang into the air. As he flew in a vast spiral over the river and meadows, he called down the astral light in a hawk's harsh voice.

Below him snow melted, and grass sprang up, green and lush. Flowers bloomed in an instant, dotting the lawns with white and yellow. In every direction, as far as he could see with a hawk's long sight, Spring returned, laughing. The hawk cried out once, then broke from his spiral and flew steadily toward the forest at the meeting of the worlds. Shaetano was hiding somewhere, most likely in the part of the Lands that had once been his. Evandar intended to find him.

Down in Deverry, the same storm that was casting its etheric shadow over Evandar's Lands raged over the northern territories. For three days snow trapped Dun Cengarn in a cage of white. The gwerbret's men spent their days in the great hall near the two huge hearths and their ever-burning fires, though they made brief forays into the stables to tend their horses. Some even brought their blankets from the barracks and slept on the straw with the servants.

Rhodry stayed mostly among the company of Prince

Daralanteriel's escort of ten elven archers, the last of the large troop he'd assembled for the past summer's war. With provisions so scarce at Cengarn, the prince had sent the rest of them home long before. Even though his kingdom lay in ruins in the mountains of the far west, by Deverry standards royal blood still ran in Dar's veins, and he ate and sat at the honour table with Gwerbret Cadmar. Protocol, however, seated his men among the warband, under the captaincy of a pale-haired archer named Vantalaber.

Since the cold draughts bothered the Westfolk men less than it did the human members of Gwerbret Cadmar's warband, they took the table nearest the back door – they were farther from the human stink that way, too, as the archers often remarked. Just like the human men, they diced to pass their time, although the elven game was a fair bit more complex. Each player took a handful of brightly-coloured wood pieces – cubes and pyramids both – shook them hard, then strewed them in a rough line. Counting the points amounted to another game in itself, with a lot of argument and token cursing from the other players. At times during these sessions one or another man from the warband would stroll over to the elven tables and watch their game, but they never asked to join, and no one invited them, either.

Every now and then a servant girl would come to the table to pour the men ale from a dented flagon or set out a meagre basket of bread. One particular evening, Rhodry realized that it was always the same girl, a buxom little blonde, when she stopped for a moment to chat with one of the archers, Melimaladar, a dark-haired fellow whose eyes were a smoky sort of green, unusual even for one of the People. They whispered together, head to head, until something he said made her giggle, and she trotted off, still smiling to herself.

Vantalaber took a sip of the ale she'd brought and nearly spat it out.

'Ye gods, it's watered!' the captain snarled, but in Elvish. 'Thin as swill!'

'The dun's running out,' Rhodry said in the same language. 'Soon enough the steward will be breaking out the vinegar.'

'What? Why would anyone drink vinegar?'

'You don't drink the stuff for itself. You just put a dollop in a tankard of well water. To make it safe, like.'

'Well, the way these people live in filth, I'm not surprised. But I don't mean to insult all of humankind. Gwerbret Cadmar's a fine man in his way.'

'He is that,' Rhodry said. 'Though I worry about his health. He doesn't have a son to inherit the rhan, and the last thing the Northlands can afford is a cursed feud over rulership.'

'That doesn't make any sense. What about his daughters?'

'Van, they can't inherit. They're women. If Cadmar were only a tieryn or a lord, maybe his vassals would back a daughter, but she could never rule as gwerbret.'

Vantalaber rolled his eyes in disgust. Melimaladar, who'd been watching his blonde as she served other tables, leaned forward to join the conversation.

'The daughters have got sons, right? What about them?'

'Cadmar can designate a grandson as heir, yes,' Rhodry said. 'But the High King will have to approve it.'

'Huh.' Mel paused, thinking. 'It's a strange place, Deverry. I don't like it. I feel like riding out right now, snow or no snow.'

'We'll all be leaving in the spring,' Rhodry said. 'What's so wrong?'

Melimaladar exchanged a look with Vantalaber. All the archers at the table had fallen silent, Rhodry realized, to listen.

'Well, look,' Van said. 'Here's our Prince Dar, and he is a prince; none of us would deny it. But he's a prince of the People, not one of your lords, and before this he's always known what that means and how he should take it. Now look at him! He's learning to give himself airs, isn't he? With all the Round-ears bowing and scraping every time he walks into a room!'

Rhodry slewed round on the bench to look across the great

hall. Near the honour hearth Cadmar was sitting in his carved chair with Prince Dar at his right hand and his favourite hounds lying at his feet. Once Cadmar had been a powerful man, but now his hair was white and his face somehow shrunken. Every now and then he would rub his twisted leg and its old injury, as if it pained him despite the warmth of the nearby fire.

By contrast Daralanteriel seemed all youth and strength, even though he sat still, contemplating the enormous sculpture of a dragon that curled around the hearth with its stone back for a mantel. He was an exceptionally handsome man even for one of the Westfolk, and Rhodry could see how a young girl like Carra would have followed him anywhere once he'd been kind to her. Over the winter his pale skin had turned even whiter, setting off his dark hair and violet eyes.

As they watched, Cadmar leaned forward to bark an order at the boys playing by the hearth. Two of them jumped up and ran off to do their lord's bidding, but not before they'd bowed to both prince and gwerbret.

'That kind of grovelling around,' Vantalaber said. 'I don't like it. None of us do.'

'Notice how the boys made their bow to Dar first?' Melimaladar put in. 'And how he smiled?'

'And look at what he's wearing,' Vantalaber went on. 'All the time now.'

Rhodry obligingly looked, though it took him a moment to see what Van meant. Around his neck on a golden chain the prince wore a gold pendant. In the firelight a jewel winked and gleamed.

'By the Dark Sun herself!' Rhodry whispered. 'It's Ranadar's Eye.'

'We all know he's royal,' Vantalaber said. 'He doesn't need to flaunt it.'

'Just so,' Rhodry said. 'Huh. I'll try to have a word with him. You're right. The People will never stand for this, not out on the grass.'

*   *   *

Despite the cold in the tower room, Dallandra often stayed up late, reading one or another of Jill's books by the silver light of the Wildfolk of Aethyr. Usually her studies led straight to her sleep work, when she went to the Gatelands to renew the magical wards that kept Rhodry's dreams safe from Raena. That particular evening she had just finished restoring the flaming stars when Niffa joined her there. For some while they merely considered each other in the red and gold glow from the wards. She was a little thing, to Dalla's elven way of thinking, not much more than five feet tall and slender with long dark hair that she wore loose over her shoulders.

'There be a need on me to thank you,' Niffa said finally. 'Your news about our Jahdo did do my mam's heart much good.'

'I'm glad to hear it,' Dallandra said. 'He worries about her and the rest of you as well.'

'Well, if you'd be so good, do tell him that Mam fares well, though in truth, she be sick again. There be naught he can do, so far away, and I'd not have him fret.'

'I'll do that, then. Is there a good herbwoman in your town?'

'One of the best, or else I'd be sore troubled about my mam. Otherwise, there be much trouble upon us and our town. Tell me if you would – Raena, is it that she does cause grief to you and yours?'

'She has in the past, truly. What's she done to you?'

'Naught that I can prove.'

'Indeed? What do you think she's done?'

'Murdered my man, that's what. I did see her in vision, like, laughing and laughing when he lay dead, but the councilman, and he be her man and not likely to bring her to trial, is he now? But the councilman, he did say it was evil spirits, and now the whole town does believe him.'

'I have no idea of what you're talking about.' Dallandra paused for a smile. 'Slowly now, lass. I don't know the councilman nor much about your town. I didn't even know you'd been married.'

Niffa's dream image blushed.

'My apologies,' the lass said. 'I do forget that you be your own self, somehow, and not just some woman in my dreams.'

'And how do you know that?'

Niffa stared at her for a long moment. All at once her image wavered, turned pale, and faded away. No doubt Dallandra's call for rational thought had woken her, because it takes long years of practice for dweomerworkers to stay lucid and rational in their dreams. Dallandra could safely assume that Niffa held no real control over her magical gifts. Someone should be teaching the lass, she thought. When she looked at the ward-stars that heralded her skill, she laughed at herself. Most likely that 'someone' was her. Paths such as hers and Niffa's never crossed by pure accident.

With the morning the clouds broke up under a cold north wind and let sunlight flood the dun. In her tower room Dallandra took the oxhides down from the windows to let in light for a task she'd been dreading. Jill's wooden chest held those few things that could be said to be personally hers, as opposed to things, such as her medicinals and dweomer books, which she had collected only to help others. Among the Westfolk, Jill's bloodkin would have taken or given away her belongings to those who should have them, but Jill had no bloodkin left. The job had fallen to Dallandra, thanks mostly to their common devotion to the dweomer, which made them clanswomen of a sort.

She pulled over the chair, sat down, and lifted the lid of the chest. One piece at a time, she took out Jill's spare clothing – two shirts, a pair of brigga, all much washed and patched, and a newish grey cloak – and laid them on the table. The cloak would do for Jahdo, who grew taller daily, or so it seemed. The others? Dallandra supposed that the gwerbret's women would cut them into useful rags. At the bottom of the chest, however, she found things of more interest: two bundles of brown cloth and a brown cloth sack.

The oblong bundle proved to be another book, a huge volume as long as her arm from fingertips to elbow. It smelled of mildew, and the leather cover was crumbling at the edges. When Dallandra opened it, she found tidy scribal writing, faded to brown, announcing that this book belonged to Nevyn, councillor to Maryn, Gwerbret Cerrmor. No wonder, then, that Jill had kept it apart from the other books on her small shelf. Carefully Dallandra turned a few of the parchment leaves, the writing faded, the sheets all ragged and splitting at the edges, and came to a diagram of concentric circles, each labelled to represent the nested spheres of the universe. The mildew made her sneeze, and she shut the book with some care.

Dallandra had met Nevyn once, towards the beginning of his unnaturally prolonged life. Thanks to her long dwelling in Evandar's Lands, to her the meeting seemed to have happened no more than a few years past, even though it had been close to four hundred years as men and elves reckon Time. He had brought the Westfolk books of dweomer lore, and she remembered sitting in the warm summer sun and turning each page, staring at the diagrams and at the words she couldn't read. Later, of course, Aderyn had taught her the Deverry alphabet. Aderyn, her husband, back then so long ago – she could still remember how it had felt to love him, though the feeling was only a memory.

'Four hundred years ago.' She said the words aloud, but they carried little meaning, just as her own age meant nothing to her. She'd been born more than four hundred years ago, but of that what had she lived, truly lived in the awareness of time passing? Thirty years perhaps, if that, because she had gone to Evandar's country so young and stayed there so long. Did she regret it? Since nothing could call the years back, regret would only be a waste of time. She returned to her inventory.

The long narrow bundle turned out to be a sword in a sheath of stained, cracking leather, an odd thing for a dweomermaster to carry with her, as it was no ritual weapon but solid Deverry steel. Dallandra drew the blade and saw marks carved near the hilt: a stylized striking falcon, and just below, a lion device that at one time had sported a touch of red pigment. Out of curiosity she held the blade up to sight along it, looking for other marks. When in the cold room her warm breath touched the steel, a little snake made of moisture squirmed and ran down the blade. Startled, she nearly dropped it. She sheathed it and laid it on the table by the book, then opened the sack.

Inside she found a silver dagger in a much newer leather sheath, and a small something wrapped in silk. She put the dagger on the table and unwrapped the silk to find a squarish bone plaque, a few inches to a side, engraved with a portrait of a Horsekin: a warrior, judging from his huge mane of hair and his facial tattoos. The delicacy and realism of the engraving marked it as elven work, and of great age.

'Meradan,' Dallandra said softly. 'Someone recorded what the invaders looked like. I wonder how long the limner lived afterwards.'

For a moment she held the plaque in both hands, as if it were a talisman that could give her knowledge of those ancient days. She felt nothing. She wrapped it up again in its silk and laid it by the other objects that Jill had treasured enough to carry with her through her wandering life. What to do with them? Dallandra had no idea.

Dallandra had known Jill only a brief time, and Jill had not been an easy person to understand. Her workings were so far beyond mine, Dallandra thought. Her knowledge of dweomer lore, too – gods, a thousand times beyond mine! On the wall hung the small shelf of books that Dallandra had begun to study under Jill's tutelage. Those, she knew, Jill would have wanted her to keep until the time came to pass them on to another student of the lore. But what she would never learn from books was the way Jill lived her dweomer, in complete surrender and service to the Light that shines beyond all the gods. Although her compassion had at times been a cold and abstract thing, it had never wavered, not even when that service had demanded her life.

And what have I been doing? Dallandra thought. Chasing after glamours, living far from the physical world, turning my back on those I was born to serve! She had come to despise the physical world, in fact, with all its stinks and pain and filth. In Evandar's fair country life flowed like mead, smooth and intoxicating. Yet like the mead its illusions of pleasure wore off soon enough, leaving the drinker muddled and more than a little sick.

Out in the corridor footsteps were coming toward the door. Dallandra stood just as Rhodry opened it and walked in, glancing at the table.

'Jill's things?' he said in Elvish.

'Just that. Here, take a look at that sword, will you? I'm curious about those marks on the blade.'

Rhodry obligingly picked the sword up, drew it full out of the sheath, and studied the devices. When he looked up, his eyes glistened with tears.

'This belonged to Jill's father, Cullyn of Cerrmor,' he said. 'She must have carried it with her for his memory's sake.'

The tears spilled and ran. For a moment he stood sobbing like a child, yet still he held the sword in a practised grasp. If someone had threatened them, Dallandra felt, Rhodry would have killed him instinctively through his tears. With one last sob he laid the sword down on the table and wiped his eyes on his sleeve.

'My apologies,' he said. 'It's still hard, thinking that she's gone.'

'So it is,' Dallandra said. 'Would you like that sword? I'm sure she'd rather you had it than anyone else.'

'Most like she would.' He picked up the blade again and sheathed it before he went on. 'But I own too many things already for a silver dagger. Here, I know. I'll give it to Dar for a wedding gift – a bit late, but then, he's cursed lucky he's getting anything from me at all.'

Dallandra laughed.

'So he is,' she said, 'and what about the silver dagger?'

Rhodry laid down the sword and picked up the dagger. When he slid it free of its sheath, the silver blade flared with a strange bluish light. Rhodry laughed and held it up while the dagger seemed to burn like an etheric torch.

'What in the name of the gods?' Dallandra took a quick step back.

'It's a dwarven dweomer working.' Rhodry sheathed the blade again and put it down on the table. 'It gives warning when anyone with elven blood touches it. It would do the same for you. The Mountain Folk consider us all thieves, you see.'

'It would scare a thief away, all right, seeing the blade burn like that! Huh, it's odd. I've always heard that the dwarven race shuns dweomer.'

'That's true. Ah, who knows?' Rhodry shrugged and considered the dagger for a long moment. 'That should have been buried with Jill.'

'I'm sorry. I didn't realize.'

'Not that it matters to her any more, I'd wager.' He looked up, his eyes bleak. 'I could take it, or wait! Jahdo shall have it, because when we captured him and Meer, he lost a knife that his grandfather had given him, and it's irked him ever since.'

'It's rather too grand for him, isn't it? What if the other boys or one of the servants steals it from him?'

'He can keep it up here.' Rhodry picked up the sheathed dagger and gestured at a heap of saddlebags and bundles stacked in the curve of the wall. 'Along with the goods Meer left him.'

'I suppose, but I don't understand. If it's important enough that it should have been buried with her, why are you going to just give it away?'

'Because what I'm really doing is throwing it onto the river of Wyrd.' All at once he laughed with a toss of his head. 'I lost my silver dagger in Bardek once, you see. But it came back to me, twenty years later, and when it did, it brought change with it. I've been thinking, just now and again, about the things you told me, Dalla, last summer, about the way that a man might get reborn – or a woman, since we're talking about Jill. And I wonder if she's meant to have this dagger back. If so, it'll find its way, when the time comes.'

Rhodry laughed again, his high berserk chortle. There were times when Dallandra wondered how she could share her bed with a madman like him. As if he heard her thought, he wiped his daft grin away and looked at her solemnly.

'But you have the last word, on this dagger,' Rhodry said. 'Give it elsewhere if you'd like.'

'No, do give it to Jahdo. You may be right about it finding Jill again. I'll keep this book, because I doubt if anyone else here could understand it.'

There remained the bone plaque.

'Shall I give this to Carra?' Dallandra said. 'For a wedding gift?'

'Why?' Rhodry smiled briefly. 'I doubt if it would mean one thing to her. She's so wretchedly young.'

Dallandra had to agree, but later that day, when she joined the dun's womenfolk in their private hall, she had a surprise coming. As usual Carra – or Princess Carramaena of the Westlands, to give her full title – sat near the fire with her infant daughter sleeping in her lap. Instead of being swaddled in tight wrappings, little Elessi wore only nappies and a loose tunic while she slept. At Carra's feet lay Lightning, her dog, though the animal looked more than half a wolf. Across the room at an uncovered window the gwerbret's lady, Labanna, and her serving woman, Lady Ocradda, sat wrapped in cloaks at a big table frame. They wore fingerless gloves to embroider upon a bed hanging, stretched out tight between them.

Dallandra sat down opposite Carra and little Elessi. For a few moments they chatted about the child, but when conversation lagged, Dallandra thought of the bone plaque, which she had carried with her, tucked into the coin pouch she wore hidden under her tunic.

'What do you think of this?' Dallandra brought it out and

handed it over. 'Don't let Elessi touch it. It's a good thousand years old.'

Carra took the plaque in both hands and stared at it with a fierce concentration.

'That old?' she whispered. 'How amazing! It shows a Horsekin, doesn't it? Who drew this?'

'One of your husband's ancestors. Well, and mine too.' Dallandra paused for a smile. 'A limner, an elven limner from one of the Seven Cities.'

'Fascinating!' Carra let out her breath in a soft sigh and went on studying the picture. 'To hold somewhat this old – ye gods, I can't find words to tell you how it makes me feel.'

The other women left their embroidery and came over to see. When Carra proffered it to Labanna, the gwerbret's lady drew back.

'I'd be afraid to touch it,' Labanna said, smiling. 'For fear I'd drop it or suchlike.'

'It's . . .' Ocradda hesitated, 'very interesting. Awfully faded though, what a pity.'

With polite smiles they returned to their work. Carra turned the bit of bone over and studied the back. 'No maker's mark or suchlike. I was rather hoping.'

'I never thought to look for one,' Dallandra said. 'But you're right, that would have been important.'

'I love things like this.' Carra laid the plaque in her palm and held it out to Dallandra. 'You'd best take it back before I turn thief.'

'Well, now, here! You should have it since you love it.'

'Oh, I couldn't. It's too valuable.'

'My dear Carramaena! You're a princess now, and you should have a few treasures in your possession.' Dallandra handed over the silk. 'Here's the wrap for it.'

'My thanks and a thousand more!' Carra took the bit of fabric from her. 'This is so wonderful, Dalla! When you hold it, you feel like you hold the past itself. As if this was a bit of

Time, turned frozen or suchlike like ice. Well, that's a clumsy way of speaking, but do you understand?'

'I certainly do. I'd no idea that things of the past mattered so much to you.'

'Well, they do. Does that make me sound silly?'

'What? Of course not!'

'Well, my thanks, but my sisters used to tease me and suchlike, saying I was such an odd duck! I always wanted to know the history of things, you see, and I drove our chamberlain half-mad, when I was a child, asking where did this come from and how old is that.' Carra paused to look at Dallandra's face, as if searching for scorn. 'I do think that's one reason I fell in love with Dar. He never told me he was a prince, but he did talk of the Seven Cities and the kingdom that had fallen to demons, all those ages ago. I'd never heard such wonderful stories, not even when a travelling bard came our way.'

'Well, it's a sweet sort of sadness,' Dallandra said, 'thinking of all that vanished splendour and brave heroes fighting to the very end.'

'Oh, that too. But best of all it explained things. About the Westfolk, I mean, why you always come and go on the border and live with your horse herds instead of in towns and duns. I'd always wondered about that. When Dar talked of the old days, it was like clouds rolling back, and you could see a strange new sky.'

Carra seemed about to say more, but Elessi woke with a complaint, wailing and throwing her arms into the air. Carra wrinkled her nose.

'Oh what a stink! I know what you need, my beloved poppet. Dalla, please hold this picture for me while I change her?'

Dallandra took the bone plaque and laid it on her knee while Carra took the baby to the far side of the room, where a table stood with a chamber pot ready and a pile of rags for nappies. As she listened to Carra croon and chat to the baby, Dallandra felt ashamed of herself. Have I ever really looked at Carra before? she wondered. She had seen what everyone else had seen in her: a young lass, besotted with love – pretty little Carra, with her heart-shaped face and blonde hair, her enormous blue eyes that stared up at her husband in limpid devotion. None of us ever thought she had a brain in her head, Dalla thought. More fool us!

'I've got a legacy to deliver to you,' Rhodry said.

'A what?' Jahdo said. 'And who would be leaving a lowly lad such as me a thing?'

'Jill, of course. Here. This is to take the place of your grandfather's knife, the one I made you lose.'

Jahdo pulled the silver dagger from its sheath and stared at it for a long long time without speaking. They were standing outside in the late afternoon sunlight, not far from the stables, where Jahdo had been shovelling snow with one of the flat mucking-out shovels.

'Oh, it be so splendid!' Jahdo held the dagger up, and the blade caught the light and flashed like a mirror. 'Here, I could never be taking this!'

'You can, and you shall,' Rhodry said, grinning. 'Though I think you'd best keep it up in Dallandra's chamber where the other lads can't find it.'

'True spoken.' Jahdo ran a fingertip down the blade. 'There be a device on it, a little falcon, like.'

'That was Jill's father's mark, and she used it too, of course.'

'He were a sorcerer, then, such as she?'

'He wasn't, but the greatest swordsman in all Deverry.'

'Ah.' Jahdo sheathed the blade, hefted the dagger for a moment, then handed it back to Rhodry. 'I do hate to give it up, but truly, it had best wait for me up in the tower.'

'I'll take it. And talking of Jill reminds me, lad. I made you a promise, didn't I? About teaching you letters. It's a fair way to spring yet, so let's make a start.'

'Oh, my thanks! I did wonder, my lord, but I did hate to vex you or suchlike –'

'No harm in reminding me, and I'm no lord.'

'Well, you be so to me, as generous as any man could be.'

For a moment Jahdo thought Rhodry was about to cry, from the way he turned away with a toss of his head.

'My thanks,' Rhodry said, and his voice was unsteady. 'Here, I'll hunt up a slate or suchlike. Cadmar's scribe should have one. And we'll start today.'

Rhodry turned and hurried off across the ward. Jahdo watched him go, then went back to his work before the head groom caught him slacking.

Jahdo was just leaving the stables when he saw a small procession coming from the broch complex. At its head trotted Carra's dog, with Carra and Lady Ocradda just behind, and two pages following along after them. Jahdo felt himself blush. Here he was, with his clothes filthy on top and sweaty inside, and the princess was heading straight for him.

'Jahdo!' Carra called out. 'It gladdens my heart to see you.'

'And mine to see you, your highness,' Jahdo said, stepping back. 'But er, I be a bit mucky right now, and so –'

'Do you think that bothers me?' Carra smiled at him. 'I've come to see how my horse fares. I thought I'd fetch him out for a bit of sun and walk him round the ward.'

Ocradda looked as sour as if she'd bitten into wormy meat. Jahdo could guess that the princess had fought a battle to be allowed to come to the stables at all.

'I'll bring Gwerlas out for you,' Jahdo said. 'You'd best not be going in there with your long dresses and all. Some of the men, well, they be careless when they do muck out their mounts' stalls.'

'Oh here! I've always cared for my own horses, all the years that I –'

'Your highness!' Ocradda interrupted. 'The lad's right. Let him wait upon you! Er, I mean, if you please.'

'Oh very well. But be careful. Gwer can be a bit bitey.'

More than a bit, or so Jahdo knew from the earlier times when he'd cared for the horse. Still, the big dun gelding seemed to be in a good mood that afternoon; he allowed Jahdo to tie a rope onto his halter and lead him out without showing so much as a tooth. Out in the sun Gwerlas snorted and tossed his mane, then spotted Carra and headed straight for her with Jahdo trotting along at his side.

'There you are!' Carra crooned. 'My darling!'

When she threw her arms around his neck, the horse snuffled at her cloak and nudged her. Lady Ocradda rolled her eyes heavenward in something like despair. For their walk around the ward, Carra insisted on leading the horse herself, but she did allow Jahdo to hold onto the loose end of the rope for appearances' sake. A disgruntled Ocradda and the pages trailed behind as they followed the exercise path, a broad swathe next to the dun walls that had been cleared of the usual sheds and clutter.

'It's good to see you, Jahdo,' Carra said. 'How do you fare these days?'

'Well enough, your highness.'

'The servitors seem to be finding you lots of work to do.'

'Oh, working be no bother to me. It does make the time pass quicker, like.'

'You must be looking forward to going home.'

'That be ever so true.'

For a few moments they walked in silence. Carra kept laying her hand on Gwerlas' neck, making sure that he wasn't raising a sweat in this chilly air from lack of exercise. Jahdo barely felt the cold, as if walking next to the princess were in some mysterious way warming his blood. If only he could think of witty, courtly remarks that would impress her! Instead, he found himself searching desperately for conversation.

'Ah well,' Jahdo ventured finally. 'I did have a bit of news. I were talking with Rhodry, and he did offer to teach me how to read.'

'How splendid! I wish I could learn.'

'Well, why not ask him, then?'

Carra risked a quick glance over her shoulder. Ocradda and

the pages were picking their way through the snow a fair distance behind, but still, Carra lowered her voice. 'I fear me that the good women of the dun would scream at the horror of it all.'

'What? Why shouldn't you learn –'

'Not the reading. It's Rhodry, he's a silver dagger. Lady Labanna classes him with the dogs and the pigs, lower even than the men in her husband's warband.'

Jahdo considered this as they walked past the cookhouses.

'I did forget about things such as that,' he said at last. 'But here, I know! Why not ask our sorceress if you mayn't learn? If the lady Dallandra does approve, no one will dare say a word about it.'

It was late in the evening before Dallandra went up to the women's hall. By the light of candles the gwerbret's wife and her serving woman were leaning close to their embroidery to finish one last patch before their eyes grew too weary to continue. Dallandra joined Carra at the hearth. Elessi was awake, propped up against her mother's stomach.

'Elessi loves the fire,' Carra remarked. 'Not for the heat, I mean, but when she's awake, she'll stare into it for hours.'

'Well, it *is* a pretty thing, fire.'

Carra smiled and stroked her daughter's thin strands of pale hair. In the fire Dallandra could see salamanders, crawling along the logs, dancing among the embers, or rubbing their backs on the iron grating. No doubt Elessi could see them, too. The Wildfolk would flock to a being such as her, one of Evandar's kind and born into the world flesh for the first time.

'I can hardly wait to show her the spring,' Carra went on, 'the flowers blooming and the trees coming into leaf. Her first spring!'

'That will be lovely.'

'And then we'll be able to travel. The gwerbret and his lady have been so generous to us, and I shall miss them, but I'm so eager to meet Dar's people and see the grasslands.'

'It's not an easy life out on the grass.'

'It's not an easy life here, is it?'

'Well, that is most certainly true.' Dalla lowered her voice. 'I'll be glad to leave myself.'

'No doubt.' Carra smiled, briefly. 'I'm just so glad Elessi got herself born, and we both lived. Whilst I was carrying her? I truly did feel half-mad.'

'It was worrisome to watch. Everything seemed to frighten you.'

'Well, there was that small matter of the Horsekin army. I think me I had good reason to be frightened.'

'The best in the world. No one could blame you.'

'Jill did.'

Old pain shivered in Carra's voice. Dallandra considered her answer carefully.

'Unfortunately, that's true,' Dallandra said. 'But Jill demanded their absolute best from everyone she met, you know. It wasn't only you. She was a warrior in her soul, but not all of us can live up to that.'

'I can't, certainly. I'm a coward.'

'Truly?' Dallandra smiled at her. 'You left your brother's dun behind forever and followed Dar.'

'Oh, but I was frightened the whole time.'

'So? Do you think warriors never feel fear? Ask Rhodry about that, and see what he says.'

Carra paused, thinking.

'Well, I know what you mean,' Carra said at last. 'But sometimes I remember the way Jill used to look at me, and I cringe all over again.'

'I can understand that. Still, you have your own strengths, and the older you grow, the more you'll know them.'

'I suppose. You know, that reminds me, in an odd sort of way. I was talking with little Jahdo earlier, and he told me that Rhodry was going to teach him to read.'

'So I understand.'

'And well —' Carra hesitated for a long moment; then her words came in a rush. 'Could I learn too? I know it's above a woman's station, but I do so much want to learn.'

'Above your — oh hogwash! Of course you may learn, if you'd like. I'll speak to Rhodry for you.'

Carra turned to her and smiled, a bright steady joy like sunlight that was exactly the same smile she got when she saw her husband walk into the room. That Carra burned with a passion to learn how to read shocked Dallandra all over again, though as she thought about it she realized that anyone with a strong interest in history would no doubt wish to read about the past. Dallandra had laboured so long and hard to get Elessi born into the physical world that in her mind Carra's role as Elessi's mother had absorbed the actual person that Carra was. What an awful thing to do to someone! Dallandra told herself. She made herself pay strict attention to the girl as she talked on.

'It's just so wonderful,' Carra was saying, 'to be able to think about things like books and letters now. Sometimes I dream about Alshandra still, and the Horsekin army at our gates. When I wake up, I have to tell myself that we're safe at last.'

Dallandra started to make some pleasantry, but a dweomer-warning like a sudden blast of cold froze her lips, or so it seemed. She felt fear run down her back like the stroke of an icy hand. Carra turned to her in alarm, but fortunately the baby woke, stretching tiny arms, and began to cry. Dallandra murmured an excuse, got up, and left.

As she hurried up to her tower room, the dweomer cold went with her, hugging her so tightly she found it hard to breathe. Twice on the staircase up it forced her to stop and rest. While she leaned against stone walls and gasped, she heard a strange rustle or murmur, so loudly that at first she thought it was sounding in the physical world. The sound, however, followed her into her own quarters, swelling to a roar and babble of voices.

Safe at last? Far from it, far far from it! Dallandra nearly fell onto the bed. She had just the presence of mind to grab the blankets and pull them over her before she sank into trance. It seemed to her that she was awake in the tower room, but she lay paralysed in a light transformed into the silvery blue of the etheric plane. All around her swirled voices in a babble of languages; some words she could understand, others escaped her entirely. The voices seemed to come from a dozen speakers, some male, some female, others strangely ambiguous. Whatever they were trying to say rang with urgency; she could hear anger and terror, both, as they babbled on and on, louder and louder.

Suddenly the harsh shriek of a raven silenced the voices. The raven cried again, and it seemed its huge black shadow covered the room.

Abruptly Dallandra woke, lying in sweat-soaked clothing in an icy dark room. She got up, staggered to the window, and leaned against the wall while she fumbled with the leather covering. Finally she managed to pull up one corner. Cold wind and a flurry of snow slapped her in the face. Night lay over the dun, but how deep or early, she could not say. She let the hide fall again. Heat, she thought. I must get out of here, go where it's warm.

On her table stood a pitcher of water. She cracked the ice on top and drank straight out of the spout. The water brought enough sensation back to her body to allow her to walk across the room and open the door, but the dark landing and stairwell beyond made her hesitate. She called upon the Wildfolk of Aethyr, who materialized to surround her with a silvery glow. In their safe light she went down and reached the great hall at last.

Apparently the evening meal had just been cleared away. In firelight and torchlight the household lingered at table, from the gwerbret and the noble-born at the table of honour to the servants sitting by their fire and eating the left-over bread. Although Dar kept Carra company at the table of honour, his archers sat together with Rhodry among them on the far side of the hall. Although by the courtesy of the thing Dallandra should have gone to the gwerbret's side, she wanted her own kind around her. She started toward the archers' table only to find walking difficult. Half-afraid she'd fall, she stopped again, swaying like a drunken woman, but Rhodry had seen her. He swung himself free of the bench and hurried over.

'Dalla, ye gods!' Rhodry spoke in Elvish. 'Are you ill?'

'No. Just exhausted. I did a working of sorts.'

Rhodry caught her arm and steadied her. Yelling for a servant lass, he steered her across the great hall and over to a table near the honour hearth, where he made her sit with her back to the roaring fire. When Carra and Labanna started to join them, he hurried over to warn them off. Dallandra propped her elbows on the table and supported her head with her hands whilst she watched him, speaking urgently.

'My lady?'

The voice made Dallandra yelp, but it was only a servant girl with a basket of bread in one hand and a tankard in the other. When Dallandra took the tankard, the yeasty scent of watered ale cleared her head.

'My thanks,' Dallandra said. 'My apologies if I startled you.'

The girl gave her a wan little smile and ran for the other side of the hall. Being a sorcerer in Deverry must be a lonely sort of life, Dalla thought. She tore a chunk of bread off the loaf and bit off a mouthful. The taste made her realize that she was ravenous. Rhodry came back along and sat next to her, watching while she stuffed in the bread like a beggar child.

'You'd best wash that down with a bit of ale,' he remarked after a while. 'Or you'll choke.'

She nodded and had a long swallow.

'That's better,' Rhodry said, in Elvish this time. 'Now, what by the Dark Sun happened to you?'

'I was overwhelmed by a vision.' Dallandra paused for another long swallow of ale. 'No, that's not the right word, but I'm too tired to think of what you'd call a lot of voices, all speaking omens.'

'Can I ask what they were telling you?'

'I couldn't understand them, actually.' She sat the tankard down and considered him – if anyone in the dun could keep a secret, it would be Rhodry. 'It didn't matter. I also heard a raven caw, and that was the heart of the omen. It had to be your old friend, Raena. She means to harm Carra somehow, or more probably the child.'

Rhodry swore in a mix of several languages. Dallandra winced.

'Sorry,' he said. 'Raena takes me that way. Why would she want to hurt them? Her wretched false goddess is dead.'

'Does she believe that?'

'Well, I was assuming she would.'

'Why?' Dallandra paused for another swallow of ale. 'She carried out Alshandra's orders to raise an army. If it weren't for Arzosah, that army might have won, too, with Raena at their head. She's had glory and excitement both, a thousand times more than any other woman, probably. What makes you think she'll just meekly go back to her needlework now?'

'True enough.' Rhodry hesitated, thinking. 'Well, if she tries to harm either of them, she'll have to go through me first.'

'Oh, I'm sure she knows that. Why do you think I keep renewing the wards over you?'

'Now there's a thought. In my vanity I was thinking she hated me for myself, but if she knows I've sworn to guard the lass –'

'You did swear a vow like that? Right out loud, I mean.'

'Yes, when Yraen and I met Carra on the road. I saw her, and I knew I was bound to her in some strange way. So I hired myself out to her for a guard.'

'Oh! You mean you swore to guard Carra, not the baby.'

'Well, I suppose I meant the baby as well. I was stinking drunk at the time, and I don't remember the details.'

'No doubt.' Dallandra yawned, stifled it, then gave up and yawned again. 'I'm sorry. I'm just so tired.'

'You'd best get some sleep. You still look pale as death. I'll come upstairs with you.'

'Ye gods, I've slept all day!'

Yet Rhodry insisted, and once she was tucked up in the blankets with him beside her, radiating welcome warmth, Dallandra fell asleep straightaway.

For some while she slept in a normal oblivion, but eventually she woke and remembered the wards in the Gatelands. This time when she slept again, her mind went straight to the etheric and her stars. After she tended them, she stood in the tall grass and considered the swollen purple moon that hung, huge and menacing, over the meadow. She wanted to talk with Niffa, but since she knew only the girl's dream image, rather than her physical presence, she could no more scry her out on the etheric than she could in the material world. Fortunately, Niffa seemed to want to talk with her, as well, because in what seemed a brief space of time, Niffa joined her. As they sat in the tall grass and talked, Niffa's lack of rational control over her sleep-visions made it difficult to hold an organized conversation, but a bit at a time Dalla pieced together the girl's story of her murdered husband and of Councilman Verrarc.

'But here,' Dallandra said at last. 'You didn't truly see Raena murder your man, did you?'

Niffa shook her head.

'And so you can't be sure she –'

'That be what they both say!' Niffa snapped. 'My mam and da, I do mean by that.'

'Well, who do they think killed him, then?'

'Evil spirits,' Niffa said. 'The councilman, he did say this, and even our herbwoman and our Spirit Talker, they do believe him now.'

'What about the rest of the town?'

'The town? Well, the folk do be terrified and talk of witch-craft and dark things. They do but wish it forgotten, so they might pretend that naught were amiss.'

'I see. You'd best be careful, you know. They might turn on you eventually.'

'My mam, she do say the same. She be powerful frightened.'

Niffa's image was growing thin, stretched out like a figure painted on cloth held against the landscape. Dallandra had to think quickly.

'You're right to mistrust Raena,' Dallandra said, 'but be careful! She's very dangerous, and –'

Niffa's image winked out. I wonder if she heard me? Dallandra thought. Well, no doubt I'll see her here again.

When she woke that morning, Niffa heard voices out in the great room – her mother's and another woman's. That best not be that miserable Raena! As she dressed, she snarled like a ferret. She found her clogs, slipped them on, then stomped into the other room, only to see Emla, Demet's mother, sitting comfortably by the fire.

'Well, there you are,' Emla said. 'I did come to see how you fare, lass. We've not seen you since –' Her voice choked with tears. 'Since the funeral rites.'

'I've not been out much,' Niffa said. 'Going out into the town does ache my heart.'

Niffa sat down on the bench next to Dera, who slipped an arm around her shoulders. Despite the grey that grew in her blonde hair, Emla looked so like her son that seeing her made Niffa's grief double in her heart.

'Sooner or later,' Dera said, 'you'll have to begin living again. I doubt me if Emla would begrudge you.'

'Not in the least.' Emla leaned forward in her chair. 'You be young, Niffa. In time there'll be another man, and I'd not have you thinking I'd take offence at your happiness.'

'I'll never marry again!'

The older women exchanged glances – sad-eyed, but with a hint of a smile. Niffa got up, took a wooden bowl from the table, and busied herself with filling it with porridge from the kettle by the hearth.

'And there be another matter,' Emla went on. 'Your mam and I did discuss this matter of Councilman Verrarc's woman. He does wish to marry her, all right and proper like, but Werda refuses to perform the rites.'

'No doubt she kens what's best,' Niffa snapped. 'She always does.'

'When it comes to spirits, no one would argue with that,' Emla said, smiling a little. 'But flesh and blood – well, that be another matter, bain't? And we all ken the history of the thing. Verro would have married his Raena years hence, had his wretched fool of a father but allowed. It does seem right to put it right, as it were.'

Niffa sat down on the bench at the far side of the table and concentrated on her porridge. How could Emla think such a thing, that Raena should be allowed into the citizenry as a redeemed woman and a proper wife?

'I do wonder, though,' Dera was choosing each word carefully, 'what sort of influence Raena might have on the councilman, if it be wholly good, that is.'

'Now that be a true question.' Emla nodded her agreement. 'But once they were married, he would have the dominion over her, bain't?'

'True, true.'

'I do think she be the sort of woman who does need a firm hand to guide her,' Emla went on. 'And Verrarc, he be a stubborn sort of man.'

'That too be a true speaking.' Dera hesitated for a long moment. 'You do know well that Verrarc, his happiness does mean much to me, ever since he did run to me for refuge when he were but a tiny lad. I do wish naught but the best for him.'

Niffa caught her mother's eye and scowled. Dera turned away and looked only at Emla.

'Just so,' Emla said. 'You do doubt, then, that Raena would make him a proper sort of wife?'

'I do,' Dera said. 'Here, she be barren for one thing. It be no fault of her own, but a man like Verrarc, with property to leave – he does need sons, bain't? Or a daughter to dower at least.'

'Huh! I'd not thought of that. But truly, she did stay with her husband for a year, and then she and Verrarc did give the gods plenty of chances to bless them.'

'Just so.'

Emla sucked her teeth for a thoughtful while. 'Verrarc be a stubborn sort of man,' she said at last. 'He'll not be giving her up easily.'

'True spoken.'

'But you know what they do say, Dera. Sometimes a man must needs get what he wants before he can see that he wants it not.'

'Now that be a very true thing.' Dera paused, considering. 'The more that the town speaks ill of her, the more loyal he'll be.'

Niffa looked up from her bowl and glared. Emla waggled a long finger in her direction.

'That porridge must be sour stuff,' Emla said, 'if I were to judge by the look on your face. What does ache your heart so badly, lass?'

Caught – Niffa could hardly tell Emla about her visions and suspicions. She laid her spoon down in the empty bowl.

'Ah well,' Niffa said at last. 'Never have I liked Raena, truly. She does seem so sly, and who can ken where she's been hiding herself this while past? She did show up in winter out of nowhere, bain't?'

'Oh, that be simple enough.' Emla was smiling. 'She did return to her father's farm when her husband cast her out. No doubt the old man's rubbed her raw with the shame of it. He always was that sort, all long nose for the looking down.'

'That be enough to drive anyone out into the snows,' Dera put in. 'The poor woman!'

If her mother's compassion had been kindled, Niffa knew, there was no use in arguing further.

'Well, Mistress Emla,' Dera went on, 'if you go to speak with Werda, then I'll be going with you to put in a word, like.'

'My thanks. The more of us, the better. I'll be off to speak with some few others of the women here.'

When Emla was leaving, Niffa managed to force out a reasonably pleasant farewell, but she spoke not another word. Dera shut the door behind their departing guest and latched it for good measure. She sat down opposite Niffa.

'Mam! How could you!'

'Hush, now! You do think that Raena had somewhat to do with Demet's death, but I be not so sure. Werda did say evil spirits, and would you be telling me that you do ken more of these matters than Werda?'

'Well, I wouldn't. But she laughed, Raena I mean, laughed at him lying dead.'

'Be you so certain of that? There be times, when a woman or a man too for that matter, when she does see some great horror, and while it does seem that she laughs, truly there be no mirth in it, just a ghastly sort of sobbing without tears.'

Niffa started to answer, but her mother's quiet voice caught her and made her think. What if she were accusing Raena falsely? That would be a terrible thing.

'Whatever you say, Mam. Mayhap you and Emla have the right of it.'

'My thanks.' Dera allowed herself a small smile. 'And I'd not worry just yet. Changing Werda's mind about any matter be a long hard task.'

It was a few days later that Dallandra heard the truth of Demet's death, when she met Evandar on the crest of Market Hill. They found each other just at nightfall under a sky so clear and cold that the stars seemed chips of ice, glittering in the silver fire of the rising moon. Wrapped in his blue cloak Evandar glowed to match the moonlight.

'And how does Salamander fare?' Dallandra asked him.

'Who? Ah, Rhodry's brother.'

'Indeed. I asked Rhodry if he knew anything about a curse Jill put on him, and Rhodry swears up and down that she'd never have done such a thing. He did say, though, that she might have sworn like a silver dagger at him, and in his madness he might be remembering it and misinterpreting.'

'Now that makes a great deal of sense. I'll try to visit him again.' Evandar frowned up at the stars. 'I've not had a moment to spare, my love, what with the trouble Shaetano's causing.'

'In Jahdo's city? I've heard another nasty tale myself, about Raena and the way she murdered a man there.'

'The young militiaman? It wasn't her who killed him. It was Shaetano.'

Dallandra found herself with nothing to say. Evandar laughed at her shock, then sobered fast.

'It's an evil thing,' he said. 'And I've no idea how he did it. Worse yet, neither does he. He's been calling himself Lord Havoc, and he seems to be living up to his name.'

'Things are even worse than I thought, then. I'd better go have a look at all of this in the spring.'

'If you wanted to go straightaway, I could take you there by the mothers of all roads.'

'I can't leave Carra and the baby.'

'We could all go, Jahdo and Rhodry too.'

'True, but Rhodry won't leave until spring, because he's waiting for Arzosah. Not that she's likely to return.'

'It was foolish of him to break that binding spell, truly. The great wyrms have devious little hearts.'

'But here, he knows – we all know, truly – her true name. Shouldn't that –'

'It's not enough. I don't care what the old tales say, but merely knowing a dragon's name is no protection for an ordinary man.

Someone who can put dweomer behind speaking the name –
well, that's different.'

'I see. Well, dragon or no, in the spring I'd better get myself
to Cerr Cawnen.'

'Shall I bring Rhodry's brother there to meet you?'

Dallandra considered this for a moment.

'I don't think so,' she said at last. 'I think he'd be better off in
the Westlands, nearer his father. But for the love of every god,
don't bring him anywhere just yet, will you? I've got enough on
my mind as it is.'

'True spoken, so I'll leave him be for now. It's not like his
poor wife has to handle him on her own.'

'That's one good thing about all those wretched acrobats.'
Dallandra glanced around and realized that all the houses she
could see had gone dark. 'Ye gods, I'd better get myself back
to the dun! The gatekeeper won't wait for me forever.'

'I'll walk with you. I don't trust these streets at night. Which
reminds me. Does Rhodry still have that bronze knife?'

It took Dallandra a moment to remember which knife
he meant.

'The ancient one?' she said. 'The one that has some strange
dweomer on it?'

'That's the one. He might need it with Alshandra's pack still
on the loose.'

'He keeps it on his belt with the silver dagger.'

'Good. Tell him to stay on guard, too.'

Together they hurried back to the dun, but at the iron-bound
gates Evandar left her. Dallandra gave the old gatekeeper a
coin for his patience, then walked into the main ward, where
torchlight danced and threw fitful shadows on stone. Not far
from the back door to the great hall she saw a crowd of the
gwerbret's riders, all arguing about some incomprehensible
thing. Out of curiosity she drifted over and found a place to
stand on the steps of one of the side-brochs.

From there she could see the trouble. In the centre of a
ring of Cadmar's sworn men stood a man of the Westfolk

and one of Cadmar's riders, both of them trembling with fury while Cadmar's captain and Prince Daralanteriel talked urgently together. Nearby a blonde servant girl stood weeping into the hem of her apron.

At the edge of the crowd stood Rhodry, his hands dangling easily by his sides. The sooty torches cast more shadow than light, but she could see him smiling with a tight twist of his mouth. When a torch flared and washed his face with light, the look in his eyes turned her cold; they were as blank and hard as a hawk's. All at once he stepped forward; it seemed the argument between Prince Daralanteriel and the gwerbret's captain was heating up. Someone in the crowd yelled, 'Filthy thieves, all of you – thieves and silver daggers!'

Rhodry moved, struck, had the fellow by the neck with both hands.

'Rhodry!' Dallandra screamed. 'Don't!'

Rhodry threw his prey to the ground and twisted free. Hands reached down and hauled the fellow to his feet; he was choking and shaking but mostly unharmed. Rhodry turned toward her and laughed in a high-pitched shriek of merriment.

'My thanks!' he called out. 'I would have killed him if it weren't for you.'

'So I thought,' Dallandra muttered, but too quietly for him to hear. 'You berserk bastard.'

The riders all turned to look at her, and she saw most of them holding up crossed fingers in the gesture of warding against witchcraft. Some stepped backwards into shadows, then turned and ran; others slipped away more slowly, but they got themselves gone nonetheless until only Rhodry and Draudd, one of the gwerbret's sworn men, stood alone in the smoke-stained torch light.

'I'm blasted glad you came along.' Draudd bowed to Dallandra. 'Ye gods, the little slut's not worth a man's life!'

'That blonde lass – she was the cause of this, then?' Dallandra asked.

'She was,' Draudd said. 'Keeping two hearths warm at once, if you take my meaning, like.'

'Will there be more trouble over this?' Dallandra said to Draudd.

'Not from any of us. Since it never came to drawn steel, the gwerbret doesn't have to know. Well, unless he heard the scuffle?'

When Dallandra went to the door of the great hall and looked in, she found the gwerbret's chair safely empty. Jahdo came running and told her that his grace had gone early to bed.

'His leg's bothering him,' the boy said. 'The twisted one.'

'No doubt, in this cold and damp,' Dallandra said. 'Well, I'll brew him up some poultices in the morning.'

For a moment she stood watching the men filing back into the hall. When she turned back, Rhodry had gone.

She found him up in their tower room, feeding twigs by candlelight into the charcoal braizer. She shut the door, but he ignored her and bent down to blow upon the coals. Finally the tinder caught; he added a few thin twigs of charcoal, then some bigger chunks.

'I think that'll take,' he said.

'Looks like it, truly.'

In the candlelight and faint glow from the brazier, his face was unreadable. With an irritable snarl, Dallandra called on the Wildfolk of Aethyr. A silver ball of light appeared, hovering over the table. Rhodry looked up. His eyes seemed huge, his dark brows straight above them, but his soft mouth hung slack; he could have been thinking murder or nothing at all.

'Would you really have killed that fellow?' she said.

'Most likely.' With a shrug he turned away from the brazier and wiped his hands on his brigga. 'I've never been a patient man. And it's been too long since I sent my Lady Death a courting-gift. She's even less patient than I am.'

'I wish you wouldn't go on like that about your Lady Death. It's such a daft fancy!'

'Is it? Why?' All at once he was grinning, his eyes narrow with delight. 'Haven't I served her faithfully all these years?

You'd think a true lover would have had his reward by now, wouldn't you?'

She could only stare at him. Ye gods! she thought. Is this the evil Wyrd that Jill saw? That he'd go mad – if it is madness? His smile faded.

'What is this?' Dallandra said suddenly. 'Are you saying you want to die?'

'Who wouldn't, after the life I've led?' Rhodry turned his back on her and walked a few steps away.

When she walked over and laid her hands on his shoulders, she could feel hard muscle, tensed and ready to spring. She let her hands fall.

'There's naught you can say to that, is there?' His voice was low and level. 'There's naught anyone can say.'

'True enough.'

Around them the Wildfolk began to appear, sprites and gnomes, and in the glow of the brazier, she saw a salamander lounging on the coals.

'You're not thinking of killing yourself, are you?' Dallandra said.

'I'm not. Not while the raven woman lives, at least.'

'Ah ye gods! Promise me you won't –'

'Won't what? Take a knife to my own throat or suchlike?' Rhodry turned around at last, and he was smiling. 'I won't. I'll swear it to you on my silver dagger. That's the one oath you know I'd never break.'

'How can you smile like that?'

He cocked his head to one side and considered her for a long moment, then wiped the smile away.

'True enough. It's no jest, is it?' He grabbed his cloak from the chair's back. 'I'll not be able to sleep. Don't wait up for me.'

He strode out of the room with the Wildfolk following him in a swirl of little lives. She sat down on the chair and held out her hands. She wasn't in the least surprised to find them shaking.

*   *   *

Although the gwerbret had seen nothing, Prince Daralanteriel proved unwilling to let the matter drop. When Rhodry walked into the great hall, the prince rose from his chair at the honour hearth and hailed him. Rhodry stood where he was and waved vaguely in Dar's direction. For a long moment, while every man in the great hall watched, the stalemate held; then with a shrug Dar grabbed his cloak from his chair and strode across the hall to join Rhodry at the door.

'You wanted to speak with me?' Rhodry said. 'What about?'

'Things.' Dar busied himself with draping his cloak over his shoulders. 'We'd best talk outside, anyway.'

Around back of the main broch they found a spot out of the wind, where flickering light from the fires inside spilled out onto the frozen mud. Both of them could see in far less light than any ordinary man, but the glow seemed somehow comforting against the night.

'That fellow called me a thief,' Dar said abruptly. 'Should I challenge him to an honour duel?'

'Do you want to?' Rhodry said.

'I don't, no. It would be stupid, and you've already given him the scare of his life. But what will the men here think of me if I don't?'

'Ah. You're starting to think like a Deverry lord.'

Dar flushed scarlet. Rhodry looked him in the face and refused to flinch. After a moment, Dar looked down.

'Maybe I am. I wish to all the gods that we could just ride out of here, but in this weather –'

'We'd never make it home. Your men are getting worried, Dar. They look at you sitting with the gwerbret and wonder if your head's getting too big for your helm.'

Dar stared at the muddy ground for a long moment, then turned on his heel and strode off. Rhodry followed him as ducked back inside the great hall. Dar hesitated briefly, then walked over to the table where the other men of the Westfolk were sitting. He spoke a few brief words to Vantalaber, then sat down on the bench at his captain's right hand. Smiling to himself, Rhodry strolled over and joined them.

In the morning Dallandra woke to find Rhodry still gone. When she went downstairs, she found him rolled in his cloak and asleep in the straw near the riders' hearth, with a couple of dogs at his back and Jahdo asleep nearby. As she hovered there, wondering whether to wake him, he solved the problem by sitting up and yawning.

'Good morrow, fair sorceress,' he said, grinning. 'I got too drunk last night to manage the stairs. Dar had squirrelled away some mead in his chamber, and he brought it down for us.'

'Ah. I see.'

Yawning, shaking his head, he rubbed his face with both hands.

'I need to shave,' he said. 'I hate getting shaggy, winter or no. Have you eaten yet?'

'I've not.'

Rhodry got up, shaking out his cloak.

'I've made a bit of a fool of myself, haven't I?'

'Not truly.' Dallandra spoke in Elvish. 'No more than the rest of the men have, at least, and I'm including the prince in that. You know, you should all get out of the dun more. Go hunting, maybe – the gods know we could use the meat if there's any deer left to bring down.'

'Good idea,' he answered her in Elvish as well. 'I'll talk with Dar. You're right. We're all going more than a little mad, shut up like this.'

With that he bowed and wandered off, muttering about finding hot water to wash in. While Dallandra waited for a servant to bring her bread, the man whom Rhodry had nearly killed came hurrying over, a narrow-eyed blond fellow with a freshly split lip and bruises on his neck just the size of Rhodry's fingers. When he bowed to her, she could see him trembling.

'I owe you my life,' he blurted. 'My thanks, my lady.'

'Well, most welcome you are. I'm just glad Rhodry listened to me.'

'Listened?' He laid a hand over the bruises. 'We all figured you cast a spell. Naught else could reach him, we figured, when he has one of his fits.'

Dallandra started to tell him otherwise, then decided that long explanations of how Rhodry's mind worked would lie beyond him.

'You seem to bear him no ill-will,' she said instead.

'Of course I don't. He's one of the god-touched.' The rider shrugged, hands out as if he were holding some truth before him. 'That trial by combat he fought – remember? It showed all of us how much the gods favour him. So it's all my own fault, what happened last night. I was drunk, I don't remember what I said, but it's no matter. You don't prod one of the god-touched.'

'I see. Well, I'm glad you came to no real harm. But you know, you'd best apologize to the prince for the things you called his men.'

'You're right. I'll do it the moment he comes down.'

By the noontide the squabble had smoothed itself over, and as far as Dallandra knew, the gwerbret never heard of it. She hoped the spring would come early that year. The sooner they were all out of the stone tents once and for all, the better.

For several nights Niffa tried to return to the meadow under the purple moon and talk with the woman who called herself Dallandra. Her dreams, however, like ill-trained horses wandered where the road looked easiest and avoided the city that once had appeared so faithfully. Finally Niffa realized that mere hope would always fail her. She began trying to picture the purple moon and Dallandra as she was falling asleep, and this technique brought success. One night when the winds howled round Citadel and shut out the world, Niffa fell straight asleep and found herself walking across the meadow toward the great warding stars, burning red and gold. Dallandra sat waiting next to them.

'It's good to see you,' the sorceress said. 'I was afraid you'd decided not to return.'

'Oh, no such thing. It were the dreams that turned stubborn when I did try to force them. Tonight I let the moon rise in my mind, like, and it brought me here.'

'Very good indeed! Now, I need to talk with you about somewhat important, but it won't make much sense at first. Tell me – you see the Wildfolk, don't you? The little creatures in the air, or in fires and running water?'

'I do, truly. How were you guessing that?'

'Jahdo told me you always watched things that no one else could see.'

'Ah.' Niffa smiled, remembering. 'He did tease me over that until at times I did feel like giving him a good clout. There be not much that our Jahdo does miss.'

'He's a sharp lad. Well, there are other spirits in the world, bigger ones, much more like men and women, and very much more powerful indeed. They appear here and there and look just like ordinary people until of all a sudden they do somewhat strange or just disappear.'

'Be those gods?'

'They're not, but a race called the Guardians.' Dallandra hesitated and seemed to be considering what to say next. 'One of them has made a bargain with Raena. He's teaching her magicks, and she's – well, how to say – well, she's doing him little favours in return.'

'I don't understand.'

'Neither do I.' All at once Dallandra laughed. 'Not completely. But this creature can appear as a fox or a man. He calls himself Lord Havoc.'

'That be an ill-omened name!'

'He's an ill-omened creature. I'm as sure as I can be that he'll bring trouble to Cerr Cawnen if someone doesn't stop him. Raena – well, she's mostly deluded. She thinks he's a god, and he's not. It's not truly her fault.'

Niffa considered for a moment.

'Well, even so,' Niffa said at last, 'would this Lord Havoc fox creature be a-troubling us if that whoring slut of a Raena hadn't brought him here?'

'You truly hate her, don't you?'

Niffa paused on the edge of a retort. She could see that Dallandra was studying her face as she waited for a reply.

'I do,' Niffa said. 'And truly, you do touch upon a riddle. At first, before my man died, I knew not why I did hate her so. From the day she came to Cerr Cawnen, and I did see her walking toward the gates, I did feel – well, it be so strange – but I did feel she'd be the ruination of us all, that some great evil walked in with her.'

'Oh, did you now? Jahdo's told me that when you have these feelings, you're usually right.'

'It's happened.' Niffa shrugged and looked away. 'Over the years I did learn to keep my mouth closed tight when the omens did beat against my lips. It did trouble everyone around us.'

'No doubt. Say naught about that omen to anyone until I get there.'

'You do plan on coming to Cerr Cawnen?'

'I do indeed, in the spring when we – Rhodry and I – bring your Jahdo home. Raena is somewhat of an enemy of mine, after all. I'd rather like a few words with her, not that she'll enjoy hearing them.'

For a moment the dream threatened to waver and dissolve in a flood of sheer relief, but Niffa focused her mind on Dallandra's face, thought of nothing but that image, and slowly the dream grew strong and clear again.

'Very good,' Dallandra said, smiling. 'For a moment I thought I'd lost you.'

'I did think I were about to go, truly. But it gladdens my heart, hearing that you be coming to Cerr Cawnen.'

'I'm glad you trust me.'

'Well, I do, though I know not why. Mayhap it's because you do hate Raena too.'

'Hate her I don't. She's but a tool in the hands of lying spirits.'

'What about the councilman? Be it that he worship this fox spirit too?'

'I have no idea. Now listen carefully. It's not Raena that murdered your man. It was Lord Havoc.'

The surprise hit like a blow and flung Niffa out of the dream. She woke to a room silver with dawn and knew that she'd not be falling asleep again, not this late in a winter's day. Her body ached, too; for a moment, she wondered if she'd somehow hurt herself by waking so fast. Then she recognized a familiar pain. Her monthly bleeding had finally begun. She sat up in bed and stared at her cold little room.

'I did want Demet's child,' she whispered. 'I did want his child so very much. Ah ye gods!'

She twisted round and grabbed the pillow, then lay down to sob into it until she ached too badly to weep the more.

'Master!' Old Korla came shuffling into the great room. 'The Spirit Talker, she be at our door.'

'Then let her in, for the gods' sake!' Verrarc said. 'Did you think I'd be turning her away or suchlike?'

Korla set her mouth in a tight line, shrugged, and shuffled back down the corridor.

Verrarc rose from his little table by the hearth. He'd been puzzling over his dweomer scroll again, and he rolled it up to hide its subject matter. With Korla following, Werda came striding in, draped in her white cloak.

'This be an honour indeed.' Verrarc bowed to her. 'Do come sit by my fire.'

'I'll not be staying but a moment,' Werda said. 'I be here to tell you but one thing. If you wish to marry your woman, I'll perform the proper rite.'

'My thanks!' Verrarc was stammering, and he felt tears rising behind his eyes. 'My humble thanks! I –'

'Some of the good women of this town did come to argue with me,' Werda went on. 'Pay your thanks to them, not me. I did listen to them with care, and with care did I think the matter through. I do suggest, councilman, that you put as much care into your choice of a wife. Think on this for seven nights. Then, if you still wish to marry Raena daughter of Marga, come to me at the temple, and I'll cast the omens to find a propitious phase of the moon.'

Before Verrarc could say another word, Werda turned on her heel and strode out, with Korla hurrying after.

'The haughty bitch!' Raena snarled from behind him.

Verrarc spun round to see her walking out of their bed chamber. She was wearing a green overdress, and she'd done her hair in thick braids, falling one on either side of her face.

'I'd not speak ill of Werda, if I were you,' he said.

'Indeed?' Raena was scowling. 'Huh! Some priestess she is, her and her little gods! Here, my love – do you not scorn my Lord Havoc and claim him but a fox spirit or suchlike? Well, the gods Werda tends are no better than that, the spirit of a mountain, the spirit of a tree!' Her mouth twisted. 'Did they give her the power to call forth silver light, as the great Alshandra gave to me?'

'They didn't, truly. But Rae, when it comes to life in this town, there be gods that Werda tends who have true power indeed.'

'Oh? And who may they be?'

'Rumour, for one.' Verrarc looked steadily at her. 'And the gods of a happy hearth and a good reputation, for others.'

Raena blushed, looked away, then sat down in her chair by the hearth. Verrarc went to the fire and knelt down to add the last of the wood from the big basket near the hearth. The flames leapt up in a swirl of golden sparks.

'This be the second happiest day of my life.' Verrarc reached for the poker. 'The first, well – truly, it will always be the day my father died.'

Raena laughed. 'Never would I begrudge you that, my love,' she said. 'It gives my heart joy, too, thinking I'll be your wife.'

Verrarc glanced over his shoulder and smiled at her just as Korla returned, her mouth still tight, her eyes narrow with what seemed to be anger. No doubt she wasn't looking forward to having another woman give her orders in her kitchen, not after so many years of keeping house for Verrarc alone. He would have to do somewhat to soften the blow, he decided.

'Korla?' he said. 'Do tell Harl to bring in more wood, will you? And it would behoove you and Magpie to be thinking of what sort of grand present I can make you to celebrate my marriage.'

Korla relented enough to smile, but all she said was, 'Harl, he be out in the woodshed now. I'll be telling him.'

Raena watched her unspeaking as the old woman crossed the room and disappeared through the door that led to the kitchen. Verrarc rose, dusting the ashes off the knees of his brigga.

'We shall have a feast on our wedding day, my love,' he said, 'the best that winter can offer us, and then in the spring when the crops come in, we'll have a proper celebration at the same time of the moon that marks our wedding.'

'That will be splendid, Verro. Truly, this day gladdens my heart. I did hear what Werda said about the townswomen. There be a need on me to go and thank them.'

'There is, at that.' Verrarc sat down in his facing chair. 'I ken not all their names, but I'll wager that Dera and Emla be among them. I do owe them thanks myself, and we'll pay our calls together.'

Raena nodded, staring into the fire with a small smile. Verrarc leaned back in his chair and stretched out his legs to the warmth.

'It will be splendid,' Raena said at last, 'to have a name again. I did get so sick to my heart of their snubs! Now, mayhap I can gain their trust, so that they'll listen to me.'

'Whose trust?'

'The women of the town, of course. I do think that they'll hear about Alshandra with more joy than the men.'

'What? Just what be you planning to do?'

'Spread the word of my goddess's coming.' Raena was looking at him with a slight frown, as if she were puzzled by his obtuseness. 'Think you I be a miser, to keep such joy to myself? I did swear to her that ever and always would I tell of her doings to all whom I would meet. Cerr Cawnen, it be a fine place to take up her charge again.'

Verrarc started to speak, then thought better of it. All at once he felt a cold that the leaping fire was powerless to dispel.

'I shall spread the word,' Raena went on, her voice soft, almost dreamy. 'I shall set her name upon Cerr Cawnen and make it a place of her altars. All the people shall rejoice in her name, and she will send them strength.'

Once again Verrarc opened his mouth, and once again held his tongue. The cold around him deepened. Had she gone mad, his beloved Raena? Or could she be speaking the truth and truly serve a goddess who could set men free from the chains of death? She turned to him, her eyes thoughtful.

'Fear not, my love. In time I'll be showing you more of her marvels, and till then, I'll not speak a word to anyone else. I do ken better than any how the ignorant will mock and scorn some new thought. I shall be all caution and soft words.'

'Well and good, then. Rae, please, you do see that I be not mocking what you say, bain't?'

'I do. Fear not! With her there be only courage.'

Verrarc smiled, but the cold had turned to a wild animal, it seemed, sinking claws of warning into his heart. Raena returned to staring into the fire and smiling to herself, as if she were hearing some grand jest. For a moment he wondered if indeed he should marry her. If she were mad and babbling of false gods, wouldn't she be a threat to his beloved city? But he could remember his father's face, flushed with drink and sneering, and hear again the insults he'd hurled at Raena and her kin. A rich pig farmer be a pig farmer still – that was the least of them.

'Well, I ken not the truth of such things as gods,' Verrarc said, 'but I do ken that I love you with all my heart, and that be enough for me.'

'Well, now,' Dera said. 'I do have some news from young Harl. Verrarc and Raena will marry in three nights, when the moon turns from dark to the first sliver in the sky.'

'It were time that he did make an honest woman of her,' Lael said.

Kiel nodded his agreement. After their mid-day meal, the family was sitting at the long table in front of their hearth. Niffa realized that they were all looking at her. She got up and began picking up the empty wooden bowls and spoons.

'Harl did say that Verrarc wished us to be there,' Dera continued in a few moments.

'I shan't go!' Niffa snapped.

She looked up to find the family still watching her. She carried the bowls to the washtub by the door and set them inside to wait until Kiel fetched water. Ever since Dallandra's warnings, Niffa had been trying to watch her words about the councilman's woman.

'It's not that I do blame Raena,' she said at last. 'To see a wedding – it would pierce my heart with grief.'

Dera's eyes filled with tears.

'Oh,' Lael said. 'Well, then, we'll let your mam and brother go to represent us, like, and I'll be staying here with you.'

Niffa covered her face with both hands and wept. She heard her father getting up, felt his arm around her shoulder.

'Here, lass, here,' he murmured. 'You have a good cry, like. I do ken how hard it be to believe this, but in time, the pain will heal up.'

'I do hope you be right,' Niffa sobbed. 'I do hope so.'

On the day of Verrarc's wedding, Kiel and Dera went off to

the celebration. Niffa and Lael passed the time by working. Since the wicker rat traps and the cage to carry the ferrets wore out fast, Lael always kept a supply of withies and leather thongs on hand. That day Niffa set some of the withies to soak in the washtub whilst Lael inspected the traps and set the broken ones onto the table. The ferrets, of course, offered their version of help, capturing any thong that moved, chewing on the wet withies, knocking over the traps, and chasing each other around the table. Laughing at them, Niffa could for a little while feel happy.

Dera and Kiel came home laden with food – loaves of bread, dried apples, a big chunk of fresh roasted pork, a skin of mead, and an entire raw pork liver for the weasels – all bounty from Verrarc. After Niffa cleared off the mended traps, they laid the food on the table, but neither of them spoke until they'd finished.

'He did pay a farmer to fatten up a hog.' Kiel gestured at the chunk of roast meat. 'So that the guests would have a proper meal.'

'He be a generous man, Verrarc,' Lael said. 'Here, woman, what be so wrong with you?'

Niffa had expected Dera to come home chattering and happy after such an event, but in truth, her mother looked solemn enough for a funeral. Dera took off her cloak and hung it on a wall peg before she answered.

'The wedding fire wouldn't light,' Dera said at last. 'Young Artha tried and tried, but no matter how many sparks she did strike, the tinder, it did smoulder, but it did refuse to burn.'

'Ye gods!' Lael said. 'Be they not married, then?'

'Oh, they are,' Kiel muttered. 'Verro, he'd not let the thing be stopped.'

'It did light, you see,' Dera added. 'In the end. Harl did help Artha, and they did get the tinder burning in the end.'

Niffa caught her breath in an audible gasp.

'Truly,' Dera said, nodding her way. 'It be a terrible, terrible omen. All this food? It were few of the guests who stayed for the feasting, so Verrarc, he did pile our arms high with it.'

'Huh,' Lael said. 'Bad omens twice over. Nah, thrice, I'd say, and three times thrice at that.'

As winter turned toward spring, Evandar began to visit Cengarn and Dallandra more often. In back of the kitchen hut he'd spotted the herb garden, dead under the last of the snow, lying at some distance from any iron. Toward dawn on one frosty morning he sent her a dream, and once the sun rose, they met there, well out of sight of the main broch.

'I'm so glad you're here,' Dallandra said.

'Indeed?' Evandar said. 'What's so wrong?'

'I'm worried about Elessario. I've just spent a long night trying to get her to go to sleep so Carra could get some rest.'

'Is she ill?'

'No, but she will be if the baby keeps running her ragged.'

'I meant Elessi.'

'Ah. No, not at all.' Dallandra hesitated for a moment, thinking. 'But she's not – she's not quite right. I don't know how to explain it, but while she looks like a normal infant, she's not. Her mind works very differently.'

'Like little Zandro?'

'Who?'

'My apologies. I forgot you wouldn't know. Salamander's youngest child. He's one of Alshandra's people, but born, I mean, into a human body now. His mother's in despair over him.'

'What? How could he –'

'I've been thinking about that very thing. When we were scheming to get our magical child born, didn't Alshandra the Hag try to stop us? She set her spies to watching and following Elessi everywhere she went. And then, when you were teaching the child what it might mean to be born into this world, didn't you take her to Bardek? The spies obviously followed you.'

'So they must have. I suppose it's possible, that one of them got fascinated with the place and its people, but –'

'Not fascinated with Bardek, my love. Fascinated with Salamander. Spirits swarm around him all the time. It's like his soul is a lantern burning out on the astral, and they're the moths.'

'Oh.' Dallandra considered this with a small frown. 'Well, that would explain it, all right. Now, what about the rest of Alshandra's pack? Have you taken them into yours yet?'

'I have not, and I shan't, either, the ugly little spawn! It's bad enough that I've saddled myself with Shaetano's creatures.'

'But if you leave them running loose in the world, they'll be working mischief.'

'I don't care. Let them fade away into naught!'

'You can't just –'

Evandar kissed her to silence her, then turned away with a laugh.

'We'll speak of these things later, my love. I'd best see to Salamander's troubles.'

'Come back here! We need to talk about this.'

Evandar walked over to the wall round the garden. In a shimmer of early light he could just see a link between the worlds.

'Evandar!' Dalla sounded furious. 'You can't leave those creatures to their own devices!'

With a smile in her direction, he sprang to the top of the wall and stepped through the link. Sure enough, one of the mother roads lay waiting. He walked onto it and followed a long shaft of sunlight south.

Although Evandar set out for Bardek, in a few moments he looked around him, saw pine-forested hills, and realized that he was heading north. He turned around and started to walk south again only to find himself circling back round, as if the road were moving under his feet. In the wind he heard a voice, whispering 'danger, grave danger' over and over again.

'Should I go to Cerr Cawnen instead?' he asked aloud.

The wind hissed out a yes.

'Oh very well then!'

The road seemed to fly of its own accord, speeding him along. He stepped down onto the peak of Citadel, then picked his way through the boulders and down into the tunnel. If there were danger in this city, he was willing to wager that Raena was bringing it, but the ruined underground temple stood empty. Evandar hurried back out. He spread his arms wide, then took off running with a sudden leap into the air. He felt his wings grow as the wind caught them, and his body shrink and change.

With a chirp a sparrow flew over Citadel, banking into the cold wind. In this form he could search for Raena unnoticed. For some long while he hovered over the town and the lake, flying this way and that, perching on windowsills to peer in or listen. Finally he remembered Councilman Verrarc's fine house near the crest of the hill. When he settled on the outer wall of the compound, he found the councilman outside, bundled in a cloak and arguing with an old woman who stood in the doorway.

'I be sick to my heart with worry,' Verrarc was saying. 'Not one soul in the town has seen her. I've asked everywhere.'

'Huh, and where would she be going, anyway?' the old woman said. 'I've not seen her since last night.'

'Ye gods. Ah ye gods!'

Where, indeed? Evandar thought to himself. Either to my lands or to Deverry, that's where, and the one leads to the other!

With a flap of wings the sparrow leapt from the wall, but as he flew, circling higher, he transformed himself into the red hawk. On long wings he flew fast, heading to his country and the magical roads.

'Those wards of yours must be powerful things,' Rhodry said. 'I've not dreamt of Raena in a long time now.'

'Good,' Dallandra said. 'I set them fresh every night.' She

paused, glancing around the great hall. 'Which reminds me. How long do you plan on being away from the dun?'

'Just the short day. The prince is no fool, and we shan't ride far.' Rhodry followed her glance: sure enough, Daralanteriel was waving at him from the main door. 'I'd best be gone.'

Out in the main ward the prince had assembled his hunting party. The men of his personal guard carried short curved bows and their shorter hunting arrows. Behind them stood a kennelman, surrounded by his pack of black and tan hounds, and a couple of servants with a pack mule to carry home their kill, though in truth they had little hope of finding game. During last summer's seige the Horsekin invaders had overhunted the countryside.

'I've told the men that they're not to bring down any does or yearlings,' Dar said. 'We need to let the herds build up again. I'm hoping we can find a buck or two. The does should all be carrying fawns by now, and one male won't be missed.'

'It'll be more meat than none,' Rhodry said. 'And it'll get us out of Cengarn for an afternoon's ride.'

Dar flashed him one of his brilliant smiles.

'I hope I never have to come back to the stone tents again,' Dar said. 'The way they stink! But it'll be spring soon, and we'll be gone, and in the meantime, let's ride!'

Despite the snow on the ground and the damp wind, the horses pranced and snorted, glad to be free of their stalls. The hounds raced this way and that, barking and sniffing the wind, tails wagging hard. As they left the dun, the men sang in elaborate elven harmonies, and on the streets of the town, the folk came to door and window to listen as they rode past. At the town gates they let the horses trot for a mile or so, then slowed them to a walk lest they sweat in the icy air. For some long while they rode north, leaving the settled farmlands behind, but the dogs raised nothing more than rabbits.

The sun had climbed to zenith when at long last the dogs flushed a deer, a button buck and thus no loss to its herd. With the dogs yapping behind, it came crashing through the sparse winter underbrush to fall dead from a few well-placed arrows. On the spot the servants butchered it, throwing the liver and other entrails to the half-starved pack.

'It's a good fat one,' Rhodry said. 'I'm surprised.'

'Don't be,' the kennelman said. 'The fewer the deer, the more winter fodder to go round, like.'

'Well, true spoken.'

'Save a bit of that liver, will you?' Dar put in. 'For my lady's dog.'

They left the servants with the kill and rode out again. Since the gwerbret's farmers cut this stretch of forest for fuel and timber, the trees thinned out to scrubby grassland. Snow lay thick in the hollows, but on the side of a hill the wind had scoured it away to expose dead grass and twiggy shrubs, a veritable banquet for deer. The kennelman called in the dogs and trotted with them on foot as they put nose to the ground and headed up the hill.

Rhodry saw the stag first, standing between two trees and watching. With a yap and a bay the dogs sighted it next and raced uphill. The stag leapt and ran, bounding across the hillside, heading up to the crest and forest cover. Rhodry yelled at the others to follow and kicked his horse forward. The stag was a fat one and pure white, an omen of good fortune as well as food. He was thinking of nothing but turning it back to the waiting archers when Dar's voice reached him on the wind.

'Come back! Don't! Dweomer, Rhodry! Come back!'

Instinctively he slowed his horse and looked ahead. Tangled in the trees at the crest of the hill hung a pale lavender mist, shot through with opalescence. Like a gigantic wave from some unseen ocean it rose up, towering above him. With a yelp he jerked his horse's head around so fast the poor beast stumbled. Rhodry kicked his feet out of the stirrups and threw himself clear as his horse went down, rolling. He scrambled up to see the horse, unhurt, doing the same. Around them the sunlight darkened. When he looked up, he saw the mist breaking like a wave and plunging down. He took one step back; then it hit, pouring over him with a blinding glitter of multi-coloured light.

By yelling curses and orders at the top of his lungs, Prince Daralanteriel managed to get all of his men, all of the dogs, and the kennelman down from the hillside and back to safety on the flat. Rhodry's gelding, reins trailing from the bridle, trotted down to join them. The kennelman caught the reins and tossed them up to Dar.

'It looks calm enough,' Dar said. 'It must not have been able to see – well, whatever that was.'

The archers nodded grimly. At the top of the hill the dweomer mist had vanished, except for a few scant shreds caught like tufts of wool on the trees, but for all he knew the wretched fog would reappear and devour them all.

'Your highness!' The kennelman was shaking so hard that he could barely speak. 'What – by the gods – where's the silver dagger?'

The elven archers were staring at him with the same question in their eyes. Dar merely shrugged and turned in the saddle to watch the torn mists. Melimaladar urged his horse up beside the prince's.

'That stag!' Mel said, in Deverrian for the kennelman's sake.

'It wasn't real,' Dar said. 'I've seen it before, last summer it was, just before the siege. I took some of my men out hunting, and the cursed stag led us too far away to get back that night.' Dar's voice tightened at the memory. 'And then the Meradan caught us by our campfire.'

'That's where Farendar died?'

'It is, and too many other good men.' Dar rose in his stirrups and shaded his eyes with one hand. 'It's dissolving, that's the last of it. Ah horseshit! We could ride around here all day and not find a trace or track of Rhodry!'

'But we can't just leave him here!' Mel said.

'He isn't here for us to leave.'

Mel started to speak, then merely shuddered. As if to agree one of the dogs whined.

'Well, what can we do?' Mel said at last. 'We can't stay here all night. We'll freeze.'

'I know that,' Dar snapped. 'I – well, ah by the black hairy ass of the Lord of Hell! I don't have one cursed idea of what we do next.'

'Ye gods, I wish Dalla was here! She'd know.'

'Wait! Maybe I can reach her.'

'But it'll take us a long time to ride back.'

'I didn't mean by riding.' Dar shot him a dark glance. 'Hear me out!'

'I will. My apologies.'

'Very well, then.' Dar paused, thinking. 'You know my bloodlines as well as I do. But the princes of the Vale of Roses were supposed to have dweomer of their own, weren't they? A kind of inborn thing that they passed on to their heirs. Well, I've got a touch of it. It was the same night I was just speaking of, when the Meradan laid a trap for us. Jill came to me in a sort of vision or sending or somewhat like that. I don't understand it, but I heard her and saw her, and she warned us about the trap. So hold your tongues, all of you. I've got some hard thinking to do.'

Dar glanced at the sky. Already the sun was hanging low in the cloudy west, sending streaks of gold across the sky like spears, aimed at their hearts. He would try to contact Dallandra, but then he would have to lead his men home to the warmth and safety of the dun, no matter how much it ached his heart to abandon Rhodry.

Dallandra was sitting in her tower room with one of Jill's books open on the table in front of her. Her mind kept drifting from the particular passage she was reading, which in the event proved a fortunate thing. Out of a daydream she heard

Daralanteriel's voice, so clear and close that she turned round in her chair, expecting to see him standing in the doorway.

'Dalla! We need help. Dalla, I hope you hear me!'

All at once a flock of Wildfolk swept into manifestation. Sprites hovered round her in the air, holding out translucent little hands. Warty grey gnomes mobbed her, grabbing her tunic's hem, pulling on her sleeves.

'What is this?' Dallandra said. 'Is the prince in danger?'

They shook their heads, but apparently someone was facing a threat. Some of the gnomes pantomimed the act of loosing arrows; others pretended to attack an invisible foe.

'Who is it?' Dallandra leapt to her feet. 'Rhodry?'

This time they nodded yes.

'Do you know where he is? Can you take me to him?'

They nodded and caught her hands. As she hurried to the window, she was thinking of Evandar, picturing him in her mind and calling out to him with her thoughts. No answer – she could only pray that he'd heard her. She pulled off her clothes, tossed them on the bed, then yanked the leather covering from the window in a cloud of dust and mildew. Icy wind slapped her and pushed past into the chamber. She ignored it and perched naked and shivering on the broad stone windowsill.

In her mind she summoned her bird form, a thought picture only, but she'd trained her mind through long years of this working to make thoughts that had a reality of their own. In an instant she first imagined, then saw the construct perched beside her on the window sill. It was strangely featureless, a smooth grey creature with a song-bird's beak and the general shape of a linnet. When she transferred her consciousness over, first she heard the usual rushy click; then she was aware of warmth. The linnet's feathers kept off the cold a fair bit better than her elven skin could. She shook her wings and with a hop leapt into the air. The linnet could fly fast when she needed to. Dallandra winged her way north with the sprites to guide her.

* * *

When the dweomer mist cleared away, Rhodry found himself standing on a dusty plain under a copper-coloured sky. Overhead dark clouds churned and roiled; off at the horizon smoke billowed in front of an enormous sun, turned blood-red and swollen. He'd seen the place once before, during the last summer's war, when Evandar's magic had brought him here.

'Evandar!' Rhodry yelled it as loudly as he could. 'Evandar! Are you here?'

Nothing but silence answered him. He realized that he was holding his silver dagger, though he couldn't remember drawing it. Something about it struck him as odd, but when he examined the blade, it looked perfectly normal, except perhaps for the oily way the metal reflected the unnatural light. Finally he realized that the heft felt wrong, perhaps twice as heavy as it should have been. With a shrug, he sheathed it and drew the bronze knife instead. The triangular wedge of the blade, bound into a cleft stick with thongs, caught the light and gleamed as bright as a candle-flame. He waved it in the air and saw long red sparks fly from the point.

'Huh, you look a cursed sight more dangerous here than in my world. It's a pity you're not a spear. I've got an ugly feeling I'm going to need a dweomer weapon soon enough.'

In his hand the bronze knife suddenly twisted like a living thing. The wood stick turned slippery, or so it seemed, and sped through his fingers. With a yelp he nearly dropped it, caught it again in both hands, and by then he needed both hands. The knife had transformed itself into a spear about six feet long, made of solid wood. When he hefted his new weapon, the bronze point still flashed with red fire.

'Well, then,' Rhodry said aloud, 'If I wish for a warband, will I get that too?'

He heard nothing but the wind, scouring dust over the coppery plain, and the spear stayed a single spear. Apparently he'd used all its dweomer. Clutching the spear, he turned around in a slow circle. Off in the direction of the perpetually setting sun, he saw a plume of what looked like dust. At first he thought it might merely be more smoke, but the plume grew taller, thicker – and faster, travelling straight for him. Slowly it resolved itself into a pair of riders, one on a black horse, the other on a blood bay. He had nowhere to hide and no speed to outrun them. He took the spear two-handed and held it ready across his body. The riders came closer, slowing to an easy walk, as if to tempt him to run.

'Ah ye gods!' Rhodry snarled. 'I might have known.'

Raena rode up on a glossy blood bay gelding. She was wearing unusual men's clothing, a shirt and tight brigga of rusty black cloth. Around her neck hung a leather thong bristling with talismans, which Rhodry recognized as Horsekin work. In her right hand she held a long black whip with a gold handle, much like the ones Horsekin officers carried as a mark of rank. Beside her on a black horse rode a creature that seemed more fox than man, though he was wearing black armour and held a black plumed helm tucked in his left arm. His pointed ears pricked like a fox's, and his shiny black nose presided over a face covered with russet fur.

'So, Rhodry Maelwaedd!' Raena spoke in the rough border patois of Deverrian. 'I've got you good and proper now!'

'Maybe so,' Rhodry said. 'If you live to take me.'

Raena laughed and cracked her whip in the air. As if it heard the sound, the spear point flamed like a torch and hissed. Her horse flung up its head and danced backwards. Rhodry could see how hard it was for her to get it back under control, what with her holding both reins in one hand. She lashed the whip again.

'And how long will you hold onto that bit of wood?' Raena said. 'I do wonder.'

Raena lifted her whip and snapped it right at his face. Rhodry flung up his spear in a parry. When the whip curled round the spear point, the braided thongs thrashed like a dying snake and hissed like one, too. With a scream Raena pulled it back, but a severed length of the lash fell, twitching, on the ground at her horse's feet. The bay whickered and threatened to rear. With a muttered oath the fox rider drew his black sword.

'Let him be!' Raena snarled. 'He's mine!'

The fox rider ignored her and spurred his horse forward. Rhodry had just time to jump to one side and swing the spear at his horse's head. The black whickered and fought the bit, but the fox rider wrenched its head around hard. Rhodry swung and smacked the black across the nose. A calculated risk – the fox rider's sword was slashing down, straight at him, but the horse squealed and reared, its forelegs pawing the air, and the rider's stroke missed. Cursing a steady stream, Raena was trying to force her horse toward Rhodry, but it too balked and tossed its head so violently she nearly lost the reins.

Rhodry howled out a berserker cry and rushed straight for the blood bay. He could hear the fox-man yelling something incomprehensible at Raena, who was trying to lash the whip with one hand whilst hanging onto the reins with the other. When her gelding saw the flaming spear heading straight for its eyes, it reared, came down hard, and kicked out. Raena tumbled inelegantly over its neck into the dirt. With one last whicker of panic, the horse bolted, galloping off toward the perpetual sunset.

Hooves sounded behind him – Rhodry spun round just in time to parry a sword slash as the fox rider charged him. The spear point slid off the sword blade as if by its own will. Rhodry snapped his wrists and swung the spear behind the fox-man's futile slash. The blazing bronze point smacked the fox rider's back – a glancing touch that should have done no harm, but the black armour shattered with a sizzle like burning fat. With a clumsy back-hand swing Rhodry brought the spear back round as the fox-man struggled to turn his horse. Another clumsy strike with his spear – this time it glanced off his enemy's black greave. Red fire shot out. The greave broke in half with a puff of black smoke and the stink of burning fur. The fox-man screamed in agony and spurred his horse hard. The horse leapt forward, and they galloped away, right past Rhodry and over the plain.

Rhodry howled in berserk laughter, so lost to the world that Raena nearly caught him. She'd got to her feet, and with a curse she lashed out with her whip. The tip seared down his back, but the pain only made him laugh the harder as he swung to face her. The black braid flashed down; he flung up the spear and twisted, caught the whip and pulled. The spear point burned through the leather and let her pull what little was left of the lash free.

'Lord Havoc!' she cried out. 'Come back!'

She turned her head to look for the fleeing fox-rider, just for an instant, but an instant was all Rhodry needed. He jumped forward and stabbed with a heft of the spear. The blade struck her flat between the breasts and flamed. With a scream of agony she dropped the whip and staggered back.

'So, you slut of a whoring bitch,' Rhodry said. 'Who's got who good and proper now?'

She flung her arms into the air and jumped, a gesture that caught him so much by surprise that he stared, paralysed. With a shriek that turned hoarse in mid-cry, an enormous raven flapped into the air and flew, circling round him once with one more cry of contempt. He stood open-mouthed and watched as the bird flew away in the general direction of the fox rider.

'By the black hairy arse of the Lord of Hell!' Rhodry muttered.

On the ground lay the remains of her black whip. Rather than touch it without knowing what it might do to his hands, he slid the spear point under it, meaning to pick it up, but the handle bubbled like bitumen in a pit and melted into a puff of ill-smelling smoke. Raena wouldn't be using that weapon again.

'That's all very well,' Rhodry said aloud. 'But how by all the ice in the hells do I get back home?'

When he looked up into the sky, he swore aloud. Unnaturally

large birds were flying straight for him, a pair of them this time. Apparently Raena and her strange ally had come back for more. He let his knees bend and crouched, waiting, spear held in front of him, as they flew closer and closer. But they proved to be no ravens – he could recognize a red hawk. The other was some strange grey bird that reminded him of a linnet.

'There he is!' The linnet sang out with Dallandra's voice. 'Thank every god in the stars!'

Rhodry laughed and waved the spear in greeting. The linnet dipped her wing, then turned with a graceful flap and headed after the raven. The hawk slowed, circled, and dropped down. As it sank it changed, shimmering with blue light as feather smoothed into flesh. For a moment Rhodry saw Evandar hovering naked in mid-air buoyed up by huge wings. With one last flap Evandar's feet hit the ground; the wings disappeared into arms. Dressed in his usual elven tunic and trousers Evandar stood before him.

'My apologies,' Evandar said. 'We tried to find you before Raena did, but you seem to have dealt with her easily enough.'

'It was luck, mostly,' Rhodry said. 'She didn't have a battle-steady horse, and then this spear – it started life as the bronze knife you gave me, all those years ago.'

'Spear or knife – it doesn't matter to the thing. It will become one or the other as you wish.'

'Handy of it. Neither Raena or her vulpine friend liked the taste of the point, especially when it caught fire.'

'Shaetano was here?'

'Who? This fellow looked more like a fox than a man, and she called him Lord Havoc.'

'Shaetano it was, then. My brother.'

'And here I thought Rhys Maelwaedd was nuisance enough as a brother! Can we get back to the real world?'

'What makes you think this world isn't as real as yours?'

'My apologies, then, but it's not as cosy, is it now?'

Evandar laughed. 'I'll grant you that. We'll leave it behind, then.'

'How? I can't fly like you can, and I left my horse behind somewhere.'

'Dar's got your horse. Dalla and I flew over him and his men on our way here. I'll call us up a pair of mounts, and we'll ride back in style.'

'Splendid! And whilst we're riding, I'd like an explanation, thank you very much, of what all this cursed dweomer means.'

With the long sight of the magical linnet, Dallandra had seen Rhodry strike Raena with the dweomer spear. While normally the raven could outfly her, she was counting on that wound to slow her quarry down. Sure enough, she'd not gone far before she saw the raven flying low to the ground on wings that trembled and beat an unsteady rhythm. Although Raena was heading toward the forest that marked the boundary of Evandar's Lands, she was tiring too badly to reach it. The trees were still a dark swell on the horizon when the raven screeched once, then settled to the dusty earth.

In human form Raena appeared, staggering as she walked a few steps toward a flat grey boulder, lying half-buried in the earth. In a near-faint she flopped down upon it. Dallandra circled overhead, then landed not far from the boulder. She transformed her image into her usual elven body, complete with clothing, an easy job here on the astral plane. Raena saw her, started to rise, then sank back onto the stone.

'Lord Havoc!' Raena threw back her head and howled the name. 'Lord Havoc! Come back!'

As Dallandra walked over, she noticed Raena's eyes, studying her in a glitter of malice. The raven was perhaps not as spent as she chose to look. She stopped a safe distance away.

'Lord Havoc's deserted you,' Dallandra said. 'He's a coward.'

'Indeed? Think you I know that not? He be so, but of use to me and my holy lady all the same.'

Dallandra started to answer, thought better of it. For a long moment they considered each other in silence.

'Here!' Raena said abruptly. 'I do know you. You be the elven witch that stands guard over the cursed silver dagger.'

'The very one. It was a foolish thing you did here today. Rhodry could have killed you, you know.'

'That I do see and most clear, like. What does move you to warn me so?'

'I'm not really sure. I feel sorry for you, mayhap.'

'Oh, do you now?' Raena tossed her head like a startled horse. 'And why?'

'Because you've been duped by lying spirits. They're not gods, Raena, not Shaetano, not Alshandra either. When they claim to be gods, they –'

'Blaspheme you not my Lady's name!' Raena rose to her feet. 'Or I'll scratch your eyes out.'

'Your "lady" is dead.'

'Not! She liveth still and someday will come to us again, no matter how you ply your foul false magics.'

'The matter's not in my hands.'

'At last you speak a true thing. She will return when she chooses, and she alone will choose. The Horsekin did prove themselves cowards, and so she hid herself from them. When they prove worthy, then will she reappear in all her glory. And I did fail her in the holy charge she laid upon me, and so I be no better than they, and no more worthy of her.'

'You don't understand. She's gone. Well and truly gone.'

'Not! I say to you, not!' Raena shook her head in fury. 'Someday she will lead us to our heritage, that which she did promise us.'

'The Slavers' country?'

'Just that. And at her return, neither you nor any other mortal shall stand against her. She be not dead but withdrawn from this world.'

She's gone mad! Dallandra thought to herself. But she's the more dangerous for it, no doubt.

'Listen to me, please!' Dallandra said aloud. 'If you keep using dweomer this way, it'll cause you great harm. You don't know how to use the power Shaetano gives you. He's leading you to your ruin.'

'I'll not hear this no more, elven witch.'

Abruptly Raena turned and ran, dodging round the boulder and heading toward the forest. Although Dalla took out after her, panic lent her quarry speed. Raena took one last step, then disappeared as suddenly as if she'd run through an invisible door and slammed it behind her.

'Ah ye gods!' Dallandra said. 'Well, at least I tried to warn her. On her own head be it!'

She stepped up onto the boulder and transformed herself back to the linnet. With a mournful cry she leapt into the air and flew off, heading for Dun Cengarn and Rhodry.

For three days and on into a fourth Raena stayed missing. With some of the militiamen Verrarc hunted for her in the farmlands surrounding Cerr Cawnen, but no one had seen her, and they found no tracks. He searched all through the city as well; again, he discovered no trace. At night he would lie awake, alone in their bed, and curse her for shaming him so. Although no one said a mean thing to his face, he knew perfectly well that behind his back the gossip was flying like the feathers when a farmer slaughters chickens.

Finally, on the fourth afternoon Verrarc went into the ruins of the temple and tried to invoke Lord Havoc; no one answered or came. He stood in the dark room and wept with both hands over his face, as if he could shove his sobs back into his throat. The sun was setting by the time he left the temple ruins. He stood for a moment at the peak of Citadel and watched the night, gathering storm clouds to cover the stars. If it snowed, and Raena were out somewhere in the countryside – he couldn't finish the thought. Far below the lake steamed around its rocks. For a moment he considered

throwing himself to his death; then he shook the evil thought
away and headed downhill to his compound.

When he came in, Korla was laying more tinder on the
fire in the hearth. She looked up and made a grunting sound
that did for a welcome, then went back to her work. Verrarc
hung his cloak up near the fire to dry, then walked into his
bedchamber to take off his boots. Raena was lying naked on
the bed, sprawled on her back. For a moment he could only
stare gape-mouthed. With a little moan she raised her head,
then fell back against the pillow.

'Ah ye gods!' Verrarc rushed over and sat down beside her.
When he laid a hand along her cheek, he found it cold and a
little damp. He could hear her breath wheezing and gurgling
in her chest.

'Oh my love!' He was stammering through tears. 'What befell
you? Where have you been?'

Raena opened her eyes and tried to speak, then fainted.
Yelling for Korla, Verrarc went to the hearth and began laying
a fire. The old woman came shuffling in, saw Raena, and
screamed.

'Witchcraft!' Korla hissed. 'How did she get in here?'

'I know not and I care not,' Verrarc snapped. 'Bring me some
fire from the other hearth! Then send Harl to town to fetch the
herbwoman!'

All that day Gwira fussed over her patient. She made Raena
breathe steam from simmering herb water, made her drink
decoctions of some green muck, mixed up still a third prep-
aration to form into a poultice for her chest. Raena coughed
and moaned, swore and spat up great lumps of greenish rheum,
then lapsed into sleep whenever Gwira allowed her. While the
herbwoman worked, Verrarc paced back and forth in the great
room by the fire. He was remembering another visit of Gwira's
to this house, when his mother lay dying from her husband's
brutality. Gwira had seemed old as the moon then, too. Korla
had taken him out of the house down to the lake to distract
him, a little lad then – how old? He could not remember, and

it didn't matter. Korla he remembered as being still vigorous, a stout woman with grey hair and a ready smile.

'Councilman?' Gwira spoke from behind him.

Verrarc spun around, his heart hammering in sudden fear.

'I do think me she'll live,' Gwira went on, 'be I able to keep her chest clear.'

'My thanks to every god!'

'Ah, but no easy hopes, lad! There be a need on us for caution. This be no light chill, cast off with a few sneezes. It will take many a day of physicking to get her well.'

'Do whatever you can, and I'll reward you twice.'

'Hush, lad! The matter may be out of my hands. I do think you'd best send Harl for Werda again. The evil spirits, they did carry her off, or so I'd think. Werda, she will ken the truth of that.'

Later that evening Verrarc was allowed to see Raena, tucked up in bed with a mound of pillows under her. He pulled up a chair and caught her hand between both of his, kissed her fingers, and held her hand just for the comfort of her living touch. She sighed and turned her head to smile at him.

'What befell you?' Verrarc said. 'Where did you go?'

'None of your affair.' Her voice was the barest whisper.

'Well, ye gods, worry's half-eaten my soul! There be a want on me to know where you went.'

She turned her head away and closed her eyes. Verrarc laid her hand gently down on the blankets, then sat back in his chair and considered her. Now that she was safe, he could realize just how furious he was. Evil spirits! he thought. Not by half! Did she have another man somewhere? He was sick to his guts of her disappearing on him! When she's well, he told himself, then will I have the truth of this! If she'll not tell me, then I'll – Well, and just what would you do? he asked himself. Throw her out? Lose her forever?

He sobbed once, then choked back tears. The shame of the thing, he knew, was eating him far more than his fear of losing her.

* * *

Evandar returned to his own true country to find that winter had won the battle with its artificial summer yet once again. In his absence the snow had stayed gone, but a freezing wind had brought ice to replace it. He swore aloud in rage and stood on the hill to survey the damage. Every tree glistened in the cold sun, each branch and twig hung sheathed in silver ice. The reeds along the river bank glittered as sharp as spear points. When he walked down the hill, the grass crunched and crackled under his feet. He looked back to see his footsteps, black marks on a silver carpet.

Near the riverbank his people huddled in the tattered pavilion. Men and women alike had wrapped themselves in cloaks and cloths and every bit of stuff that might warm them. When Evandar strode up, Menw rose and ran to meet him.

'The ice, my lord,' Menw said. 'It cuts and stings.'

His people moaned and stretched out pale hands. When he'd been making the illusions of the bodies they wore, Evandar had modelled them upon the elves, tall and slender with pale skin, though some of the folk had chosen richly dark skins like those that humans wore in Bardek. He'd given them the illusions of clothing, too, long dresses for the women, tunics for the men, but now everyone had wrapped themselves in their heavy cloaks; they clung together against the cold.

'My lord!' they cried out. 'Bring back the spring!'

'And if I do, how long will it endure?' Evandar said.

Everyone began talking at once while he listened, aware only of their pain, not of the meaning of the words, with his rage troubling his mind. What could he do? No matter how often he restored the spring, the moment he left, this wretched winter would sneak in behind him and take over again. Yet how could he stay on guard? Rhodry, Dallandra, all his schemes in the physical world – they demanded him as well. He snarled aloud like a wolf. Menw jumped back.

'Have we offended you, my lord?'

'Nah nah nah, and my apologies. I don't know what to do, that's all.'

Everyone gasped, staring at him. Never before had they seen him thwarted like this. And what will happen to them once I'm gone? he thought.

Apparently the winter had laid ice all through the Lands, because he suddenly heard distant horns. With Menw right behind him Evandar ran out of the pavilion. The rest of his folk hurried after and stood blinking in the ice-bright sun. Across the glittering meadow another army came riding, waving bits of white cloth to signal peace and surrender.

'The Unseelie Host, it is!' Evandar said. 'Shaetano's pack!'

'No, my lord,' Menw said. 'They're your vassals now.'

'Just so. I'd forgotten.'

The riders were both male and female, dressed in black armour made of enamelled copper. Long ago Shaetano had made them clumsy bodies, a mix of beast and human, some furred and snouted like Westlands bears, others sporting glittery little eyes and warty flesh like a Bardek crocodile. A few of the riders seemed almost human until they raised a paw, not a hand, in salute; others were like great wolves, running behind the horses. A fair number seemed stitched together from three or four creatures – the head of a boar with human hands and a dog's tail, perhaps, or dwarven torsos on animal legs, human heads, cat heads, dog faces, braided manes like the Horsekin, dwarven hands, elven hands, ears like mules, hair striped like tigers or stippled like leopards.

At their head, carrying a herald's staff wound round with ribands, rode an old man, a hunchback, his face all swollen and pouched, his skin hanging in great folds of warty flesh round his neck.

'My lord Evandar!' the herald cried out. 'We've come to beg your aid! Our Lands are cold, and we hunger as well. Please, take us in to your feast!'

'Come and be welcome,' Evandar said. 'Dismount, all of you, and we'll go to the pavilion.'

His people screamed and swore; they drew back, they wrapped their cloaks tight around them as they shrank away from the pack. They all began to shout insults, most of which amounted to 'They're too ugly, don't let them near us!' The old herald and all his followers began to weep in a cacophony of moans and wails. At that moment Evandar saw what he must do, the only thing he could do, truly.

'Peace!' Evandar raised both hands. 'Hear me out!'

Slowly both Hosts fell silent.

'A long while ago,' Evandar said, 'I promised you and yours a reward, good herald. New bodies, bodies fair and true – do you remember?'

'We do, my lord,' the herald said. 'And we long for them.'

'Very well, but there's only one way that I can do what I promised, and only one place I can do it in.' He turned to the Seelie Host. 'If we go there, you'll be free of this sorcerous winter. Will you all follow me?'

Unseelie and Seelie Host both joined together in a wordless shout of joy. Evandar spread his hands and looked at them – it seemed to him that his fingers should wear gloves of ice, he felt so cold in his heart. The Hosts fell silent and waited, watching him.

'It's time for you all to follow Elessario,' Evandar called out. 'Time to be born in the world of Time.'

They shouted again, but this time he heard fear sing amidst the rejoicing.

'And what of you, my lord?' Menw said.

'I shall stay here and make you a safe place in that world.'

'And then will you follow?'

'Of course.' The lie came easily. 'Once everything is ready, I'll follow.'

The two Hosts cheered him for a third time.

On his golden stallion Evandar led his people in one last circuit of the Lands, the long green meadows, the twisted ancient forest, the ruins of palaces, the dead cities of forgotten kings. As they rode their circle it seemed that the Lands changed under them and above them. The sky turned silver with mist; then the mist turned to a sullen purple, streaked here and there with violet light. The trees and the ice disappeared, and they rode through fields of purple flowers. When they returned to where the river should have been, it had disappeared. Evandar called for the halt and the dismount. As soon as they stood upon ground, their horses vanished.

'Follow me!' Evandar called out. 'It's not far.'

Evandar led them through a field of white flowers, nodding in a light the colour of silver but tinged with violet. On the far side of the flower meadow lay a river of shifting mists, not quite water, not quite air. Overhead a huge violet moon hung in an indigo sky, but no stars shone. Behind him the chattering Hosts fell silent. When he glanced back, he found them all still following, their heads turning this way and that as they stared at the marvels. He stopped on the riverbank and turned to face them.

'To this place,' Evandar said, 'did Dallandra bring me and Elessario, when it was her time to go down to the world of Time and be born. Now it's the gate through which you must pass. You must wade through the river and walk into that mist.'

'I see, my lord.' Menw's voice trembled.

When Evandar looked at him, he found his lieutenant standing naked, his slender body as white as alabaster and as translucent. The rest of the souls who followed him had become the same: pale, shimmering, and stripped of the false features he had given them. His brother's pack had lost their fur and fangs, transformed their snouts and paws; they stood straight and laughed in joy at the new images of themselves. The old herald – a stately and white-haired envoy now, came forward to speak for them all.

'Our thanks! You have given us what you promised us, so long ago.'

But Evandar knew that he himself had done nothing. He felt the wind pick up, a cold wind that slapped at him in a flood and surge of raw power. Through the meadow beings were coming, all clothed in golden light, huge and towering above the mists and death-pale flowers. Were they human? He could not tell in the glow of their coming. One raised a hand; they had no need of words.

'To the river!' Evandar called to his people. 'Into the river and beyond!'

For the last time the Hosts obeyed him. It seemed they flew, rising above the flowers and swirling like dead leaves caught in the rising wind. The Great Ones flew with them in a huge waft of golden light that washed over them, swirled them around one last time, and carried them into the mist on the far side of the white river. Three enormous knocks like thunder boomed over the meadow. Without thinking Evandar sank to his knees and flung up his arms.

For a moment the river mist shone in a burst of gold; then slowly the colour faded away. The white river ran once more under the white mist. The white flowers trembled once, then held still. Evandar rose and turned to see one last figure walking toward him: a human being with dark skin and curly white hair, dressed in a coarse brown robe and carrying an apple in one hand and a knife in the other.

'You're here?' Evandar said to him.

'I am.' The old man paused to cut off a slice of apple. 'I turn up in the most cursed strange places, don't I?' He handed Evandar the slice. 'You've done splendidly.'

'Have I?' Evandar put the slice in his mouth and found it tasted wonderfully sweet, far better even than the mead from his own stores.

'Just so: splendidly well. What about you, now?'

Evandar merely looked at him.

'A while back we traded questions,' the old man said. 'And I laid up a few in store. You owe me some answers.'

'So I do, good sir. Well then, here's one of them. I have too much work afoot in the world of Time to follow my people.'

'Work can always be jobbed out. Do you want to go across?'

'I don't! Never shall I be born in the world of slime and blood and decay! Better to fade away than that!'

'Ah.' The old man considered him for a moment. 'You know, I wonder if you could be born, even if you wanted to. I doubt it.'

'What do you mean?'

'You're a man of great power. Look at you, still whole and dressed all fancy, even here in this place.'

Evandar glanced down to see his familiar green tunic and buckskin leggings.

'The mists usually dissolve such things clean away,' the old man went on. 'You're a marvel, you are, but I'll wager there's one thing you're too weak to do. No doubt you could never strip yourself of enough power to cross that river.'

'Indeed?' Evandar heard his voice snarl. 'Well, then, it's a good thing I don't want to, isn't it now?'

'It is at that.' The old man was smiling at him. 'But if you're ever of a mind to, we could meet here and lay a wager on it.'

'If I ever have time to, we could at that. Not, of course, that I want to do any such thing. Be born, I mean.'

'Of course.'

For a moment they considered each other; then the old man turned away; Evandar suspected him of hiding a smile.

'Well, a good day to you, then. I'd best be getting back.'

Without another word he strolled off. Evandar glowered after him, then strode off in the opposite direction to head for the mothers of all roads and home.

When he returned to his country, he found it white, wrapped in a silence of snow. For a long time he stood on the hill top and looked, merely looked, at the ruin of what he'd created, the garden dead, the long meadows wrapped in frost, the river frozen and still. Although he knew he should be gone hunting his brother down, he had no heart for it.

And while Evandar mourned the death and birth of his people, Time passed in the world of men and elves below.

*   *   *

On her mother's bed, Elessi lay face down, trying to turn herself over. She floundered, rocked back and forth, tipped her head back and glared as she beat at the blanket with one chubby hand. All at once she let out a high, thin wail; her face reddened, and the wail turned to a howl of sheer rage. Screaming, she arched her back and swayed so hard that she turned herself over, but she lay waving her arms and legs and screeching at the top of her lungs. Carra perched on the edge of the bed and smiled at her daughter.

'You did it!' Carra said. 'You did it! Look, look! You're on your back!'

Elessi ignored her and went on screaming until Carra picked her up and cradled her against one shoulder. In her mother's arms she fell silent, then grabbed a strand of Carra's hair in one fist. She sucked on the golden strand while Carra murmured to her and rocked back and forth. Dallandra and Lady Ocradda, standing nearby at the foot of the bed, exchanged glances.

'Oh you can say it,' Carra snapped. 'She's got an awful temper. I know it better than you do.'

'I'm sure you do, your highness,' Ocradda said.

'She absolutely hates to be thwarted. If she can't have somewhat she wants the very moment she wants it, she screams like this and carries on so. I've not been around many babies. Is she all right, do you think?'

'Well, my dear princess,' Ocradda said, smiling. 'She's a bit young to learn patience.'

Dallandra nodded her agreement, but she was remembering the things Evandar had been telling her about Salamander's little son. She was seeing a hideous similarity between him and Elessi – the utter frustrations of a soul to whom everything in the world was first-time new.

For some days, in fact, she'd been trying to reach Evandar, both by forming images of him in her mind and, when that failed, sending the Wildfolk in search of him. Finally, on a morning when the sunlight actually felt warm, and the snow

lay thin and streaky, he appeared, meeting her in the copse on
Market Hill. He seemed dreadfully thin to her, that morning,
and so pale that the sour cherry colour of his lips flamed scarlet.
Without thinking she laid a hand along his face, which felt as
cool and silky as always.

'What are you doing?' Evandar said.

'I thought you might be feverish or suchlike, that's all. Have
you been ill? Or is that a silly question for the likes of you?'

'I don't know if it is or not. I've done some strange things
since last we met.'

'Indeed? What?'

'I learned that I'm not the master of my own Lands, for
one, and an evil thing that was – though a good did come
out of it.'

'Indeed? What do you mean, or is this one of your tedious
riddles?'

'It's not. But it was just a little thing. Perhaps you'd not be
interested.'

'Evandar, please don't tease me!'

All at once he laughed aloud.

'It's come true, your wish for my people.' He was grinning
at her. 'They've crossed the white river. They chose life, and
I gave it to them.'

Dallandra let her hand drop and stared at him like a lackwit.
His smiled faded, and he cocked his head to one side.

'Aren't you pleased?'

'Of course.' She found her voice at last. 'You just took me
utterly by surprise. That's wonderful, my love. I'm so happy
for them! And I'm so proud of you.'

His smile returned in force, and he strutted a little, walking
back and forth through the dirty snow. Dallandra heard her
own thoughts as a distant rumble of thunder: why now? Why,
just when she'd realized that all her scheming to get these souls
born might be dangerous to them and those around them, why
now had he finally done what she'd been begging him to do for
four hundred years? But what else was there to be done?

'They have their birthright at last,' she said aloud. 'They ride the wheel of Time now.'

'And they'll not fade away when they die?'

'Never. They'll have life again and again, round and round. But what of you, my love? Won't you –'

'Hush!' He held up one hand flat for silence. 'I'll not discuss it any more.'

Dallandra set her hands on her hips and glared at him, while he considered her with all traces of feeling stripped from his face. All at once it seemed to her that someone was standing behind her. She spun round to find no one there, but the feeling of a presence remained.

'Is Shaetano nearby?' she said.

'What? He isn't, no. I always know when he's around.'

'But someone's watching us.'

From high up in a leafless tree she heard a faint wail, a ghost of a cry rather than a real sound. She glanced up and saw, clinging to the branches, a withered little creature with a face like bark and hands like twigs. With huge dark eyes it stared at her, then vanished.

'One of Alshandra's pack,' Evandar said. 'Naught more. There's nothing there to worry us.'

'Isn't there? I gather you left them behind.'

'Quite right. They're too ugly to bother with.' He hesitated briefly. 'Oh now here! You're not expecting me to help them, are you?'

'I'm not expecting you to do anything.' All at once Dallandra felt profoundly tired. 'No doubt I'd best just try to do it myself.'

With a toss of her long hair she strode off, fuming. What had she expected, she asked herself? Some glorious moment of victory, she supposed, when she could look back at all her efforts to give Evandar's people life and think how worthwhile the trouble had been. Somehow in her fancy for this moment there had been an admiring crowd, too, all marvelling at what she'd done. Instead, she had a flawed triumph, an irritating success, and not one shred of honest gloating to enjoy.

'Ah well,' she muttered. 'That's what life is like, here beneath the moon! Why am I even surprised?'

And then and only then did she hear, in some deep recess of her soul, an echo of those three great knocks and know that the Great Ones were pleased. She burst out laughing and strode off to the dun, smiling to herself. Trouble there would be, no doubt, for those souls so suddenly brought into life, but she would deal with it when it happened and not worry herself till then.

Although she eventually recovered, Raena's illness – a deep rheum of the chest, a fever that burned in her face – lasted weeks. In the boredom of winter, Cerr Cawnen gossiped endlessly. Why had she been out, wandering round in the snows? Some said that Verrarc's new wife probably had some other man; after all, a woman who'd betray one man would doubtless cheat on the next. Others whispered of things more sinister, black witchcraft and evil spirits. The spirits had come to Raena twice now, had they not? And why would they do such a thing unless she were attracting them?

Niffa, of course, knew perfectly well that the latter tale was the true one, but she refused to cause her mother grief by telling that truth. Dera, in her loyalty to Councilman Verrarc, had decided that the third theory going round was the correct one, that Raena was subject to sudden fits of madness and thus deserved pity, not censure.

'She never had a child, poor thing,' Dera would say. 'And truly, it be not likely now that she will. It must have been preying on her mind, like, her just married and all.'

Niffa would hold her tongue and smile, but in her heart she hated Raena as much as ever, even though she knew now that the woman hadn't killed Demet herself. She would wonder, though, in softer moments, just where her hatred sprang from.

Little could she know that this poisoned tree had its roots back in a time when the evil dweomers Raena worked had had grave consequences, destroying lives and threatening the entire kingdom of Deverry long after the actual death of the body and the personality she'd then worn. And to Niffa, her daughter in that life, had fallen the ill-omened task of setting right her wrongs.

PART TWO

Deverry

The year 849. Autumn came. Evil portents
troubled our High Priest Retyc. We wondered
if Prince Maryn were truly meant to be king.
But then a woman on temple lands gave birth
to twins, and one died. Retyc declared this a
good omen.

The Holy Chronicles of Lughcarn

I n summer, the fog from the Southern Sea crept in daily at sunset and covered Dun Cerrmor with grey mist, swirling so thick along the ground that one could see it move. On the evening before she gave birth to her second son, Princess Bellyra stood at a window in the women's hall, high up in the royal broch, and watched the fog advance. The setting sun off to the west turned the first ranks to gold, promising splendour, but once the mist invested the town, the gold faded to a cold, relentless light.

'Your highness?' Elyssa came up beside her. 'What's wrong? You look so distressed.'

'I was watching the fog. Did you see it turn from gold to grey?'

'It always does that, your highness, this time of year.'

'I know, but I was just thinking that my life's rather been like that, all gold when I married, and now . . .'

Elyssa stared, her dark blue eyes narrowed in puzzlement. Although the serving woman was the older by a few years, they had been friends since childhood, but now, Bellyra supposed, Elyssa hardly knew what to make of her. She hardly knew what to make of herself at times.

'It's just the baby,' Elyssa said at last. 'It should come soon.'

'Very soon.' Bellyra laid both hands on her swollen belly. 'He feels ready to move down.'

'You're so sure it's a lad.' Elyssa smiled at her. 'I hope you're not disappointed.'

'I won't be. No lass would kick her mother's guts as hard as this little beast has.'

'Let's hope, anyway.' Elyssa considered her, the smile gone. 'Are you frightened?'

'Very, but not of the labour or suchlike. It's what came after.'

Elyssa reached out and caught the princess's hand twixt both of hers.

'You'll do splendidly this time. I swear it. I've made ever so many prayers to the Goddess.'

'But did the Goddess give you an answer back? Oh, I'm sorry, Lyss, please, don't look so distressed. We'll deal with what comes if it comes.'

In the middle of the night Bellyra woke sopping wet and in pain. Her water had broken. She got out of bed, stood for a moment considering her contraction – not too bad, but strong – then flung open her bedroom door and yelled to her serving women.

'It's begun. Send for the midwife!'

She sat down on a wooden chest and let herself sprawl, legs akimbo. In a few moments Elyssa and Degwa came hurrying in, carrying candle lanterns. Degwa's dark hair hung in two tidy braids, while Elyssa's fair hair tumbled down her back, all tousled.

'Let me just put a dress over this nightgown,' Degwa said, 'and then I'll go down and wake the pages.'

'Send young Donno,' Elyssa said. 'He knows the town well. And get a couple of serving lasses up here to light a fire and suchlike.'

Panting from the pain, Bellyra leaned back against the wall and let their concern cover her like a warm quilt. Servant girls came soon, and after them the midwife. By the time the dawn broke, her labour filled her world. She clung to the birthing rope and thought of naught else but the child fighting within her to get out. The pain, oddly enough, helped keep the fear at bay. When the sun was well over the horizon, the baby came with one huge squall of rage at being shoved into the light.

'A lad!' the midwife crowed. 'Ah, the Goddess has favoured you again, your highness.'

'I told you,' Bellyra whispered. 'Give me some water.'

The afterbirth came clean and whole. Only then did she truly feel safe. Once again, she'd had an easy birth, or so the midwife told her. Laughing and chattering, her women washed her and brought her dry nightclothes, then tucked her up in her freshly-made bed. By the time they'd drawn the hangings around her, she was asleep.

In a little while they woke her. When Degwa brought the new prince to her bed, he mewled like a kitten. Bellyra took him with unsteady hands and settled him at her breast. He grabbed the nipple in his mouth and began to suck the false milk so hard that her breast ached.

'Oh, he's so beautiful,' Degwa crooned. 'What a little love, isn't he?'

'Just so,' Elyssa said. 'What lovely little hands he has!'

In truth, Bellyra thought, Marro was red, wrinkled, and squashed-looking about the face still. His sprinkling of pale hair lay coarsely on his skull. She lay back on the mounded pillows and stared up at the bed hangings, embroidered with a repeating design of three ships bound round with inter-lacements. The ships were brown, the waves blue, and the interlacements red. She could remember embroidering them, back when she was first married and still happy.

'You must be so proud,' Degwa said. 'Two sons for your lord!'

'I'd hoped for a daughter, in truth,' Bellyra said. 'But you remind me. How is Casyl? Jealous?'

'Of course.' Elyssa was smiling. 'But I explained to him that he'll always be the oldest and the Marked Prince, while his brother will have to make do with a lordship. I don't think he truly understood, but he was the happier for it.'

Bellyra smiled, and at that moment her new son opened his cloudy-blue eyes and looked up at her with such an intense animal devotion that she laughed.

'You *are* precious!'

He shut his eyes tight and slept. When Bellyra handed him back to Degwa, she could read the profound relief in her dark eyes. Elyssa too was smiling.

'We need to send the prince the news,' Bellyra said.

'I thought we'd best wait a few days,' Elyssa said, hesitating. 'Just to make sure that little Marro lives.'

'True spoken. Unfortunately. Still, Casyl was healthy enough, so I have hope.'

Bellyra spent the next few days in a pleasant sort of exhaustion. Although all the important men in the kingdom had followed the prince off to war, the noblewomen who lived within a day's ride all came to see the new princeling and to offer her their congratulations. All morning she would sit with the guests and gossip. In the middle of the day the sun poured into the women's hall; she sat in a chair at a window with her women while they embroidered the pieces of the dress she would wear when her husband was finally invested as high king. Yet every night the fog slid over the town and turned her heart cold.

All too soon the morning came that she'd been fearing. She woke, sat up, pulled back a bed curtain and burst into tears at the sight of the chamber beyond. She flung the hanging closed. For a long while she wept, until Elyssa heard and came hurrying in. She pulled back the hanging and peered round the edge.

'I'm just so tired,' Bellyra stammered. 'It's all the visitors and such. Just let me sleep a bit more.'

And yet she stayed abed all that day. Finally in the evening, when Degwa carried in the new prince for a feeding, Elyssa insisted on pulling back the bed curtains.

'To let some air in, your highness,' Elyssa said. 'There. Isn't that better?'

The cold grey fog light hung in the chamber and seemed to pick out every detail in an unnatural glare. The streaks and chips on the stone wall, the grain on the wood windowsill all seemed marks in some mysterious writing. If she could read them, she knew, they would tell her tales horrible beyond her imagining. She forced herself to look away. In the breeze from the open window the hangings swayed. The ships seemed to bob up and down on their embroidered waves.

'Your highness?' Elyssa's voice had turned tentative. 'You seem so sad. Would you like us to sing to you?'

'I wouldn't.' Bellyra looked at her suckling and wished she didn't hate him. 'Get him away from me! Get him a wet nurse! It's all starting again.'

She felt the tears run, but sitting up to wipe them away lay beyond her. Clucking and murmuring, her serving women swept the squalling baby away and at last left her alone. She managed to flop onto her side and weep into the pillow. Some long while later, Elyssa came back.

'One of the kitchen lasses has a year-old son and lots of milk. Degwa's making her have a bath, and then she'll come up and take little Marro over.'

'It's very odd, these tears,' Bellyra said. 'They fall of their own accord.'

'Ah, my lady! It aches my heart to see you like this again! What – I wish I could – if we only understood –'

'I want to go to sleep. Please leave me alone.'

'It's not good for you to –'

'Get out of here!' Bellyra propped herself up on her elbows. 'Get out of here and leave me alone!'

Elyssa fled. Bellyra could hear her whispering with other women just beyond the door, but she could understand nothing of what they said. She flopped back down onto the pillows and stared at the hangings until at last she fell asleep.

Dun Deverry lay so far to the north of sea-coast Cerrmor that the son was nearly a fortnight old before his father learned he'd been born. The messenger rode in with the news late on a sticky-hot afternoon when low clouds threatened rain. Servants rushed every which way until they at last found Prince Maryn on an outer wall of the royal dun.

With the man everyone called 'lord' Nevyn, his most trusted councillor, the prince was leaning over the wall, looking down at the ruins of what had once been a flourishing city, now reduced to rubble by the long years of sieges and the fires they always seemed to bring. What was left of the houses and shops stretched across a valley to another low hill, crowned with the walls and the tree-tops of the sacred grove surrounding the temple of Bel.

'I hope to all the gods that the folk come back to rebuild,' Maryn was saying.

'So do I,' Nevyn said with a wry grin. 'But remember, there are inducements you can offer.'

They heard voices calling and turned to see a pair of pages racing down the hill, their tabards flapping around them.

'Your highness, your highness! Messages from Cerrmor! Your lady's given you another son!'

'Splendid!' Maryn called to them. 'Where's the messenger?'

'Up in the great hall, your highness.'

Nevyn followed Maryn down the rickety ladder. Ahead of them the grassy hill, ringed by three more walls, climbed to the fortress at the crest. With the pages leading the way they trudged up the spiralling road toward the inner fortress. Black against grey, three ravens flew overhead, cawing. With their passing the day fell hushed in homage to the coming storm. Nevyn wiped enough sweat from his face onto his sleeve to leave a wet spot.

'You look grim,' Maryn said abruptly.

'Do I, my liege? I do hope the princess is truly well.'

'And not as she was the last time? Ye gods, I've never seen a woman so sad, and all for no reason. I thought she'd gone daft.'

'She hadn't. There were medical reasons.' Nevyn put steel in his voice. 'Childbirth takes some women that way.'

'Well, so you said at the time. My apologies.'

'Watery humours collect in a woman's womb to feed the child. These are expelled at birth. In a few cases, there are dregs left behind, and these corrupt to vapours, producing the illness.'

'These women's matters!' Maryn shuddered. 'I thank the

gods for making me a man, frankly, when I think on such things. But here, Nevyn, if this illness falls upon her again, she'll be more comfortable in Cerrmor, and safer as well. The journey upriver might be hard on her.'

'Don't you want her here?'

'What? That's not it! Of course I do! It's just that – well, I fear for her, that's all. My lady has given me another son. She's done great service to the kingdom and to my line, and I'd not risk her health in any way.'

It was all true enough, yet Maryn couldn't look him in the eye. Oho! Nevyn thought. What's all this?

'I see,' Nevyn said aloud. 'Well, we can wait to send for her. I'll send a message to her women and see how she fares.'

'That's a splendid idea. And it will be good to have her here. She's got more common sense than ten men, when she's herself at least. I truly respect her opinions, you know. It's a pity that she's not able to rule in her own right. I'd give her the blasted Cerrmor rhan and put an end to all the cursed conniving over it.'

'By rights it would belong to her, truly.' Nevyn considered for a moment. 'Alas, I doubt me if we could convince either your vassals or the priests.'

Maryn laughed, nodding his agreement.

'Don't let me forget,' the prince went on, 'to send messengers to my father with this news.'

'I'm always mindful of Pyrdon, never fear. Once you've settled things with the Boar clan, it'll be time to look west, and I fear me we won't care for the view.'

'Oh, I agree. As soon as I claim Pyrdon, we have a war with the Eldidd on our hands.'

'Of course. The Eldidd king is likely to back your brother, you know, as a claimant for the Pyrdon throne.'

'Riddmar has no claim. I'm the eldest by a great many years and I have sons.'

'Just so. But I truly wish your father's new wife had given him a daughter.'

As they walked on, Nevyn was feeling grim. Despite the prince's spectacular victories of this summer, they had yet to achieve the final peace. Fighting over spoils had kept many a war alive before this. And hovering on the western horizon like a sunset storm lay the kingdom of Eldidd, whose tentative claim to the Deverry throne had helped prolong the civil wars for a hundred years.

Toward noon the rain finally hit, driving everyone indoors to the great hall of the royal broch. While servants set about bringing the men ale, Councillor Oggyn bustled in. He was a stout man, Oggyn, barrel-chested and egg-bald, though his brindled black and grey beard bristled with enough hair for two men. He climbed onto a bench so he could be seen and shouted at the top of his lungs for silence. When he got it, he called out the news of the birth of the prince's second son. The noble lords in attendance, and there were a good many of them, all cheered and clapped at the prince's good fortune.

'It's their good fortune, too,' Maddyn said. 'It's a hard thing to fight for a new king only to see his line shrivel and die.'

'Just so.' Owaen raised his tankard in semi-salute, then drank the ale off in one long swallow. 'Two sons make a four-fold blessing for a lord.' He burped profoundly. 'Pardon.'

The two silver daggers were sitting near the hearth they shared with the riders in the various lords' warbands, across the circular great hall from the noble-born themselves. Most of Prince Maryn's enormous army still camped at the bottom of the hill behind the outer ring of dun fortifications. Custom, however, demanded that each lord have an escort of picked men near them at all times, and the prince had his guards as well, all quartered within the dun proper.

Or what was left the Prince's Guard, all twenty-three of them, when once a hundred men had worn the silver dagger as their badge. They had lost the rest and their leader, Caradoc, in the summer's fighting. Now Maddyn, who was something of a bard, and Owaen, one of the best swordsmen in the entire kingdom, were supposedly leading the unit together, as Caradoc had wished. Supposedly – Maddyn doubted that the arrangement would last much longer. He cared little for command, while to Owaen it was everything.

'We need to recruit,' Maddyn said. 'The prince needs more guards than our handful.'

'Just so.' Owaen wiped his blond moustache dry on the back of his left hand, which sported a clot of scar tissue where the little finger should have been. 'I've been approached by some of the regular Cerrmor riders.'

'Any of them any good?'

'They weren't. But I've got my eye on a couple of other lads who can swing a sword well enough. Don't know if they'll fit in. What about you talk with them? You're better at that kind of thing.'

'Very well. Point them out to me.'

Owaen swung a leg over the bench and stood straddling it while he looked round the great hall.

'They're not here,' he said finally. 'Let's see if we can find them outside somewhere.'

'Ye gods, it's storming out there!'

Owaen gave him a look of such disgust that Maddyn rose to join him.

'Oh very well. Truly, it won't shorten my days to get wet.'

They left the hall but stood for a moment under the shelter of the doorway. Rain pounded down on the cobbled ward, one of many at the heart of the fortress. Dun Deverry stood on the crest of a high hill and spilled over it, too, trailing down the sides in a jumble of towers and barracks, storage sheds and brochs. Here and there low walls surrounded a particular cluster of buildings, marked off a random-seeming ward, or cut across open space for no particular reason. Most of the buildings were squat in the broch style, wider at the base than the top.

A few slender towers rose up over the confusion, though they seemed to have been built off true, because they leaned over the wards below.

Thunder cracked overhead and rolled around the towers. Owaen looked up at the dark sky and scratched his stomach in a thoughtful sort of way.

'They won't be out and about,' Maddyn said, 'these lads of yours.'

'Maybe not. Here! What's that?'

At the gates someone was yelling, demanding entry, and men came running to swing them wide. Escorted by pages, a rider on a black horse jogged through. He was carrying a staff wound with many-coloured ribands, plastered down at the moment with rain. His boots and brigga and his mount's legs and belly dripped dark mud.

'It's a herald,' Owaen said.

'True spoken,' Maddyn said. 'And isn't that the Boar crest on his saddle-bags?'

The herald handed his staff down to a page, then dismounted and reclaimed the soggy emblem of his office. As a stableboy led the black away, the silver daggers could see the Boar rampant quite clearly, stamped on the saddle-skirts as well as the saddle-bags.

'Isn't that interesting?' Maddyn said. 'I wonder what Lord Braemys has to say to our prince?'

'The gall of the man!' Prince Maryn snarled. 'The stinking spiteful gall!'

'Well, truly, your highness,' Oggyn said. 'It bodes ill.'

Nevyn propped his elbows on the table and considered the piece of parchment lying in front of him. The three men were sitting in the prince's private council chamber, where the prince had pressed Nevyn into service as a scribe to read privately the letter from Braemys of the Boar. A cold wind flapped the cowhides hanging over the windows and swirled round the stone room. The candles guttered dangerously low. Nevyn grabbed the parchment and held it flat.

'I must admit,' the prince said, 'that I'm not looking forward to spending a winter here. The summer storms are bad enough. Listen to that rain come down!'

'True spoken, my liege,' Nevyn said. 'But if this is how Braemys thinks a man sues for peace, then you'd best not leave Dun Deverry. He might move right in and call himself king.'

'Just so, my prince,' Oggyn put in. 'His arrogance astounds me.'

'He mentions Tibryn's son, the new gwerbret. What is he, still a child?'

'Just that, my liege, about seven years old,' Oggyn said. 'By a second wife. Nevyn, what did you say the child's name was?'

Nevyn read the letter aloud once again. 'To the Usurper, Maryn, Prince of Pyrdon. It is my understanding that you hold among your court's womenfolk Lillorigga, daughter of the Boar clan. Since she has been formally betrothed to me, I demand her immediate release and return to me at Cantrae. Braemys of the Boar, Regent to Lwvan, Gwerbret Cantrae.'

That was all, but the salutation spoke clearly enough for a stack of parchments.

'So!' the prince said. 'He wants war.'

'Just so, my liege,' Nevyn said. 'He's taken on his father's feud.'

'Well, it's his right, and he's doing the honourable thing.' Maryn frowned down at the table. 'But I wish he'd seen his way clear to taking my pardon instead.'

Nevyn nodded agreement. Before this summer's fighting had given Maryn control of Dun Deverry, the lords of the Boar clan – Braemys's father and uncle – had ruled in their half of the divided kingdom, though technically in the name of another child, young Olaen, who claimed to be king. They were all dead now, the would-be king and the two Boar lords as well, but the civil wars, it seemed, were not yet over, not with the Boar's son to carry them on.

'Perhaps we can use the lass as a bargaining point,' Oggyn said. 'I always knew she would come in handy, like.'

'Have you gone daft?' Maryn leaned forward and looked Oggyn square in the face. 'Ye gods, after everything Lilli did for me, do you think I'd turn her over to my enemies?'

Oggyn blushed a sunset-red from his beard up and over his bald pate.

'My apologies, my prince. I fear me I've overspoke myself.'

'You have. Remember from now on that Lady Lillorigga is my guest, not some sort of hostage.'

'I will, my prince. I most humbly beg your pardon.'

'Granted, of course. But I'd not hear of this again.'

Slowly Oggyn's colour faded to normal. Maryn leaned back in his chair and looked away absently.

'Unless Lilli wants to marry the man, of course,' Nevyn said. 'Then Braemys's loyalty can be the bride-price you exact.'

Maryn turned to face him and looked for a brief moment murderous.

'I'd not thought of that.' The prince buried the rage in a brief smile. 'Perhaps the lady should be asked.'

'It would be courteous, my liege.' Nevyn stood with a bow his way. 'I'll just go look for her. I hope you'll forgive me if it takes some small while?'

'Of course,' Maryn said. 'This dun is as cursed confusing as a rabbit warren, I swear it!'

In actuality, Nevyn knew where to find Lilli, up in her chamber in the royal broch, a narrow wedge of a room with bare stone walls. Dressed in green, Lilli herself was sitting cross-legged on her bed and staring at a page of the big leather-bound book lying in front of her. When Nevyn came in she looked up and smiled. Her blonde hair, cropped short at the jawline, hung untidily around her slender face.

'How are you doing with the reading?' Nevyn nodded toward the book. 'Do you remember all the letters?'

'I do, but sounding them out one at a time is so tedious.'

'No doubt, but it's the best we can do for lessons. At the

moment, anyway. When winter comes we'll either be back in Cerrmor, or I'll send for a scribe's teaching book.'

'Do you think we'll go back?'

'I have no idea.' Nevyn sat down on a wooden chest under the single window. 'The prince will winter here, certainly.'

Lilli glanced at the book and concentrated on closing it.

'If the princess returns to Cerrmor,' Nevyn went on, 'I'll go, too. As my apprentice, you'll come with me.'

'Of course, my lord.' Her voice held steady. 'We'll be much more comfortable there.'

'And safer. We've heard from Braemys.'

Lilli looked up and laid a hand at her throat.

'He still wants to marry you,' Nevyn said. 'He claims you as his betrothed.'

'Oh curse him!'

'I just made a show in council of asking your opinion on the matter, but I'll wager you don't want to go through with the marriage.'

She shook her head.

'Don't let it trouble your heart,' Nevyn said. 'If he turns nasty and tries to press the matter, I'll reveal the truth.'

'That he's my . . .' Lilli forced out the word, 'brother?'

'Well, you only share a father, but that will be more than sufficient for the priests. They'll forbid the marriage in an instant.'

'Indeed. You know, sometimes I dream about my mother, and in the dreams I can feel just how much I hate her. She would have let me marry Braemys. She would have let me – well, she saw naught wrong with sleeping in her own brother's bed, did she?' Lilli's voice dropped. 'Her brother. My father!'

'Try not to hate her.' Nevyn made his voice soft. 'It will only bind you to her memory.'

Lilli started to speak, then coughed, a deep rasping noise that made her clap her hand over her mouth. She twisted round on the bed to hide her face, but he could hear her spitting something up. With her other hand she took a scrap of rag out of her kirtle and wiped her mouth and hand both.

'That sounds nasty,' Nevyn said. 'How long have you been coughing like this?'

'Just since this morning.' Lilli turned back. 'It's the damp. I always get like this in the summer rains.'

'Indeed? I'll make you up some herbwater, and you'd best have a poultice for your chest, too.'

'It's naught.'

'Huh! You'll drink the herbwater anyway. As hot as you can stand it.'

'Oh very well.' Lilli reached up to shove a strand of her awkward hair back behind her ear. 'It'll be a comfort, I'll admit it.'

'I'll be back as soon as the prince has no need of me.'

When Nevyn returned to the council chamber, he found Maryn waiting there alone, standing at the window and staring out at the rain. He turned when Nevyn shut the door.

'I gave Oggyn leave to go,' Maryn said. 'His blunder was eating at him.'

'That was kind of you, my liege.'

'Politic, anyway.' Maryn shrugged. 'What does Lilli say?'

'She has absolutely no desire to marry Braemys, your highness.'

'Splendid! We'll send the herald back with a message that will blister Lord Braemys's ears for him.'

'Shall we compose it now, my liege?'

'Let me think on it a bit. We'll consult later, and then I'll summon a scribe – wait. Braemys sent his herald to carry a letter, but his herald shall hear my answer. Let it look like I'm not taking him seriously enough to have it written out.'

Nevyn left the prince and went up to his own chamber, a small round room perched at the very top of a tower. It held a narrow cot, a single chair, a small unsteady table, a charcoal brazier, and a large pile of his belongings – sacks and small chests, mostly crammed with packets of herbs and roots, as well as what few pieces of spare clothing he owned. Into an empty sack he put the medicaments he needed, mostly liquorice root and a few simples, then went back down.

But when he reached Lilli's chamber, he found the door open and her gone. Inside, one of her maidservants was setting down a basket of charcoal near the bronze brazier that stood near the head of the bed.

'Where's your mistress, lass?' Nevyn said.

'Gone off somewhere, my lord. A man from the king's guards came up a little while ago and asked her to talk with him.'

'One of the silver daggers? Which one?'

'Branoic, my lord.'

'Ah. I thought it might be he.' Nevyn paused as a thought struck him. 'Here, about Prince Maryn? He's not king yet.'

'Oh, we all know what the priests say, my lord, but he's king enough for us.'

'I see.' Nevyn had to smile. 'Well, my thanks. I'll just leave these things here, then, for later. Don't touch them.'

'Have no fear of that, my lord!' The lass looked at his bundle with deep suspicion. 'Are evil spirits going to pop out of that?'

'I doubt it very much. Just don't touch it, and you won't be in any danger.'

Nevyn was walking back down the corridor to the stairs when he met Oggyn, hurrying toward him and carrying an armload of the sort of parchment rolls chamberlains use to note taxes and other dues.

'Lord Nevyn, a moment of your time,' Oggyn said. 'There's somewhat I want to lay before the prince, but after my horrible blunder, I'm afeared to.'

'Oh here!' Nevyn said. 'I'd not worry about that if I were you. The prince has forgiven and forgotten.'

'I truly hope you're right. At any rate, it concerns the taxes and dues from this demesne, Dun Deverry's own lands and holdings, I mean. Could you tell me when he's well disposed to consider such things?'

'Most assuredly, but I do think you could approach him yourself without harm.'

'It's not just that cursed blunder.' Oggyn looked puzzled. 'Lately he's been much distracted. Deciphering his moods is a difficult thing.'

'Well, of course! Ye gods, he spent his whole life battling toward this day, when he'd have Dun Deverry for his own. Ever since he was a child, truly – and now he has it. And so it's over, that entire part of his life. It's left him feeling spent.'

'I see. Ah, how I wish I had your wise knowledge of the hearts of men!'

Nevyn refrained from making a sharp remark about hearts that resort to flattering those they in truth dislike. It was better to have Oggyn indebted to him, after all, than at odds.

In the great hall of Dun Deverry low fires smouldered in the pair of hearths to drive off the damp. Although the draughts won the battle for the centre of the room, near the fire it was warm enough for Lilli to breathe easily. She sat with Branoic on a bench close to the honour hearth, where her noble birth gave her the right to be. Branoic looked so uneasy at being out of his usual place among the prince's guard that she laughed at him. Every time someone walked toward them he would half-rise from his seat, an act that only made him the more noticeable. Even for a Deverry warrior he was a big man, a good head over six feet tall and broad in the shoulders. When she'd first met him, the spring past, she'd thought him beefy, but the summer's fighting had turned him hard-muscled and lean.

'Oh, do sit still!' she said. 'No one's going to chase you away like a dog or suchlike.'

'Well, I wouldn't be too sure of that. I keep wondering what your foster-brother would say if he saw me at your side.'

'I doubt if he'd say anything.'

'Huh! As if he doesn't know that I'm common-born and a
bastard to boot, while you're a –'

'A lady, sure enough, but one with no dowry, no land, and
no kin but him. I see no reason to give myself airs.'

'So!' Branoic grinned at her. 'You don't really enjoy my
company. I'm merely the best suitor you can get, eh?'

'Oh hold your tongue! What would you do if I said you
were right?'

They shared a laugh. Over the general noise in the hall, Lilli
heard pages shouting, 'The prince, the prince!' She looked up
and saw Maryn coming down the stone staircase with pages
marching before him and Nevyn and Oggyn trailing after,
hard-pressed to keep up. Maryn never simply walked; he
strode, always ready to leap like a stag, it seemed, just for the
sheer joy of it. Although he was a handsome man, with blond
hair and deep-set grey eyes, he could have been ugly and still
captivated. Whenever he walked into a room, it seemed that he
brought with him life and power, spilling over onto everything
he touched and everyone he acknowledged. The entire great
hall fell silent to watch him do something as simple as coming
down the stairs.

When she realized that Maryn was heading for them, Lilli
stood and curtsied. Branoic slid off the bench and knelt on
one knee, his head bent respectfully.

'Good morrow, Lady Lillorigga,' Maryn said. 'Branno, you
can get up if you'd like.'

'My thanks, my prince,' Branoic said. 'My apologies for being
where I don't belong.'

'Oh come now!' Maryn was smiling at him. 'And how could
I hold it against any man for wanting the company of such a
beautiful lass as our Lilli?'

Lilli felt her face burning with a blush. Maryn glanced her
way, and for a moment their eyes met, just the briefest of
moments before his gaze travelled on, but all at once she
wondered if her hopeless feeling for him was so hopeless
after all. She hastily looked away and saw Nevyn, watching

all of this with his hands on his hips and steel in his ice-blue eyes. Behind him Councillor Oggyn stood clasping an untidy heap of parchments to his chest.

'My liege?' Nevyn said. 'My apprentice and I have work to do. If you'll excuse us?'

'Of course,' Maryn said. 'You have my leave to go.'

'My thanks. Oggyn wishes to discuss some important matters of finance with you, should that please your highness. I strongly suggest that you do so. Lilli, come along.'

Nevyn turned on his heel and started back across the great hall. Lilli curtsied again to the prince, smiled at Branoic, then rushed after the old man.

In silence they walked up the stairway, slowly to let her catch her breath, but once they reached her chamber and the door was safely barred, Nevyn turned to her.

'I've warned you before,' he snapped. 'The prince may amuse himself with women as he chooses. For the women in question, it's not such a light-hearted thing.'

'I know, my lord.'

'Then try to remember it! Here, Lilli, I'm sorry. I don't mean to be harsh, but I don't want to see you become a cast-off woman with a bastard child – and no place at court any more because the princess hates you. I doubt me if you'd like the life you'd have then.'

'I wouldn't, my lord. I know you're right, but I feel ensorcelled or suchlike. When he walks into a room, it's like the sun follows him in, and everything becomes larger and more alive.'

Nevyn stared at her for a moment, then did the last thing she would have expected: he laughed.

'Well, after a manner of speaking,' Nevyn said at last, 'you *have* been ensorcelled, you and half the kingdom with you. Some years ago, when I was desperately hoping for peace and doubting that I'd ever see it again, Maddyn the bard gave me a idea. If a prince came along who seemed be dweomer, everyone would flock to his banners. And so I found Maryn and made him look as magical as a king out of the Dawntime.

Wildfolk follow him everywhere, Lilli. They cast glamours over him like cloaks.'

Caught without words, Lilli sat down on the edge of the bed.

'You no doubt respond more than most people,' Nevyn went on. 'You have the dweomer gifts, even if you can't see the elemental spirits yet for yourself. In time you will, and then you'll understand what I mean about the glamour.'

'Oh ye gods! I feel like such a dolt.'

'Why? I happen to cast a rather good spell. It's fooled thousands of other people, after all.'

At that Lilli could look up and find him smiling at her. She started to laugh, but in the damp air of her chamber her lungs ached. The laugh turned into a racking cough.

'Huh, that sounds worse and worse,' Nevyn said. 'I've brought some medicinals for it. Let me brew you up some, and then I need to ask Oggyn about getting you a chamber with a proper hearth. I'd forgotten about this dun, how cold it always seems to be.'

'Did you live here once?'

'Once. Before you were born. A very very long time ago.'

Although Lilli wanted to ask more, he turned away and began to rummage through his sack of medicinals so resolutely that she knew the subject had been closed.

That evening the prince summoned Nevyn to his private quarters in the heart of the royal broch. A page led him up a winding stone stair to a heavy oak door, worn smooth and grimy with age and smoke. It opened into a dim suite of rooms hung with threadbare tapestries and stuffed with decrepit furniture. Fat candles burned in smoke-stained sconces on the stone walls. Nevyn picked his way around three carved chests to sit in one of the many chairs the prince offered him. It creaked alarmingly under him. The prince himself perched on the edge of a wobbly table.

'The splendour of the royal palace!' Maryn said, grinning.

'Indeed, my liege. These people certainly never rid themselves of anything, did they?'

'Not their chairs nor their kingdom, not willingly. Though if the siege had gone on all winter, most of this would have ended up as firewood.'

'Most likely, truly.'

The prince paused, as if thinking something through. Nevyn folded his hands in his lap and waited. The guttering light from the candles threw shadows across the beamed ceiling and made him remember a time when torches had lit this room, two hundred years ago. He'd been young and a prince himself, then, and this broch new-built. More than two hundred years now, he thought. Gods! no wonder I grow weary!

'There's a matter I need attended to,' Maryn said abruptly. 'It concerns the Lady Lillorigga.'

'How so, your highness?'

'No matter how much we consider Lilli a daughter of the Rams of Hendyr, and certainly Tieryn Anasyn calls her naught but sister, by birthright she's still a Boar. When I proscribe the Boar clan and attaint their lands, it will go ill with her if she falls under the dominion of the proclamation.'

'I'm very glad you remembered that. I'm afraid I'd quite forgotten.' Nevyn was more than a little annoyed with himself for it. 'I'll speak to the priests of Bel tomorrow and take Anasyn with me. Before the god they can proclaim her kinship.'

'Splendid! Do that, please.'

'I take it that you don't hold out much hope for Braemys swearing fealty.'

'Do you?' Maryn smiled with a twist of his mouth.

'None, my liege.' Nevyn got up. 'When do we ride out?'

'Soon. We'll give the herald a decent head start for the honour of the thing, but we can't wait long. My vassals are growing restless. They need to return to their lands to receive the autumn taxes and suchlike. I'm hoping that Braemys's loyal lords are just as eager to quit the field.'

'No doubt. They can't have much stomach for more fighting. There aren't very many of them left.'

'Just so. We have about four thousand fighting men in good health. Braemys can't have more than a bare thousand at the uttermost.'

'He does have one strong ally, of course. Distance. It's well over two hundred miles from here to Cantrae.'

Maryn swore briefly.

'The road runs through some hilly country as well,' Nevyn went on. 'If I may make a suggestion, my liege?'

'Of course.'

'You'd best hold a council of war soon. Gwerbret Daeryc of Glasloc is going to be invaluable. Glasloc lies between here and Cantrae.'

'It does?' Maryn stared in puzzlement. 'What's he doing as overlord to the Rams, then? Hendyr lies to the west.'

'You know, I haven't the slightest idea. I'd best ask him.'

When Nevyn left the prince, he started to return to his own chamber, but living in Dun Deverry was bringing back memories. He himself had lived in a chamber in a side broch that no longer seemed to exist – if indeed he'd correctly puzzled out the overall plan of the palace. He glanced at the candle in the lantern he carried and judged it good for a long while's burning. Much to his surprise, he went straight to the little door that led to an obscure stairwell. He remembered climbing these steeply wound stairs two at a time; now he paused several times to rest. The stairs led him to a window little more than an arrow slit. Just opposite it there had once been a door, leading into the side broch and, eventually, to his suite. When he held up the lantern, he saw that some of the stonework formed a patch, roughly door-shaped, and much newer than the rest. His old tower, then, was indeed gone.

The stairs continued up, however, and out of curiosity he followed them to the old storeroom at the top of the royal broch. A splintering door hung at an angle from a single hinge. In his long-ago youth, two guards always stood before this door, which led to the royal treasury, but now, when Nevyn pushed the door open, he saw a pair of splayed wooden chests and a lot of dust. He heard little things scuttling away in the shadows, rats and spiders, he supposed. Holding the lantern high he took a few steps in.

Outside the tower, the wind howled, whistling through the arrow slits. In the draughts the candle flame danced, throwing drunken shadows. Nevyn hung the lantern on a rusty metal hook driven between two stones on the wall, then out of sheer idle curiosity opened the first chest. It held nothing but a pile of cloth so old it had turned stiff as straw. The other chest stood empty as well, except for a water-stain. With a shrug he turned his back on the door and retrieved his lantern.

Suddenly Nevyn knew that he wasn't alone. He had heard no one walk up the stairs, heard no rustle of skirts or cloak, but the hairs on the back of his neck rose. Cold damp worse than that of the stones made him shiver. Someone – or something – had followed him in.

'And a good evening to you,' he said.

No answer. Holding the lantern high he turned around. In the doorway stood a woman, wrapped in a black mourning cloak. Her honey-blonde hair hung free, all matted and dishevelled, over her shoulders. She had built her illusions so well that had he not known dweomer, Nevyn would have thought her human. As it was, he noticed that her eyes never blinked. He turned his head to look at her with his peripheral vision and saw etheric substance playing at the edges of her form like glimmers of far-distant lightning.

'A spirit, then,' Nevyn said aloud. 'What do you want here?'

Her lips parted, but instead of speaking she moaned.

'What torments you?' he said. 'Let me help you find peace.'

'My child.'

Nevyn felt his stomach clench. There had been a dead baby buried with the tablet that cursed Prince Maryn.

'Your new-born son?' he said.

'Nah, nah, nah! My daughter, my beautiful little daughter. They plan to steal her away from me.'

'Who? Let me help you!'

She flickered like a dying candle and vanished. Nevyn swore under his breath. She was no ghost, he was sure of that, but a being of great power from some other plane. He remembered the apparition he'd seen when he had sent Lady Merodda's ghost to the Great Ones. Could this be the same being? He would have to meditate on that, but for now, he no longer wanted to stay here, alone with the wind's howls. He hurried down the stairs and retreated to his chamber, where Wildfolk danced to greet him. Late into the night, he studied his dweomer books, hunting for clues as to what sort of spirit the apparition may have been. He found none.

By the morrow morning the storm had travelled on, leaving wet roofs steaming in the summer sun. In the ward outside the great hall, Prince Maryn, with Nevyn in attendance, summoned his highest ranking allies to witness his message to Braemys. A foraging servant had found a length of cloth in the green and brown plaid of the royal city; Maryn wore it as a makeshift cloak, pinned at one shoulder with the pair of silver ring brooches that marked him Prince of Pyrdon and Gwerbret Cerrmor.

It was interesting, Nevyn thought, to see how the lords arranged themselves. Those who had fought alongside the prince from the beginning, such as Tieryn Gauryc, stood to one side of their liege lord, while those who had gone over to him during the summer, such as Tieryn Anasyn, Lilli's foster-brother, stood on the other. Aside from this self-imposed sorting, they seemed friendly enough here in the prince's presence. Over the winter, Nevyn supposed, a few old grudges would be settled by the sword off in the countryside, a secretive distance from their new overlord's justice.

The Cantrae herald, Avyr, was waiting in the ward. While a page held his black horse by the gates, Gavlyn, the prince's own herald, escorted Avyr into the presence of the noble-born.

Avyr bowed, then knelt with a swing of his staff that sent the ribands swirling. Maryn acknowledged him with a small nod.

'Now, concerning the Lady Lillorigga, tell Lord Braemys this,' Maryn said. 'The lady now belongs to the Rams of Hendyr. Her brother has proclaimed the betrothal broken and disavowed. From me, tell him this: I shall forgive him for referring to me as a usurper provided he forswear his rebellious behaviour. He may swear fealty to me or leave my lands forever. Those are his choices.'

'I see, your highness.' The herald looked away – rudeness in another man, but in his case, a sign that he was memorizing the prince's exact words. 'I shall tell him.'

'Good. Here's more: I'll be riding out soon for Cantrae. He may meet me along the road to parley if he chooses.'

'Very well, your highness. I shall convey your answer with all speed.'

'My thanks. Let us all hope the gods let your lord choose peace.'

Avyr smiled and rose, bowing. Not one man in the crowd expected Braemys to swear the vow of fealty – Nevyn would have wagered high on that – but there were rituals to these things, as unforgiving as those of any temple.

Once the herald had ridden on his way, the little crowd around the prince began to thin out. Nevyn noticed Gwerbret Daeryc strolling off toward the stables and hurried to catch up with him.

'Your grace!' Nevyn called out. 'A word with you?'

The gwerbret stopped and turned around, smiling pleasantly, or rather, he smiled in a way he meant to be pleasant. Since he'd lost all the teeth on one side of his mouth, he kept his lips shut and twisted, giving him the look of a bear in pain.

'The prince asked me to lay this question before you,' Nevyn said. 'It concerns the Rams of Hendyr. Glasloc's well off to the east of Dun Deverry, and Hendyr's in the west, and yet you're overlord to the Rams.'

'Ah. No doubt that pricked his curiosity, truly. Glasloc's mine in name only, good councillor. My lands lie north of Hendyr. My father inherited a goodly demesne near Mabyndyr, and when we lost Glasloc, we made them our home.'

'Lost Glasloc?'

'Well, I call it as a loss. My father traded it away for the right to rule as gwerbret in Mabyndyr. A lot of the common folk who fled Dun Deverry settled near there, which meant dues and taxes to support a gwerbretrhyn. So the Boars proclaimed the new rhan for him, you see, because they coveted the lands near Glasloc. He could give them Glasloc or lose everything – that was the bargain they offered.'

'But he kept the honorific?'

'My father didn't. I took it back when I inherited, and there was naught that Regent Burcan could say or do, because the slimy bastard knew he needed me and my men.'

'Ah. You say the Boars did the proclaiming?'

'Well, the words came out of the mouth of the king – poor little Olaen's grandfather, that was – but we all knew who'd put them there.' Daeryc paused to spit onto the cobbles. 'Burcan's father was gwerbret then, and a worse man than his sons.' He looked up. 'A word to the wise, councillor. Some of the northern lords will desert back to Braemys over the winter, and I'd bet a good horse that Nantyn will be one of them. But I won't. You have my sworn word on that.'

'My thanks, but you know, I never doubted you for an instant.'

'Indeed? Why?'

'Tieryn Peddyc would never have honoured a man who changed sides out of anything less than true conviction.'

'My thanks.' Daeryc nodded, looking down at the ground. 'I'll miss Peddyc. Closest thing to a friend I ever had. Ah well, the fortunes of war, eh?'

The gwerbret turned on his heel and strode off fast. Let us hope, Nevyn thought, that the fighting stays over. It was a feeble hope, he supposed. With a shake of his head he went into the royal broch to find Oggyn, who had by default as much as merit managed to appoint himself chamberlain.

Much to his surprise he saw his fellow councillor over by the riders' hearth, talking with one of the men from the Cerrmor warband. As he walked over, Nevyn saw the rider give Oggyn a coin, but he thought little of it – some wager, perhaps. When Oggyn saw him approaching, he came bustling over, all smiles.

'My apprentice needs a better chamber,' Nevyn said. 'One with a proper hearth and suchlike.'

'Of course. Just come upstairs with me.'

'We'll just collect Lilli on the way.'

As they climbed the stairs, Nevyn glanced back and noticed the Cerrmor rider watching Oggyn still. He could have sworn that the man looked furious.

'What about this one?' Oggyn said. 'It's much larger and it has a hearth.'

'Oh, this will do splendidly!' Lilli said, but she glanced at Nevyn. 'I've never had so much room.'

'I heartily approve.' Nevyn answered her unspoken question. 'The air here should be quite wholesome.'

They were standing in a bedchamber once set aside for guests. As well as the hearth, it sported a big window with proper wooden shutters, braided rushes on the floor, and a sufficiency of tapestries, faded and torn though they were, to keep the damp off the walls. Near the hearth stood a chair and a solid round table. The morning sun poured in and fell across the bed like a gold blanket. Lilli sat down on the edge of the mattress and stretched out her arms to the warmth.

'This is lovely!'

'Very well, then,' Oggyn said. 'I'll be on my way. I'll send a couple of pages to help your servants move your things over.'

'And make sure they fetch firewood, too,' Nevyn said to him. 'If you don't mind.'

'Not at all, my pleasure.' With a bow to Lilli, Oggyn bustled out, shutting the door behind him.

'My thanks, Nevyn!' Lilli said. 'Oggyn never would have given me such a fine chamber if I'd asked him myself.'

'Most welcome. And once you're settled, I expect you to get right to the work I set you.'

'I will, my lord.'

'Good. I'll be gone all afternoon, running an errand with your foster-brother.'

'So he told me, my lord. It will gladden my heart to be a true daughter of the Ram.'

Lilli kept her promise after Clodda and Nalla had brought her possessions to the new chamber. Thanks to Nevyn's confession about the spells he'd cast on Prince Maryn, she was particularly eager to learn how to see the elemental spirits, or the Wildfolk as they were commonly called. On her table she placed a silver basin filled with water, then sat in the chair and let her breathing slow as Nevyn had taught her. The shaft of sunlight had moved on to fall upon the floor. Motes danced in the slight breeze, while the surface of the water in the silver bowl trembled. She waited, she watched her breaths, she became aware of nothing but moving air, sunlight, water, dancing dust.

Like a shadow flitting something moved at the edge of her vision. She concentrated on breathing. The shadow came a little closer, grew solid, then disappeared. She waited still longer, while the shaft of sunlight crept across the floor. All at once a creature appeared, a strange grey fellow, about two feet high and shaped roughly like a human child, with a big head and a protruding belly. It looked at her out of narrow purple eyes. Lilli gasped aloud, and it vanished. Though she sat a long while more, nothing, or no one, appeared to her.

'Still,' Nevyn said when he returned, 'you've made a splendid start. I'm very proud of the progress you're making.'

Lilli felt her face warm with a blush. No praise had ever meant so much to her as his.

'I have a message for you. Your brother wants you to dine with him tonight in his chambers,' Nevyn went on. 'I told him that you'd doubtless agree.'

'Of course! What did the priests say?'

'That neither they nor their god had any objections to your adoption by the clan of the Ram. There's a small matter of a fee for the drawing up of the proclamation, but we'll take care of that on the morrow, and the matter will be settled.'

'I'm glad it was so easy.'

'Well, the prince proclaimed your new kinship in the ward this morning. That certainly didn't hurt your cause.'

When the sun hung low in the sky, Lilli went to her foster-brother's quarters. Since Anasyn was newly married, he'd been given chambers in the royal broch itself – a decent-sized suite with a small wedge-shaped reception chamber as well as a bedroom. When she knocked, his page opened the door and ushered her inside. Some of the chairs she recognized and the table as well – once this furniture had been her mother's, but it had joined the general booty of the dun, handed out to the victors. A pair of maidservants were laying out a cold meal from a pair of big baskets onto the table. She could remember the bowl of black ink sitting on that same cloth, waiting to swallow her mind. She shuddered, suddenly cold.

'What's wrong, Lilli?' Abrwnna said.

'Oh naught. Just geese walking on my grave.'

Abrwnna, Anasyn's wife, was sitting in a high-backed chair by the empty hearth. She was beautiful, Abrwnna, with long red hair and big green eyes, but Lilli found herself thinking of her as a child – odd, since Abrwnna was near her own age and twice-married now, not that her first marriage, to the child-king, had ever been consummated. She smiled and waved Lilli over.

'Come in, sister,' Abrwnna said. 'My lord is off somewhere, but no doubt he'll join us soon. Do have that chair with the cushions.'

'My thanks.' Lilli nearly dropped her a curtsey out of sheer habit. 'You're looking well.'

'Am I? Truly, I count myself the luckiest of women these days. When I think of what might have happened to me after the siege was over –' Abrwnna laid a pale hand on her paler throat. 'We should all be thankful that our prince is a merciful man.'

'Just so.'

Abrwnna hesitated, glancing at the servants. Until they'd done setting out the food, she said nothing more, then dismissed them. The page hovered near the door.

'Do go see if you can find our lord, will you?' Abrwnna said. 'Tell him his sister is here.'

'I will, my lady,' the page bowed, then hurried off.

Once the door had closed behind him, Abrwnna leaned back in her chair and let out her breath in a long sigh.

'I've not seen you to have two private words together, truly,' Abrwnna said, 'not since the dun fell. Why, Lilli? Why did you run away like that and go over to the prince?'

Silence hung between them like smoke. Lilli felt like a dolt for being surprised – of course Abrwnna would want to know, of course all the women left behind to suffer in the taking of Dun Deverry would want to know.

'Why did I betray you?' Lilli said at last. 'Is that what you mean?'

'It's not, truly it isn't. I – well, I just wanted to know – well, was it because of Lady Bevyan?'

'It was. After my mother had her murdered, how could I stay here and pretend to be her dutiful daughter?'

'You couldn't.' Abrwnna hesitated for a long moment. 'But I still don't understand what happened. The servants told me that Merodda murdered Bevyan. I thought she'd been killed by Cerrmor raiders. I don't understand.'

'Hasn't Anasyn told you?'

'Not a word.' Abrwnna's voice was shaking badly. 'I'll tell you somewhat. In the great hall that day, when your brother asked the prince for me, I truly thought he only wanted vengeance. I feared he was going to beat me to death, once I was his wife and no one could say him nay.'

'Sanno would never!'

'I know that now.' Abrwnna was whispering again. 'But at first I was afraid to say two words to him. He did tell me Bevva's death was none of my doing. When I asked why, he swore at me and said never to mention it again.'

'Well, those Cerrmor raiders? They weren't real. After you sent Bevyan away, Uncle Burcan followed her with some of his men and killed her and everyone with her. They left some Cerrmor shields behind as a ruse. But my mother was the one who wanted Bevva dead. She put him up to it.'

Abrwnna dropped her face into her hands and sobbed. Lilli sat stone-still, barely able to think, watching her weep, rocking back and forth like a troubled child.

'Here, here,' Lilli said at last. 'What's so wrong?'

'What's wrong?' Abrwnna let her hands drop. 'I sent her away, just as you said. It's my fault she was out on the roads. Oh ye gods, you must hate me!' She paused, wiping her face on the sleeve of her dress. 'And your mother was the one – ah, Goddess! I thought she was my friend.'

Lilli stood and walked over to lay a hand on Abrwnna's trembling shoulder.

'I don't hate you. I've no doubt at all that my mother worked on you to send Bevva away. I'll wager you didn't even know she was using you, either.'

'We did talk, truly, just before.' Abrwnna stared up at her and shook. 'She told me, well, things. She told me Bevva was telling people I was a slut or suchlike.'

'Never! Bevva never would have done that. You see? It's not your fault. If you'd not sent her away, then my mother only would have poisoned her or found some other way to do her murdering.'

'Do you think so?'

'I truly do.'

'You don't hate me?'

'Did you think I would?'

Abrwnna nodded, then leaned her head back against the chair.

'Do you hate me for aiding the prince?' Lilli went on.

'I don't. You know what the worst thing is? I keep dreaming about the taking of the dun, that last awful day. Or sometimes I dream about poor little Olaen, and the way he died, poisoned like that. And in the dreams I can't stop screaming. I see all the horrible things all over again and just keep screaming and screaming.' Abrwnna paused to run shaking hands through her hair. 'But then I wake up. And there's Anasyn next to me, and I know I'm safe. And I can't help thinking, I'm glad Prince Maryn won. I'm glad I'm Anasyn's lady and not queen any more. And I feel so horrible because I'm glad.'

Abrwnna began to weep again, a thin trickle of silent tears. Lilli took a napkin from the table and handed it to her, then sat down again.

'If you're a traitor, Lilli, then so am I.' Abrwnna began to wipe her face. 'A thousand times a day.'

'Oh here! The gods are the ones who ordained Maryn the true king, aren't they? It's his Wyrd, and there's naught that you or I can do about it. It must be your Wyrd, too, that you're the lady of Hendyr now.'

Abrwnna merely shrugged, then wiped her face. The linen napkin shook in her hands.

'Would you like me to pour you a little mead?' Lilli said.

'None, but my thanks.' Abrwnna let the napkin fall onto her lap. 'Your mother! Ah gods, it was all true, then, the gossip. She truly was some sort of witch.'

'She was.' Lilli felt as if the words had stuck in her throat and were choking her. 'I suppose there was a lot of gossip that I never heard.'

'How could anyone tell you? It was evil evil stuff, and I refused to believe any of it, truly I did, but you know what? Now I suppose I should have.'

'About her poisons, you mean?'

'Just that. And spells and things. Everyone thought she cast spells on herself to look so young.'

'That was only herbs and some sort of elixir she brewed up.'

'Ah. Truly? And here I believed it about the spells! Some of the women said she had lots of lovers, you see, and that's why she'd use magic to keep her looks.'

Lilli's breath caught in her chest. Had anyone guessed that Merodda's brother had sired her daughter?

'Lovers?' Lilli said. 'Why would they think that?'

'Well, I don't remember exactly.' Abrwnna thought for a moment. 'It all seems so paltry now, the gossip I mean.'

Lilli found it hard to breathe. Old gossip, swept away by the summer's tide of blood and the horrors of siege – of course the other women would scorn such chatter now. But to her, it might mean the difference between having a place at court or losing one as a landless bastard.

'I do wonder,' Lilli said. 'There must have been a lot of talk that I was never allowed to hear.'

'Well, it was all nasty stuff. There were a few tales that would have branded her a fiend if they were true. Like that child, the one she birthed after your father was slain, and everyone told me it wasn't really his anyway.'

'What? What child? I never knew about that.'

'Well, it died a little while after it was born. Merodda left court and shut herself up in Dun Cantrae to birth it, and all the old gossips said she ran away because she was so shamed, but I wasn't at court then, so I wouldn't know the truth of that. When she came back in the spring she told everyone the child had died of fever. But ah Goddess, knowing what I know now, maybe the gossip was all true, and it wasn't Lord Garedd's child, and she smothered it or suchlike.'

'Indeed?' Lilli found it harder and harder to talk. 'And whose was the child, then? Did they say?'

'A demon's.' Abrwnna leaned forward in her chair to look

at Lilli wide-eyed. 'They said she'd been got with child by a demon she'd conjured up, and that's why the baby was so sickly. But that couldn't be true, could it?'

'I doubt it very much.' Lilli nearly laughed from sheer relief. 'I truly do. Don't the priests always say that demons don't have real bodies? How could they sire anything without them?'

'You're right, aren't you? But that didn't stop the gossip. All the old cats were still talking about the scandal when my father brought me to court to marry Olaen.'

No doubt it was sickly, Lilli thought. It was another child of incest, wasn't it?

'And then the gossips said that one of Merodda's retainers was a demon, too, so they thought he was the father.' Abrwnna paused, listening. 'I hear voices in the hall. It's probably Sanno.'

The chamber door opened: Anasyn indeed, followed by his page. The tieryn was by no means a handsome man, though not ugly, either, with his long face and long thin nose, but Abrwnna smiled at him as if he were a vision of Bel himself.

'There you are, beloved,' Abrwnna said.

'My apologies for being late,' Anasyn said. 'I met old Gauryc in the great hall, and he wouldn't let me go till he'd had his say.'

'About what?' Lilli put in.

'The gwerbretrhyn of Cerrmor. When he's seated as king, the prince will have to give it up. Gauryc wants it. Badly.' Anasyn smiled briefly. 'And to get it, he'll need every ally on the Council of Electors that he can scrounge up. He's not the only one with his eye on the rhan.'

'No doubt.' Lilli glanced at Abrwnna. 'I've been there, and ye gods! It's the richest place I've ever seen.'

'You simply must tell me all about it.' Abrwnna turned to the page. 'Very well, you may serve your lord, and then Lilli and I will serve ourselves, and then you may take what you wish.'

For the rest of that evening their talk centred on the politics of the new court that Maryn was forming. Every now and then, though, Abrwnna would fall silent for a long while, and Lilli would notice her staring at the empty air as if she were seeing horrors drawn upon it.

Over the next two days the prince held councils of war. In the oldest broch stood a big round room that had been the great hall when Nevyn was young. Maryn took it over for his councils, and servants carried in all the extra chairs they could find for the assembly. By ancient laws and courtesies both, every noble-born man in Deverry who served royalty had the right to speak out in council when a high king was making plans for war. As a mere prince, Maryn had to be more respectful of these rights and customs than a king would have been. A wrong word or act of arrogance would lose him allies.

Although Daeryc's clan no longer ruled Glasloc, he knew the territory between Dun Deverry and Cantrae well. So did Nevyn, but he mostly held his tongue. Admitting his knowledge of the area would mean admitting when he'd lived there, and that in turn would bring awkward questions about his unnaturally long life. Dun Cantrae, the stronghold of the Boar clan, lay inside the town of Cantrae proper, which meant a double ring of walls to take should the matter come to siege. The town lay on what was at that time the furthest border of the kingdom, a good two hundred and thirty miles to the north-east.

'For the first part of the journey,' Daeryc said, 'the roads will be good ones, and the country's flat. But past Glasloc you get into the hills.'

'That's not good,' Maryn said. 'The army moves slow enough on the flat.'

'Just so.' Tieryn Gauryc, a skinny man with hair cropped close to his skull, rose to speak. 'We made what? Twelve miles a day when we marched from Cerrmor?'

'No more than that, truly,' Maryn said.

In the back of the chamber some lord or other let out a loud long snore. Everyone laughed and woke the man, who grinned sheepishly while he rubbed his eyes.

'My lords, I think we've had an omen,' Maryn said, smiling. 'Let's leave this lie for today.'

The assembled company cheered him. When the council disbanded, Maryn held Nevyn back for a private word.

'I need your opinion on somewhat,' Maryn said. 'Oggyn approached me with this daft-sounding scheme. He wants to take a couple of scribes and ride around the royal demesne, writing down everything he finds there. Well, not everything, but how many farms, and how many bondmen, and so on and so forth.'

'That doesn't sound daft to me, my liege. It sounds cursed sensible. We don't have the slightest idea of what you can expect in dues and taxes.'

'So Oggyn says.' Maryn considered for a moment. 'Well, rebuilding the Holy City is going to take coin, not just bound labour.'

'True spoken. Oggyn's real worth lies in such matters. He understands coin, and more to the point he understands mustering labour and assigning duties and so on.'

'Very well. I'll tell him to go ahead and start the survey. There's no use in his coming along with the army, when we're only riding on what amounts to a feint.'

When he left the prince, Nevyn went looking for Lady Merodda's old chambers. He'd not forgotten the mysterious spirit presence who had appeared to him, and Merodda was the only clue he had. When he asked the servants about the chambers, they pointed them out readily enough. Since the taking of the dun, they'd stood empty, because no one wanted to sleep in a room where someone had practised witchcraft and poisoning. It was amazing, he thought, how quickly the rumours about the lady had spread. The men of Maryn's army and retinue hadn't even known she existed six months ago. Now they all feared her, even in death.

When Nevyn walked into the suite, he found it bare. Not so

much as a stick of furniture or firewood remained. She might have been feared, but apparently her possessions weren't. In the emptiness Nevyn's footsteps echoed; dust puffed and fell at his feet. He asked himself what exactly he expected to find, but he had no answer. He wandered into the empty bedchamber, looked around for a moment, and wandered back out. Near the hearth a half-round chair had appeared, and in it sat Merodda – or a perfect illusion of her. Nevyn turned cold with little gasp of breath. The spirit had reproduced her image down to the unnatural shininess of her skin – a blonde woman, once beautiful, dressed in flowing blue, she sat with a simulacrum of a book open in her lap.

'I know you're not her ghost,' Nevyn said. 'I exorcised her myself.'

'Oh, I remember that,' the spirit said – in Elvish.

'Very well. Then what are you doing, mimicking her?'

'I'll not answer that unless you answer me a question.'

'I'll agree to that if you answer mine first.'

The spirit considered him with eyes that never blinked. In her lap the book turned transparent and disappeared.

'Done then,' she said at last. 'Becoming her I know her.'

'I see. What's your question?'

'You stole her daughter from her, didn't you? Just like they plan to steal mine.'

'I didn't. Her daughter left her of her own will.'

The spirit screamed in such murderous rage that Nevyn stepped back. In that instant spirit and chair both vanished.

By all the gods! he thought. What is she? And why did that anger her so?

With a shake of his head Nevyn left the room. He would have to meditate on the question. Lilli might well know something, too, if her mother had ever mentioned having some sort of astral visitor. But although he looked in her chamber and in the great hall, he couldn't find Lilli to ask her. Finally he stopped a passing page.

'Have you seen Lady Lillorigga of the Ram?'

'I've not, my lord,' the boy said.

'Well, then, have you seen Branoic the Silver Dagger?'

'Not him either, my lord.' The boy smiled in a sly sort of way. 'Shall I look for them?'

'Most definitely not. She'll turn up sooner or later of her own accord.'

Maddyn had no illusions about his skill as a harper. Over the years he'd brutalized his hands with sword and shield until his fingers could bend only so far and travel the strings only so fast and no more. He did, however, take his music seriously, and every morning he found a private spot in one of the dun's many odd corners to practise far away from the noise and crowds in barracks and great hall. Sound carries, of course, and thanks to his music he was always easy to find.

'Ah, uh, captain?'

Maddyn looked up, startled. Standing in front of him was a young man who looked vaguely familiar – pale hair, pale eyes, and the high cheekbones of a southern man to go with the Cerrmor blazons on his shirt.

'I hate to disturb you,' the fellow went on, 'but one of the silver daggers, that truly tall fellow with the broad shoulders, told me I should speak to you.'

'Branoic, was it?'

'That's his name. Mine's Alwyn.'

'Very well. What did you want to speak to me about?'

Alwyn turned and looked behind him, then glanced off in the direction of the broch complex.

'Well, it's about Councillor Oggyn,' Alwyn said at last. 'I want to join the silver daggers, you see. Oggyn told me that it would cost a silver piece for him to introduce me to Owaen.'

'What? The filthy gall of the man!'

'Branoic said somewhat like that, too. I paid the coin over, you see, and Owaen talked with me and had me meet some of the other men in the troop. And so I was drinking with Branoic last night, and I mentioned the councillor and his silver piece. And some of the other new men spoke up and said the same had happened to them. Branoic was fair furious, he was.'

'Cursed right, too! That little pissproud glorified scribe! Come along, lad. Let me stow my harp in the barracks, and then we'll go find Owaen.'

Owaen, however, turned out to be in the barracks, sitting on his bunk and polishing his mail. His sword belt lay beside him on the blanket, but even unarmed there was something dangerous about Owaen. He was frowning as he pulled a scrap of rag through each ring with a quick gesture born of years of practice; his ice-blue eyes glared as if he were killing Boarsmen, not rust. Maddyn knew better than to get too close to him when he was in such a reverie. He stopped a couple of bunks away and called out.

'Owaen? A word with you?'

Startled, Owaen was on his feet and reaching for his sword. The mail slid off his lap and chimed onto the floor.

'Oh.' Owaen said. 'It's just you.'

He sat back down and picked up the mail. Maddyn led Alwyn over.

'This lad has a very interesting tale to tell. Councillor Oggyn's been charging a fee to send men our way.'

While Alwyn repeated his story, Owaen said not a word. His expression went perfectly calm, perfectly blank, and when the lad was done, Owaen merely nodded. He laid the mail aside, got up, and buckled on his sword belt.

'Let's have a word with our councillor.' Owaen's voice was perfectly soft and calm. 'Follow me.'

Alwyn hesitated, visibly puzzled, as if perhaps he wondered if he'd been believed. Maddyn winked at him and shepherded him out of the barracks. They followed Owaen's broad back across the ward and into the great hall, which here in mid-morning stood mostly empty. A few riders lingered on their side of the big round room; a few servants wandered back and forth, wiping up scraps from the tables and throwing them to the waiting dogs. Oggyn was standing by the honour hearth and gazing at the staircase, as if he were waiting for someone. Owaen paused and turned to Alwyn.

'You'll swear to this?'

'I will, and there's six other lads in the same spot as me.'

'Done, then.' Owaen allowed himself a brief twitch of his mouth that might have been a smile. 'Follow me.'

As they strode over, Oggyn looked up and saw them coming. He froze, started to back away, realized that Owaen was too close to outrun, and finally arranged a commanding stare on his face and crossed his arms over his chest as well.

'You wish to speak with me?' Oggyn bellowed.

Owaen took one long stride, grabbed him by the shirt with both hands, and slammed him back against the wall. Oggyn squeaked and howled and kicked; Owaen slammed him again, and Oggyn held still, gasping for breath. Those few people in the hall stopped what they were doing and turned to watch. Maddyn glanced around, but no one was rushing to the councillor's aid.

'Listen, you,' Owaen said. 'You've been extorting fees, haven't you? Demanding coin from men who want to meet me or Maddyn?'

'Not! Lies!'

'Horseshit! There are seven men ready to swear you took their coins.' Owaen shook him. 'You're paying every copper back.'

'Won't! Can't! It's not true!'

'Then you won't object if we go straight to the prince with this matter.'

'I'll pay!'

Owaen smiled and let Oggyn go. Moaning and fussing, the councillor smoothed down his shirt, then reached inside it and pulled out a fat pouch, hanging round his neck from a gold chain. Alwyn was staring at Owaen with a look suitable to viewing a god come down to earth. Swearing under his breath, Oggyn gave Alwyn a silver piece, then counted out six more into Owaen's waiting palm.

'And one more,' Owaen said, 'for the troop's general coffer. Consider it lwdd.'

'May the gods piss upon you!' Oggyn snarled – but he paid.

Still muttering, Oggyn trotted to the staircase on the far side of the great hall to the accompaniment of snickers and downright laughter from the servants and riders present. Owaen's face had gone blank again, but he stood jingling the coins and watching the councillor hurry up the stairs.

'Branoic's good for somewhat after all,' Owaen said at last.

'Truly,' Maddyn said. 'I'm glad our new men found him easy to talk to.'

'Where is he, anyway?' Owaen glanced around.

'I've no idea.'

The bard, however, was lying. Branoic was off courting the Lady Lillorigga, and Maddyn knew it. He simply saw no reason to give Owaen anything more to hold over Branno's head.

Although Dun Deverry sported no proper gardens like those in Cerrmor, it did have a kitchen garden out behind the cookhouses and storage sheds. In search of a little privacy, Lilli and Branoic found it one morning when the summer air hung warm and heavy. They sat down on a wood bench and breathed the scents of rosemary, sage and spicy thyme. Branoic lounged back and laid one long arm on the bench back behind her. She could feel the warmth of it, it seemed, and she stared straight out ahead of her.

In a little eddy of dust a big grey gnome appeared. He set his twiggy hands on his hips and cocked his head to one side like a miniature silver dagger. Lilli felt herself smiling, then stifled it. What if Branoic had noticed her watching invisible things? But when she glanced his way, she found him smiling as well, his eyes moving as the gnome strutted back and forth.

'You see him,' she whispered.

'Ye gods!' Branoic swung his head round to look at her. 'So do you.'

For a long moment they merely stared at each other, each a little aghast. I don't know this man, Lilli thought. I thought I knew exactly what he was, but I was wrong!

'Ah well,' Branoic said, and his voice was just barely above a whisper. 'Either we're both daft, or the cursed little things do exist after all.'

'Not daft,' Lilli said. 'Does Nevyn know you see them?'

'He doesn't, and I'll beg you, my lady, to never let him know. Or anyone else, either.'

'Why not?'

'What do you mean why not?' Branoic turned on the bench and crossed his arms over his chest. 'Should be cursed obvious.'

'It isn't.'

He scowled at her, and then, without any reason that she could see, they both burst out laughing.

'Well, I do understand,' Lilli said. 'I shan't say a word to anyone. I was just teasing you.'

'I'd rather have teasing from you than flattery from any other lass.' All at once he turned solemn. 'We're riding out tomorrow. Will you miss me?'

Because he deserved an honest answer, she considered her feelings while he waited, watching her solemnly.

'I will,' she said at last. 'It aches my heart, having someone to fear for, but I do worry about what could happen to you. Please ride back again?'

'If my Wyrd allows it, I will. And you stay safe for me.'

'I'll do my best.'

For a moment they sat smiling at each other. She thought that he might kiss her, but he rose and bowed instead.

'Shall we walk back, my lady? I'd not have anyone speaking scandal about you.'

'My thanks, but I doubt if they would.' She rose to join him. 'I'm not important enough.'

'Well, most likely that's a blessing, you know.'

'True spoken.'

When he offered her his arm, she slipped hers through it, and they walked together back to the great hall. At the door, however, she heard Nevyn calling her name and turned to see the old man striding toward them. His energy always amazed her; with his white hair and frog-spotted skin he looked ancient in repose, but when he moved, he seemed more vigorous than many a young warrior. She gave Branoic's arm a pat, then pulled hers free.

'You go on in,' Lilli said. 'Nevyn seems to need me for somewhat.'

'Well and good, then, my lady.' Branoic bowed to her. 'It's doubtless best that the noble-born don't see us together, anyway.'

Nevyn did indeed wish to speak with her, as it turned out. Cautioning secrecy, he escorted her up to her new chamber, where the maids had finished tidying up her things. Lilli sat down on the chair while Nevyn perched on the wide windowsill.

'I need you to put your memory to the test,' Nevyn said. 'About your mother.'

'Very well.' Lilli folded her hands in her lap to keep them from shaking.

'I hate to distress you, but this could be extremely important.'

'Oh, I do understand. I just hate thinking about the way – the way she died.'

'No doubt.' Nevyn hesitated, his ice-blue eyes sympathetic. 'But did she ever talk with you much about her dweomer workings?'

'At times, my lord, and Brour did let things slip now and then.'

'Good. Did either of them ever mention that she talked with spirits? Or to be precise, one particular spirit, who would have appeared to her as a woman?'

'I don't think so, although – wait.' Lilli paused, letting her mind wander around an image of her mother, sitting in a candle-lit room and speaking. 'She did mention once that she had seen a ghost walking these halls, a woman dressed in mourning.'

'Indeed? Go on.'

'Brour remarked that a lot of women had died miserably here, in childbed and suchlike, and my mother laughed and agreed.'

'Laughed?'

'Well, it was one of those ghastly nervous laughs. She didn't see any humour in it or suchlike. And then she said that mayhap she'd try to find out what the poor restless soul wanted. But that's all I remember.'

'It may very well be enough. My thanks.' Nevyn rose, glancing at the table and the book lying upon it. 'I'd like you to work upon your studies this afternoon. We have much to cover before I leave with the prince and his army.'

When Prince Maryn rode out, some days later, he left over half of his army behind on fortguard. As much as he wanted to make an overwhelming show of force, the full contingent of four thousand men would travel too slowly. Time and supplies were both running out. Every day the night fell a little faster. If they stripped much more food from the countryside, farm families would begin to starve, and then, as Nevyn was quick to point out, who would grow the next crop? The vassals talked openly of riding home to their own lands as soon as the prince would allow.

'If Braemys meets us on the road, well and good,' Maryn told Nevyn. 'If not, we won't be able to ride all the way to Cantrae, and we couldn't mount a siege if we got there, and I suspect he knows that as well as I do.'

'No doubt,' Nevyn said. 'It's a pity, though. I can't help wondering how many of your newest allies will come to your muster in the spring.'

'Some, certainly. More than we had before, which will mean Braemys will have less, and that will be all to the good. Even if they all desert, what will it amount to? Another five hundred riders, more or less, and we'll still outnumber Braemys handily. I doubt if any of the northern lords will strip their fortguards for the Boar cause again.'

'Now that's true spoken. Well, it's in the laps of the gods now.'

For three days the army travelled north-east, following the main road that led from Dun Deverry to Cantrae. Every dun they passed belonged to one or another of the prince's new allies. At each, the lord who held it would open the gates to the prince himself and greet him by grasping his stirrup in a show of fealty. These lords, Nevyn decided, were likely to hold true to Maryn's cause – not because of their ritual greeting, but because their duns were too small and shabby to stand off an attack by the prince's forces.

The army was still a fair ways from Glasloc, and it had just made camp for the night in a meadow, when the Cantrae herald returned. Nevyn heard the commotion among the camp guards and trotted out to see what was wrong. His beribboned staff in one hand, his black horse's reins in the other, Avyr was walking into camp with two guards on either side of him.

'Good morrow, good herald,' Nevyn said. 'I trust you've got a message for the prince?'

'Just so. If his lordship would be so kind as to take me to him?'

They found Maryn sitting in a chair in front of his tent with some of his lords standing nearby, talking over the day's ride. Behind him, stiff at attention, stood Branoic and another silver dagger. A page boy took the herald's horse, and Avyr bowed low to the prince.

'Lord Braemys would have me speak to several points, your highness,' Avyr began. 'First, if the Rams of Hendyr refuse to honour the betrothal of Lady Lillorigga, they then owe him twenty-five horses as lwdd for their offence.'

Maryn laughed, one sharp bark of utter amazement. The men standing nearby either did the same or shook their heads in disbelief.

'Your lord doesn't lack for gall, does he?' Maryn said.

'There's naught I can say about that, your highness.'

'Well, of course you can't. What else does Lord Braemys wish me to hear?'

Avyr hesitated, looking round the circle of lords. Nevyn had the distinct feeling that the man was wondering if he'd live out the night. At length he licked his lips and began.

'Lord Braemys begs to point out, your highness, that as yet you are but Prince of Pyrdon and Gwerbret Cerrmor. He has received no word that the priests of Bel have declared you king. If such should happen, that is, if the priests should so declare, he begs you to send him a messenger with all speed so that he may reconsider your claim to be his liege lord.'

Maryn's face went dead white, then reddened. The herald stepped back as if to put himself out of reach of a blow and nearly stepped on Gwerbret Daeryc's feet. Daeryc patted him on the shoulder with the same motion he'd use to calm a nervous horse.

'Here, here, lad,' Daeryc muttered. 'Our prince is an honourable man. He doesn't go about slaying heralds.'

'Just so.' Maryn's voice was more of a growl; he paused to collect himself with a pair of deep breaths. 'Very well, good herald. Rest in our camp tonight, and on the morrow I'll give you a message to take back to your lord the regent.'

The news spread fast. Before Maryn could call for a council, it assembled itself as his noble-born allies came running to his tent. Nevyn had never seen Maryn so angry. The entire time he talked, he paced back and forth, one hand on the hilt of his sword. Yet there was little that anyone could suggest that would ease the situation or end it. After wrangling deep into the night, the lords disbanded at last to get some sleep, but for most of the night Maryn waked, walking back and forth in front of his tent with a lantern in his hand.

Toward dawn Nevyn gave up on sleep and went over to join him there.

'My liege?' Nevyn said. 'Is somewhat wrong?'

'Naught,' Maryn said, yawning. 'I've been thinking about my answer to Braemys, that's all.'

'I rather did assume you were.'

'Oh of course.' Maryn suddenly grinned at him. 'Do you remember a dream I had once, back when I was but a little child, and you'd just become my tutor? I dreamt that I was in a battle in Cantrae, and everyone was calling me the king of all Deverry.'

'I do remember it, oddly enough. It was a very important dream.'

'So it was, and you know, it looks like it's going to come true.' Maryn yawned again, hugely, covering his mouth with both hands. 'So, I told myself, I shouldn't be surprised that Braemys is spoiling for a fight. It's a thing of Wyrd for both of us, and there's no arguing with Wyrd.'

'So there's not, your highness. And that said, I suggest you get some sleep.'

In the morning, the camp slept late, but the prince was up before many of his men. After he'd eaten, Maryn called the herald and his allies as well to him to hear his answer. Avyr bowed, then stood ready to memorize.

'Tell your lord this for me,' Maryn said. 'The high priest of Bel in Dun Deverry charged me with the holy task of bringing peace to the kingdom. If your lord refuses to make peace, then he defies the will of the gods themselves. If he surrenders now, the Boar clan will continue to hold the Cantrae rhan. Should he continue to defy the gods, he will lose it.'

The herald winced and bowed for want of anything else he could do.

'As for the other thing,' Maryn went on. 'I cannot settle this matter betwixt him and Tieryn Anasyn of the Ram because Lord Braemys refuses to acknowledge me as heir to the king-ship. Should he wish me to hold malover upon the matter, he may swear fealty to me, and then I'll be happy to give him a fair hearing.'

'So I shall tell him, your highness,' Avyr said. 'Every word.'

The prince, his councillor, and some of his lords walked with the herald to the edge of the camp, where a servant stood holding his black horse. Avyr bowed all round, mounted, and rode out fast. Maryn stood by the road and watched until the dust of his leaving had settled.

'Cursed little bastard,' Maryn remarked. 'And I don't mean the herald.'

'He's much like his father,' Anasyn said. 'There always was a lot of inbreeding among the Boars. My mother used to say that if they were dogs their kennelman would have to drown half their pups for having two tails.'

'Braemys may not live to grow old, dog or not, if he keeps on like this, not that I'll be drowning him, exactly.' Maryn was glaring down the road as if he could see his enemy lurking on the horizon. 'Pissproud little whoreson! He drew me out of Dun Deverry just to make us waste our days and provisions.'

'And to infuriate you,' Nevyn said. 'Angry men don't think as clearly as they might.'

'Your point is well taken.' Maryn took another long deep breath. 'Very well, my lords. Let's get our men ready to ride. The sooner we return to the Holy City, the sooner you may all disperse to your own lands.'

By the time the army left camp, the sun hung near its zenith. At the very head of the line rode two men carrying the red wyvern banners; next were Maryn and Nevyn, who generally rode beside the prince. Just behind them came the silver daggers, with Owaen and Maddyn at their head. Branoic rode about half-way back in the troop, out of reach of Owaen's sarcasm. Although he understood why Caradoc had made Owaen his heir, he didn't have to like it. Ever since he'd taken over, Owaen had made Branoic's life miserable – assigning him the worst duties, giving him the worst horses, chewing him out over every petty thing he could find. It was time, Branoic decided, to ask the prince for that boon he'd promised. Although he never would have left the silver daggers while Caradoc lived, Caradoc was riding in the Otherlands these days. Branoic decided that he'd rather be cursed than ride under Owaen for another summer's fighting.

With such a late start the army didn't get far. They camped in fallow fields near a stream that fed into a farmer's duck pond. Although a couple of the silver daggers speculated about those ducks and how easy they'd be to catch, the prince himself forbade the stealing of a single one.

'And not a single apple from that tree, either,' Maryn said. 'Pass the word around the riders, will you? We've taken enough from my people, and we're not taking any more.'

Once the silver daggers had pitched their tents, Owaen strolled through their section of the camp and assigned guard duty. Branoic wasn't in the least surprised that he drew the middle watch – the worst, as it broke a man's sleep and then sent him back to his blankets with only a few hours left before dawn. Oddly enough, though, in the event he would be grateful to Owaen.

In the dark of the night, when his predecessor woke him, Branoic went to Maryn's tent to stand guard. Yawning and shivering in the chilly air, he stood outside the tent flap on the off-chance, he supposed, that an enemy would manage to creep unseen and unheard through an army of several thousand to murder the prince. He had just taken up a comfortable stance when he heard Maryn moving around inside. In a few moments more the prince came out to join him.

'I couldn't sleep,' Maryn remarked. 'I've been having trouble that way, just of late.'

'That saddens my heart to hear, your highness,' Branoic said. 'Can't Nevyn brew you up some herbs?'

'He won't. I did ask, but he says a man gets used to them after a while and then can't sleep without them.'

'Well, then, they sound a bit dangerous.'

For a few moments they stood looking up at the clear sky, where the Snowy Road glittered and the bright stars hung like candles in a vast lantern. By the sky's light Branoic could distinguish the dark shapes of the tents, spread out through the silent camp, and beyond them the supply wagons.

'Excuse me, your highness,' Branoic said. 'I'll just be taking a look round back, like.'

Maryn nodded his permission. Branoic glanced this way and that as he strolled around the tent, found nothing, then paused for a moment. He had a clear view, between two straight rows of tents, of the tethered horses in the distant meadow. Something – someone – was moving among them. Several someones, and he saw a glint of light that might have come from a knife. Branoic yelled the alarm at the top of his lungs.

'Guards! Wake up! Raiders!'

He kept screaming until he could see and hear others rousing. Since his first duty lay with the prince, he started round the tent only to find Maryn coming to meet him and buckling on his sword belt as he moved.

'Let's go!' Maryn was laughing. 'We'll spread the alarm!'

They both drew their weapons, then ran, yelling like banshees, through the camp. By then they were part of a mob, men half-dressed and half-awake, waving swords as they rushed to defend their mounts. Out in the meadow they found chaos. Panicked horses raced away, trailing cut tether ropes, whilst others reared neighing as they tried to pull their tethers and run. Over the general noise Branoic heard one he recognized all too well.

'Armed men riding!' he bellowed. 'Ware!'

In the uncertain light he could see mounted riders turning off the road. They charged across the meadow straight for the horses. Branoic had one dreadful moment to realize that while the Cantrae men were fully armed, he was one of the few men in the entire army wearing his mail. He sheathed his sword and grabbed Maryn by the arm.

'Your highness! I'm getting you out of here!'

'Don't! You get your hands off me!'

Branoic ignored him and yanked him back. Although Maryn was no weakling, few men could argue with Branoic when it came to brute strength. Branoic threw both arms around the prince from behind, clasped him in an unbreakable grip, and began frog-marching him back toward the tents while the prince yelled and swore and cursed him with every foul thing he could think of. Behind them they heard a roar and shouting, men screaming, horses neighing and shrieking, and the unmistakable sound of metal clashing with metal.

'Good lad!' It was Nevyn, running toward him. 'Owaen's right behind me.'

Owaen and twenty silver daggers as well – they poured around Branoic and the struggling prince like water round a stone. Branoic felt in his heart that they were all doomed. In this sort of surprise attack their superior numbers meant little. Nevyn reappeared with the prince's mail. The men passed it back, and Branoic helped Maryn get it on and laced. Maddyn raced up, his arms full of shields. In the confusion Maryn ended up with a shield bearing the blue device of Glasloc, but no one bothered to change it.

As the fighting in the meadow raged on, more men came running from the tents, some fully dressed and armed, others half-naked and barefoot, waving their weapons as they ran. Owaen began commandeering the battle-ready men to make a stand around their prince. Grimly they fell into position in the living wall.

'For the gods' sakes!' Maryn snapped. 'I can't stand here forever! We've got to get to the fighting.'

Owaen considered, then nodded.

'Formation round the prince!' Owaen yelled. 'Then march!'

Like a ragged animal with too many legs, they headed for the battle. They had just reached the edge of camp when Branoic spotted Nevyn again. The old man was standing among the last row of tents with his arms held high over his head as if he were waiting for someone to throw him something from above. Branoic stared, wondering if Nevyn had gone daft, but a sudden shout and a flare of light from the battle distracted him.

On the far side of the yelling, neighing mob of men and horses in the meadow, a line of horsemen was trotting purposefully along, wheeling around the edge of the field and heading for the tents. Each carried a flaming torch.

'May the gods rot their balls!' Owaen snarled. 'They're going to fire the camp!'

'We've got to stop them,' Maryn shouted. 'Form up and we'll make a stand.'

Maryn broke free of his guards and started running to meet the oncoming charge. Screaming at the top of his lungs, Branoic took out after him. He could hear Owaen swearing and the rest of their pack pounding along behind. The light from the torches flared, and he could see the Boar blazon on the horsemen's shields – and they must have seen the shield Maryn was carrying and its Glasloc device. The leader of the torchbearers was yelling out commands, a young man whose voice cracked with excitement.

'Swing around, lads, swing around! Get the tents! Don't stop to fight!'

Braemys's very cleverness cost him the chance to kill Maryn and gain a throne. The line of torchbearers swung their horses' heads round and bypassed the prince's ragged, half-armed line. Maryn and his men turned to follow them just as thunder boomed from the clear sky above. Or not so clear now – Branoic glanced up and saw clouds racing in from only the gods knew where. Prince Maryn threw his head back and howled with berserk laughter. The thunder crashed again, rolling around the battlefield.

'There wasn't any lightning!' Branoic yelled.

For an answer Maryn went on laughing, half-choking, half-screaming with it. The torchbearers were shouting and reining in their spooked horses just a bare hundred yards from the first line of tents. Branoic could hear their leader screaming in rage.

All at once rain poured from the massive clouds, a deluge as solid as if the gods had emptied giant buckets onto the earth below. The torches went out. Yelling in rage and frustration the horsemen turned and swept back into the battlefield, but Branoic could hear silver horns crying out through the rain as the Boar sounded the retreat.

All at once lightning did flash, and in the brief glare Branoic could see that the battle on the meadow was disintegrating into chaos. The prince's forces were falling back toward camp. The Boarsmen were galloping away northward. The lightning flashed down and struck the road behind them, as if the gods were ordering them to keep riding. They did. Maryn had stopped his berserk laughter and stood panting for breath.

'Surround the prince,' Owaen called out. 'Let's get him back to camp.'

Slipping in the sudden mud, the clumsy formation staggered back to the tents. The rain slacked, and when Branoic looked up, he saw the clouds scudding away before a fast wind. In the east the sky was turning the colour of steel. He'd never been so glad to see a sunrise in his life. Nevyn trotted up and fell in beside the prince.

'My thanks,' Maryn said.

'Most welcome,' Nevyn said casually. 'And from now on I think I'd best do a little scrying every night. Those blasted Boars caught me off-guard.'

It took the army the entire day to get itself ordered. All morning soldiers carried a steady procession of the wounded over to the wagons where the chirurgeons had set up an improvised surgery. Without armour of any kind, the men had sustained some of the ugliest stabs and tears that Nevyn, or any of the other physicians, had ever seen. Most of the badly wounded died under their hands. No wounded Cantrae men found on the field lived to reach the chirurgeons.

When the sun had reached its height, Nevyn poured a couple

of buckets of water over himself to clean up and returned to the prince's side to find Maryn holding a council of sorts. Various lords would hurry up to him and recount their losses or tell him how the horse hunt was going. They had detailed most of their riders to go out and search for the lost mounts; some had been found, and others over the course of the day returned voluntarily to their herd. Still, several hundred head of battle-ready mounts were gone – and doubtless into Cantrae hands.

By late afternoon Nevyn and Maryn managed to sort out what had happened. Braemys's men had crept up on the outer ring of guards and murdered them where they stood. They then had slipped in among the horses to cut tethers before the main body of Cantrae men charged the sleeping camp. If Branoic hadn't chanced to see them and give the alarm early, Braemys might well have ridden straight through the camp and managed to kill an unarmed Prince Maryn or at the least trampled a good many of his vassals. Their tents and food would have gone up in flames as well.

'Slimy little cub!' Tieryn Gauryc snapped. 'A coward and the son of a pig, all right.'

The other lords in council nodded their agreement.

'Tonight we put up double rings of guards,' Maryn said. 'And when we march tomorrow, we put men at point and off to our flanks. We'd best dispose guards along the supply train, as well.'

No one argued with him.

That night passed without any further attacks, and in the morning the army set off even more slowly than before, what with all the extra scouts to come and go from the main line of march and the wounded men to nurse along. Despite the banners and the show of force, every man in the army knew that they were crawling for home, and that against all odds and despite the dweomer on their side, Braemys had scored a victory.

*   *   *

Since the prince sent messengers on ahead to announce his return, those left behind turned out to cheer him on the day that he marched home. His men swarmed the walls, the main wards, even the road leading uphill to the broch so thickly that Lilli went upstairs in one of the side towers rather than fight for a place. She found a window that gave her a good view down into the main ward. She had just perched on the wide stone sill when she heard the distant shouting that meant the prince was arriving. She leaned out at a dangerous angle to watch the army climbing the hill.

Just behind the banners she could make out Prince Maryn, riding unhelmed, with his golden hair gleaming in the sunlight. Her heart pounded just at this distant sight of him, but then she spotted Nevyn, riding alongside like a warning. Behind them came the silver daggers. Even in the middle of the troop Branoic stood out because of his height. She realized that he was looking up, studying the windows above him as if he were hoping to see a particular someone. As the troop filed into the main ward, she leaned out a little farther.

'Branoic!' she called out. 'Branno!'

With a laugh he waved at her, and she waved back. Perhaps the prince would notice and realize that she wasn't lacking in suitors. She left the window and hurried down to the main ward, a thundering confusion of men and horses. It took her some while to make her way across. In the great hall Nevyn was nowhere to be seen, but a page had heard him remark that he was going to his chamber.

'More stairs!' Lilli said. 'I don't know why he had to pick the highest chamber in the whole wretched palace!'

By the time she reached his door, Lilli was gasping for breath. Nevyn opened it before she knocked and ushered her in.

'Sit down,' he said. 'It gladdens my heart to see you, but there was no need to run all the way here.'

'I didn't,' Lilli gasped. 'Took my time.'

She sat on the offered chair and let herself simply breathe.

Nevyn cocked his head to one side and considered her with eyes that seemed oddly out of focus. After a moment he glanced away, back to normal.

'This illness is beginning to worry me,' Nevyn said.

'But I've not been ill.'

'You may not have been aware of it, but you were and are. I'm glad I'm back.'

'Well, so am I. Which reminds me.' Lilli reached into her kirtle and brought out a silver message tube. 'While you were gone, my lord, a messenger brought you a letter from the princess's women.' Lilli handed it over. 'He gave it to me for safekeeping.'

'My thanks.' Nevyn cracked the wax seal and slid the rolled parchment out. 'I hope this isn't the news I've been dreading.'

Yet on the outermost bit of the roll Lilli saw the words, 'a return of her old trouble'. Swearing under his breath, Nevyn smoothed the parchment out and read it silently – a great marvel in those days, for someone to read without speaking each word to hear its meaning.

'Bad news indeed,' Nevyn said at last. 'It's the madness again. From childbirth, I mean – her mother was prone to this as well, from what the servants told me. It's a terrible sadness that overwhelms her rational faculties. Have you ever seen this disease?'

'I have,' Lilli said. 'One of the women here in the dun got that way with her first baby. Bevva told me it was vapours from the womb.'

'Precisely. In time they dissipate of their own accord, and a good thing, too, because I've never found the cure, not in books nor from midwives.'

'Will we go back to Cerrmor to care for her?'

'I don't know. It depends on when the prince summons her here.'

'Of course. I'd forgotten that.'

Lilli knew that he was studying her, waiting to see how she would take the news that Bellyra would some day join her husband. Lilli got up, casually she hoped, and began to straighten the clutter on his table – parchments, dirty cups, magical diagrams, little cloth sacks of herbs, and books, all jumbled together.

'Naught else of import happened while you were gone,' she said. She was pleased that her voice sounded steady. 'I was ever so glad to see Branoic safe.'

'Good. We had entirely too much excitement one night, but doubtless he'll want to tell you about it himself. He saved the prince's life.'

'He did? How splendid!'

'It was. Tell me somewhat, Lilli. Did you know Braemys well?'

'I did when he was a child, but once he went back to his father I barely saw him.'

'I see. When he was a lad, did he impress people as being quite clever?'

'Oh, he did, truly. I remember him beating everyone at games like carnoic and gwyddbwcl, and he was always leading the other boys in mock battles and suchlike. Everyone said that it was a pity he wouldn't inherit Cantrae instead of Uncle Tibryn's son.'

'I see. Life would be much simpler if only he were stupid.'

After Nevyn gave her leave to go, Lilli sought out Branoic and found him in the great hall, sitting with Maddyn and a few other silver daggers on the riders' side of the room. The men from the various warbands filled the tables around him, and they were drinking heavily, teasing the servant girls who were trying to bring them ale and bread. Lilli had no desire to walk through the mob, nor did she want to ask a page to take him a message, not here where half the people in the dun could see. As she stood by the honour hearth, debating what to do, Branoic solved the problem by looking up and seeing her. He stood, waved at her, and came trotting over.

'It's so good to see you,' Branoic said.

'And it gladdens my heart to see you safe,' Lilli said. 'Old Nevyn told me an interesting thing about you, just now.'

'Oh, did he? What?'

'That your quick thinking saved our prince's life.'

Branoic looked modestly down at the floor.

'Ah well,' he said at last. 'I did naught that any other man wouldn't have done.'

'Truly?'

He shrugged and sat on the bench. Lilli glanced around and realized that Maryn and his retinue were coming down the staircase.

'Somewhat like that deserves a reward,' Lilli said. She leaned over and kissed Branoic on the cheek.

'I'll take that for a reward over any favour of princes or priests,' he said, smiling. 'My thanks, my lady.'

Lilli sat down next to him but a decorous distance away. Out of the corner of her eye she was aware of Maryn, walking across the great hall with Nevyn while pages trailed along behind. If Maryn had seen the kiss, he showed no sign of caring one way or the other. The two men sat down at the honour table some distance away, well out of earshot. She turned her attention resolutely to Branoic.

'You must tell me about the battle,' Lilli said. 'Nevyn didn't tell me much.'

'Well, the details aren't fit for your ears, my lady. Our prince acquitted himself well, though. Maybe a little too well. All I really did was keep him from making some kind of hopeless charge into the thick of the enemy.'

'Well, tell me about it!'

Branoic rolled his eyes heavenward, but tell her he did, though she knew he was leaving out a fair bit of mayhem. Speaking of their prince together was oddly satisfying, she realized. Branoic could show her the part of Maryn's life that otherwise she wouldn't see, and it was fascinating. Now and then she'd glance up, but she looked directly only at Nevyn, who smiled at her in approval. Yet always she was aware of the prince, sitting at his distance, like a fire blazing with warmth felt half-way across a room.

After the evening meal in the great hall, Nevyn retired to his chamber. He lit candles, then laid a leather-bound book, as tall as his forearm, onto the table. Although he'd owned this book for many years, it had only recently returned to him after spending some time in the hands of a thief, and he couldn't remember if it held the information he wanted or not. He had just found a page listing the various kinds of spirits when he heard someone coming up the stairs with a tread far too heavy to belong to Lilli.

'My lord Nevyn!' It was Oggyn's voice, puffing from the climb. 'Nevyn, are you in?'

'I am!' Nevyn laid a scrap of cloth in to keep his place, then closed the book. 'I'm on my way.'

Nevyn got up and opened the door to find a winded Oggyn, his arms full of parchments. In the dim light spilling out of the chamber, he looked terrified.

'What's so wrong?' Nevyn said.

'A private word with you, if I may. Somewhat's very wrong indeed.'

Nevyn ushered him inside. Oggyn dumped his parchments onto the table and then sank onto the only chair. He pulled a rag out of his pocket and mopped the sweat from his bald scalp. Nevyn sat down opposite on the edge of his bed.

'Whilst you were gone, I rode around the royal demesnes to draw up my lists, just as I'd planned.' Oggyn waved at the heap on the table. 'I made some very unpleasant discoveries. As soon as he gives up Cerrmor, our liege is going to be a poor man.'

'Oh ye gods.' Nevyn felt as if he'd been slapped awake. 'I should have realized! After all these years of war –'

'Precisely, and it was the territory around Dun Deverry that bore the worst of the fighting. I mean, by the Lord of Hell's balls! Look at the city! Well, the royal farmlands are in much the same condition.'

'But we've passed prosperous-looking –'

'Those all belong to the priesthood of Bel.' Oggyn paused, scowling within his black beard. 'No one was going to risk the wrath of the gods by overrunning *them*, were they? Over the years the Boars wangled plenty of favours from the priests, and their rewards always came out of the king's lands, not theirs.'

Nevyn swore like a silver dagger about the personal habits of the Boar clan. Oggyn nodded in vigorous approval.

'We've been wondering, you and I,' Oggyn went on, 'just how the Boars got such an upper hand over the kings. Well, now we know. The kings needed them, Nevyn, needed them desperately. By the end, the royal house couldn't have been able to raise and feed more than a hundred men from their own holdings.'

Nevyn found he couldn't even swear. Oggyn mopped his head one last time and stuffed the rag back into his pocket.

'Have you spoken to our liege about this?' Nevyn said at last.

'I've not. I wanted to consult with you first. You're the man who knows the priests. I was wondering, is there any chance they'd turn some of that land back over to the royal line?'

'On the same day that horses sprout wings and fly.'

'I feared that, truly. Ah ye gods, I don't know what we're going to do! Our prince is going to be at the mercy of his vassals now, just like Olaen was. Whoever holds the Cerrmor rhan is going to hold a knife at Maryn's throat.'

For some while they sat without speaking, watching the candle-thrown shadows dance over the walls. Nevyn could see all his schemes, his hopes, his long campaign to end the wars crumble like a lump of sand on the Cerrmor beach, washed out on a tide of ambition and arrogance. The ocean, indeed, and all those merchant taxes and dues that had made both Cerrmor and its gwerbret rich.

'Oh ye gods!' Nevyn said. 'I've got an idea.'

'I don't,' Oggyn said gloomily. 'I know my place, my lord. I can see the little things, how they lie close at hand, but the long view escapes me.'

Only then did Nevyn realize how frightened Oggyn truly was, that he'd be so honest to a man he saw as a rival.

'Well, this may not work,' Nevyn said. 'But what if Cerrmor and its attendant lands remained in the prince's control?'

'It would save the entire situation. He'd have eight hundred riders of his own and the contingent of spearmen as well, though truly, I think me the town will balk at such a large levy once the wars are done.'

'What if the levy made them a free city for a hundred years and a day?'

Oggyn's smile shone like the sun through storm clouds.

'I thought so,' Nevyn went on. 'Now listen, I don't know if we can bring this off, but if we can, it will catch a pair of rabbits in one snare. Maryn will be free of the burden of apportioning the rhan to someone, thereby disappointing everyone else, and he'll have troops sworn to him alone. The taxes due him from the merchant trade will support those riders, while the town can easily outfit the spearmen from what they save in gwerbretal dues and have a good bit left over.'

Oggyn nodded and went on smiling.

'First things first,' Nevyn said. 'You're an important man in Cerrmor. Can you get the town council to agree to such a scheme?'

'My dear Nevyn, an idiot child could get the council to agree to this! They'll be free of one entire set of taxes and so will their children and grandchildren. There's going to be grumbling from the noble-born, though.'

'Grumbling is a mild word for it. Especially the circle around Gauryc. I don't want them pulling out of the alliance.'

'I was worrying about them, truly. Gauryc's been sidling up to me, flattering and suchlike, just because I have the ear of the prince.'

'Truly?' Nevyn made a great effort and managed to look surprised.

'Truly. A sad sad thing! But here, I just had another thought. Once he gets rid of Braemys, the prince will have Cantrae to hand out for a prize. It's not as rich as Cerrmor, but it'll be a goodly sop nonetheless.'

'Just so.'

'One last thing.' Oggyn hesitated, staring down at the table. 'What will our prince think of breaking precedents and precedence this way?'

'I think we'd best go ask him.'

Prince Maryn, it turned out, had already retired to his private chambers. Since Nevyn was one of the few men in the kingdom who could follow him there, he got a candle-lantern and led the way with a nervous Oggyn trailing behind him. Maryn greeted them both courteously and ushered them into his reception chamber, now free of most of the battered furniture. A low fire smouldered in the hearth, and candles blazed in their wall sconces.

'I was tired of the noise in the great hall,' Maryn said. 'This business of not sleeping all night – it wears a man down.'

'My apologies, my liege,' Nevyn said, 'if we woke you.'

'No such luck. Be seated, good councillors.'

Maryn flopped into a half-round chair and slouched down, crossing his long legs in front of him at the ankle. In the candlelight his skin looked as smooth as a child's, and Nevyn found himself remembering that handsome little boy of years past, who had been so eager to be king.

'Oggyn?' Nevyn said. 'I suggest you lay your findings before our prince.'

Oggyn explained, with much flapping of parchments, the poverty of Maryn's new realm. Maryn listened intently, but his face was absolutely unreadable, and he said not a word, not even when Oggyn read off the dismal lists of burnt villages and unploughed fields. When Oggyn fell silent, Nevyn laid out their plan to grant Cerrmor a limited charter in return for revenues. He'd not quite finished when the prince interrupted.

'I can't do that,' Maryn snapped. 'What will happen when the hundred years are over and the town refuses to accept a gwerbret?'

'My liege!' Oggyn said. 'None of us will be alive in a hundred years.'

'So?' Maryn got to his feet and began pacing back and forth by the fire. 'That's not the point. It's the honour of the thing.'

Since the prince was standing, Nevyn and Oggyn had to stand as well. Oggyn laid his parchments down carefully on a table and tried again.

'My liege, do you disagree with my words about the state of affairs here in Dun Deverry?'

'Not at all,' Maryn said. 'I meant to commend you on your hard work, in fact. There's no doubt it's worrisome, but by Great Bel himself, how can I release Cerrmor from the dues it owes its rightful lords?'

'Once you're seated as king, my liege,' Nevyn said, 'Cerrmor will have no rightful lord.'

'Oh come now!' Maryn stopped pacing and turned to face him. 'Aren't you the one who taught me how important order and the laws and honour and such are to the kingdom? There have always been gwerbretion in Cerrmor. That's the way the gods and the laws both intend the city to be ruled. How can I take my place as high king if I overthrow those laws, even to –' Maryn hesitated for a long moment. 'Even to save my rule?'

'There are times,' Nevyn said, 'when a man must break the words of laws in order to honour their spirit. If the kingdom's to have peace, there absolutely must be strong kings in Dun Deverry.'

'Well then! How can my vassals respect me if I've thrown Cerrmor to the common folk?'

At that point Nevyn realized that he would never change the prince's mind, not if he argued the entire winter through. He glanced at Oggyn, standing head down and defeated nearby.

'Our liege has spoken,' Nevyn said. 'Good councillor, I think we'd best come up with some other remedy.'

'Just so.' Oggyn made the prince a low bow. 'If your highness will excuse us?'

'Of course. And please understand that I appreciate your efforts on my behalf.'

'My prince?' Nevyn said. 'A boon, if I may be so bold.'

'When couldn't you ask me for anything?'

'My thanks. Your silence on this matter is absolutely necessary until your councillors find a solution.'

'That I can promise you.'

'Splendid! And my thanks yet once again.'

Maryn crossed to a window and stood staring out at the night whilst Oggyn, with Nevyn's help, gathered up his parchments. They let themselves out, shut the heavy door carefully, and stood staring at each other by the light of Nevyn's lantern.

'Stubborn mule of a man!' Nevyn whispered. 'I wish he were still a lad so I could give him a good clout. Knock some sense into him!'

'But he's not.' Oggyn too kept his voice barely audible. 'Shall we retire and discuss this further?'

To spare Oggyn the stairs they went to the quarters he, as chamberlain, had assigned himself, a pair of large rooms that during the day would be sunny and cheerful. During the leisurely sack of the dun after the siege, Oggyn had acquired some of the best chairs, the newest cushions, and a selection of tapestries that were if not splendid then at least less threadbare than most. On his mantel sat a small silver wyvern and a silver flagon. He dumped his parchments onto a long oak table banded with delicate carving, then took Nevyn's candle and trotted around, lighting more in their silver sconces.

'May I offer you mead?' Oggyn said when he was done.

'None for me, but my thanks. I need to think.'

'True.' Oggyn sat down in a chair opposite him. 'I see no use in trying to hide my deep disappointment in our prince's opinion.'

'I see none either. Ye gods!'

'We're at such a critical juncture of the war. If we could only keep the problem at bay till Maryn's brought Braemys to heel!'

'Well, he remains Gwerbret Cerrmor till the priests declare him king.'

'A most excellent point! But afterwards –'

'Indeed. Let me think on this. There has to be a solution.'

'I hope to every god that you come up with it, whatever it may be.'

'Until then, no one else had better learn of this situation.'

'Just so. You can count on my silence.' Oggyn rose and began tidying his parchments. 'But if the prince sees this as a matter of honour, then he'll start his reign so heavily indebted that he'll be king in name only.'

On the morrow morning, the prince's vassals, released from their summer's service to their liege lord, assembled their men and broke camp, heading for their own lands. Lilli sat in her tower window and watched as one after the other the lords knelt before Maryn to promise him their prompt return, either in the spring or in his great need, whichever came the sooner. By then Lilli saw the Wildfolk as easily as she saw objects on the physical plane, and she studied them as the spirits swarmed around the prince and lent him their energies to augment his own. They supplied the brightness in the air, the private breeze that ruffled his hair, the spring in his walk, even. The Wildfolk of Aethyr swelled his aura to an enormous golden cloud, a crackling globe of sheer astral force that enlivened everyone who came in contact with it.

Lilli had to admit that she understood now what Nevyn had meant. Maryn's unnatural allure did lie in the dweomers his councillor worked. She also realized that the admission had brought her to the edge of tears.

'Oh stop it!' she told herself. 'You've got more important

things to do, anyway, than day-dreaming about Prince Maryn.'

Tieryn Anasyn, her true brother now, was among the last to leave Dun Deverry. All of the northern lords who'd come over to Maryn the summer past were leaving behind some of their men – technically an extra levy for the prince's fortguard, but in actuality hostages of a sort. Lilli waited down in the ward while Anasyn commended ten of his best riders to the prince's care. Abrwnna was already mounted on her palfrey at the head of her husband's warband. Seeing her there, the new lady of Hendyr, made Lilli weep. Her sister-in-law's position was the final, irrevocable sign that Lady Bevyan lay dead, that never again would she preside in Hendyr's great hall.

Anasyn came hurrying over and flung one arm around Lilli's shoulders.

'Here, here,' he said. 'I'll be back in the spring.'

'Oh, I know.' Lilli snuffled back tears. 'I was thinking about Bevva.'

Anasyn nodded, suddenly solemn.

'Hardly a day goes by that I don't think about her and Father, too,' Anasyn said finally. 'Which reminds me. Father wanted you properly settled in life. Abrwnna tells me that there's been gossip about you and Branoic the silver dagger.'

'What? The gall! What sort of gossip?'

'Naught terrible.' He grinned, and she realized that he was teasing her. 'He's a fine man, Branno. But I doubt me if he can support a wife.'

'Well, he told me that the prince has promised him a boon, and that he's going to ask for land.'

'Oh? Oh, well then! If he can support you decently, I've no objections to him.'

'My thanks, brother. It gladdens my heart.'

'I thought it might. And now I'd best be off. If you want to come visit us this winter, send me a messenger, and I'll send men to fetch you.'

'My thanks! I will!'

Yet Lilli knew that she'd not have the courage to return to

Hendyr so soon, not with Bevyan's death so fresh in her mind. She ran to the gates of the main ward to wave Anasyn and Abrwnna out, then slowly, thinking of very little, she walked back to the cluster of brochs. Maryn was standing on the steps, waiting for her. She stopped and stared at the wonder of it, that he would wait for her, standing on the steps alone like an ordinary man.

'Good morrow, Lady Lillorigga,' the prince said.

'A good morrow to you, your highness.' Lilli curtsied and felt her heart flutter like a trapped bird. 'I was just seeing my brother off.'

'So I noticed. He's a good man, Anasyn.'

She smiled, Maryn smiled, and neither, it seemed, could think of a word to say. The Wildfolk swarmed round them both, gnomes and sprites and like crystals in the air, the sylphs, but she could strip the dweomer away, she realized, and see the man himself. He's still splendid, she thought. I'd find him wondrous if he were the kitchen boy.

'Lilli!' It was Nevyn's voice, and the Wildfolk vanished in a burst of fear. 'There you are, eh?'

Lilli spun around, blushing so hard she felt her face burning. Nevyn was striding across the ward.

'I am, my lord,' she stammered. 'Have you need of me?'

'I do.' Nevyn glanced at the prince. 'If you'll excuse me, your highness? My apprentice and I have important work to do.'

'Of course,' Maryn said. 'And I need to talk with the gwerbret of Yvrodur. He's doubtless impatient to be on the road.'

All the way up to Nevyn's chamber Lilli trembled, sure she was in for the worst lecture of her life. Instead he merely opened his book of dweomers and set her to work memorizing the names and formal terms of address for all the spirits of all the Elemental Courts, kings, queens, champions and princesses, every last one of them. It was so tedious that, she realized, he'd given her work of a sort to drive all thoughts of Maryn out of her mind.

*   *   *

In the council chamber of the royal broch the last of the afternoon's sun fell across the maps spread across the table. The three men studying them stood leaning over the tattered parchments. Although each map purported to show Deverry and the bordering lands, each was so different from the others that Nevyn despaired of ever forming a clear idea of the shape of the kingdom.

'What matters, though,' Nevyn said, 'is simple enough. Eldidd lies west of Deverry, and so does Pyrdon. Pyrdon lies north of Eldidd. When Maryn becomes king of Deverry and Pyrdon, Eldidd will be like a piece of meat between two jaws.'

'Just so,' Maddyn said. 'And I doubt me if Aenycyr of Eldidd is so blind that he hasn't seen it too.'

'It's a bad situation, all right,' Owaen said. 'But we've all known about it for years. You called us here for some cursed reason, councillor. Why don't you just drop this feint and tell us?'

Maddyn glared at his fellow silver dagger, but Owaen ignored the black look. There were times when Nevyn wished he actually could blast a man with fire or turn one into a frog, and Owaen always seemed to be the person who inspired those moments.

'Very well,' Nevyn said. 'I want to know how your recruiting efforts are going. I'd like to see the silver daggers brought up to strength as soon as possible.'

'Do you think I wouldn't?' Owaen said.

'Oh hold your tongue, you hound!' Maddyn broke in. 'We're doing pretty well, Nevyn. We've now got fifty-six men, fifty-seven if Red-haired Trevyr can ever fight again.'

Owaen ostentatiously picked up a map and carried it over to the window to study. With him gone, a blue sprite materialized on the table, a pretty little thing except for her mouthful of fangs. She stuck her tongue out at Owaen, then hopped onto Maddyn's shoulder.

'I wouldn't count Trevyr,' Nevyn said. 'It's a miracle that he lived at all.'

'So we tell him. Daily.' Maddyn smiled in a wry sort of way. 'You must be expecting trouble soon, if you're worrying about the prince's guard.'

'I am. In Eldidd the winters are mild. There's no reason for King Aenycyr to wait till spring to cause trouble. I've had reports that he's considering how he might exploit Maryn's half-brother to keep Pyrdon out of Deverry hands.'

'Ah horseshit! That's the last thing we need. How old is Riddmar, anyway? He's but a child, isn't he?'

'He was born nine summers ago, if I remember rightly. Casyl of Pyrdon's not in good health. When he dies, who can blame his wife if she's ambitious for her son? She's never so much as met Maryn, and he's the living memorial to Casyl's first wife, anyway.'

Owaen turned round and lowered the map to listen. The sprite, whom of course he couldn't see, stuck her thumbs in her ears and waggled her fingers at him.

'I hadn't heard about King Casyl being ill,' Maddyn said. 'That saddens my heart. He was generous to us silver daggers when we were in Pyrdon.'

'He's a good man, truly.' Nevyn sighed, genuinely saddened himself. 'But be that as it may, when Casyl dies, Maryn inherits, Pyrdon becomes part of Deverry, and there's Eldidd, squeezed on both its borders. Aenycyr will do anything he can to stop it.'

'And Riddmar's the logical weapon for him to wield.' Maddyn considered for a moment. 'Is there any way to bind Riddmar to Maryn? Some practical thing, that is. Family sentiment never seems to burn brightly among the noble-born.'

'That's it!' Nevyn suddenly burst out laughing. 'Maddo, you've done it again!'

'Er, I beg your pardon?' Maddyn said.

'Given me a splendid idea, that is.' Nevyn did a few quick steps of a jig, then calmed himself. 'I must go speak with Councillor Oggyn. Do carry on, lads, with your recruiting. The more men in the prince's guard, the better.'

Nevyn practically ran down to the great hall. He found a page and sent him off to look for Oggyn, who appeared promptly. They stood in the curve of the wall out of the general confusion to talk.

'My apologies for disturbing you,' Nevyn said. 'But I've had an idea about that problem we discussed the other night. I suggest that we lay it before the prince straight-away.'

But the prince proved much harder to find. Nevyn and Oggyn sat at a table in the great hall whilst the pages searched all over the broch complex. No one had seen the prince ride out of the dun, no one had seen him retire to his private chambers. After a long irritating while, Nevyn suddenly realized where Maryn must be.

'If you'll come with me, Oggyn,' Nevyn said, 'let's go up to my chamber while the pages keep looking. I'll tell you this idea privately.'

'A wise move, no doubt,' Oggyn said.

Sure enough, when Nevyn opened the door to his chamber, there was Maryn, half-sitting, half-leaning on the table while Lilli sat opposite, the book open in front of her. She was giggling, smiling up at the prince while he grinned back at her, but at the sight of Nevyn she yelped like a kicked dog. The prince blushed sunset-red and stood up. Nevyn bowed to him.

'Ah, my apologies, my liege,' Nevyn said. 'But we have a grave matter to lay before you. Lady Lillorigga, if you would attend to the work I set you? It's of the utmost importance, tedious though I know it must be.'

In the council chamber the maps still lay on the table where Owaen and Maddyn had left them, but the sun had sunk below the walls of the dun, and shadows filled the room. Nevyn glanced around, saw half-burnt candles in the sconces, and lit them all with one quick flick of his wrist. Oggyn shuddered.

'I've not got used to that yet,' the councillor said with a small sigh. 'I doubt me if I ever will.'

'My apologies.' Nevyn turned to the prince. 'Your highness, you'll remember the problem of the Cerrmor rhan?'

'I do, indeed,' Maryn said. 'It kept me awake half the night past.'

'Councillor Oggyn,' Nevyn went on, 'how many years do you think must pass before the royal demesnes are prosperous again?'

'I'm not truly sure.' Oggyn frowned, thinking. 'Much depends upon the number of men available to farm them and of course the weather. There are bondfolk still in the villages, but they've been too dispirited to work very hard, and truly, who can blame them? If we fed them decently and got them the seed corn they need, in but three or four years the fields would bloom again. Five, mayhap.'

'Good,' Nevyn said. 'And in five or six years, Riddmar of Pyrdon, our prince's half-brother, will be on the edge of manhood – and able to rule Cerrmor without his brother's aid as regent.'

For a long moment both prince and councillor stared at him. Then Maryn laughed, tossing back his head.

'Oh, splendid, splendid!' Maryn said, grinning. 'Why should Riddmar listen to Eldidd if I give him such a splendid prize?'

'And how can he deny you troops, with you as regent?' Nevyn said. 'And who among your vassals will argue with you about it? Gauryc can nurse his disappointments all he wants, but he knows you have to hold Eldidd at bay. He's greedy, not stupid.'

Oggyn was smiling as if the Goddess of the Fields had appeared to him, her arms laden with bounty.

'The long view,' Oggyn said. 'Lord Nevyn, truly you're a master of the long view.'

'My thanks.' Nevyn wondered what Oggyn would think if he knew just how long his view was. 'But it was Maddyn the bard who started me thinking about this.'

'Then he shall eat at my table tonight,' Maryn said. 'When shall we announce our choice, good councillors?'

'First, my liege, I suggest we get messengers on their way to Pyrdon,' Nevyn said, 'before the snows set in.'

'I'll fetch a scribe, my liege,' Oggyn said, all smiles, 'should you wish me to.'

'My thanks.' Maryn nodded at him. 'You have my leave to go.'

With Oggyn gone, another matter occurred to Nevyn, now that he had a moment of the prince's attention.

'If I have my liege's permission, I'd like to travel to Cerrmor,' Nevyn said. 'There are a few things I left behind that I want to fetch, things that servants have no business handling, if you take my meaning.'

'Of course. Here, can you leave soon? One of the Cerrmor galleys is standing on the river down past the falls. I could send a messenger to hold it there, and you could ride down and take it over.'

'My thanks, my liege. That would save a great deal of time.'

'And what about your apprentice?' Maryn made a slight bit too much of a show of looking away. 'Will she accompany you?'

Until that moment Nevyn had been planning on leaving Lilli behind.

'She will, my liege. I'll need her help with packing these things for the journey.'

Maryn's eyes had gone cold and distant. Nevyn could work out what he was trying to hide: disappointed lust. When Oggyn came bustling in with the scribe, Nevyn was glad to turn his mind elsewhere.

Toward the end of summer in Cerrmor, the fog disappeared and left the weather glorious. In the hot afternoons Princess Bellyra and her women would take their needlework out to the rose garden by the marble fountain. Even though she knew the sun would be good for her, it took all of Bellyra's

courage and a good bit of coaxing as well to get her into the
garden each day. The bright light seemed to turn the world as
flat and as unreal as the red wyverns she embroidered upon a
shirt for her husband. Often she would run her needle into
the cloth and let the work lie in her lap while she stared out
across the garden, splashed with scarlet roses, to the trees
beyond. She could never remember what she thought about
during these lapses.

The new prince turned two months old on a particularly
lovely day. The nursemaids brought both children into the
garden, Marro to sleep in his basket, Casso to play at his
mother's feet, and Bellyra found that she could smile at them
now and again. She caught her serving women watching her,
though, and snarled.

'I wish you wouldn't stare at me like that!'

'My apologies, your highness,' Degwa said.

'Lyrra, we're just concerned.' Elyssa shot back. 'Can you
blame us?'

'I can't, truly, but –'

'I have a surprise for you.' Elyssa spoke firmly, cutting her
off. 'I was looking for more thread in one of the chests, and I
saw this.' She leaned down to rummage in her work basket,
then brought out a book, or more precisely, a codex. 'I didn't
know what it might be, so I showed it to the scribe, and he
told me it was somewhat that you'd treasured, back when you
were a lass.'

With her first laugh in two months Bellyra took it, a history
of Dun Cerrmor started long ago by some anonymous scribe.
In the blank pages at the back, however, she had added to the
story with precise descriptions of the dun as she'd known it as
a child.

'If we might be so bold,' Degwa said, 'could we ask her
highness to read to us? It would make the time pass so
pleasantly.'

'And truly,' Elyssa chimed in, 'it's such a marvel to know a
woman who can read.'

'Oh huh!' Bellyra wrinkled her nose at them. 'You rehearsed that, didn't you? But you know, I think I'd like to. Here's a bit about King Glyn's sorcerer that I used to love when I was a child. His name was Nevyn, too, and our Nevyn is his grandson.'

'Indeed?' Degwa's eyes grew wide. 'I never knew that! But the first Nevyn – that's the man who helped my clan keep its name.'

'Truly? Well, then, we simply have to read about him.'

Bellyra cleared her throat and began. Her small audience listened with a flattering attention, caught by the magic that allowed her to turn little marks on parchment into words that they could understand. And perhaps that book did have dweomer of a sort. As she read, she felt her black mood lightening; later that evening, after all her servants and serving women had gone to bed, she sat in the women's hall and read the passages she'd written as a girl until the flickering candlelight made her eyes water. When at last she went to bed, she lay awake for a while, considering entries she might make to continue her description of the buildings and rooms. She fell asleep happy.

In the morning the pleasant mood stayed with her so long as she kept her mind on her book. As soon as the daily life of the dun intruded, she felt the black sadness take her over again, but the book had one last dweomer to offer. Late in the afternoon, while she read to her women, Nevyn himself arrived. She looked up from the book to see him striding through the garden with pages scurrying ahead of him and the Lady Lillorigga trotting after, unable to keep up with the old man. Bellyra shut the book with a snap.

'I swear it, we've conjured him up!' Bellyra said, pointing. 'Look!'

Degwa and Elyssa turned on the bench and burst out laughing.

'So it seems, your highness,' Elyssa said.

'And our little Boarswoman too,' Degwa murmured. 'How very nice.'

'Oh Decci, stop it!' Elyssa snapped. 'She belongs to the Rams of Hendyr now.'

'Once a person has been raised in an unwholesome manner,' Degwa said, 'it's very hard for them to change their ways.'

'Hush!' Bellyra said. 'Or she'll hear you!'

Degwa arranged a smile and held her tongue. In a flurry of greetings and laughter, Nevyn and Lilli joined them. Lilli sank down onto the bench next to Elyssa to catch her breath, but as always Nevyn seemed full of boundless energy.

'And what brings you here, Nevyn?' Bellyra said.

'A great many small errands,' Nevyn said.

'Ah, I see. And how long will you stay?'

'Not too long, alas. Your husband has need of me back in the Holy City.'

'It's too bad he has no need of me.'

The words had slipped out unbidden. Bellyra laid a hand over her mouth as if she might shove them back in. They were all watching her, staring at her in undeniable pity, a soft sad-eyed patronizing pity. She leapt up, clutching her book to her chest.

'Well, do you think I don't know?' Bellyra snapped. 'My husband hasn't seen fit to invite me to his new demesne, has he? He's not so much as mentioned my joining him in Dun Deverry now that he has the victory.'

No one spoke, no one moved. Bellyra felt tears running down her face. All at once she could no longer bear the sight of any of them.

'Leave me alone!' She knew that she was screaming and no longer cared. 'Go away, all of you! Just go away and leave me alone!'

The nursemaids jumped up and scooped up the children. The other women rose more slowly, but at a sign from Nevyn they left as well, following the servant girls back to the dun. Nevyn sat himself down on the bench.

'I'm not leaving,' he said. 'Why don't you join me?'

The tears had stopped. Bellyra wiped her face on the silk sleeve of her dress, then sat back down in her chair.

'I'm sorry,' she said.

'For what? Speaking the truths of your heart?'

'A princess isn't supposed to have a heart. If she had a second womb instead the men would be well-pleased.'

Nevyn winced.

'Well,' Bellyra went on. 'Do you think I'm wrong?'

'I've never lied to you, have I? I told you from the first that your position was a difficult one.'

'So you did.' She held up the codex. 'I wrote that down, too, all those years ago. I suppose I've no right to complain. It was exceptionally stupid of me to fall in love with my husband. Most women in my position have the good sense to avoid that particular trap, but then, most of them have rather repellent husbands, so it's easier for them.'

Nevyn laughed, and after a moment, she smiled.

'If you didn't have so much common sense,' Nevyn said, 'your life would be easier. You could find comfort in throwing fits.'

'Mayhap, mayhap not. I've no mind to try.'

'I certainly do understand how it must rankle, sitting here in Cerrmor and wondering when you'll be summoned.'

Bellyra nodded, sighed, looked away at the green view, glowing in the sun.

'I'm also truly sorry you've been ill,' Nevyn went on.

'So am I. But you know, I do think it's beginning to pass off.'

'I cannot tell you how much that gladdens my heart to hear.'

'If my monthly bleeding would only start again!'

'It will. The Goddess hasn't cursed you. You have my word on that.'

Bellyra managed a smile.

'And I'll tell you somewhat,' Nevyn went on, 'and it's the very soul of truth and not some fancy I'm telling you for comfort's sake. Maryn hasn't sent for you because he worries about your well-being. Dun Deverry's a grim place, as shabby as a hunting lodge after all these years of war, and the fighting's not yet over. He told me in so many words that he'd not risk you in any way.'

'Oh!' Bellyra felt tears threaten, but she managed to choke them back. 'Really?'

'Really. Maryn has the greatest respect for you. He told me that he values your opinion above those of ten men. I know it's not what you'd hoped for, but –'

'But it's a far greater thing than most noble wives are ever offered. I'm mindful of that, Nevyn. Truly I am.'

He smiled, but sadly. Bellyra rose, holding her book in one hand and smoothing down her dress with the other. He got up to join her.

'Shall we go in?' she said. 'You must be weary after your journey.'

'I wouldn't mind getting out of this sun. It's blazing out here.'

'I suppose it is. Often I feel so cold, no matter where I am.' When she looked around, the world seemed to have turned flat and pale, as if some demon had sucked all the colour from it. 'But truly, I'm ready to go in.'

'That's what we've come to fetch,' Nevyn said, pointing.

'I thought it might be,' Lilli said.

The silver casket, engraved with a design of roses, sat gleaming in the sunlight on the table. Although Wildfolk swarmed all over the women's hall, they refused to go anywhere near the casket itself. Other than the Wildfolk, they had the big sunny room to themselves. Bellyra was sleeping, and Elyssa and Degwa had gone off about their own business in the dun.

'I bitterly regret leaving the casket with the princess,' Nevyn said. 'But I didn't know what else to do with the wretched thing. I couldn't trust anyone else with it, and I could hardly take it with me on campaign.'

'I should think not, my lord!' Lilli said. 'It might have got you killed.'

'Or the prince, worse yet.'

'Is that what's made her so ill, the casket I mean?'

'It's not. That's quite another matter.'

A greenish-grey gnome climbed into Lilli's lap like a cat. She stroked its nubbly back and almost, it seemed, could hear it sigh in contentment. Nevyn walked over to the table and stood scowling at the casket as if he could force it to speak.

'My lord? You've never told me what's in it,' Lilli said. 'All I know is that I can't bear to touch it.'

'And that's a mystery in itself. I put so many dweomer seals on it that I doubt if the Kings of the Elements themselves could get through them, yet you felt the evil without half-trying.' He shook his head in irritation. 'But what it's hiding is at root simple: a curse tablet. Have you ever seen one of those?'

'I've not.'

'They're strips of soft lead, hammered very thin – you engrave the words of your curse on it with a sharp bit of stick or suchlike.'

'What did this one say?'

'As this so that. Maryn king Maryn king Maryn. Death never dying. Aranrhodda rica rica rica Bubo lubo.' He smiled briefly. 'Are you any the wiser?'

'Well, everyone knows who Aranrhodda is, and the death part is clear enough.'

'Unfortunately. Tell me, did your mother ever talk of Aranrhodda?'

'Not that I remember. What I wonder about is the bit that says 'as this so that'. It bothers me. What's the 'this'?'

'Ah, here's the nastiest thing of all. It had been buried in a box with the corpse of an infant boy.'

'They didn't kill the child on purpose, did they, just for this spell?'

'I'm afraid they must have. He was badly mutilated, too. It takes a lot to shake me, but I was shaken, I'll admit it.'

'How horrible.' Lilli felt on the edge of nausea. 'The baby's not in there, is it?'

'What? Of course not! I had the local priests bury the poor little fellow properly.'

'That gladdens my heart. How long have you had this casket?'

'Six years or so. I found it buried in Pyrdon, just before Maryn started his march to Cerrmor. The Lords of the Elements warned me that there was dark dweomer nearby, you see. They told me where the cursed little bastards had sheltered, and I found the child's grave when I was poking around.'

'Dark dweomer? You mean like that retainer of my mother's, the one my uncle killed?'

'Exactly. I'm guessing that it was the same man, in fact.'

The nausea rose with a taste of bile in her mouth. Six years ago. Olaen was but five summers old when he died, and he'd been betrothed to Abrwnna when he was new-born.

'Is somewhat wrong?' Nevyn said.

'I'm not sure. I'm trying to think – there's a thing I heard – but I'm not sure when it happened.' She hesitated for a silent prayer that she might be wrong. 'That child, the one buried with the tablet. How old was it?'

'Some weeks. I'm afraid it had been dead for some time, and I couldn't be sure of its age. Lilli, you've gone pale as death! What's so wrong?'

'I think the child was my brother.'

Nevyn goggled at her, his mouth slack.

'Abrwnna told me some gossip about my mother,' Lilli went on. 'Abrwnna came to court about five years ago, but there was still talk of somewhat that had happened when my father – I mean, my mother's husband – died, the year before she arrived. My mother left the court to give birth to a child. When she returned, she said the baby had died of a fever, just a few weeks after it was born.'

Nevyn shut his mouth with a snap. He left the table and half-sat, half-leaned on the windowsill. She had never known anyone who could turn as quiet as the old man could.

'We'll need to find out more about this,' he said at last.

'If I'm right –' Lilli said. 'Oh ych! it's too disgusting!'

'Quite so.' Nevyn made a sour face. 'Are you thinking that Merodda gave the child over to her tame wizard?'

'I am.'

'If the baby was your blood kin, it would certainly explain your peculiar link to the casket. Or to the evil within it, I should say.'

'How can we find out if it's true? I suppose some of the older servants in Dun Deverry might remember things, but I don't know if I could bear to ask them.'

'They wouldn't tell you anyway, most likely. When we get back, leave this task to me.'

'Gladly. Ah ye gods, if it's true? It's just too vile!'

'It is that. I –' Nevyn paused, holding up his hand for silence.

A footstep scraped in the hall outside. Lilli rose, thinking that Degwa might be eavesdropping, but when the door opened, Bellyra stood there. As the princess came in, Nevyn got up to bow, and Lilli curtsied.

'Did you rest well, your highness?' Lilli said.

'I did, truly.'

Lilli fetched Bellyra's favourite chair, and the princess sat down with a murmur of thanks. Lilli was shocked at how thin Bellyra had become. Her pale skin stretched over the bones of her face so tightly that it seemed a smile might crack it and make her bleed.

'We were discussing the casket, your highness,' Nevyn said. 'It's time I took it away.'

'I'll be glad of that.'

The silence hung there, heavy in the room. Lilli desperately searched for something pleasant to say, but the casket, glittering in the sun like a vial of poison, seemed to make any pleasant chatter impossible. Nevyn at last took pity on her.

'Lilli, would you find a page to bring me some ale?' he said. 'And perhaps some sweetmeats for her highness.'

'And for you,' Bellyra broke in, 'if you'd like some, Lilli.'

'My thanks.' Lilli rose. 'I'll go down to the kitchens and see what Cook has on hand.'

Lilli curtsied, then fled the women's hall. Her mother's curse – had she been as desperate as all that, to sacrifice her own son to serve the Boar clan's cause?

'Will we never be free of these wars?' Lilli whispered.

She stepped out of the broch to the pleasant sunshine, bright on the pale slate roofs of Dun Cerrmor, but to her inner sight it seemed that storm clouds gathered, dark and evil, over them all.

With the summer's fighting past and done, time lay heavy on the silver daggers. Every morning Branoic would groom his horse, sweep out its stall, then go riding for some short while to keep the horse fit and himself as well. He filled part of his day with talking with the new men, like Alwyn. Every now and then the prince wanted to go riding around his new lands; the entire troop of silver daggers went with him on these occasions. But for the most part, life reduced itself to drinking in the great hall and wishing that Lilli would get herself back from Cerrmor.

'Tell me,' Maddyn said one evening, 'how's your suit proceeding? I haven't forgotten our wager.'

Branoic had. 'What suit?'

'Your courtship of Lady Lillorigga. You bet me one silver piece to ten that you could gain her favour.'

'Oh, that suit! It's going well, truly.'

'Indeed? Words are cheap, my friend. What counts is the horse race.'

'Maddo, lad, cheap or not, you'd best watch how you spend yours. Say one wrong thing about the lady, and I'll cram the words down your throat.'

Maddyn stared at him for a long moment.

'My apologies,' the bard said at last. 'I'd not realized that this was a serious thing to you.'

'It is. I've been trying to get up my courage to ask our prince for that boon he promised me.'

'And what do you want to ask for?'

'Enough land to support a wife.'

'Truly serious, then.' Maddyn whistled under his breath. 'You'll never hear a wrong word about the lady from me.'

'My thanks. I figured I could rely on you to see things right, like.'

Maddyn waved down a passing servant and had her refill their tankards. For a while they drank in silence, watching Prince Maryn on the far side of the hall. The prince never allowed himself to sit at the head of the table of honour, a place reserved for the king; instead he sat in the place that would have been at the king's right. Tonight Councillor Oggyn was kneeling beside him, talking earnestly with much waving of hands.

'I wonder what Slimy Oggo's up to,' Maddyn said.

'No good, no doubt,' Branoic said.

'I've not trusted the man since I caught him out over those weevily oats he gave our horses.'

'I remember that, truly. You should make a song about him, Maddo.'

'There's a thought.' Maddyn suddenly grinned. 'I wouldn't mention his name of course. An animal song, mayhap.' He hummed a few notes of a tune. 'Oh, the fox went to the henhouse once too often, he found a wolf on guard. That kind of song.'

'Sounds like a splendid idea!'

Across the hall Oggyn rose, bowed, and hurried out.

'Tell me somewhat, Maddo,' Branoic said. 'Can the prince settle land upon a man now or will he have to wait till he's proclaimed king?'

'I've not the slightest idea. You'll have to ask Nevyn when he gets back. But here, are you that eager to leave the silver daggers?'

'It's not the leaving of the troop, you dolt. It's the gaining of the wife.'

'Oh. Well, I suppose so. I've never cared that much about a woman in my life.'

'Huh!' Branoic gave him a grin. 'Don't brag where the gods can hear you, Maddo lad. You'll tempt them.'

Maddyn laughed.

'Scoff all you want,' Branoic went on. 'But as for me, I'm looking forward to settling down, like, with my lady.'

On the morrow, Branoic got the answers he needed from the prince himself. He was walking rather aimlessly through the ward when he chanced upon Maryn, doing much the same though with two pages and Councillor Oggyn in attendance. Branoic bowed low, then went down on one knee to let him pass, but the prince stopped and hailed him.

'Good morrow, Branno. Are things well with you?'

'They are, your highness,' Branoic said.

'Splendid! When are you going to ask me for that boon?'

The prince was smiling, as if perhaps he were making a small jest, but Branoic decided that he might as well test his Wyrd right there and then.

'I've been thinking about that, your highness,' Branoic said. 'I've just not been sure when the fit time to ask you might be.'

'Now, if you'd like.' Maryn turned solemn. 'I gave my word, and I meant it.'

'Very well, then, your highness.' Branoic took a deep breath. 'I'd like a holding with enough land to support a wife, your highness, if that's not too much to be asking for.'

'Not in the least! The gods all know there are plenty of demesnes that have lost their lords in the wars, and I see no reason why you shouldn't have one and the title to go with it.'

Branoic tried to speak, but the words failed him. He could feel himself grinning like a half-wit. Maryn laughed and gave him a friendly cuff on the shoulder.

'Tell you what, Branno,' Maryn said, 'when you get that title, we'll give you your eagle device back.'

'Ye gods! You remember that, your highness?'

'How could I not, with Owaen ragging you about it for all these years?'

Had protocol allowed, Branoic would have grabbed the prince's hand and kissed it. It's the little things, he told himself, the things like this, that make us all willing to risk our necks for him!

'Oggyn?' Maryn went on. 'I charge you with finding a solid demesne and a lordship for our Branoic here. Once I'm truly the king, we'll bestow it upon him right and proper.'

'Very well, my liege.' Oggyn looked sour but resigned.

'Tell me, Branno,' Maryn said, grinning. 'You must have the wife in mind to be asking me for the land. Who is she?'

'Well, begging your pardon, your highness, but I'd like to keep her name to myself until I'm sure she'll have me.'

Maryn laughed, and Oggyn smiled, doubtless because the prince was and for no other reason.

'A wise policy,' the prince said. 'Done, then. I'll get you the land, and you get yourself the lass, and that will be that.'

'My thanks, your highness. I – ah ye gods! My humble thanks!'

The next few days Branoic spent mostly pacing back and forth, wondering when Lilli would arrive. He took to going down to the town walls, where he could climb to the catwalks and watch the river road that ran to Cerrmor. On the fourth day after Maryn granted his boon, his patience paid off, late on a golden afternoon, when he saw a cloud of dust coming up from the south. Slowly it resolved itself into horses and riders. A small company of armed guards, with the three ships blazon on their shield, surrounded an old man with white hair, and next to him, riding astride like a lad, a blonde lass. Behind them came a cart and more riders.

Branoic let out a whoop, climbed down the ladder, and ran to his horse, tied nearby in the shade. By the time he mounted, the party was just coming in through the gates. Branoic paused his horse by the side of the road till they reached him, then fell in beside Lilli. She turned in the saddle to laugh at him.

'What are you doing here?' she said.

'What do you think? Waiting for you, of course.' Branoic leaned forward and called to Nevyn. 'Good morrow, my lord!'

Nevyn waved. Branoic turned his attention back to Lilli.

'I thought you travelled by galley,' Branoic said.

'We did on the way down,' Lilli said. 'But it's too hard a row back with passengers and suchlike, and barges are too slow.'

'Ah. Well, it gladdens my heart to see you safe. I hope you didn't meet with any trouble on the road.'

'None. I doubt me if there'd be any bandits around, with all of Maryn's vassals gone back to patrol their lands.'

'True spoken.' He paused, gathering courage. 'Uh, speaking of lands, like –'

Lilli caught her breath. For a long moment they stared at each other, half-smiling, half-afraid. Their horses ambled on, following the others just ahead.

'I asked him.' Branoic could think of no other way than a blurt. 'He granted it.'

Lilli laughed, one boyish whoop of delight, cut short when Nevyn turned in the saddle and frowned at her. Branoic concentrated on the road ahead, but he could feel his heart pounding. She's willing to marry me, he thought. She wouldn't be so blasted pleased if she weren't.

Although the previous king's high-ranking servants as well as his noble-born servitors had left Dun Deverry after Maryn's victory, the lowest ranks stayed for the simple reason that they had nowhere else to go. Many of them had been born in the royal dun and inherited their work and its meagre privileges from their parents. By asking here and there, Nevyn found such an old woman, the swineherd's widow, Vena, still living in a hut upwind of the pigsties, who had spun wool for the queens of Dun Deverry for many a long year. White-haired and thin as a stick, she was nearly blind, and throwing a drop-spindle for days and years on end had left her hands and wrists swollen and twisted.

While he brewed up herbs to ease her pain, Nevyn chatted with her and decided that her mind was still sharper than many a youngster's. A low fire crackled in her little hearth under a big cast-iron hook. He hung his iron pot of herbs and water from the hook, then added a few sticks of wood to the fire.

'It's good of you to leave off physicking the prince to help an old woman,' Vena said.

'The prince is young. He doesn't need much in the way of herbcraft.'

'As long as there be no battles, eh?'

'True spoken. And as long as no one tries to poison him.'

'Let's pray that never happens.' For a moment she sat silently. 'Well, I heard they were a-hanging of Lady Merodda, so mayhap he's safe enough.'

'You think she was a poisoner, then? Most people in the dun seem to.'

'I do, and not only from the gossip, neither. Many a long year it was now, but she did give my man a handful of copper coins for a piglet. We found the thing dead out on the dung heap some while later, and when one of the dogs did eat of it, he died too, and slowly, poor beast.'

Nevyn whistled under his breath. She smiled and turned on her wooden chair toward the sound.

'You think the same, eh?' she said, 'that she was a-making sure her evil potions would do the job.'

'I do indeed. You know, ever since I've been in this dun I've heard tales of Lady Merodda's misdeeds, but that's a new one.'

'Well, don't believe everything you hear, good sir. You know how the gossips are. Many a time I'd be attending to my work, and the lasses with me would be spinning more tales than wool. And every time a tale got itself told, the more exciting, like, it would be.'

Nevyn nodded, smiling. 'Now, someone told me a thing

about Merodda just the other day,' he said. 'That she'd had
a bastard child after her husband was slain.'

'She had a child, sure enough, but it were only some seven
months after he'd ridden away to war. So it could have been
his easy enough.'

'They say the baby died. Did she poison it, do you think?'

'Well, when she come back in the spring, she was all tears,
weeping for her dead little son. A fever, said she. Didn't believe
the tears, I didn't, but the winter's a powerful bad time to get
yourself born. It could have been a fever.'

'A son, huh?'

'It was. Now, the lady's maidservant told us that she'd never
seen the poor little thing's body, and so some of the lasses did
insist that a demon had carried the child off in the middle of
the night. That's what I mean about tales getting puffed up,
like. A demon! Now I ask you!'

'A ridiculous idea, indeed.'

But what if a man of flesh and blood had taken the baby
away? Nevyn asked himself. Not so ridiculous, and in fact,
entirely too possible.

'Now, I'll leave these herbs with you,' Nevyn said at last.
'You heat them up and soak your hands in them twice a day.
The willow bark will help ease the pain. I'll stop back by in a
few days to see how you fare.'

'I'll do that, my lord, and you have my humble thanks.'

Nevyn went back to the great hall to look for a servant lass
named Pavva. By chance he'd run across her when the prince
had first taken the dun, and he remembered her as having
some association with Lady Merodda. It was late in the day,
and most of the servants were in the great hall, laying out food
for the evening meal while a few at time, the men from the
dun's garrison strolled in and sat down. Not far from the table
of honour, a small mob of silver daggers were standing around
some central point. Fearing trouble, Nevyn walked over, but
in their midst he saw Maddyn, sitting cross-legged on a table
and tuning his harp.

'Good morrow, my lord,' Branoic said to Nevyn. 'Maddyn's going to sing us a new song.'

'Indeed? Well, that'll be worth hearing.'

'I think so, truly.' Branoic grinned, profoundly sly. 'Let me know what you think of the words, like.'

Nevyn would have asked more, but Maddyn began. He had a decent voice for a man who'd never received a moment's training, particularly suitable for songs such as the new one proved to be, a light little tune with lyrics concerning a fox who tried to steal chickens from a farmer named Owaen. As Nevyn listened, though, he realized that the fox was meant to be a human being, Councillor Oggyn, in fact. Not only was the fox stout from being so greedy but by the end of the song he was bald. The farmer's trap caught him by the hair on his head and pulled it all off when he escaped. Back in his den the foolish animal decided to cut some hair from his tail to cover the bald spot, but he glued it under his chin by mistake.

'So instead of plump fowl he ate beard for his dinner' was the closing sentiment before the final chorus.

At the end the silver daggers howled with laughter. Even Owaen managed to crack a smile. Nevyn was about to say something to Branoic when he realized that Oggyn had been standing on the staircase the entire time. Branoic saw him there as well.

'And what's he going to say?' Branoic said to Nevyn. 'If he takes umbrage, he'll have to admit the song's about him.'

'Oh, you won't hear a word about it,' Nevyn said. 'But Maddyn's made himself an enemy all the same. Oggyn will remember this, never fear.'

'So will Owaen.' Branoic grinned at him. 'And that's where I'd lay my money for a wager.'

'That's not going to make the situation better, lad.'

At that moment Nevyn saw Pavva coming in the back door. She was carrying an armful of bread loaves, while her baby slept, strapped on her back.

'My apologies, Branno,' Nevyn said. 'But I've got to be off.'

Nevyn caught up with the girl as she deposited the bread in an enormous basket by the riders' hearth. Since she was going back to the kitchen hut, he walked with her.

'Tell me, Pavva,' Nevyn said, 'how long did you know Lady Merodda? Were you in her service?'

'I wasn't, my lord. She never took no notice of me till that last horrible day. Of the siege, I mean.'

'I see. Did you ever hear a tale about a baby she was supposed to have had, one sired by a demon?'

'Oh, that!' Pavva laughed, wrinkling her nose. 'The women did say the strangest things about that, but I never believed none of it.'

'I don't suppose you know when she supposedly had this child?'

'I don't, my lord.'

Nevyn handed her a couple of coppers and let her get back to work. By then he'd forgotten the flyting song. Later, of course, he would curse himself for a fool.

'Good morrow, Lilli.'

Lilli spun around and curtsied. Lost in shadows the prince was standing in the doorway of the main broch. Out in the sunny day she'd walked straight past without seeing him.

'My apologies, my liege,' she said. 'I'm much distracted, I fear, with my studies.'

'So it would seem.' Maryn turned, glanced into the great hall, then stepped outside. 'Will you honour me by taking a little stroll?'

'If my liege commands.'

Maryn stepped back as if she'd slapped him. Lilli looked demurely down at the cobbles, but she felt as if she were shaking with fever. Never in her life had she wanted anything, it seemed, as badly as she wanted the prince.

'I'd not command anything,' Maryn said at last. 'It was just a passing thought.'

'I thank my liege for thinking of me, but –'

'But you have work on hand for Nevyn?'

'Just that, my liege.'

'Oh well, then, far be it from me to interfere.' Maryn turned on his heel and strode back into the great hall.

Lilli let out her breath in a sharp sigh and walked on, heading for the side broch and Nevyn's chamber. She found Nevyn downstairs, however, standing just inside the outer door, where he'd apparently watched her exchange with the prince.

'That was very well done,' Nevyn said. 'I'm proud of you.'

'My thanks.' Lilli felt tears gathering and irritably wiped them away on the back of her hand. 'I keep thinking about the princess, my lord.'

'Good. I was hoping that was the case. Maryn's a man like any other, and he'll take his amusements as they do, but the princess, unfortunately, is not the usual noble-born wife.'

'So I can see. And she's been so good and so generous to me.'

'So she has.'

'Did you see the prince lurking and come down to meet me?'

'I didn't. I'm waiting for Otho, the silver daggers' smith.' Nevyn suddenly smiled. 'You look so surprised! But don't forget, Otho's the man who made our wretched casket. I want to discuss it with him.'

Otho arrived not long after, carrying a leather bag, clanking with tools. A short man but heavily muscled, with a neatly trimmed grey beard and grey grizzled hair, he wore a leather apron over a dirty pair of brigga and linen shirt pock-marked with tiny burns.

'Morrow,' he said. 'So. What's happened to the casket?'

'Naught, I think,' Nevyn said. 'But I have to be sure.'

The three of them went up to Nevyn's chamber. Nevyn had carried the casket back from Cerrmor wrapped in straw inside a rough wooden box, decorated on each side with five-pointed stars and other magical symbols, which he'd drawn with a swab of cloth dipped into ink to make bold lines. In turn he'd hidden his handiwork inside three old cloth sacks. This whole arrangement had been sitting under his table ever since they'd arrived back.

Nevyn dragged it out, stripped off the outer layers, and set the silver casket on the table. Otho picked it up and studied it, turning it this way and that, holding it over his head to examine the bottom.

'Well, now,' Otho said. 'It looks solid. If someone had tampered with it, my lord, I'd know it.'

When he pressed the catch, the lid popped open to reveal the smooth silver interior.

'No marks on it here, either.' Otho tapped the flat bottom with one finger. 'Under this, Lady Lilli, is the curse tablet, in a sealed compartment of its own.'

'And of course, there are magical seals set upon it as well,' Nevyn said. 'Can you see them, Lilli? Let your eyes go slack, the way I showed you, and look at it out of the corner of your eye.'

Lilli did as she was told. In a moment she could see, hovering just above the surface, tiny five-pointed stars that seemed to be woven of strands of golden light, about as thick as straws. She let her normal vision, with all its expectations of how the world should look, focus on the far wall and waited, merely waited, to see what more might show up. All at once she realized that the casket lay in the centre of a six-pointed star – no, many such stars, shimmering and floating until it seemed they formed a sphere of light around and over the casket.

'Oh! I do see them!'

Her delight, however, lost her the vision.

'Don't worry,' Nevyn said, 'you're doing well. One of these days you'll be able to concentrate on such things. But did you see any trace that struck you as evil? Any sign that someone had tampered with the seal?'

'I'm not sure what that would be. A demon face or suchlike?'

'Nothing so spectacular. Now, the emanations we're looking for are very strange. They don't exist in the physical world, but they send shadows on to the physical. Think of a fire burning in a room – it sends light through the window, and if some object is standing in that light, its shadow will fall upon the ground. So, the curse exists on the astral and radiates evil onto the lead tablet.'

'And the shadow on the ground is what I see or feel here, like the way the casket hurts my hands?'

'Exactly! Now, these astral shadows are so cloudy and tenuous that your mind has to cloak them in images before you can be aware of them at all. You'd think you were seeing smoke, perhaps, or dust in the air, or perhaps mould or slime on the surface.'

'I saw none of that.' Lilli held her hand over the casket. 'But I don't even need to touch it. It feels cold and horrid even when I hold my hand this far away.'

'That's how your mind represents the shadow, then. It doesn't have to be an image. A sensation will do as well. Well, Otho, I was thinking. Shall we have that curse tablet out?'

'Have you gone daft?' Otho snapped.

'Not so as I've noticed. I thought if we removed the tablet, the princess could have her casket back, and I could get another good look at the wretched thing.'

'You're the sorcerer, not me,' Otho said. 'I can dig out the tablet right here, but I'll have to take the casket to my forge to repair the damage, and I'm not so sure I want it anywhere near my place of working.'

'With the tablet out, it'll just be an ordinary bit of silver.'

'Imph.' Otho stroked his beard whilst he studied the casket. 'Do I have your sworn word on that, my lord?'

'You do.'

'Well and good, then. Let's see what we can do.'

Otho opened his leather sack, peered inside, then brought out, one after the other, little hammers and tiny chisels. He laid them in a row on the table, then spent some time examining the base of the casket. Finally he picked up a chisel and hammer. Lilli watched fascinated while he tapped round the edge of the base. What had seemed so solid began to split apart along a seam, as neatly as if the smith ran a knife through leather. Otho laid the tools down, took the casket and deftly twirled it right side up with a little shake. The entire bottom dropped out, and with it came a strip of lead, hammered into a narrow sheet as thin as parchment.

Lilli nearly screamed. She stuffed the side of her hand into her mouth and took two fast steps back from the table.

'What do you see?' Nevyn said softly.

'Maggots. The whole thing is crawling with them!'

'Those are just the shadows.'

The moment she heard his words, the maggots disappeared.

'Ye gods,' she whispered. 'That's horrible.'

'Isn't it?' Nevyn took one of the sacks that had hidden the crate, wrapped it around his hand, and only then picked up the lead strip. He dropped it into the symbol-decorated wood box.

'I'll seal this up again and hide it,' Nevyn said. 'You leave with Otho, though. You're not quite ready to witness this working. But before you do, try touching the silver casket again.'

When Lilli laid her fingers on the lid, she felt nothing but smooth cool metal.

'It's not cursed any more,' she said. 'Truly, Otho, I don't think you have to worry.'

'You'd better be right,' Otho growled. 'Very well, lass, come along. We'll leave your master to his spells, and let's all hope they work.'

As they walked across the ward, Lilli saw Prince Maryn again, but he was discussing something with the captain of his guard while Oggyn and a pair of pages waited nearby. She gained the safety of the great hall without his seeing her.

*   *   *

For several days Nevyn considered what he might do about Princess Bellyra. On the one hand, Maryn was right enough that Dun Deverry offered plenty of discomforts and dangers. On the other, a private danger threatened her in Dun Cerrmor. The memory of her grief haunted him until at length he made his decision.

Just that morning he'd received letters from High Priest Retyc of Lughcarn, and he used those as an excuse for a confidential audience with the prince. Since last he'd been in Maryn's chambers, servants had made some effort to give Maryn's reception room a royal air. They'd found Bardek carpets for the floor and laid them over each other in such a way as to hide the threadbare portions. The tapestries on the walls had been washed and mended as well, with patches of new yarn embroidered over torn weaving. All the furniture had cushions, now, and the brass work at the hearth and the silver sconces on the walls glittered in the morning sun. On the mantel sat the silver wyvern that Nevyn had seen previously in Oggyn's quarters.

'This all looks most impressive, my liege,' Nevyn said.

'Oggyn set some of the dun's women to work,' Maryn said, glancing around. 'I suppose it's necessary. I needed somewhere to receive my vassals and such.'

'You did, truly.'

Maryn sat down on the wide sill of one of the windows and gestured to a nearby chair. Nevyn sat, then reached into his shirt and took out the letters. The prince waved them away.

'Just tell me what they say.'

'As his highness wishes.'

Nevyn felt suddenly troubled. Never before had he seen Maryn so careless about affairs of state. Even while Nevyn summarized the letters, Maryn seemed as much interested in the view from his window as he did in the news from the second most powerful priest in Deverry. At length Nevyn stopped talking and waited to see if the prince would notice. After some moments, he did.

'My apologies,' Maryn said. 'Did they say they'd found the white mare?'

'Only that they'd sent to your father in Pyrdon for one. My liege seems much distracted today.'

'Your liege hasn't slept well in too long.'

'As your physician, my liege, as well as your councillor, may I make a recommendation?'

'Of course.'

'Bring your wife here.'

Maryn looked away again, his jaw set so tightly that Nevyn could see a vein throbbing on his forehead.

'A good thought,' Maryn said at last. 'But who will be my regent in Cerrmor?'

'Your highness has a seneschal and a chamberlain who are both fine men and quite capable of keeping the dun from sliding into the sea. The only thing they cannot do is hold malover, and neither can the princess.'

'True spoken. Very well. Send me a scribe, and I'll get the messengers on the way.'

When Nevyn rose to leave, the prince walked with him to the door.

'Oh, by the way,' Maryn said with a studied casualness, 'how does your apprentice fare these days?'

'She has a gift for dweomer, your highness,' Nevyn said, 'and she works very hard at her studies. I'm quite pleased with her progress.'

'Good, good, it gladdens my heart to hear that.'

'Not everyone with a gift can use it well, of course. The dweomer makes enormous demands on a person. Concentration, the power of the will, and above all, time – developing the gift the gods gave her requires all of those.'

'No doubt. She's lucky she's found such a good teacher.'

'My thanks, my liege. She truly is my apprentice, you know, as much as she might be apprenticed to weaving or some other craft. Her well-being is my responsibility now, and it's one I take quite seriously.'

Maryn tossed up his head like a startled horse. The message had struck home. Nevyn smiled pleasantly and waited.

'You have my leave to go,' Maryn snapped.

The prince turned and stalked back to his seat in the window. Nevyn allowed himself a sour smile at his retreating back, then let himself out the door.

Since Retyc had asked him to take the letters on to High Priest Gwaevyr, Nevyn had an ostler saddle him a horse, then left the dun. He rode through the valley ruins and up the road that spiralled around the second highest hill in the city. On its crest, behind high walls, stood the temple of Bel, the holiest land in all Deverry, or so its priests claimed. Since Nevyn was known there, the two neophytes guarding the gates let him in without a challenge, and a third ran off to deliver the news of his coming to the high priest.

While he waited, Nevyn handed his horse over to a servant and walked in the sacred oak grove among the graves of Deverry's high kings. Fresh grass was growing on the newest, a pitifully short mound over little Olaen. Nevyn stood for a moment with bowed head and asked the child's soul to forgive him. Although he knew that Councillor Oggyn had murdered the child-king, he'd done nothing to bring him to justice. Oggyn was proving his worth now, with his surveys and prudent plans, just as Nevyn had known he would. Still the memory haunted him, of the child's death-pale face and unseeing eyes as he lay on his soiled bed.

'Lord Nevyn?' A soft voice hailed him from behind.

Nevyn spun around to find a middle-aged priest, shaved bald as his kind always were and wearing a simple linen tunic with a rope belt. At his waist hung a small golden sickle.

'My name is Trinyn. I'm afraid His Holiness is unwell and not receiving visitors.'

'Is there anything I can do? I've studied physic for many a long year.'

'We have our own healers.'

'Of course.' Nevyn inclined his head in Trinyn's direction. 'I don't mean to intrude.'

Trinyn smiled thinly. Nevyn reached into his shirt and brought out the message tube.

'Letters from Retyc of Lughcarn,' Nevyn said. 'He asked me to ensure that His Holiness received them.'

'My thanks.' Trinyn's smile grew a trifle more hospitable. 'I appreciate your delivering these yourself.'

'No doubt they contain important matters. I'd best leave you to the reading of them.'

As he rode back to the dun, Nevyn puzzled over the cold reception he'd received. Retyc's letters had been nothing but reassuring; the Lughcarn temple was confident that they would find a white mare, all the omens seemed good, and the politicking between their temple and Dun Deverry had died down to a caution born of old distrust.

'I don't understand,' Nevyn said to the prince. 'I see no real obstacles to their proclaiming you king once the white mare turns up.'

'If you don't understand it,' Maryn said, 'then I fear the worst.'

'What?' Nevyn went on. 'That they'll never make the proclamation? I doubt that, my liege, very much indeed.'

'So do I. I'm afraid that they'll wait so long that my allies will start deserting. I've cobbled together this reign on Wyrd and fancy promises, after all. Some men lose patience with such.'

Nevyn sighed. The candle-flames in their sconces bobbed in the draught from the windows as if agreeing.

'That's real enough,' Nevyn said at last. 'Ah well, there's naught to do about it now. We'll have to fight that battle when it rides our way – if indeed it does.'

'All right, lads,' Owaen said. 'The prince has asked me to detail some men to ride to Cerrmor and escort the princess on her journey here. Branoic, you'll be going with them.'

'Now here!' Maddyn snapped. 'Branno's got important matters afoot here in the dun.'

Branoic started to speak, but Owaen was too fast for him.

'So what if he does?' Owaen said. 'I say he's going. Are you going to argue with me, bard?'

'Am I going to make a song about you that will have the great hall howling with laughter?'

Owaen took a step back, his face dangerously blank. They were standing in one of the many odd private corners found in Dun Deverry's wards, an awkward triangle twixt a narrow tower and a wall. If there had been onlookers, Branoic would never have given in to Owaen, but as it was, keeping peace in the troop mattered.

'Maddo, it's not worth fighting about,' Branoic said. 'It'll be a pleasant thing, seeing Cerrmor again.'

'If you're sure?' Maddyn said.

'I am. Come with me, why not?'

'I'll do that.' Maddyn turned to Owaen. 'One of us should go anyway, out of deference to the prince's lady.'

'You're right. If you want the duty, take it.'

'I will, then. I take it you'll have no objection if I choose the men to go with us?'

'None.' Owaen kept his voice flat. 'The prince wants you on your way on the morrow.'

'Then that's what we'll do,' Branoic said. 'It'll be an honour to bring his lady to her new home.'

Without another word Owaen stomped away. Maddyn set his hands on his hips and glowered until his co-captain was well out of earshot.

'One of these days,' Maddyn said quietly, 'I'm going to make such a flyting song about Owaen that he'll never hold his ugly head up again. I'm beginning to understand why you want to get out of the troop.'

'I never would have left it before the prince came into his own,' Branoic said. 'You do know that, don't you?'

'I do.' Maddyn hesitated on the verge of speaking, then

shrugged. 'Ah well. Let's think about the matter at hand. I say we take Red-Haired Trevyr with us, for starters. It'll do him good.'

'By all means. Let's take all the men who –' Much to his surprise, Branoic heard his voice catch. 'Who rode under Caradoc.'

'Good idea. You tell them. I'll hunt up Slimy Oggo and get some supplies out of him.'

Getting the honour guard ready for the journey kept Branoic so busy that he had no time to speak to Lilli that day. In the morning, though, when the silver daggers were assembling in the main ward, she came down to say farewell. She was wearing a pair of green dresses, and her hair, once so short, was long enough to frame her face and lift in the early morning breeze. When she laid a soft hand on his arm he felt like the luckiest man in the world.

'Take good care of our princess for me,' Lilli said.

'I will. And you take good care of yourself. You're my princess.'

She smiled with such pleasure that he leaned down and kissed her, just a chaste brush of his mouth on hers, there in front of the troop. All at once he saw the Wildfolk, popping into manifestation, flapping their skinny little hands at him as if to warn him of some danger. Startled he looked up to see Prince Maryn striding over, accompanied by pages and his two councillors. Lilli went decidedly white about the mouth. With a murmured farewell she walked off fast, heading for nowhere, it seemed, disappearing among the confusion of walls and towers.

'Branno, 'ware,' Maddyn whispered. 'I think me the prince has some interest in your lady himself.'

Branoic felt as if he'd been kicked in the stomach, but he managed a decent bow. When he started to kneel, Maryn stopped him, smiling a little, but his eyes had gone as hard as steel.

'My thanks, silver daggers,' Maryn said. 'I'll charge you to bring my lady and her women back with all possible speed.'

'Then so we shall, your highness,' Maddyn said. 'Nevyn, do you have letters for the princess?'

'I do.' Nevyn handed the bard a pair of silver message tubes. 'And may your journey be a pleasant one.'

With the usual shouting of orders and the confusion of horses, the troop mounted up and rode out. Behind them creaked a slab-sided cart, filled with supplies for the journey. As they filed out of the dun, Branoic rode up and down the line, chivvying everyone into a decent marching order. He said a few cheery words to the pair of men stuck behind the cart in the dusty rearguard, then trotted back to fall in beside Maddyn. The troop rode clear of the final wall around the fortress and headed through the ruined city for the south gates.

'What was that again, Maddo lad?' Branoic said. 'About the prince?'

Maddyn glanced back, judging the distance between them and the first pair of riders.

'I can't be sure,' Maddyn said. 'But I'll wager that the prince envies you your lady. I didn't like the way he was looking at you.'

'Ah. Oh horseshit!'

'Just so.'

'If I were a lass, and I had a choice twixt the high king of all Deverry and a silver dagger, and a silver dagger I am still, whether I get that land or no, I doubt me if I'd think twice about which I'd choose.'

'Oh, I don't know. You've told Lilli you want an honourable marriage. Who knows how long the prince's fancy for the lass will last? He has his pick of half the women in the kingdom, and the other half are too old.'

When Maddyn laughed, Branoic glowered at him until the bard fell silent.

'My apologies,' Maddyn said. 'I don't mean to twist a knife in a wound.'

Branoic shrugged the concern away. He thought hard, but he found only one thing worth saying.

'Ah horseshit!'

Prince Maryn and his entourage stayed in the ward until the silver daggers had ridden out of sight. As he turned to go, Maryn hesitated and gestured Nevyn over. Oggyn and the pages waited expectantly, but the prince waved them away. The pages ran off shouting to join the other boys at the far end of the ward. Oggyn withdrew so slowly that he practically crawled into the great hall. Maryn waited until he was well gone.

'Branoic told me wanted to marry,' Maryn said. 'I take it that Lilli is the woman.'

'She is, your highness,' Nevyn said.

Maryn's face might have been carved of wood. For a moment the silence held.

'Will you prevent them?' Nevyn said finally.

'Of course not! Ye gods, what do you think I am?' Maryn's composure splintered into rage. 'Your wretched apprentice has made it clear that she thinks me beneath her, and by the Lord of Hell's arse, that's that!'

Maryn stormed off, heading for the stables. So that's what's wounded him! Nevyn thought to himself. He allowed himself the luxury of wishing that he could take his apprentice and go off into the wilderness where they could both devote themselves to the dweomer and dweomer alone. Unfortunately, the kingdom needed him just where he was.

It seemed to Lilli that wherever she walked in the dun, Maryn would be waiting. Most times he was accompanied by his entourage, and he would restrain himself to a glance her way or a few pleasant words. She would curtsy and keep her eyes modestly turned down, just as Bevyan had taught her, until he walked on and released her. Every now and then, however, she would come face to face with him alone in some empty corridor or isolated corner of the ward. At those times court manners did her no good. He never pressed her, never came within two feet of her, in fact, but he could have been half-way across a room and still her traitor body would have responded to his smile.

On a rainy morning she woke suddenly to the sound of a rustle at the door. She sat up on the verge of screaming. The memory of her mother's ghost oozing around her chamber was all too fresh in her mind. In the grey light and early shadows nothing moved. When she summoned her courage and looked at the door, she saw a scrap of something white lying on the floor. A letter of some sort? She rose, picked it up, and scurried back to her warm bed to study it. Although she was making good progress in learning to read, she still had to sound out most words a letter or so at a time.

'There is someone whose heart aches each night when he dreams of you.'

That was all it said, no signature, no hint of who this someone might be. Maryn was her first thought, but she couldn't imagine the prince entrusting this sort of sentiment to a scribe. She puzzled over the letter for a long while. Perfectly clear letters formed graceful words – perhaps she had captured the interest of one of the heralds? Finally she hid it under her pillow, then dressed and began her day. Down in the great hall she got chunks of bread and some apples, wrapped them in a napkin, then dashed through the rain to the half-broch that housed Nevyn's chamber.

Just inside the door Maryn stood waiting for her. With her hands full of breakfast she couldn't even drop a proper curtsy. He smiled at her, then looked her over with a hungry appreciation.

'Tell me, Lady Lillorigga,' he said at last. 'Did you sleep well last night?'

Could he be referring to the note?

'I did, my liege.'

He stepped toward her, she stepped back and reached the wall. Maryn put one hand on the wall near her head and leaned toward her, but he kept himself from actually touching her. Lilli felt her heart pounding and clutched her bundle to her chest.

'My liege,' she stammered, 'Nevyn could come down any moment.'

'Would it distress you if he did?'

'It would most assuredly distress him!'

At that he laughed, straightened up, and stepped back.

'My lady speaks true,' Maryn said. 'And it's not a pretty sight, Nevyn distressed.'

The prince bowed to her, then left, striding across the ward as if not even a downpour could trouble his dignity. Lilli took to the stairs, but the climb bothered her more than usual. By the time she knocked on Nevyn's door, she was gasping. Nevyn opened the door, caught her arm, and helped her inside. She laid the bundle down on the table and sat down heavily in the chair.

'What's so wrong?' Nevyn said.

'Rain. Thick air.'

'I begin to worry about the winter. How it will affect you, I mean.' Nevyn opened the napkin. 'Ah, my thanks! You'd best rest before you try to eat.'

Lilli nodded for want of breath to speak. Nevyn took half the bread and one apple, then sat on the wide windowsill to eat. He was looking down at the ward, and all of a sudden he scowled.

'I wish our prince had enough sense to get in out of the rain,' Nevyn remarked.

'Is he still out there?'

'He is, staring up at this window. What was he doing, lying in wait when you walked over from the great hall?'

'Just that. I don't understand! He could have any woman in this dun. I'm not even that pretty. Everyone tells me I'm too thin, and I puff and gasp all the time.'

'My dear child!' Nevyn turned away from the window. 'I'm afraid you've worked a mighty act of dweomer that's captured his very soul.'

'I never meant to! What did I do?'

'You said him nay. I don't suppose there's been one lass in his entire life who ever refused him before.'

Lilli stared, feeling utterly stupid. Nevyn was smiling, but in the most kindly way possible.

'You see,' he went on, 'now that you've rebuffed him, he's not able to leave you alone. It's the challenge of the thing. Not, I hasten to add, that the challenge is more important than your charms. But the former adds considerably to the latter.'

'I do see. And I suppose my being fond of Branoic's not helped the matter any.'

'It's not. Are you truly fond of Branno?'

'I am. He's the only man I've ever met who listens to me. Well, except for you, my lord.'

'That recommends him, indeed.' Nevyn considered for a long moment. 'I don't know how your Wyrd will run, Lilli, when it comes to mastering the dweomer. You've got gifts, but many do, and it's a rare soul who can master them. But I do know Tieryn Peddyc wanted to see you settled in a good place in life, and so do I. I'm not a young man any more, and I'd hate to think what might happen if I weren't here to protect you.'

Lilli turned ice-cold and laid a hand at her throat.

'I'd hate to think as well,' she whispered. 'If I couldn't stay at court, I'd end up living on my brother's charity.'

'Now, here, I've upset you! Forgive me. I'm not planning on dying any time soon, I promise you.' Nevyn smiled at her. 'Eat your breakfast, and we'll put these matters to one side.' He glanced back down at the ward. 'Ah, the prince has gone in. Later I'd best attend him to make sure he's not given himself the rheum.'

Lilli giggled and helped herself to bread.

'My lord?' she said. 'The strangest thing happened this morning. Someone slipped a love-note under my door. I've not the slightest idea who did it.'

'The prince, most like.'

'Well, but surely he wouldn't let a scribe know?'

'Ah.' Nevyn suddenly smiled. 'Of course you don't realize that Maryn can read and write. His father was a most far-seeing man and insisted upon it. Here, you've gone as red as a beet!'

'Well, I was thinking that it couldn't have been him, because I've never known a noble-born man who knew letters.'

'This one, alas, does. Don't answer it.'

'I shan't, my lord. Never fear.'

'But ye gods! It gripes my soul to think of him sneaking through the corridors of the dun. There are times when even natural dignity fails a man, and when he makes a fool of himself over a lass is one of them.'

'True spoken. Maybe he sent someone else to deliver it.'

'I'll hope so.'

Yet later Lilli wondered, when she was thinking over what Nevyn had told her, if not answering would only provoke Maryn further. She could not honestly say if she feared or hoped that it would.

Despite the rain the silver daggers had an easy ride down to Cerrmor and reached the dun after an eightnight on the road. Since the prince had sent speeded couriers ahead of them, Lord Tammael, the chamberlain, had their old barracks ready. They turned their horses over to the servants, stowed their gear, then went to the great hall for the evening meal.

It was just sunset, and the last bloom of light gilded the pale slate roofs of the towers. A sea breeze caught the pennants and snapped them out, while the red wyvern banners on the walls swelled and rustled. The ward stood empty and quiet, the cobbles freshly swept. The men walked slowly, in deference to Red-Haired Trevyr's limp, and spoke only in low voices, as if they were afraid to break this moment of peace.

'I'll miss Cerrmor,' Maddyn said.

'It's a better place to be barracked, truly,' Branoic said. 'Dun Deverry crimps a man's soul.'

In the great hall candles glimmered; in both hearths peat

fires smouldered to keep the autumnal chill off the stone walls. Up on the dais, at the table of honour, the princess and her women were already seated, wearing dresses of bright silks, green, gold, blue. The silver daggers reclaimed their old places at the tables directly below. Maddyn took the message tubes out of his shirt and walked over to the dais. When the princess acknowledged him with a nod, he bowed to her.

'Letters from Nevyn, your highness.'

'Oh, splendid!' Bellyra said. 'Here, page! Fetch those from Maddyn, will you?'

A boy trotted over, and Maddyn handed the letters up.

'Did you have a decent ride down?' Bellyra went on. 'I didn't expect to see my escort so soon.'

'We did, your highness. Your husband's vassals gave us shelter and suchlike, so the horses never tired.'

'Good, good. You'll have a slower ride back, no doubt. Lord Tammael convinced me that we need to travel by barge.'

'That's wise, your highness. You'll want to bring some of your fine furnishings with you. Dun Deverry's a poor sort of place these days. It's seen too much fighting.'

The three women exchanged grim glances.

'My thanks for the warning,' Bellyra said. 'But don't let me keep you standing there. You must be good and tired. Do sit down and have some ale and suchlike.'

'My thanks.'

The rest of the silver daggers were already tearing into chunks of bread and washing them down with Cerrmor's good dark ale. Maddyn took his place at the head of the table nearest the dais. As captain he had a proper chair, and it was good to lean back comfortably with a tankard.

'The princess looks well,' Branoic remarked.

'She does at that. I'm glad to see it.'

The two serving women were discussing some matter, perhaps the furnishings, but Bellyra had opened Nevyn's letters and was reading them, holding them up at an angle to catch the last of the sunlight in the room. Her pale hair, caught back in a little kerchief as casually as a farm wife's, rippled down nearly to her waist and glimmered in the light. She was frowning, her striking green eyes narrowed in thought as she read, but now and again she smiled, no doubt at some jest of Nevyn's.

Branoic had just said something to him. Maddyn turned to him with a smile.

'What?' Maddyn said. 'Sorry.'

'Do you want more ale? The lass is here with the flagon.' Branoic jerked his thumb in the general direction of the servant girl.

'I don't, my thanks. I've barely tasted this.'

'So I thought. Is somewhat wrong?'

'It's not. I'm tired, truly, after the long ride down. I'm not as old as Nevyn yet, but ye gods, there are times when I feel my years.'

Tired or no, in the morning Maddyn woke long before the rest of the silver daggers. He dressed without waking anyone, then took his harp in its big leather bag and crept out of the barracks. In the centre of Dun Cerrmor stood a royal garden, where an ancient willow tree grew next to a stream and roses bloomed. When the silver daggers had first come to Cerrmor, Princess Bellyra had given Maddyn leave to visit it as he wished, and it was his favourite place to sit and practise his music. Among the echoing stones the harp sounded so sweetly that he could almost convince himself that he was a decent harper.

When he played, the Wildfolk gathered to listen, sylphs and gnomes, while in the stream undines rose up and clustered at the grassy bank. This particular morning the music drew another listener as well. Maddyn had just finished a difficult set of runs when he heard the little door in the wall open behind him. He glanced back and saw the princess.

'Don't get up or suchlike,' Bellyra said. 'I'll just join you if I may.'

'I'd be honoured, your highness.'

Bellyra walked over and sat down facing him. She was wearing a pair of linen dresses, worn soft and shiny. She wiggled her bare feet in the grass like a child.

'It's nice out here, in the cool of the morning,' she remarked.

'It is, indeed. I hope I didn't wake you.'

'Oh, hardly! Degwa and Elyssa have been up since dawn, packing up things and running here and there to make sure they've not forgotten anything. We'll need two barges if they keep this up. Is the royal dun truly awful?'

'Truly. Black grim stone, and ye gods, it's crammed with towers and broken walls and suchlike. I think half the furnishings must have gone as firewood during the sieges. I remember how Cerrmor was, when we first brought the prince here. Well, Dun Deverry's far worse.'

Bellyra made a sour face.

'Then Decci's right,' she said. 'We do need to take lots of tapestries and carpets. And the silverwork, of course. That will help brighten things up.'

'Which reminds me. Otho sends his best to you, your highness.'

'Dear Otho! It gladdens my heart to hear that he's well. I rather worried about him.'

'You can rest assured that he went nowhere near the fighting. Now, the looting was another matter entirely. He asked me to tell you that he's picked up some old silver here and there, for the melting down, and so he'll have a surprise for you when you reach Dun Deverry.'

'Ooh, lovely! What is it?'

'I can't tell you, your highness. Otho would skin me alive.'

She laughed, wrinkling her nose at him, then wrapped her arms around her knees and leaned back, looking up at the patch of sky above the pale stone walls.

'Play something, Maddo,' she said. 'Songs or airs, it doesn't matter. I do love the sound of that old harp of yours. You do know that the other bards would all love to get it away from you, don't you?'

'I do. Several of them have offered me gold, over the years, but I always turned it down.'

'What makes it so sweet? It's all nicked and suchlike.'

'The Wildfolk enchanted it for me.'

She laughed again, and he smiled, but he'd told her naught but the simple truth. When he played, the gnomes swarmed closer, lying on the grass to listen with their little heads pillowed on their warty hands. One bold sprite even stroked the princess's hair as if admiring its colour. He had no idea of how long they sat together while he played through the pieces he'd learned from the court bards.

'Princess!' The voice took them both by surprise. 'My dear princess! Your highness!'

Bellyra jumped up like a guilty child. The owner of the voice, Lady Degwa of the Wolf, came trotting out of the door in the wall. All at once Maddyn realized that the woman meant to be queen of all Deverry had been unwise to sit around half-dressed with one of her husband's retainers. All round eyes and fluttering hands, Degwa kept trying to be properly servile, but she was having trouble finding words.

'Oh do stop it, Decci!' Bellyra said at last. 'I know I've been scandalous and terribly improper and all of that. But Maddyn's known me since I was but a child, and I do so love the sound of his harp.'

'My apologies, your highness.' Degwa calmed, slightly. 'I fear me I forgot myself. It was the surprise. We've been looking for you, and then I heard the music, and I thought I'd see if the harper had seen you, and never did I expect —'

'I know.' Bellyra cut her off. 'But if I were going to besmirch my honour with a silver dagger, I wouldn't do it in broad daylight out in the middle of a garden.'

'Er.' Degwa's round little face had gone red. 'Ah. Um. Of course not. Ah.'

'Let's go in.' Bellyra smiled at Maddyn. 'My thanks for the music.'

'You're most welcome, your highness.'

Bellyra slipped her arm through Degwa's and marched her back into the broch. Maddyn slacked the strings on his harp, then slid it back into the leather bag. I *have* known her since she was a child, he thought to himself. He could remember her as a skinny girl who had just taken her hair out of plaits, married off to a boy she'd met but a fortnight before. It made him smile, remembering them as a pair of beautiful children thrust into a situation that would have drowned many a grown man. But they had survived, both prince and princess, and brought the kingdom with them safely into harbour.

She was a child no longer. Most certainly not a child.

Maddyn felt his heart turn over. He grabbed his harp and fled the garden for the safety of the great hall, where the rest of the silver daggers were already seated and eating. Maddyn laid his harp carefully on the floor next to his chair and sat down. Carrying his bowl of porridge, Branoic left another table to sit on the bench at his right.

'Practising?' Branoic nodded at the harp.

'I was, truly. Here, Branno, I just had a thought. When you get that house and land, you'll be needing a bard.'

'So I will.' Branoic grinned at him. 'You don't need to hint around, you know. You'll always be welcome at my table.'

'My thanks. We'll let Owaen have the prince's guard to himself. It will do us both good to get away from court.'

'My dear princess,' Degwa said. 'I hate to rebuke someone so far above my station in life, but the queen's honour is the very soul of the kingdom.'

'Why do you think I don't know that?' Bellyra said.

Degwa stopped, her mouth open, and blinked rapidly several times. Finally she pursed her lips.

'My apologies, your highness.' Degwa curtsied, then glanced at Elyssa, as if for support.

Standing amidst baled tapestries, Elyssa said nothing. With a deep dramatic sigh, Degwa walked to the other side of the women's hall, where a heap of straw and several wooden barrels stood ready to receive the princess's collection of silver oddments. Bellyra flopped into her favourite chair and stared out the window at the blue sky.

'Were I but a little bird, I'd fly unto my love,' she sang, then merely spoke. 'But instead of flying we'll be absolutely crawling upriver on a barge.'

'Better than remaining here,' Elyssa said. 'Or so I hope.'

'Better for me, anyway,' Bellyra said. 'I do worry about you and Decci. If the dun's as ghastly as everyone says, it won't be very pleasant, living at court. Maybe you should stay here in Cerrmor till the new gwerbret's named.'

'You took us into your service when we had naught.' Elyssa looked up sharply. 'I'll not be deserting you now.'

'Nor I,' Degwa put in. 'Especially not now when it seems you need us more than ever.'

'Oh, Decci! You're still worrying about Maddo, aren't you?' Bellyra shook her head and grinned. 'Don't you ever let anything drop?'

With her hands full of straw, Degwa stopped wrapping to consider this seriously.

'Perhaps I don't,' Degwa said at last. 'But if I were you, your highness, I'd not be using his nickname so freely.'

Bellyra laid her head on the back of the chair and groaned.

'Don't be a silly goose, Decci,' Elyssa put in, amiably. 'Your highness, I think we've got all the valuables packed, or we will when Decci finishes the silver. The servants can deal with the bedding and the rest.'

'Splendid!' Bellyra sat up straight again. 'When shall we leave? On the morrow?'

'I think me that might be too soon,' Elyssa said, 'judging from what Tammael told me. But after a pair of nights, surely.'

'Thank the Goddess!'

Bellyra got up and walked to the window to lean upon the sill. Down below she could see the polished ward of the dun and its beautiful stonework. She'd miss it, she supposed, but then, to her anywhere her husband might be was the most beautiful place in the world. Not long now, she told herself, and you'll see him. She wondered if he would pretend to be glad that she'd arrived.

In the end they did take two barges with them to Dun Deverry, thanks to the taxes due Maryn as Gwerbret Cerrmor and the servants due to Bellyra as his wife. What with the nursemaids, the children, the scribes and the maids of her chamber, she travelled in a crowd. As for the taxes, live hogs, live chickens, the food to feed them on, plus sacks of meal, salt fish, dried beef, apples, cabbages and cheeses made up Maryn's dues from the farmers of his rhan, and the city folk owed him tanned leathers, lengths of cloth, refined salt, baskets, ceramic pots and barrels of ale. A few merchants, those who held the charters to trade with Bardek, paid in silver coins, carefully weighed as well as counted and wrapped in bits of fine cloth. All of it needed hauling upriver along with the princess, her women, and their furnishings. Each barge was so laden that the bargemen hitched up a foursome of heavy horses instead of a pair to pull each barge.

'I feel like the richest farm wife in the world,' Bellyra said. 'Those are fine pigs, aren't they? And we have eggs to offer you as well, bard.'

Maddyn laughed. Along with the serving women they were standing on the river pier up at what was then the village of Dai Aver, where they were waiting for the servant girls to finish stowing the baggage. Their barge would travel first, of course, upwind from the livestock. Behind them in the road the silver daggers waited, each man standing beside his horse, or in a few cases, beside two horses. The escort would lead the women's palfreys, ready for the last few miles to Dun Deverry, when the river road grew too steep for the barge horses. A parade of carts would meet them to carry the furnishings and goods. Bellyra glanced at the cloudy sky.

'I hope the weather holds,' the princess said. 'It's going to take us long enough to get there as it is.'

'At least you'll have shelter on the barge, your highness,' Maddyn said. 'But I wish the prince had summoned you before this. Summer's all but gone.'

'So it is. I had rather hoped to be summoned before this as well.'

Maddyn winced.

'My apologies,' Bellyra said. 'With half the folk in the kingdom starved and turned out of their homes, I've no call to be pitying myself. Here, Maddo, if the weather holds, will you bring your harp on board to entertain us now and again?'

'I'd be honoured, your highness. If of course your women won't object?'

Degwa set her mouth to a tight line and said nothing. Elyssa hesitated, then gave bard and princess both a watery smile that might have meant anything.

'Well, once they hear your harp, they'll understand. Ah, look. The bargeman's sending one of the pages for us. We'll talk later.'

Maddyn made her a bow and strode off to his men. Elyssa watched him go.

'There's grey in his hair, but he's a good-looking man still,' Elyssa said.

'It's his music that commends him to me.' Bellyra put a touch of steel in her voice. 'Shall we go on board?'

In the autumn rains Lilli coughed. She always had, and she always would, she supposed, even though the proper hearth in her new chamber helped considerably. While the rain poured over the dun she spent long afternoons in her chair by the fire and worked on her visualization exercises. The work – learning to create mental images and then hold them steady – was tedious in the extreme, but to her it became a refuge. When she was visualizing the elaborate pictures Nevyn set her, she simply could not think about Maryn, and as long as she was working in her chamber, Maryn could not trick her into his company.

Besides the visualization, she had breathing exercises to do, and these seemed more like real dweomer to her. Nevyn had told her that soon she would combine the two halves of this programme in a practice that would lead her to proper, controlled visions rather than the upwelling of omens that had so troubled her before. She spent long hours on her work, brooded over her work, lived for her work, until at times she dreamt about her work.

Yet the cough continued, troubling her concentration. Nevyn seemed worried about it as well. One particularly nasty afternoon he came to her chamber with an iron pot and bags of herbs. Whilst he brewed up infusions of pennyroyal and horehound, he asked her detailed questions about when and where she found herself coughing.

'It's much much better by the fire, my lord,' Lilli said. 'I truly do doubt if it matters.'

Nevyn considered her for a long moment.

'You're all wrapped up in shawls,' he said. 'But you still look far too thin. Your face glows with fever whenever you get tired. It matters, Lilli.'

'Well, perhaps so.'

'You know, I think I may have made a mistake. I thought the trouble you have breathing was a result of the ghastly way your mother and Brour misused your dweomer gifts. You know enough now to see how important proper breathing is to the work.'

'I do, my lord. It's like I can suck up aethyr from the air or suchlike, and it feeds me.'

'It should, most certainly. But I look at you and I wonder if it's draining you instead. I begin to wonder if your troubles stem from such a basic and ordinary root that I've overlooked it.'

'What would that be?'

'An illness.' Nevyn gave her a rueful smile. 'A congenital

weakness of the lungs due to imbalanced humours. You most assuredly seem to have an excess of the cold and moist humours, because such an excess collects in the lungs. Your body would try to balance it out with the warm and dry humours of the air, you see.'

'Oh. That sounds worrisome.'

'It is. I think you'd best devote yourself to getting well. Lay aside those dweomer exercises I gave you, just for a fortnight, say.'

'But I was finally getting somewhere with them!'

'I realize that, but you'll be able to pick them up again. Not quite where you left off, I'll admit it, but close enough. You need to rest.'

When she opened her mouth to argue he caught her glance and held it. What could she do, confess that she wanted the work to keep Maryn out of her mind and heart?

'I'm just the apprentice,' Lilli said at last. 'As you wish, my lord.'

Under Nevyn's orders she began spending much of her day in bed. Although he visited regularly, she spent most of the day alone, longing for distractions. Needlework she could do in bed, sitting up propped by pillows. On the third morning she got out the pieces of the wedding shirt that would have been Braemys's and laid them out flat on her table. They might be made to fit Branoic if she added extra panels down the sides. She would have to pick off the Boar blazon, of course, from the front yokes and substitute whatever device the heralds might draw up for him.

Bevyan had embroidered those blazons. The thought of destroying even these small pieces of her work drove Lilli to tears. She folded the front section back up and returned it to her chest. She would use the back and sleeves of the shirt and simply work a new front, matching the bands at hem and yoke.

With a rustle a note slid under the door. Lilli sprang, grabbed the handle, and flung the door open. Councillor

Oggyn stood there, dead pale from his beard to his naked scalp.

'You?' Lilli snapped. 'You're the one who –'

'Not!' Oggyn squeaked. 'I'm but the page, delivering these.'

'Well, no insult meant, good councillor, but that gladdens my heart.'

Oggyn smiled and returned to his normal colour.

'No insult taken,' he said. 'I'm old enough to be your grandfather, my lady.'

'Just so. Very well, Oggyn. I've caught you red-handed, and so you have to confess. Who's writing me these notes?'

'Oh come now! Surely you must know without my having to name him out?'

'I want him named out. I hate not being sure.'

'Let me put it this way. He's a man of the highest possible estate.'

'No riddles! Is it Prince Maryn or isn't it?'

'Oh, of course it is!'

Oggyn bowed, then hurriedly trotted away before she could ask any more questions. Lilli shut the door and sat on her bed to sound out the words.

'You trouble my dreams and my waking hours. When will you take pity on me?'

Huh! Lilli thought. What would happen if I gave in to him? I suppose he'd find me tedious without the challenge. She put the letter down on the bed beside her, then arranged her pillows and lay down to drowse the afternoon away. Although she was tired, she was no longer exhausted, and she realized that she'd not coughed much at all that day. Nevyn was right, she told herself. I've been ill.

She dozed off, then woke not long after. The sound that had wakened her came again – a knock at the door, Nevyn most like.

'Come in, my lord,' she called out.

Maryn stepped in, shut the door behind him, and barred it. For a moment he stood leaning against the door and smiling, on the verge of laughter, really, as he watched her. She sat up, crossing her arms over her chest, so sleep-muddled that for a moment she thought she was dreaming.

'Oggyn told me you caught him,' Maryn said, smiling. 'I thought, well, since you know, I might as well come make my plea myself.'

'My liege –' Lilli found herself stammering.

'Don't.' He sat down beside her, and his smile was gone. 'Don't call me that. Not my liege, not your highness, none of that. I'm not the prince, Lilli, but a man who can't sleep for love of you.'

He sat close, leaning toward her, and she had no strength to pull away. She felt as if she'd drunk mead; his warmth flooded her and made it difficult to think. His eyes were as grey as storm clouds and as dangerous.

'What shall I call you, then?' She could hear her voice shaking.

'Marro will do.' He moved closer, smiling. 'Do you want me to leave? I will if you ask me.'

She knew that she should send him away. She remembered all her worries and her fears, remembered Nevyn's strictures and even Bellyra's unhappiness, but they were all voices heard in some distant room, barely comprehensible. Slowly he bent his head, hesitated, his lips half-parted, waiting perhaps for her to tell him to leave. She knew that she should force herself to speak and send him away. He reached out with one hand and touched her face with his fingertips, stroked her cheek, brushed her hair back, his touch gentle, soft. All at once she realized that he was trembling, afraid perhaps that she would still speak and forbid him. That he could find her capable of wounding him trapped her. When his fingers touched her lips, she turned her head and kissed them.

Early in the afternoon, Nevyn collected the proper herbs from his chamber, then went downstairs, heading for the royal broch and Lilli. Although she'd seemed improved that morning, her illness troubled him. He was keeping from her the truth that such a disease threatened to end her dweomer studies unless he could rid her of it once and for all. Studying dweomer with weak lungs could lead to a deadly imbalance of aethyr by bringing more of the fifth element into the blood than the person could assimilate – or so the lore ran. Whether it was accurate or not, the end result was all too well known: consumptions and fevers that could kill the student. As he was crossing the great hall on his way to the staircase, Oggyn hailed him. Nevyn waited and let the councillor catch up.

'May I have a moment?' Oggyn said. 'The prince has charged me with finding a suitable holding to settle upon Branoic the silver dagger, and truly, this raises all manner of vexing questions.'

'Such as?' Nevyn said.

'Well, if I make the holding too small, I insult Branoic. If it's too large, then I'm insulting our liege's noble-born vassals. And then there are all the other silver daggers, or I should say, those to whom our liege extended a boon. How many of them, do you think, will want land? If the whole three and twenty do, things could turn ugly.'

'Oh, come now! The Boar clan's holdings are huge. There'll be plenty of land to go round when the prince attaints them.'

'Your point's well-taken, but the prince's vassals will want those attainted lands for themselves or for their younger sons.' Oggyn paused, chewing on his lower lip. 'I've got maps up in the council chamber. Could you come look them over with me? I'd like to settle these matters as soon as possible.'

'No doubt, but you've got months to do it in. Maryn won't be able to dispose land till he's been given the kingship.'

'Ah, I didn't know that. Could you tell me precisely how it's done, then?'

'I'll be glad to, but I've got to go look in on my apprentice first.' Nevyn hefted the packets in his hand. 'I need to brew up some medicaments for that cough of hers.'

'Uh, well, I really would appreciate your immediate help.' Oggyn's voice, normally so fluid, carried just a trace of desperation – only a trace, but quite enough.

'And what's all this?' Nevyn snarled. 'Has the prince told you to decoy me off while he goes hunting Lilli?'

Sweat broke out on Oggyn's bald head.

'Of all the –' Nevyn stepped around Oggyn and headed for the staircase.

'Wait!' Oggyn came chasing after him. 'Please, good Nevyn! Let us at least discuss this matter privately.'

'Very well. Come along, then, and we'll get clear of the great hall. You're right enough – everyone's staring at us.'

They went upstairs to the council chamber, where a new set of maps and parchments lay thick as snow on the table.

'Assorted letters patent,' Oggyn said with a wave. 'Now about this matter of your apprentice –'

'I dislike being lied to,' Nevyn snarled. 'That's the true issue here, not what Lilli may choose to do. I realize that you could hardly refuse to do what the prince commanded.'

'Just so. Truly, this entire thing has struck me as lacking in dignity from the first. I'm much too old to be a go-between. The prince should be considering affairs of state, not shoving love notes under doors.'

'Precisely. I take it he went to her chamber, and you were supposed to hold me off?'

'Just that. Apparently he's there still. He told me he'd come down to the great hall once he'd spoken with her. He was expecting her to send him right away, you see, but that was some while ago. Most likely she's finally allowed him to dip his bucket in her well.'

Nevyn relieved his feelings with a few foul words.

'I only hope,' Oggyn went on, 'that his highness will get his fill of the lass and end this affair sooner rather than later.'

'No matter what the lass may think about it, eh?'

'That's no concern of mine. I hope I may count on your aid to get this matter tidied away as soon as possible.'

'You mayn't, actually. You're forgetting that Lilli is my apprentice, and her welfare is my concern.'

Oggyn took a sharp step back at this veiled reminder of dweomer.

'Eventually the prince may well tire of her,' Nevyn went on. 'But I'll not have your meddling bring that day sooner than it needs arrive.'

'Well, by the gods!' Oggyn snarled. 'If you're so concerned, then consider this! A speeded courier rode in this morning with news of Princess Bellyra. The barges are making good progress despite the rains, and she's likely to arrive within the eightnight. It lies well within the princess's power to make little Lilli's life miserable.'

'It does, but she won't. I'll see to that. It's you I'm worried about.'

'You are in no position to tell me what I may or may not do.'

'Indeed? I think me you misconstrue my position. Let us consider another matter for a moment, that of the child king's unexplained death. I have a witness to the lad's death who can testify he was poisoned. I happen to know that you had access to the poison that killed him.'

Oggyn went dead white.

'Arrogance is a luxury you can't afford,' Nevyn went on. 'I've refrained from laying the evidence before the prince simply because Olaen was doomed. If you'd not killed him, there would have been some sort of quasi-legal execution. But if Maryn knew that you personally murdered a child, even if he only suspected it, his honour would demand retribution – even though you did the killing for his sake. You know him well enough to know that.'

Oggyn nodded. Sweat trickled down his face and began to soak his beard. His eyes flicked this way and that around the chamber, as if he were searching for more ways out than the door.

'Now, then,' Nevyn said, 'I suggest that you allow this affair to run its natural course. Do we understand each other?'

'Perfectly.' Oggyn's voice shook. He pulled a rag out of his pocket and began wiping his face.

'You know, you sweat much too easily. In a man of your age it's a bad sign. I'd attend to my health if I were you.'

Nevyn stalked out of the chamber without looking back. All that afternoon he waited in the great hall for Maryn to show himself, but it was close to the evening meal before the prince finally came down the staircase with his usual bounding walk. He looked better rested than he had in weeks, smiling and somehow sleek, like a cat who's just been fed. With him were Oggyn and the usual pages, but Nevyn was willing to wager that the councillor had told the prince nothing about their earlier conversation.

Nevyn waited until Maryn was seated, then gathered up his medicinals and went to Lilli's chamber. At the closed door he paused, reminding himself that being harsh with her would do no good for anyone, then knocked. No one answered, and he knocked again, more loudly. Still no answer, and he tested the door. It opened just enough for him to look in and see Lilli, sound asleep, wrapped in a tangled blanket on top of her bed. Her green dresses lay crumpled on the floor, doubtless where they'd been thrown. He started to close the door, but she woke, sitting up with a little cry.

'Lilli?' Nevyn said.

'Oh, it's you, my lord.' She clutched the blanket around her. 'Thank every god! I was dreaming about my mother.'

'Shall I come in?'

'Please!'

While Lilli dressed, Nevyn busied himself at the hearth, lighting a fire and hanging a pot of water from the iron hook.

'You must know,' Lilli said suddenly.

'About the prince's visit? It's a bit obvious.'

'Do you hate me?'

'What?' Nevyn glanced over his shoulder and saw her honestly frightened. 'Whatever gave you that idea?'

'Well, I did what you told me was a wrong thing to do.'

'Not in any absolute sense. Dangerous is perhaps the better word.' He got up, wiping his sooty hands on his brigga. 'Come sit down, and we'll talk while your medicine is heating.'

Lilli came over, comb in hand, and sat down in a chair while he perched on the windowsill. Outside the last of the sunset brightened the dark towers of the dun, but the wards lay in shadow. The wind flowed, cool against his face.

'It's getting dark noticeably earlier every night,' Nevyn remarked. 'Winter will be here soon with the snows, and you know what that means. Going elsewhere, to your brother's dun, for instance, will be difficult.'

'I do know.' Lilli was concentrating on combing her hair. 'I'll need to be very careful. That's what you're saying, isn't it? With the princess here and all.'

'Not just the princess. What about Branoic?'

Lilli looked up on the verge of tears.

'I should have just sent Maryn away,' she said. 'I knew I should have. I wouldn't hurt Branno for the world.' All at once she was crying. 'I've been such a dolt!' She dropped the comb into her lap and hid her face behind her hands.

'Here, here,' Nevyn said. 'Don't – or truly, why not cry? You'll feel better for it. Lilli, my apologies. I forget how young you are. And this is the day that changes a woman forever, or so they always say.'

Nevyn got up, glanced around, then fetched her a damp rag from the washbasin in the corner of the room. When he handed it to her, she wiped her face. He was pleased to notice that the tears hadn't brought on her cough.

'I truly don't blame you for anything,' Nevyn said. 'Maryn is another matter.'

Lilli crumpled the rag and tossed it onto the table.

'Please don't berate him,' she said miserably.

'I'll try not to for your sake. Not his.'

Lilli stared at the comb in her lap as if she were trying to memorize its image, then at last looked up.

'I've heard that, too,' she said. 'About the first time a man beds you being the most important day in a lass's life. Well, that's not true for me. You know what day truly changed me, my lord?'

'I don't. Which?'

'The night my mother made me scry, and I saw you in the vision. Today with Maryn? Well, first it hurt and then it was wonderful, but ye gods, I grew up in a country dun. I saw lots of horses and dogs and suchlike doing the same.' All at once she smiled with some of her old spirit. 'But the dweomer – that's worth having, my lord. And that's why I wept when I thought you might cast me off. I feel like I could die, just from loving Maryn so much, but to give up the dweomer – I really would die then, I think.'

'If that's truly how you feel,' Nevyn said, 'then you've no need to worry about having to give it up.'

'Truly?'

'Truly. Though I warn you: you're going to have to proceed slowly with that weak chest of yours. Working dweomer puts a tremendous strain on the physical body. It's like, well what? Like running for miles, say. If you're fit and strong, you can run half the day, but if you're not, then running that far would kill you.'

'True spoken.' Lilli considered for a moment. 'I do understand, my lord, but couldn't I just practise my reading in the lore book? It's been dreadful, lying here ill with naught to do. If I only read and don't try to do the work'

'Very well. Humph. If I'd not let you get so bored, mayhap you would have had the sense to turn the prince down.'

She looked up startled, then laughed. Nevyn found himself laughing with her. Well, that's that, he told himself. No use in cursing over spilt ale! What mattered now would be how well he could ease the inevitable heartbreaks when they came. As long as Maryn didn't get Lilli with child before he tired of her, she would weather this affair well enough.

*   *   *

As the barges made their slow way upriver, the silver daggers rode on the towpath. When it rained, and it rained for most of the trip, the women could retreat into the wooden shelter built on deck, and the chickens could have their coops covered with canvas, but the men rode wet as their horses plodded along. Fortunately, a great many of Maryn's vassals, old and new, had duns along the river, and at night the princess and her women sheltered with them. Her escort most often slept in the stables, but since the stables were warm and dry, no one complained.

Finally, though, when they reached Camrydd Bridge, the weather cleared. Princess Bellyra invited Maddyn and his harp onto the barge to play for her and her women. He had to admit that it was pleasant, sitting in the sun while the barge glided noiselessly through the water. The princess had a chair; her serving women sat on crates; the nursemaids and the little princes sat on the deck with Maddyn, though he insisted that the nurses keep the boys away from his harp. He knew a fair number of instrumental pieces and played mostly those, not trusting his voice in front of discerning noblewomen, but eventually Bellyra asked him outright for a song.

'Your highness, truly, I'm not much of a singer.'

'Don't be so modest.' Bellyra gave him a wicked grin. 'Besides, we're bored, so we won't care.'

'Now really, your highness,' Elyssa said, laughing. 'Don't be unkind to the poor man! You play most charmingly, Maddyn, silver dagger or no.'

'My thanks, my lady. Very well, your highness. If you won't banish me from your lands, I'll sing for you.'

Although Maddyn started off with ballads, and the women listened with sincere interest, those grim tales of death and love betrayed, of cattle raids and blood feuds, soon struck him as out of place on such a lovely morning. Under the rain-washed sky the river ran full and silently between green banks. In the trees by the riverbank, birds sang. Out in the meadows grazed white cattle with rusty-red ears, and now and again a cowherd and a pair of dogs sat in the grass, keeping guard.

'I don't know very many courtly songs,' Maddyn said. 'I've not the voice for them.'

'Oh, do stop being modest!' Bellyra said. 'What about something droll? You know, those ones about the jolly tavernmen and suchlike.'

'My dear princess!' Degwa broke in. 'I doubt if any of those are suitable.'

'Your doubts are quite correct, my lady,' Maddyn said. 'Well, let me think. Here's a song I made up about a fox who was too clever for his own good.'

As he sang about Farmer Owaen's chickens and the greedy fox, the women laughed, and Elyssa even began singing harmony to the nonsense chorus. Prince Casyl favoured him with a stare of intense interest as well. When he finished, Bellyra clapped.

'Very nice,' she said, smiling. 'Though I wonder, truly, what inspired you, bard. That fox and his comeuppance – I think me I've met him. What did Oggo do to deserve this?'

Suddenly Lady Degwa folded her hands in her lap and set her mouth in a sour line.

'I trust I've not offended your ladyship,' Maddyn said.

Degwa made a small snorting sound, got up, and swept inside the wood shelter.

'Oh curse my tongue!' Bellyra muttered. 'I forgot about Decci.'

'So did I,' Elyssa said. 'I'll just go speak to her.'

Maddyn waited until Elyssa had gone inside. The walls on the barge's cabin were so thin that he could hear the women murmuring, but the words were incomprehensible.

'What have I done, your highness?' Maddyn said.

'Don't blame yourself,' Bellyra said. 'I should never have said anything, and then she'd have missed the point. Degwa can be a bit dense.'

'But –'

Bellyra leaned forward and lowered her voice.

'Oggyn's courting her,' she said. 'He fancies himself with a noble-born wife, and ye gods, she was widowed so young, I can't begrudge her the pleasure she takes in his attentions.'

'Oh by the gods! I feel like the worst dolt in the world! I'd not have wounded the lady's feelings had I known.'

'And you wouldn't have, truly, had I held my tongue. Now don't go troubling yourself about it.' She glanced over her shoulder. 'They'll be a while. So you absolutely must tell me what Oggyn did to earn a flyting.'

When Maddyn told her of the councillor's bribe-taking, the nursemaids leaned closer, all ears. Bellyra giggled, then turned solemn.

'I shouldn't laugh. That was truly greedy of Oggyn, and ye gods, Owaen might have killed him.'

'I was afeared he might, truly.'

'I've seen Owaen, over the years and all, in my husband's company, and he frightens me. He looks to me as if he might kill a man for one wrong word.'

'Your highness has the right of it.'

Bellyra shuddered, turning away, looking out over the sunny meadows.

'I hope to every god that the wars will be over soon,' she said. 'Do you think they will be, Maddo?'

'I do, your highness. Next summer there should be one good battle, and that'll be the end of it.'

'I'll pray you're right, and that my husband lives to enjoy the peace. I've never fancied myself regent to an infant son.'

'Now here, your highness! The prince has men like me all round him, and we'd rather die ourselves than let the least harm come to him.'

'Would you?' She turned back, and tears glistened in her emerald eyes. 'Ah Maddo!'

'We would, every last one of us.'

His hands ached from wanting to reach out and envelop

hers, to hold them tight and draw her close. He looked down and began slacking the strings on his harp.

'I doubt me if I can play more today, your highness,' he said.

'You've entertained us long enough. Shall I have the barge-man put into shore? No doubt you'd prefer riding with your men, and I suppose I'd best go soothe Degwa.'

As worrisome as the curse tablet might be, the matter of the Cerrmor gwerbretrhyn presented a more direct danger to the prince's dominion. Messages had come in from Pyrdon, finally, which lay far off to the west, a long ride even for speeded couriers. King Casyl was overjoyed that Maryn had remembered his half-brother so generously.

'He wants to send Riddmar to live at my court,' Maryn said. 'It seems a prudent move. If Eldidd does makes a strike on Pyrdon, then its second heir will be away and safe. And once the lad's here, Eldidd won't be heaping blandishments upon him, either.'

'Your father was always a far-seeing man, my liege,' Nevyn said.

Maryn nodded. He was holding the rolled letter in one hand, slapping it rhythmically on the other palm.

'Father wants to send him here straightaway, before the snows,' Maryn said. 'I'd best send an escort to meet him halfway.'

'That would be wise. Now that Hendyr's lord is your vassal, Riddmar will be in no danger, but the honour of the thing matters.'

'I'm sending men from the Cerrmor warband. After all, they'll be Riddmar's men once I've won the kingship. And then as a gesture Oggyn thought some of the silver daggers should accompany them as my personal envoys.'

'That sounds good.'

'I thought of putting Branoic in command of the whole lot.'

Defiance edged into Maryn's voice. 'It would be a considerable honour for him.'

'My liege, that's unworthy of you.'

Maryn tossed the rolled letter on the table. Nevyn folded his hands in his lap and waited. At last Maryn looked at him.

'True spoken,' the prince said. 'I'll send Owaen.'

'My thanks.'

Maryn smiled, but ruefully.

'It will be good to get Cerrmor settled,' Nevyn said.

'It will. I wonder if the Council of Electors will see fit to support my candidate.'

'So do I. We'll have to put some thought into that.'

Maryn got up and started pacing. He went from window to wall and back again, over and over, until Nevyn felt like screaming at him to sit down.

'What's troubling you so badly, my liege?' Nevyn said instead.

'All this talk and politicking and weaselling around! Ye gods, I used to think that once the wars were over, once I held Dun Deverry, then I'd be king, and everything would fall into place. Apparently I was a fool for thinking that.'

'Not a fool, your highness. Merely uninformed.'

Maryn stopped pacing and smiled.

'My thanks,' Maryn said, grinning. 'I much prefer your way of putting it.'

'I thought you might, my liege. But truly, the talk's every bit as dangerous as the fighting. You won Dun Deverry by the sword, but keeping it – that you'll do with words. A wrong decision now could lose you everything.'

After he left the prince, Nevyn returned to his own chamber, where the problem of the curse tablet lay waiting for him inside a little wooden box of the sort that holds tools for scribes. He'd marked the wood all over with wards and sigils, then built astral seals over it as well, renewing them five times a day at the changing of the astral tides. Once the seals were freshly set, he would perform a banishing to dispel any accidental evil that might have accrued upon it. After all these precautions he would take the tablet out and handle it, hoping to gain some fragmentary visions or hear a voice, deep in his mind, that might tell him how to unwrap the dweomer twined around it. Nothing ever came to him.

He hated to exploit Lilli's affinity for the tablet. She was young, just beginning her training, and always on the edge of illness. Yet he had no other weapons at his command.

'I begin to think that you must be right,' Nevyn said to her. 'The baby must have been your brother. We'll never have proof, but nothing else will explain the way the tablet affects you.'

'I was afraid of that,' Lilli said. 'It's so odd. My mother's been dead for months now, but it's as if she's still here, working her horrible magic.'

They were sitting in his chamber, late of an evening, with the tablet lying between them in a pool of candlelight. It was such an ugly thing, with its sullen curse scratched in crude letters, to hold such power.

'You slept much of the day, you told me?' Nevyn said.

'I did,' Lilli said. 'Which is why I can't sleep now.'

Nevyn opened the second sight and studied her aura: stronger, brighter, than it had been in all the time he'd known her. He closed down his vision and considered her physical body, less gaunt than ever before. His herbs and Maryn's attentions had apparently both been good for her.

'I'm thinking of asking you to try a dangerous trick,' Nevyn said. 'Are you game?'

'I am, my lord. Do you want me to touch it again?'

'Just that, but very lightly. I want you to see what comes into your mind when your fingertips are lying on the tablet.'

Lilli obligingly reached out and laid her fingers just on the edge of the lead strip. She frowned in concentration while the candlelight danced around her. All at once she began to speak in a hollow voice, dark enough for a young man.

'Bind him round. He must die slowly.' Her head tilted back, and her eyes rolled up. 'Burcan's child to bind him. Burcan's death brings his. As this so that.'

Nevyn leapt up so fast that he nearly knocked over the candles. He used his whole arm to scribe a pentagram in the air and thrust the banishing forward to envelop her like a net.

'Lilli! Come back!'

With a sob Lilli straightened up in her chair. Nevyn rushed around the table and grabbed her hands, pulled her to her feet, and flung an arm around her shoulders.

'Forgive me!' he said. 'I'd forgotten how fast the trance takes you over.'

'What did I say? I can't remember.'

'Some very grim things. Here, sit down and rest while I seal this loathsome thing up again.'

Once the tablet was sealed and bound, he put it back in its box, then hid it deep within one of his herbman's packs. He wanted to ensure that no casual visitor or careless servant would pick it up by mistake or out of curiosity. Lilli sat exhausted in the chair, slumped back, with one arm dangling over the side.

'I'll walk you back to your chamber,' Nevyn said. 'You need to sleep.'

'I do, truly. But I do wish you'd tell me what I said.'

'In the morning, when it's light.'

That night Nevyn walked for long hours outside in the silent fortress. Overhead the wheel of the stars hung close to earth in the crisp fall air, yet dark towers broke and bounded his view. Merodda's nasty little sorcerer had been a clever man, all right, who knew enough lore to turn his curse into a trap. He had used Burcan's son, that pitiful child buried with the curse, as surrogate to link Prince Maryn to Burcan. If Burcan died, Maryn's death would follow – if, of course, this dark dweomerman had the actual power to back up his lore. He had certainly managed to energize the tablet to some degree, or Lilli would not have felt the link so strongly.

And Burcan was already dead.

*   *   *

In dark night Lilli woke at the sound of her door closing. She could make out a figure standing by her bed, a dark shadow against the grey. She sat up, stifling a scream.

'It's just me,' Maryn said.

'Oh, good! You startled me, that's all.'

'Were you having one of your bad dreams?' He sat down on the edge of the bed and began to pull off his boots.

'I was. I'm so glad you're here.'

When he held out his arms she nestled close to him. His mouth brushed her cheek, then found her lips. His kisses were familiar, now – it always amazed her, that she would know his body so well, when once she'd thought him beyond her. He let her go, then stood up to pull back the blankets. She lay down, stretching with a little sigh of anticipated pleasure. He laughed and lay down next to her.

'I trust, my lady,' he said, 'that this isn't just a grim duty you perform for your prince?'

Laughing she rolled into his arms. He kissed her again, letting his mouth linger on hers while his hand lingered on her breast. She loved the way he touched her, forceful but slow, loved the way he took control of her, catching her hands, moving them where he wished her to touch him. She could lie back in a warm sea of trust and let his strange magnetism envelop her. That night she had never been more aware of the force that seemed to pour from him; in the dark room she could see it, a golden cloud that gushed from his body to wrap around them both.

His hand slid between her legs, and she whimpered, shutting her eyes, but still it seemed she was aware of that spiral of gold, wrapping her around more and more tightly. He moved, knelt between her legs, and entered her at last. She cried out as the pleasure of it swept over her, but in some small part of her mind she knew that this time was different, that his raw male force had found her too open, dangerously open. Lying clasped in her arms his entire body went rigid, stopped moving, and she heard the soft sigh that was the only sound he ever allowed himself.

He moved again, lying beside her, turning on his side to pull her into his arms. The cool air touched her sweaty back. She twisted away just in time and coughed, felt her back arch like a strung bow, coughed again, pulled free of his arms and sat up, covering her mouth with both hands to gasp for breath.

'Lilli, ye gods! What's wrong?'

'I don't know,' she mumbled. 'I'll be all right in a moment.'

She got up, staggered around the chamber, and finally found a rag lying on her table. As delicately as possible she coughed up what was troubling her lungs. She could hear Maryn moving behind her.

'Shall I go fetch Nevyn?' he said.

'I'll be all right. Please don't.'

'As my lady commands, then.' Maryn sounded worried. 'You don't have a banked fire in this hearth, do you? I wish we had a bit of light, so I could see how you fare.'

Lilli found her way to the shutters and swung them open. The chill night air smelled wonderfully fresh. The starlight and the last glow of a waning moon turned the chamber a bit brighter, enough so she could see him hunkering down by the hearth.

'Get back under the covers,' Maryn snapped. 'You'll catch your death of cold, standing there naked like that.'

'I was just going to have a drink of water.'

'Go lie down and get warm. Now!'

Maryn found the water jug and cup, then fetched her a drink like a page. She took it in both hands and drank it slowly, lying propped by pillows. He sat down next to her, took the cup, and set it on the floor.

'Shall I go away?' he said.

'Please don't!'

He laughed and kissed her, but gently, then stood up and walked back to the other side of the bed. She could see him silhouetted against the open window and the stars, but she fell asleep before he lay down next to her.

When she woke in the morning, Maryn still lay beside her,

sound asleep on his back and snoring. In the silver dawn light she allowed herself the luxury of looking at him, simply looking for a long silent while. Out in the corridor voices passed, servants, perhaps.

'Marro? Marro, you'd best wake up.'

'Imph?' He sat up, yawning, staring at the open window. 'Ye gods! It's light. I've got to be gone.'

Hurriedly he dressed, then lingered at her door for one last kiss.

'Hold me in your heart, my lady,' he said, smiling.

'Always, my prince.'

He kissed her once more, then opened the door, looked around, and slipped out, running down the hall and bounding up the stairs. Lilli shut the door and stood yawning for a moment. She crossed to the window to close the shutters and took a deep breath of the cool dawn air. Like knives it sliced through her lungs. She gasped, nearly fell, caught the table edge and steadied herself. The rag she'd used the night before lay on the table. It was stained with dry blood.

Lilli sat down heavily on a chair. She should dress and run to Nevyn, she knew, but fear turned her so heavy and cold that she only managed to cross the room and crawl back into bed. Although she fell straight asleep, a pounding on her door woke her.

'Lilli, are you in there?' Nevyn's voice.

'Come in, my lord. It's not barred.'

Nevyn strode in, his arms full of cloth sacks. Wildfolk and the scent of strong herbs swirled around him.

'The prince told me you're ill.'

'I am. I coughed up blood last night.'

Nevyn froze, staring at her.

'It wasn't much, truly,' Lilli said.

'Any is too much,' Nevyn said. 'From now on the only dweomer you're going to study is the lore in my book. We've got to get you well.'

*   *   *

In those days, when there were no locks and weirs, barges on the Belaver could travel no farther upstream than the South Downs. At the village of Lauddbry the promised carts were waiting for Princess Bellyra and her party, and with them the local lord, a member of the western branch of the Stag clan, come to offer her and her people his hospitality for the night. While his warband helped her servants unload the barges and load up the carts, Bellyra, her serving women, and the nursemaids, carrying the two young princes, walked down to the river bank away from the dust. With a shout for them to wait, Maddyn and a swarm of silver daggers came running.

'You'd best not walk about alone, your highness,' Maddyn said. 'We'll keep well back if you'd rather not be overheard and all.'

'Of course,' Bellyra said. 'Silly of me to forget. We're not in Cerrmor any more, where things were safe.'

'That's true.' Degwa looked around nervously, as if she expected to see bandits in every bush and garden. 'Oh, I'll be so glad to be inside a proper dun!'

Safely escorted they headed for the river again, the royal women first, the nursemaids and the silver daggers trailing after. As Bellyra watched the water, flowing fast here and churning toward the south, it occurred to her that she might never see Cerrmor again. Somehow she'd not allowed herself that thought. In letters Maryn had told her of his plan to give Cerrmor to his half-brother, an idea so clever that she assumed Nevyn had thought of it. Occasionally, she supposed, Gwerbret Riddmar would invite the royal family to take his hospitality. Otherwise her life would belong to Dun Deverry rather than the city where she'd been born and raised. She shivered, glancing around. Trees rustled in the cool wind, and already their north-facing leaves were turning yellow.

'Mama?' Prince Casso said suddenly. 'I want to get down.'

'Do you, love?' Bellyra turned to the nursemaid. 'I'll take him for a bit.'

When Arda set the young prince down, Bellyra grabbed his hand fast before he could run off. She let him lead her a little way downstream. Maddyn and four silver daggers hurriedly followed.

'Oh really, Maddo!' Bellyra said. 'What do you think will happen? That someone will seize us for ransom or suchlike?'

'Don't mock, your highness. The lords hereabouts haven't been the prince's vassals for long.'

'True spoken.' It seemed to her that the wind had turned even colder. 'Very well. Come along, Casso. Let's go back and join the others.'

After an uncomfortable night in a shabby dun, they set out early on the morrow morning. Some of the silver daggers rode ahead of the women, some rode behind, and a few rode off to either side, scouting down the side lanes for possible dangers. The carts, creaking and complaining, brought up the rear. Bellyra took Casso from his nursemaid and let him sit in front of her on the saddle. Baby Marro and his nursemaid rode in one of the carts, which made Casso feel quite grown up and important. In a few more months he'd be three years old, she realized. She would have to have Maryn's equerry find him a pony and begin teaching him to ride.

Since the carts were so slow, and wheels broke with tedious regularity, they travelled only some twelve miles a day. They were making about the same speed, Maddyn told her, as the army had over this same route. She was just thankful that the weather held cool but sunny, sparing them a ride in the rain. At night they imposed themselves on one or another of Maryn's new vassals, who, it struck her, were much more interested in pleasing the new Marked Prince than kidnapping his wife. The lords and their womenfolk grovelled and spared no hospitality to show their gratitude for Maryn's pardon. Still, Bellyra was always aware of the silver daggers, standing nearby, hands on their sword hilts, ready for the least sign of treachery.

Every day's journey seemed an eightnight long to Bellyra, but finally the dawn came when Maddyn could tell her with confidence that Dun Deverry lay only a few days away. Toward noon one of the carts laden with taxes broke a wheel, and Bellyra decided that they all might as well eat while the carters were repairing it. Maddyn had just helped her dismount when, distantly, she heard horses coming and the jingling of tack and mail that implied armed men. Maddyn swore and rushed away, yelling to the silver daggers to mount up.

'Take shelter,' Bellyra shouted to the servants. 'Decci, Lyss, all of you! Get in among the carts!'

She scooped up a terrified Casso and ran, heading for the circle of carts that would at least slow an attacker down. The other women huddled around her; Marro began to howl in his nursemaid's arms; the nearby pigs began to squeal, picking up the general mood. The silver daggers were shouting, turning their horses and milling in what at first seemed to be panic but which proved to be practised efficiency. In but a few moments they sorted themselves out into a protective ring around the carts and women.

Ahead on the road horsemen were trotting straight for them, about fifty of them, as far as Bellyra could estimate, since they travelled in a cloud of dust. Nearer and nearer – Casso suddenly laughed and pointed.

'Da!' he crowed. 'It's Da! Look! The big bird banners!'

What he always called the big bird was indeed the red wyvern device. Bellyra broke out laughing, and the other women joined her.

'Call off the silver daggers, Maddyn!' she shouted. 'It's my lord.'

Bellyra let Casso down, grabbed his hand, and then walked with him free of the carts. As they hurried to the roadside, Maryn kicked his horse and jogged out ahead of his men to ride first into camp. He dismounted with the fluid ease of a man who had spent half his life on horseback and tossed the reins of his mount to a servant. Bellyra curtsied as he strode over. He was unhelmed, but despite the quiet countryside he was wearing mail, though he'd tied a tabard over it.

'Well, my lady,' he said, smiling. 'Once you left the river old Nevyn could scry you out and tell me where to find you. So I thought I'd come escort you to your new home.'

'It gladdens my heart to see you, my lord.' Never had she said anything so true, or so she felt. She wished she could run to him and throw herself into his arms. 'You look well.'

'I am, at that. Now, who's this with you?'

Laughing, Bellyra let the straining Casso go. He could and did rush to his father, who scooped him up and settled him on one hip. For a moment they smiled at each other, two blond heads close together, and from the grey eyes and the profile they shared no man would ever doubt Prince Casyl's paternity.

'And have you been brave?' Maryn said.

'I have.' Casso reached out and touched the tabard. 'The big red bird.'

Everyone laughed. By then the silver daggers had dismounted, and Maddyn walked over to kneel before the prince.

'It looks like you've done a splendid job guarding my lady,' Maryn said. 'My thanks.'

'It's been an honour, your highness.'

'I'm about to repay you ill for your efforts.' Maryn smiled with a twist to his mouth. 'I'm going to take her and the children and suchlike back with me and my men. You get to follow along and guard these cursed carts.' He turned to Bellyra. 'That way we can reach the city on the morrow. We'll let the taxes come creaking in whenever they get there.'

'That would be splendid, my lord,' Bellyra said. 'I assume my women are included in the suchlike.'

'If you wish, certainly.' Maryn turned to look over the camp. 'Maddyn, we'll let everyone eat and then split our forces for the ride back.'

That night they sheltered with a certain Tieryn Cardomaen, or rather, his mother the regent made them welcome, since the tieryn was no older than Prince Casyl. His father had been killed the year before in the summer's warfare, or so

Maryn told her, fighting on the side of the Boar clan. That the Lady Therra was now forced to feed and shelter the man who was ultimately responsible for her husband's death made Bellyra squirm, but in truth, the lady seemed welcoming enough. During the evening meal she only referred to her husband once, and then she called him by his full name and title. They had had, Bellyra supposed, the usual marriage.

That night Lady Therra personally showed them to the dun's best bedchamber, which sported a pair of chairs as well as a bed with a full set of embroidered hangings. The walls, however, were bare, and the windows had not so much as a tanned hide to cover them. A low fire burned in the hearth. Maryn's page pulled off his lord's riding boots, then hurried out to join the other servants in the stables. Maryn tossed the boots onto the pile of the mail he'd taken off earlier, then sat down on the edge of the bed with a sigh.

'It gladdens my heart to have you with me,' Maryn said.

'Does it?' Bellyra smiled at him.

'I need your good sense. Lyrra, things are so tangled at court that I don't know what to believe. And then there's Braemys. Did Nevyn tell you about his gall?'

'He did.'

'Good. That'll save me the trouble of repeating it all.'

She busied herself with unwrapping her kirtle. I will not let him see me cry, she told herself. I will not, not, not!

'What's wrong?' he said.

'I'm just weary. It's been a long journey.'

'So it has. I wish that it had been safe to send for you earlier, when the weather was better, but it wasn't. I can only hope it's truly safe now.'

She merely nodded and concentrated on folding the kirtle. She heard the bed creak as he got up. He walked over and put his hands on her shoulders. Her pride was goading her to stiffen and move away, but she leaned back against him and felt herself tremble.

'You're truly weary,' he said. 'I should let you take your rest. My apologies.'

He let her go with a little pat on the shoulder, such as he might give a dog, and turned away so easily that it wrung her heart. And yet, she told herself, what was he being but more considerate than most noble-born men would ever be? She was so exhausted that she fell right asleep, and in the morning when she woke she found him gone before her.

During that day's ride north the landscape around them changed. They'd ridden half the morning before Bellyra fully realized what she was seeing. Although the meadows were lush, no cattle grazed in them. The fields were green and tall with weeds, not wheat. When they passed farmsteads, either empty buildings or burnt ruins stood behind their packed earth walls.

'Ye gods, Marro!' Bellyra said finally. 'There's no people.'

'Not along the river, truly,' Maryn said. 'One army too many took their crops and livestock, and they fled. I can't say I blame them, either, even if they're supposed to be bound to me. But wait until you see the city. You'll see why I've been scheming to keep Cerrmor under my control.'

See it she did, late that afternoon, when with the sunset they rode through the massive outer walls of Dun Deverry and into a wasteland. Siege after siege, fire after fire, the looting of soldiers in the summer and the thieving of desperate neighbours in the winter – she saw barely two houses standing together in all the long ride through to the hill where the dun stood. As they rode up to the outer wall of the dun proper, Maryn pointed across a shallow valley to a hill crowned with oaks.

'Things fare better there,' he said. 'That's the temple of Bel, and they managed to protect the people on the hillside.'

'I see. Do you think the folk will return?'

'Nevyn insists they will. I can only hope he's right.'

Slowly they walked their horses up the spiral road into the dun itself. At first Bellyra could make no sense out of what she was seeing. Twilight was darkening the sky, turning the jumble of brochs, towers, walls, and sheds into an incomprehensible mass of stonework. Their procession made one last turn and came out into what she assumed was the main ward, a huge cobbled open space surrounding a complex of brochs, half-brochs, and oddly random-seeming towers. Torches flared in sconces on the outer walls of a huge squat broch, and by their light she saw, waiting for them on the steps, Nevyn, Oggyn, and off to one side, Otho the smith.

'Welcome home, Lyrra,' Maryn said, grinning. 'It gets worse inside.'

It was weep or laugh, but she was happy enough at seeing Nevyn and Otho that she laughed. Maryn dismounted, then hurried round to the side of her horse to help her down. She looked back and saw servants trotting forward to help her serving women and the nursemaids. Once she was down, Maryn hurried off to give orders to the captain of his riders, but Nevyn came forward and offered her his arm. She took it gratefully.

'You made him come to meet me,' she said, 'didn't you?'

'I wish you were less perceptive,' Nevyn said. 'You'd be happier.'

'Well, I appreciate it, actually.' She patted his arm with her free hand. 'Otho! It gladdens my heart to see you!'

The dwarven smith stammered, blushed, and ran off.

'His manners haven't improved,' Nevyn said.

'Oh, from him that greeting's worth a thousand flattering words from some courtier,' Bellyra said. 'Where's Lilli?'

'Ill, I'm afraid. That cough of hers troubles me.'

Bellyra could feel him go as stiff as boiled leather. She could only think of one thing such tension might mean.

'Will the poor child live?' Bellyra said.

'Most likely. My apologies – I didn't mean to make it sound so grave.' Nevyn smiled, but only briefly. 'Ah, here's your husband, come to escort you inside.'

When Maryn strode over, Nevyn released Bellyra's hand, but Maryn made no move to take it.

'What's this about Lilli?' Maryn said.

'She's ill, my liege,' Nevyn said.

'Ah.' Maryn's face went perfectly bland. 'A pity.'

At that moment Bellyra knew, just as she always knew when he tried to hide his other women. She was tempted, bitterly tempted, to ask ever so casually if Lilli were with child, but for Nevyn's sake she kept silent. Maryn finally offered her his arm, and, smiling, she took it, to let him lead her into Dun Deverry's great hall.

For some days after the princess's arrival, Lilli barely saw Prince Maryn. Although she left her door unbarred at night, he never came to her chamber. During the day he would walk in the ward, but always with his councillors and pages. When their paths crossed, she would drop him a curtsy, and he would acknowledge her with a smile. At times she saw him in the great hall, but often the princess sat with him; at other times he was surrounded by his men. Even though she felt stronger every day, Lilli was at first glad of her illness, simply because it gave her such a perfect excuse to stay away from the women's hall. Quite regularly Elyssa would stop by her chamber and ask after her health, and Lilli could always answer in perfect honesty, 'Nevyn's worried about it.'

Branoic was another matter. During the brief times when Nevyn allowed her to go out and about the dun, Branoic kept her constant company. He was so solicitous, bringing her food or drink when she needed it, letting her lean upon his arm when they walked together. Once, when she'd walked much too far, he insisted on carrying her up the staircase to spare her the effort. Guilt began to gnaw at her soul. How could she let him dote upon her like this, in happy ignorance, when the truth about her affair with Maryn would doubtless drive him away? Finally, on a morning when she'd slept better than usual and thus felt she had the strength, she made up her mind for honesty.

'I can't stand it any more,' Lilli said. 'There's a thing I've got to tell you, Branno.'

'Indeed?' Branoic smiled at her. 'What?'

Seeing how easily he smiled hurt. She found herself on the verge of gasping for air and for a long moment could do no more than look at him. Despite the grey sky and the chill in the air, they were sitting on their usual bench in the kitchen garden, one of the few places that, Lilli could be sure, Maryn would never go. She wrapped her cloak tight around her and tried to think. Her carefully prepared speech had deserted her mind.

'What's so wrong?' Branoic said at last.

'I can't marry you.'

'Ah ye gods!' Branoic slumped down on the bench with his legs stuck out in front of him and crossed his arms over his chest. 'Your brother's spoken against me, hasn't he? I always knew he would.'

'It's not that! Anasyn thinks you're a fine man. He's already told me that we can marry provided you can support me. It's – well –' She paused, gathering breath. 'It's the prince. He's taken – I mean, I'm his –' The words stuck in her throat so badly that she wondered if she were going to cry.

Branoic uncrossed his arms and turned on the bench to face her. She'd expected rage, but he seemed merely solemn.

'I've heard rumours,' he said at last. 'So they're true?'

She nodded, swallowing hard. She should have known, she supposed, that the court would be speculating. Branoic laid one long arm on the back of the bench behind her.

'I couldn't go on lying to you,' she said.

'And you have my thanks for that. But I've got to say that I'm disappointed in our prince. It's more than a bit selfish of the man to forbid you to marry. You need a place of your own at court. Just in case things change, like.'

'What? He didn't forbid me anything.'

'Then why can't you marry me?'

Lilli could not have been more surprised if the day had turned to night around her.

'You mean you would?' she whispered. 'Still marry me anyway?'

'A lord whose wife has the king's favour is a lucky man.' Branoic considered her for a moment. 'Lilli, I'm not saying this because I'm jealous, though I am that, or to be harsh and get a little of my own back. But truly, I've seen somewhat of the world, and a bit more of our prince, and how long do you think Maryn will dote upon you, anyway? Half the women at court will be setting their caps at him, and he'll not see any reason to deny them.'

The tears did come, rough and painful, as if she wept hot sand. She covered her face with both hands and sobbed. Branoic put a brotherly arm around her shoulders.

'There, there, hush,' he said. 'Forgive me, will you? But I think me I've only said aloud what you've been thinking.'

'Just that.' She managed to force the words out between sobs. 'Just that.'

One sob too many, and she felt her chest tighten so hard she began to cough and weep at the same time. She fumbled in her kirtle for the cloth she'd tucked away there, but she just couldn't seem to find it, and the frustration made her sob the more. Branoic fished into the folds of cloth, pulled the rag free, and handed it to her.

'Blow your nose,' he said.

She did, then wiped her face on the clean part of the cloth. She crumpled the soggy mess in her fist while she breathed, forcing herself to inhale long and calmly. When she looked up, she found Branoic smiling at her, but sadly.

'What does old Nevyn think of this?' he said.

'Oh, he was ever so angry. He'd told me not to give in to the prince.'

'I guessed that. What will he think if we marry?'

'I don't know. I've not said a word about it. I just assumed you wouldn't want me any more.'

'Well, you were wrong. Why not talk to the old man about it today, like? You're his apprentice now, anyway, and it's up to him to announce the betrothal.'

'So it is. Oh ye gods, I just thought of somewhat! If people have been gossiping, the princess must know.' Lilli held a hand out in front of her and found it trembling. 'How am I going to face her? Branno, I feel so wretched. I'm not worthy of you, truly I'm not.'

'That's a stupid thing to say. If I thought that, I'd have spurned you on the rumours alone. Your Maryn's said he'll make me a lord, but in my heart I'm still a silver dagger, and ye gods, I'll not be giving myself airs.'

'But I'm not being fair to you!'

'Fair?' Branoic shrugged the comment away. 'Fair is where you go to see the pigs race, my lady.'

She managed a smile.

'That's better,' he said, grinning. 'Now, if you'll have me, I'll work out a way to get to Hendyr and ask your brother, all formal-like. Well, if Nevyn gives his approval, that is. I'll risk Maryn's jealousy, but cursed if I'll cross Nevyn. I've never wanted to be turned into a frog or suchlike.'

'Oh don't be silly! Dweomer can't turn men into frogs.'

'Well, that's a relief, but I'm not crossing him anyway.' He grinned at her. 'But I think me he'll be sensible about this.'

'So do I. He worried, he told me, about what would become of me if he should die or suchlike.'

'And he's not getting any younger. So you tell him what we've decided.'

'I will, but I want to sit here with you for a bit.'

Branoic smiled, and all at once she wondered what it would be like to sleep with him. She knew, now, what love meant. As if he'd caught the drift of her thoughts, he took her hand in both of his, drew her close, and kissed her on the mouth. Pleasant, warm – a congenial sort of kiss, she felt, but next to the passion she shared with Maryn, it held all the excitement of a bowl of warm porridge, another pleasant companion on a cold day. Still, for his sake she slipped her arms around his neck and let him kiss her again.

'You know what?' she said. 'I've been sewing on your wedding shirt.'

'Have you now?' He grinned, so genuinely pleased that she began to share his pleasure. 'When did you start that?'

'A fair bit ago. After you left for Cerrmor.'

'Huh. You're lucky I didn't change my mind.'

They shared a laugh, then another kiss. Lilli felt a gratitude so immense that she could almost mistake it for love. A marriage with Branoic would keep her steady and safe, the way a keel steadies a boat when it runs before a storm, desperate for harbour.

'My lord?' It was Lilli, standing in the doorway. 'May I speak with you?'

'By all means,' Nevyn said. 'Come in and shut the door.'

Lilli did so, sitting in the chair when he offered it to her. He was pleased to see her calmer than she'd been in days.

'Branoic still wants us to marry,' Lilli said. 'Even though he knows about the prince.'

'Indeed? Well, that's large-hearted of him! Do you want to marry him?'

'I do, but will it interfere with my dweomer work?'

'I doubt it. Branoic will be at best a very minor lord, so his household will be simple for you to run.'

'We'll be glorified farmers, more like.' Lilli smiled. 'I can't imagine Branno sitting in his hall doing naught when there's work to be done outside, no matter how much land owes him dues.'

'No more can I, frankly. Well, then, my blessings on you both.'

'Oh, my thanks! You know, Sanno's already given me his permission, so you could announce the betrothal if you'd like. I mean, you're my master in a craft.'

'So I am! You know, I'd not thought of it that way.'

'Although – well, they announced my betrothal to Braemys here in the great hall.' Her smile vanished. 'It seems like a bad omen, to announce a second betrothal there.'

'So it does. I'll just spread the word around to those who need to know.'

'Like the prince?'

'Him and others.'

'My thanks. It's going to be a long while before Branno gets that land, anyway. I gather Maryn can't give it to him until he's the king.'

'Just that.' Nevyn hesitated for a moment. 'And that means bringing Braemys to heel, one way or another.'

'So it does,' Lilli said. 'It aches my heart, my lord, to think of him being slain. He always was my cousin, and now I know he's my brother as well. I wish he'd just surrender and swear to Maryn. Do you think if I wrote him a letter it might help?'

'Now that's a thought. It might at that. Let me ponder the idea for a bit.'

Late that night, when most of the dun had long since gone to bed, Nevyn had another visitor. He was studying certain obscure sigils relating to the planetary spirits when he heard a noise that might have been a timid knock upon the door. He rose and shut the book. The noise came again.

'Is someone there?' Nevyn called out.

'There is.' A woman's voice, and tremulous.

Nevyn crossed to the door and opened it. Princess Bellyra stood on the landing, wearing a plain linen dress and a shawl over her head and shoulders. She clutched the halves of the shawl together at the neck, so that with a flick of her wrist she would have been able to hide her face from passers-by.

'Do come in, your highness,' Nevyn said. 'I hope you're not ill.'

'I'm not. I've come to see if you can make me a love charm.'

Nevyn started to answer, then merely sighed. Bellyra walked

in and sat down in his only chair. She let the shawl fall back over her shoulders, then reached up and ran a hand through her hair, hanging loose and dishevelled.

'I'd wager you can't, actually,' Bellyra went on. 'Love charms have the fine ring of legend about them.'

'You're quite right.' Nevyn sat down on the edge of his bed. 'And it's just as well. The legends are built around all the troubles they cause, you know.'

'What I really want is a potion that makes a person fall out of love.'

'If I had one I'd make Lilli drink it.'

'Oh, not for her! I don't blame Lilli for one single thing. She's so young. How was she supposed to resist Maryn once he'd set his heart on having her? I certainly never could, so I'll not be finding fault with her.' Bellyra paused, and oddly enough she was smiling. 'The potion would be for me. It would solve so many inconveniences.'

'Ah. Well, there I have to agree with you. Unfortunately, I don't have any such thing among my medicinals.'

'So I feared.'

'Here's a thought to hold, though. No matter how many mistresses Maryn might have, you'll always be his only wife.'

'Not true! Once the priests proclaim him king, he'll marry again, won't he? And to his one true love, I think me, beyond any lass of the moment or me.'

Nevyn sighed, nodding his agreement.

'You warned me,' Bellyra went on. 'I wrote it down in my book at the time. Maryn will always love the kingdom more than anything else, you told me. And I fear me you were right. I suppose that's why his women don't bother me. They don't have his heart either.'

'That's certainly true. You know, your highness, once Maryn is seated as king, the kingdom will belong to you as well as to him. He needs you rather badly. Your advice he'll always be able to trust. You won't be flattering him to get land and honours out of him.'

'Just so. I know there'll be plenty of compensations. I also wish I weren't so given to self-pity.'

'Oh come now! I can imagine other women in your position taking things a great deal more badly than this.'

'My thanks. I do appreciate it.' Bellyra paused, thinking. 'I wish I had somewhat that was all my own. My station in life I owe to Maryn. My children are Maryn's. My duties are those of Maryn's wife. He's blasted lucky I love him so much, or I'd hate him.'

They shared another laugh.

'Well, then,' Nevyn said. 'Perhaps you should find a thing that's yours alone. What makes you happy?'

'The most peculiar things. Truly, I should be positively giddy with joy over this dun. There are so many odd corners of it to poke around in. I loved doing that in Cerrmor, poking around in old rooms and learning odd bits of the history of the place.'

'Then here's what your herbman prescribes. Get the heralds to cut you up some calfskins and turn them into parchments. Go poking around to your heart's content and write everything down, just like you did in Cerrmor. By sheerest chance I know a fair bit about the oldest broch, and you can start there.'

Bellyra laughed, seemed to be about to speak, and from her smile she was about to mock the idea. Then she let the smile fade.

'You know, I think me I'll do that,' she said at last. 'It sounds a bit daft, but truly, Dun Deverry is the most important holding under the high king's dominion. Why not write its tale down? And I'll hold you to that promise about the lore.'

'Have no fear. I'll honour it.'

'I should go,' Bellyra went on. 'Probably Elyssa and Degwa are frantic by now, wondering where I am.'

'No doubt. I'll walk back with you.'

'My thanks. Do come visit us in the women's hall, will you?'

'Gladly. What's it like?'

'Oh gods!' Bellyra rolled her eyes. 'It might do to house

prize cattle. It's a good thing we brought so many furnishings with us.'

Nevyn got a cloak, and they went downstairs. Just outside the door a man stood in the ward, walking back and forth as if he were waiting for someone. Nevyn held up his lantern and caught the fellow in its light.

'Maddyn?' Nevyn said. 'What are you doing here?'

'My apologies, my lord.' Maddyn bowed to Bellyra. 'Begging your pardon and all, your highness, but I happened to see you crossing the ward, and I wondered if somewhat was wrong, like. I thought I'd wait to see if you needed an escort back to the women's hall.'

'I think,' Nevyn broke in, 'that it would be far more politic if I escorted the lady.'

'Oh probably so,' Bellyra said. 'But come with us, Maddo, if you'd like.'

Her use of the bard's nickname struck Nevyn like a warning. Don't be a fool! he told himself. What's the source of her sorrow, anyway, but her being entirely too faithful to her husband?

When Owaen led the honour guard out, Branoic went down to the ward to bid them farewell. The autumn morning was so crisp he wrapped himself in a warm cloak. To escort Lord Riddmar to Dun Deverry the prince was sending two hundred men, a hundred and fifty from the Cerrmor warband and fifty silver daggers. Men and horses milled around whilst they tried to draw up in some sort of decent order. Branoic stood on the steps, out of the way, where Maddyn eventually joined him.

'I'm cursed glad I'm not riding with this detail,' Branoic said. 'Look at Owaen strut! He's taking the prince's command as seriously as a wretched priest.'

As if to continue the thought a silver horn blew six urgent notes. Carrying the horn, Owaen was riding up and down the line on his grey gelding, yelling at everyone to get ready to fall in when the troop began to move out of the gates. At last the men seemed to have sorted themselves out well enough to please him. He took his place at the head of the line and shouted the order to march. The mob of men and horses unwound like a spiral, riding two abreast out the gates and down.

'Where will they be meeting our prince's brother?' Branoic said.

'Half-brother,' Maddyn said. 'At Hendyr. I'm surprised you didn't ride with them to ask Tieryn Anasyn for his sister's hand.'

'He already told Lilli he had no objections. Old Nevyn's sent him a letter, to make everything right and proper, like.'

'A tieryn's sister, is it? You'll be rising high in the world, Lord Branoic.'

'Ah hold your tongue or I'll shove it down your throat!'

When the last of the troop had ridden out, Branoic and Maddyn returned to the great hall. They fetched themselves ale, then sat down not far from the table of honour, empty at this hour.

'We're almost up to strength,' Maddyn remarked. 'I'll keep my eye out for good men whilst Owaen's gone.'

'How many silver daggers did Owaen leave behind?'

'About twenty. It should be enough to guard the prince in the middle of his own fortress.'

Branoic was about to answer when he saw Lilli coming down the staircase. He started to rise and join her when he saw Councillor Oggyn hurrying to meet her. Oggyn took something out of his shirt and handed it to Lilli so furtively that he might as well have shouted aloud that he was trying to keep a secret. Now what's all this? Branoic thought. Lilli took the mysterious something, slipped it into her kirtle, then turned and went back up the stairs, while Oggyn came back down to the hall.

'I wonder what that was about,' Maddyn said quietly.

'Slimy Oggo, you mean?' Branoic said. 'I wonder too. Mayhap it was just a gift from the prince or suchlike.'

'Branno, can you really go through with this wedding?'

'Why wouldn't I?'

'Well, aren't you jealous of him?'

Branoic considered the question seriously while Maddyn watched, his dark eyes full of honest concern.

'I am,' Branoic said at last. 'But not enough so that it matters. Now, if it were any man but our prince, we'd have this out with cold steel.'

'Very well, then. If it were me, I'd be cursing him daily, prince or no.'

Maddyn was leaning back in his chair, looking absently away, but something in his voice caught Branoic's attention, something painful. Since he had no idea of what to say to address it, he said nothing.

Lilli was so eager to read the prince's note that she climbed the stairs too fast. At the top she had to rest longer than she liked, but she gained her chamber without coughing – a solid victory. She sat on a chair in the sunlight and read Maryn's letter twice through.

'Forgive me, my lady. I hold you in no less esteem than before, but affairs of state have much distracted me. Stay in your chamber this afternoon, unless Nevyn has need of you, of course.'

Lilli kissed the writing, then got up and hid the letter with his others.

The afternoon dragged itself along. She practised her reading and embroidered a band of knotwork on Branoic's shirt. She kept breaking off whatever she was doing to go lean out of her window and squint at the sun. When it disappeared behind the dun, she judged its progress by the shadows creeping across the ground below.

That afternoon Lilli realized what a treasure she'd thrown away by cutting herself off from the princess and her women. Always before she had lived her real life in the women's hall among other women who did the same. Men came and went; their fighting determined the course of women's lives, just as they gave their women children. But when it came to raising the children, or living with the inevitable widow-hood, women had other women, and they were the ones who mattered.

'I've got no one to talk with,' Lilli said aloud. 'Oh Goddess, what have I done?'

Sunset touched the sky with flame, but still Maryn didn't come. At last, when she could see the first star blooming in the pale evening sky, the door opened. She spun around just as he slipped in, carrying a candle lantern.

'I brought you some fire,' he said. 'It's growing cold out, Lilli, and so you'd best light that wood I see in your hearth.'

'My thanks, my prince. It's so wonderful to see you.'

'Is it?' Maryn set the lantern down on the mantel. 'I can't stay but a few moments.'

Tears came before she could stop them and slid down her cheeks. Maryn crossed the room in a few quick strides and enfolded her in his arms. She clung to him while he stroked her hair.

'Forgive me. My days aren't my own any more.'

'I know.' At last she managed to staunch the shameful tears. 'Of course.'

He kissed her, but she could feel the distance he'd set between them. With a long sigh he let her go.

'I'd best be off,' Maryn said. 'Till tomorrow afternoon, my lady. I'll do my best to get away then.'

'That will be splendid.'

Maryn kissed her one last time and left. For a moment she stood looking at the closed door. This is what being the king's mistress will mean, she thought. Waiting and waiting for the few moments the wretched kingdom will let him give me! Her heart seemed to chill and sink within her. And yet, even in the midst of his delicate manoeuvres, devolving the Cerrmor rhan, trying to outguess the king of Eldidd – even then he had worried about her being cold. She'd never known another lord who would have done the same.

She took the candle lantern and knelt down by the hearth, extracted the burning candle and touched it to the waiting tinder. The straw caught with a crackle; a fine web of fire blazed over the kindling, which smoked, then caught as well. Lilli sat back on her heels and returned the candle to the lantern. The smaller logs were beginning to burn, and the warmth swept over her. Salamanders appeared to caper in the flames. She got up and went to her window to close the shutters, but lingered to see the night sky deepen to a field of stars. She wondered if Maryn would come to her on the morrow or if she'd watch the stars alone then, too.

Her days devolved into a tedious pattern of waiting for one man or another. In the mornings she could walk abroad, but in the afternoons she waited for her prince. Maryn sent notes, and occasionally he came to her chamber for a few quick words and kisses. Nevyn was much concerned with the priests of Bel and their stubborn refusal to name a day when Maryn would become king. Without her dweomer work, all Lilli could do was read lore, and whilst the dweomer demands a great deal of memorizing, lore work alone can chill the soul. Nevyn at least would appear at the end of the day. They would eat together while they discussed her reading and her health.

'The weather's getting quite cold,' Nevyn said one evening. 'You should spend as little time outside as possible.'

'Ah ye gods! I'll go mad!'

Nevyn raised one bushy eyebrow.

'It's so awful,' Lilli went on, 'sitting here alone all day.'

'Why don't you go join the other women?'

'And face the princess?'

'Lilli, Bellyra blames you for naught.'

Lilli picked up a slice of bread and broke it in half.

'Come now,' Nevyn said. 'Ask Elyssa if you don't believe me.'

'It's not that I don't believe you. Maryn's asked me to wait here for him in case he can get away.'

'It would do him good to show up here one day and find you gone.'

'But then I'd miss my chance to see him.'

Nevyn rolled his eyes heavenward.

'Things are about to get worse when it comes to demands upon the prince,' Nevyn said. 'Gwerbret Ammerwdd of Yvrodur is on his way here to discuss the devolvement of the Cerrmor rhan. He heads the Council of Electors, you see.'

Lilli began shredding the bread into crumbs. After a moment she heard him sigh.

'I'm being so strict about your health for a reason,' Nevyn said at last. 'At the moment your cough results only from a congestion of the lungs. What if it turns into a consumption?'

Lilli looked up fast and felt as if all the blood were draining from her face. Nevyn leaned back in his chair; never before had she thought of him as truly old, despite his white hair, but that night he did look old and sad as well.

'It's a terrible thing to have your youth eaten up by illness,' Nevyn said. 'But it's better than dying young.'

'Just so.' Lilli felt her voice shake. 'I didn't realize this cough was so perilous.'

'Well, it is. Will you swear to me you'll guard your health, no matter what the prince may or may not do?'

'I will, truly. I'm so frightened.'

'I'd hoped to spare you that, but mayhap I wasn't being wise. You deserve to know the truth. I brought back my books of physick and herb lore when we visited Cerrmor, and I've been studying them most carefully. There seems to be little to be done for a consumption in the lungs. Not Galyn, not the great Ippocratrix himself, not even the Bardekian Karliko know how to cure it. Ippocratrix does say that if a lass be losing flesh and having trouble with her breathing, the best preventative is intercourse with a man. I have my doubts, but then, you've taken that medicament on your own.'

Lilli blushed, and he laughed at her.

After Nevyn left, Lilli dragged her chair over to the fire and sat down close to the warmth. Life seemed so bitterly unfair. She'd blossomed as a woman and found the great love of her life – but had everything ended so soon? She could see herself ending up a prisoner to ill health in the grim towers of Dun Deverry, or at the best becoming Branoic's poor frail wife that everyone pitied. On the hearth the fire crackled and blazed in a shower of sparks, glorious and gold only to die away in a few heartbeats. Perhaps her life would do the same.

And what of Branoic? she asked herself. She'd not seen him in days, shut away as she'd been. Once before she'd managed to call him to her by dweomer. She thought of him, sounded his name in her thoughts, and all at once she saw him in the fire. First it seemed that he and Maddyn the bard were sitting, as tiny as dolls, in among the logs; then her vision suddenly swooped into the flames, and it seemed that she stood near them at a table in the great hall. She could hear nothing, however, but the crackling of the fire in her hearth. A puzzled Branoic was looking around him. He got up, said a few words to Maddyn, then headed for the stairs.

Her triumph died when she remembered that Nevyn had forbidden her to work any dweomer, not even simple exercises, and scrying was far from simple. She broke the vision and found herself back in front of her fire. The warmth, the feel of the chair under her, the smell of pine smoke – they were all so solid that she decided she really hadn't had a vision. She'd fallen asleep and dreamt it; that was all. In the fire a log slipped in a fine spray of flame-red jewels. She got up, looking for the poker, just as Branoic knocked on her door and called her name.

Lilli screamed. She stuffed her hand into her mouth to stifle it just as Branoic shoved the door open and strode in, reaching for his sword's hilt.

'I'm all right,' she said. 'You just startled me.'

'Did I? I could have sworn I heard you calling me.'

'Well, so I did, but I never thought it would work.'

Branoic stared at her, then burst out laughing. He turned and shut the door.

'We're a fine pair, aren't we?' He walked over to the hearth. 'Here, I'll mend up the fire for you.'

'My thanks.' She handed him the poker. 'My maidservants brought up some big logs – there, under the window.'

Lilli sat back down and watched him fussing with the fire. He picked up in one hand a log that would have strained her to lift with two and set it carefully in place.

'That should do for a while.' Branoic laid the poker down. 'Is this why you called me? To tend your hearth?'

'It wasn't. I just wanted to see you.'

'That gladdens my heart. I've been worrying. I keep asking old Nevyn how you fare, and he keeps shaking his head and looking grim.'

'Well, it's not that I'm horribly ill yet. It's that I could be, if I don't take care of myself.'

Branoic smiled, so sincerely pleased that she rose and laid her hands on his chest. Obligingly he kissed her, then took another. She realized that it wasn't only Maryn she missed, but his lovemaking.

'Branno?' Lilli said. 'I just thought of somewhat.'

'Indeed?' He smiled down at her. 'What?'

'We're betrothed in everyone's eyes.'

He considered this, his head cocked a little to one side; then he smiled, slowly this time.

'So we are,' he said. 'You honour me, my lady.'

When she slid her arms around his neck, he stooped, caught her, and picked her up to carry her to the bed.

Making parchment from calfskin is not such an easy thing. Bellyra was expecting to wait weeks for the materials for her new book, but fortunately the prince's heralds had brought blank sheets with them, ready for writs of attainder and banishment, should the fortunes of war require such. Gavlyn delivered her a share himself, although he had to wait until Maryn was in attendance upon his wife in the women's hall before he could enter. On a sunny morning he laid the parchments down on a table by a window. Bellyra ran her hand over them, just the colour of cream and as smooth, neatly scored with a blunt stylus to mark out the writing lines and the margins.

'My thanks, good herald,' she said. 'These will do splendidly.'

'Most welcome, your highness,' Gavlyn said. 'May you fill them with happiness as well as words.'

Gavlyn bowed again, walked backwards, and bowed himself out of the door. Maryn strolled over to examine her new treasure. He ran his fingertips down the surface of one piece and nodded his approval.

'What are you planning on using these for?' he said.

'Lore about Dun Deverry. What's in it, and its history, and any oddities I can discover.'

Maryn looked utterly baffled.

'Like the book I found down in Dun Cerrmor,' she said, 'and then I finished out the blank pages.'

'Ah. I do remember that, truly. Very well, if it amuses you. Except – wait a moment. I remember what you were like then, poking around filthy old chambers and sitting with the servants in the kitchens and suchlike. You're not going to do that again, are you?'

'I am. How else can I find out what I want to know?'

'Well, I don't want you to go about alone. Some of the floors in these old towers are half rotted through. And it's not seemly, anyway.'

'I'll take one of the pages.'

'That's not sufficient. Take a pair of men from my guard.'

'They'll get in the way. The old people aren't going to talk freely if they've got a great hulking pair of silver daggers looming over them.'

'Only one man then, and some pages, but I'll not have my wife wandering around alone like some servant lass. Here, I know. What about Maddyn? He's a bard; he'll find the lore interesting.'

'Done, then. I shan't mind him as much. Which reminds me.' Bellyra laughed, feeling pleasantly wicked. 'Have you heard his song about the fox who's really Councillor Oggyn?'

'What?' He picked up her mood and grinned. 'Shall I ask him to play it?'

'Not right out in the great hall where poor Oggyn could hear it. It's a flyting, because Oggyn tried to extort some coin out of men who wanted to be silver daggers. He made them pay him for introductions to Owaen.'

'Ye gods! Owaen might have killed him for that.'

'He nearly did, apparently.'

'Huh, no wonder Oggyn kept urging me to send him off to fetch Riddmar.' Maryn shook his head in mock sadness. 'How Oggo's greedy little heart must have ached! I will ask Maddyn, if I have a moment, but when that will be, the gods only know. And now I'd best be off, my lady. Nevyn will be waiting for me.'

Bellyra sent one of her servant girls off to find a page, and him she sent off to find Maddyn. Although she couldn't receive the bard in the women's hall, she saw nothing wrong with standing just outside the open door and talking with him in the corridor. When she explained her new venture, he seemed genuinely pleased to be invited along.

'Our prince thinks I need guarding,' Bellyra said.

'Treasures should be guarded, your highness,' Maddyn said. 'And a treasure you are.'

'Oh, get along with you! What's this? The wars really must be over, if silver daggers are turning into courtiers.'

Maddyn laughed. 'Maybe so,' he said. 'But I'll be honoured to be your guard, your highness.'

'Splendid! What I want to do first is just walk around and see everything. Such as the bolt hole. Maryn's told me about the silver daggers opening the gates.' She felt her sunny mood disappear. 'My heart aches, thinking of your losses. I'll write about Caradoc in my book, so he'll be remembered.'

Maddyn's eyes filled with tears. Hastily he turned away,

wiping his face on the sleeve of his shirt. The silver dagger device embroidered there, she realized, summed up his life, his honour, and his loyalties beyond even those he paid to her husband. Losing so many comrades must have wounded him worse than a sword.

'My apologies, your highness,' he mumbled. 'You took me by surprise, like.'

'None needed. I know you honoured the captain. So did my husband, and he's told me that he misses Caradoc still.'

'Well, so we all do.' Maddyn managed a smile. 'My thanks for the honour you'll be paying him.'

'Most welcome. I'll get my cloak.'

Bellyra returned to the women's hall to find Degwa, standing off to one side but close enough to the door to hear anything that might have been said. Degwa dropped her a distracted sort of curtsy.

'I'll be back in a bit,' Bellyra said. 'Make sure nothing happens to my parchments.'

'Of course, your highness. They're ever so lovely.'

When she left the broch with her silver dagger in attendance, Bellyra took a pair of the youngest pages with them as well, as much to give the boys a chance to run around and play as for the propriety of the thing. Maddyn led her through the maze of walls, sheds, towers, and wards to the ruins that hid the bolt hole. Men of the fortguard stood on duty there all day and all night, matched by another guard far away, inside the ruins where the escape tunnel debouched beyond the dun walls.

'Our prince is talking of rebuilding that dun and settling it upon some particularly loyal lord,' Bellyra told him.

'That's a good idea, your highness,' Maddyn said. 'It would be a fitting demesne for Branoic, if I can presume to offer my advice.'

'You may. It's a good idea. I'll mention it to the prince.'

'We'd best do somewhat about getting Branoic and his lady married soon,' Maddyn went on, 'before he gets her with child. Well, if he hasn't already.'

'Oh indeed? And why are you worrying about that?'

'There are nights when he doesn't sleep in the barracks, and Branoic's never been a man for sleeping out in the rain. One of the other lads twitted him about it, and I had to step between them. Branno was ready to kill him over the insult to his betrothed.'

Bellyra smiled, and this time her wicked feeling had little of the pleasant about it. Revenge upon her husband tasted sweet, but beyond that Lilli's unfaithfulness to Maryn had its practical advantages. The prince would tire of Lilli sooner or later, no doubt, but now, when she had a child, there'd be no talk of it being another royal bastard. Having one of those out in fosterage was quite enough.

It also occurred to her, as they walked through the sunny ward, that Lilli was young, so dreadfully young that she might well not realize just how dangerous her situation was, caught between two men like the hull of a boat twixt rocks. Since she could hardly warn Lilli herself, she decided to send Elyssa for as honest a talk as Lilli would allow.

Nevyn set the wood box in the centre of his table, then opened his dweomer sight and inspected each etheric seal. They held strong, but he was aware of a feeling emanating through the wood, the touch of some force that manifested as a deep unease. When he shut down his dweomer sight it appeared ordinary enough.

'I swear the wretched curse is gathering strength!' Nevyn said. 'Look at it, Lilli, but don't touch it. Do you see anything odd?'

'I do, my lord. It's almost like it's glowing, or maybe it's making the air tremble, but it's all oily and strange. Oh here, that doesn't make any sense.'

'I'm afraid that it does. It's drawing power from a very unpleasant part of the Inner Lands.'

On a stormy afternoon they were sitting in Nevyn's tower

chamber. Rain splashed down onto the roof overhead, and the wind moaned, trembling the leather drapes over the windows. Every now and then it would flip up the edge of a hide and come rushing into the room until Nevyn had despaired of keeping candles lit. Huge balls of glowing silver light clung to the walls and lit the chamber with a peculiarly even glow.

'We'd best have a good look at the thing,' Nevyn said. 'Shall I take it out of the box?'

With a little cry Lilli laid a hand to her throat. Nevyn's first thought was that the curse tablet was terrifying her, but then he realized that she was staring at something behind him. He turned round and saw the spirit who aped Lady Merodda, standing just inside the doorway.

'A good evening to you,' Nevyn said. 'Have you come to let me help you?'

The spirit laughed. 'I'm not so easy to trick, old man. What you have in that box belongs to Lady Merodda. Did you steal it, too?'

'I won't be answering your questions until you answer some of mine.'

'That I won't do.'

'Then I'll tell you naught.' Nevyn leaned over the box and started to open it. 'You'd best be gone. I'll be drawing a dweomer circle in a moment, and it might trap you.'

'Well, I might answer one question.' The spirit took a step closer.

'Very well.' Nevyn let the box lie. 'You say this belongs to Lady Merodda. Did she create it, then?'

'She didn't, but that ugly man who served her.' She glanced at Lilli. 'Your uncle slew him.'

Lilli nodded, her face dead-pale. 'So I heard.'

'I found a baby with this tablet,' Nevyn said to the spirit. 'Was he Merodda's own?'

'I'll not answer that till you answer one for me. Where is she now?'

'She's dead.'

'What does that mean?'

'She's gone to the Otherlands. She no longer lives on the earth.'

'Where does she live?'

'She doesn't live at all. Here.' Nevyn glanced around, saw a bit of charcoal lying on the table, and picked it up. 'She's all broken and gone, like this.' He crushed the charcoal in his fingers and let the black dust sift to the floor.

'And just what is that supposed to mean?'

'I don't know how to make you understand.'

'You lie, old man. You must know where she is.'

'I tried to tell you.'

The spirit snarled like an animal. Her careful image of Merodda wavered and swelled like an image reflected in a pool of water when a breeze disturbs it.

'I shall find her, old man. I warn you. I shall find her, and then together we will come get her daughter back.'

'I was not stolen,' Lilli snapped. 'I came of my own free will.'

The spirit ignored her.

'You can't find Merodda,' Nevyn said. 'She's dead and gone.'

The spirit screeched like an angry lynx and slapped at him. Nevyn flung up one hand and sketched a banishing pentagram in the air. With one last snarl she vanished. Nevyn let out his breath in a puff of relief.

'Will she keep troubling us?' Lilli said.

'I have no idea.' Nevyn paused, considering her. 'Are you frightened of her?'

'Not truly. When she appears, she always startles me, but then I remind myself that she's not truly my mother.' Lilli grinned at him. 'No spirit could be as bad as that.'

'That speaks volumes, doesn't it? Very well, then.' Nevyn laid one finger on the wood box. He could feel nothing particularly unusual, but the spirit's appearance had troubled him, breaking his concentration. 'I think I'll put this back for the nonce. But sooner or later, I'll have to think of a way to deal with it.'

'Well and good, my lord. Uh, do you have further need of me?'

'Not in particular. Why? Is Branoic waiting for you?'

'He is.'

'Then by all means go keep your tryst.'

'My thanks.' Lilli blushed, then got up, turning quickly as if to hide it. 'Will I see you at nightfall?'

'Not tonight. I'm having dinner with the prince and Gwerbret Ammerwdd.' Nevyn paused, sighing. 'I suppose I'd best put on a clean shirt, come to think of it. That fancy one with all the blazons. Irritating, but there we are. The prince needs must act like a king these days, and so I'll play the part of a courtier.'

Late that evening Elyssa came to Lilli's chamber, but instead of asking her how she felt and leaving again, she sat herself down without being invited in one of the chairs. A fire was burning in the hearth, and Lilli had closed the shutters over the windows, so that the room glowed warm with comfortable firelight.

'It's good to see you.' Lilli sat down in the other chair.

'Well, we've missed you,' Elyssa said, smiling. 'Lilli, is it truly your illness that's kept you out of the women's hall?'

Lilli felt her face burn with a blush worse than any fever.

'The princess herself asked me to speak to you,' Elyssa went on. 'She thinks that you must fear her, and that distresses her. She bears you no ill will.'

'Truly?'

'Truly. It's not like you're the first lass her husband's fancied.'

'So Nevyn says, too.'

'That must be a hurtful thing to think on.' Elyssa was watching her in concern.

'Well, it is,' Lilli said. 'Everyone tells me that, and they think I'm supposed to feel the better for it, but I don't. I feel like a prize mare, either bred or locked in the stables at her master's whim.'

'That's not far wrong, is it?'

'True spoken. And I keep wondering when he'll find some other horse to ride.'

'He might not, you know. Who knows why men do what they do? Mayhap he's finally found the one lass he's been looking for all these years. If so, won't that ease the princess's heart rather than vex it?'

Lilli considered this with a feeling much like shock.

'You know,' Lilli said at last, 'that's true spoken, but I hadn't thought of it that way.'

'There's a great deal to think about, isn't there? It will take time for you to sort through it all.'

'Just so. And then there's Branoic.'

'The prince will never forbid you that marriage. I hope you realize that.'

'Oh, I do. He has his own sort of honour, Maryn.'

For a moment they sat in silence.

'Tell me to hold my tongue if I'm prying,' Elyssa said at last. 'But do you think you might be with child?'

'Not yet, but truly, it might happen.'

'It will happen, sooner or later.'

'Oh I suppose, but I don't want to think about that.'

'Lilli, Lilli, how old are you? Do you have any clear idea?'

'Well, I was twelve when I came here out of fosterage, and that was over two years ago now. I was born in midsummer, my mother told me once.'

'So let's think: you've seen maybe fifteen years? I've seen a fair few more, and I know it would be for the best if you started thinking about this possible child now. Will it be Maryn's, or could it be your silver dagger's?'

'Either, I suppose.' Lilli shrugged, feeling increasingly miserable. 'I'd never ask the prince to claim it.'

'It's you I'm worried about. What will Branoic say if he thinks the child's not his?'

'You don't understand. Branoic is as devoted to the prince as I am. Why else would he want to marry me, knowing what he knows?'

'He knows?' Elyssa stared for a long moment. 'Well, then!' She rose, smiling. 'I think me you've made a good choice for your husband. Now, please remember to come to us tomorrow, in the late morning, say, or early afternoon. You can help tease Decci about Oggyn.'

Only later, long after Elyssa had gone, did it occur to Lilli to wonder how she'd known that Branoic had been sleeping in her chamber now and again. She felt suddenly sick, wondering if Maryn knew it as well.

On the morrow, Lilli woke up convinced that she'd continue to avoid the other women as she'd been doing, but as the morning dragged on, her fat conviction faded into a thin fear. Finally, not long before noon, she decided that she was tired of her own cowardice. She left her chamber and went up to the next floor of the broch to the women's hall. The sight of the door, and the thought of opening it, filled her with a sudden revulsion, so strong that she finally realized it had little to do with Bellyra. She'd spent time in this hall with both Bevyan and her mother. For a moment she thought she could see them, pale grey wraiths, walking down the corridor toward her, yet she knew she was only seeing her own memories. They clawed her heart worse than any ghost.

With one last gasp for breath, Lilli pushed open the door and walked in. Across the big sunny room Bellyra, Degwa and Elyssa were sitting at a wooden table frame, stitching on a bed hanging. For a moment Lilli could neither speak nor move, not, however, from the sight.

'It's so different,' Lilli blurted out. 'The hall, I mean.'

'It certainly is,' Bellyra said, smiling. 'I couldn't believe how awful it was when we first arrived. Do come in, Lilli, and have a look around.'

'My thanks, your highness.' Lilli curtsied, then shut the door. 'It's truly lovely.'

All the old furnishings had been replaced by the princess's own. Bright tapestries graced the walls, and Bardek carpets lay like little gardens upon the polished floor. The chairs, the cushions, Bellyra's little tables with her silver oddments – she had brought Cerrmor with her. None of Lilli's memories belonged to this hall.

'It's splendid,' Lilli said.

Out of sheer habit she took a chair and brought it over to the frame. When she sat down, Elyssa handed her a needle threaded with bright red wool.

'If you'll start on that wyvern there,' Elyssa said, 'I'll just finish off these spirals.'

Lilli brought her thread through to the front of the hanging and began to stitch, one hand below, one above, in a rhythm so familiar that her self-imposed exile struck her as one of the stupidest things she'd ever done. And the talk, the news of the dun, news of Maryn's allies and the negotiations over Cerrmor – after the silences of her sickroom no bard song had ever sounded so sweet.

'Lilli,' Bellyra said eventually. 'You're so quiet today!'

'Well, your highness, my life's been terribly dull. I've been shut up so long.'

'Oh huh! And what about Branoic? Is he dull?'

Everyone laughed, including Lilli. As they talked about Branoic, and the sort of demesne that Maryn would settle upon him, Lilli began to feel that her affair with the prince had perhaps never happened. Most certainly it had lasted only a brief time, and perhaps it had ended already. If so, she decided, she could not only live without him – she was also in some deep way relieved.

And yet, about the middle of the afternoon, Maryn opened the door to the women's hall and started to walk in. For a moment he froze, his face utterly expressionless as he considered the group at the embroidery frame. When the women began to rise, he waved at them to sit, turned on his heel, and left, slamming the door behind him.

'How very odd,' Elyssa remarked. 'Well, our prince is much distracted these days, what with the electors to worry about.'

'How kind you are,' Bellyra said, grinning. 'He looked terrified to me.'

Lilli bent her head and paid strict attention to her stitches. She could feel her heart pounding like a traitor, crying out that she loved him still.

After the dinner hour Lilli was sitting with Nevyn in her chamber when Maryn appeared. He walked in without knocking, then stood hesitating at the sight of his councillor.

'I assume, my liege,' Nevyn said, 'that you'd like me to leave.'

'I would, truly.'

Nevyn smiled, gathered up the book he'd been showing her, and with a bow to the prince, left. Lilli felt as if she were crouching in her chair, half-afraid Maryn would leave quickly, half-afraid he'd stay for a long while. He sat himself down in the chair Nevyn had just vacated and stretched his long legs out toward the fire.

'I take it the princess asked you to attend upon her today,' Maryn said.

'She did, your highness.'

'Don't call me that!'

'My apologies.'

For a long while Maryn scowled into the fire, which leapt over big logs in the stone hearth. The salamanders lurking in the caves of glowing coals glowered right back, but fortunately of course he couldn't see them. Lilli folded her hands in her lap and tried to think of something to say.

'Forgive me, my lady,' Maryn said at last. 'I don't know what's wrong with me these days.'

'It's all the waiting, isn't it? Sitting around and talking and waiting for summer. It must be dreadful for a man like you.'

'I suppose it is. But what is this creature, a man like me?'

Lilli was too surprised to answer. Maryn looked up with a peculiar lopsided smile.

'Don't let me spoil this little span of time we have, my lady.' He stood up, glancing around. 'Come lie down with me instead.'

Yet after his lovemaking, when he'd dressed and gone, Lilli lay awake for a long while, wondering what his question meant, and what could have driven him to ask it. Finally she fell asleep without an answer.

Gwerbret Ammerwdd of Yvrodur stood nearly as tall as Branoic, and he was as broad in the shoulders. Grey streaked his dark hair and stained his moustache. As he talked, he reached up to stroke the moustache repeatedly with one wide hand, as if he feared he'd lost it. Since the prince had given him leave to stand, he leaned against the wall next to the hearth in the prince's reception room and considered his sworn liege lord with cold dark eyes. Maryn, lounging in a chair, looked steadily back.

'I understand your reasoning,' Ammerwdd said at last. 'But there's going to be a cursed lot of grumbling about your handing Cerrmor over to a lad.'

'He'll be a man before long,' Maryn said, 'and is that truly what the grumbling will be about?'

Ammerwdd smiled, glancing at Nevyn and Oggyn, who sat at a table off to one side, then back to the prince. When Oggyn looked as if he might speak, Nevyn raised a hand and silenced him.

'Cerrmor's a rich prize,' the gwerbret said. 'I'd never deny that.'

Maryn got up, beckoned to Ammerwdd to follow him, and joined his two councillors at the table, where a map of Deverry lay spread out. Maryn pointed to the north-east corner and laid a fingertip on one town.

'This is Cantrae,' Maryn said. 'It belongs to the Boars. Follow the river down, your grace, and we have Glasloc, also in the Boar's hands. Then there's the old Wolf lands. They have a claim on Lughcarn as well, and the gwerbret there is trying to see which way the wind blows before he pledges to me. He doesn't know it, but he's waited too long. If the summer's fighting goes well, all these will be mine by attainder. I intend to be generous to my Cerrmor vassals.'

Ammerwdd nodded, stroking his moustache.

'These lands are all a cursed long ride from the Belaver,' the gwerbret said at last. 'Men who have land there aren't going to want to give it up and move north.'

'Who says they have to give up their old holdings? Well, whoever the Electors appoint as Gwerbret Cantrae will, and then Lughcarn as well. But the lesser lords won't be under that sort of obligation.'

Ammerwdd started to speak, then laughed, a short bark that sounded as angry as it did merry.

'I like that,' the gwerbret said. 'Divide their holdings; let them spend half the year riding back and forth; keep them out of trouble.'

'So I thought.' Maryn turned to Nevyn. 'Tell me, councillor. If Glasloc returns to Gwerbret Daeryc, will he give up Mabyndyr?'

'He will, your highness,' Nevyn said. 'And Mabyndyr's worth more than Glasloc.'

'And then, my liege, there are the northern demesnes,' Oggyn put in.

'That's quite true.' Ammerwdd swept his hand across northern Gwaentaer. 'How many of these lords will hold loyal to you in the spring?'

'I don't know,' Maryn said. 'Probably none of them.'

Both men laughed, a hard grim chuckle. Their cynicism was justified, Nevyn assumed, but not long after something happened that proved him wrong.

On a day when the chill wind hinted of autumn coming, one of Maryn's new vassals rode in with his honour guard of fifteen men, and it was the last one that any of them would have expected: Lord Nantyn. As soon as he saw his horses

well stabled and his men housed, Nantyn stomped into the
great hall and yelled for the prince. He was a burly man still,
Nantyn, even though his white hair lay thin on his skull; he
had watery blue eyes and a face pocked with old scars. Nevyn,
who happened to be in the hall, came hurrying to greet him
with a bow.

'Well, good morrow, my lord,' Nevyn said. 'I've sent a page
off to fetch Prince Maryn.'

'Good.' Nantyn peered at him for a moment. 'Ah, that's right.
You're that cursed sorcerer. Well, I've come on an important
matter.'

Nevyn seated the lord at the honour table and sent a servant
for mead. Since Nevyn had heard the gossip about Nantyn, that
he'd beaten at least one wife to death for no particular reason,
he was predisposed to detest him, and small talk was difficult.
Fortunately Maryn came trotting down the stairs soon after.
Nantyn rose, made a sort of bend at the knees coupled with
a bob of his head that would have to do for a kneel, and got
right to the point.

'Braemys is scouring the countryside for bandits,' Nantyn
said. 'Enlisting them, I mean, not hanging them like he should
be doing. There's a cursed lot of desperate men out there, my
liege, and he's offered them all a place in his warband.'

'Ah horseshit!' Maryn matched his way of speaking to his
hearer. 'There's more than one way to raise an army, eh?'

'Just so.' Nantyn sat back down without being asked
and picked up his goblet again. 'I figured you'd better know
it now.'

'You have my sincere thanks.' Maryn sat and motioned to
the servant. 'Mead for me and the councillor, lad. I'm surprised
you'd ride all this way to tell me.'

'So am I, your highness.' Nantyn laughed, a sound more
like another man's death rattle. 'But winter gives a man time
to think. I'm sick as I can be of the cursed pissproud Boars.
Suppose they win. Once they take all the good land south of
them, they'll be coming after my land and anyone else's they

can get their trotters on. I want my grandson to inherit, not some stinking Boarling.'

Nevyn opened his dweomer sight and studied the lord. Nantyn's aura was a ghastly sort of blood-red, not surprising, considering the sort of life he'd led. Nevyn could tell, though, that he was undeniably sincere in his loyalty to the new king. He was also telling the absolute truth as he saw it about Braemys's recruiting tactics. *The last lord I ever would have expected to hold loyal!* Nevyn thought to himself.

It was the best omen he'd had in a long time. If men like Nantyn were sick of fighting, then the astral tides had turned for certain, washing the kingdom toward peace. If only the wretched priests would see it, too! Yet as the conversation went on, Nantyn solved that on-going problem for him as well.

'I was hoping to send for all my vassals soon,' Maryn said at one point, 'to celebrate my assuming the kingship.'

'Huh!' Nantyn snorted. 'That won't happen, my liege, till you've defeated Braemys.'

'Truly? Why?'

'I forget you don't know the priests here in Dun Deverry. They've made themselves rich out of these wars. They're not going to declare for one candidate till they know beyond doubting he's won.' Nantyn paused for a swallow of mead. 'Greedy bastards, but they're not stupid. Bring them Braemys's head on a pike, and they'll seat you as high king quick enough.'

'I should have seen that long ago,' Nevyn muttered.

Nantyn shrugged, reached across the table for the flagon, and poured himself more mead.

'Well and good, then,' Maryn said, 'Come the summer, and we'll do just that.'

Nantyn laughed and saluted him with his goblet. With muttered excuses Nevyn left Nantyn to the prince and fled the great hall.

Long shadows lay across the ward. When Nevyn glanced up at the sky he saw a streak of mackerel clouds coming in from the north, signalling a rainstorm, he supposed, since it was far too early for snow. As he was walking over to the side broch that held his chamber, he saw Princess Bellyra and something of a retinue – Maddyn, two pages, and Otho – all standing with their heads tipped back. They appeared to be looking at a narrow tower that graced one of the newer buildings. When Nevyn joined them, Bellyra explained their odd posture.

'Look how it leans,' she said. 'I was wondering why.'

Nevyn looked and saw the alarming angle the tower made to the ward below.

'It's badly built, that's why,' Otho snapped. 'They just stuck it on top, like, instead of starting at the ground and digging a proper foundation.'

'It does look dangerous,' Nevyn said. 'One of these days it could come down of its own weight. Well, or so I think. Otho?'

'I agree, my lord. A bad job all round.'

'I've looked through some old accounts Oggyn found,' Bellyra said. 'The tower was built about fifty years back. The accounts even tell where the stone came from, up in Gwaentaer. They barged it down. Fascinating, I thought.'

Otho nodded his agreement.

'Well, your highness,' Maddyn put in. 'In the last day's fighting, when we finally broke through and took this area, some of the Boar's men were up there dropping stones from the roof. Thanks to the lean the stones fell straight down without bouncing off the walls. So I thought they'd built it that way on purpose, like.'

'Now that I hadn't thought of.' Otho looked profoundly sour. 'You may be right, bard. But it's not stable anyway.'

'Eventually I'm sure our prince will have it down,' Bellyra said. 'But this is all very interesting indeed. I'll have to write about this tower.'

'There's another one round back,' Otho said. 'And just as rickety as this.'

'Oh good! Let's go see!'

The princess and her retinue trooped off, heading around

the central broch complex. Nevyn, however, went back to his chamber where it was warm. There were times when the magical forces that prolonged his life ignored his aching joints.

It was Bellyra's habit to compose in her head, then commit her words to the expensive parchment only after she had them right. Normally she would write in the morning, when the sun came strongly through the windows, but at times she would find herself adding a line or two in the evenings by candlelight. Often forming letters absorbed her until her eyes ached when, as on that evening, she'd found some particularly interesting lore to record.

'Nevyn's told me lots about this broch,' she remarked to Maryn. 'The one we're in. Did you know it was the oldest?'

'I didn't,' Maryn said, yawning.

She turned in her chair to look at him, lounging half-dressed and half-asleep on their bed.

'You find this tedious,' she said.

'I don't. Go on.'

'Well, there was somewhat so odd about the way Nevyn told me about the broch. He was so caught up in it, like, and he made it seem so real. It made me feel that he'd been there and seen it with his own eyes.'

'Oh come now! He's old, truly, but not that old.'

'I do rather know that. It was just his way of telling.' She glanced at the piece of parchment. 'I've got it all down now. But anyway, the king who built it believed in keeping the old ways, and in his time the old ways included sacrificing horses and putting their corpses under the foundations of a new broch, so that's what he did.'

'They must have rotted away by now,' Maryn said. 'Bones and all.'

'Just so. Perhaps that's why your army could take the dun. The old king thought it would never be captured as long as the spirit horses guarded it. Nevyn told me that he'd read in a book that in the Dawntime, the kings would have sacrificed children and buried them instead of horses.'

'Ye gods! Truly?'

'Truly. Oh, and count yourself lucky, my lord and husband, that they don't consecrate kings now the way they did in the Dawntime. You wouldn't have just ridden that white mare in the procession. You would have had to mount her and ride her like a wife, and right in front of everybody, too, so they could be sure you'd really done it and didn't just say you had.'

Maryn blushed scarlet to the tips of his ears, and she laughed at him.

'You're inventing that,' he snarled.

'I'm not. Ask Nevyn if you don't believe me.'

'I'll do naught of the sort!'

'Well, it's true. Nevyn found it in a book that was ever so old.'

'Then you're right: I do count myself lucky. Ye gods!' All at once he smiled at her. 'You've got ink on your nose.'

She also had ink on her fingers, she realized, and her reed pen had gone all mashed at the tip. It's a good thing I seasoned more of them, she thought. She tossed it into the fire, where it burned with a hiss. She wiped her hands on a rag, then blew out the candles. By the light of the fire she walked over to the bed.

'Do you think you could have?' she said to Maryn. 'Taken the mare, I mean, if you had to in order to be king?'

'I have no idea, and I don't care to dwell upon it.'

'Well, I'm just curious. I'm not a man, so how would I know? You couldn't even get drunk first, not too drunk anyway, or you wouldn't be able to do anything at all.'

Maryn rolled his eyes heavenward. She picked up a bone comb from the wood chest under the window and began to comb her hair.

'You're thinking about it,' she said. 'Aren't you?'

'I'm not!'

'I'll wager you are. I hope they washed the mare off first.'

'Just hold your tongue about it!'

'Have I made you angry?'

'What? You haven't. To tell you the truth, I like seeing you like this, so joyous about your lore. It's like you've come alive again.'

'Well, so it is.' She stopped combing and considered for a moment. 'I'd not realized it, but that's true.'

He sat up, smiling at her.

'Come here,' he said. 'There's no use in your combing that out if I'm only going to tousle it for you.'

'And are you, then?'

'You can pretend you're the mare.'

'You beast!' She threw the comb at him.

He ducked, laughing. When she sat down next to him, he took her by the shoulders and kissed her. Wrapped in his arms she could forget everything, good and bad alike.

But later, when he'd fallen asleep, she lay awake, thinking. In a way she was the white mare, she realized. By marrying her, Maryn had married the Cerrmor rhan and the claim on the high kingship with it, just as in the old days the sexual intercourse between king and mare had served as his marriage – but not to the kingdom itself, exactly. To the sovereignty of the kingdom, she thought. That's what they married, and then the ruling is a separate thing from the land itself! The idea was so interesting that she got up, lit a candle from the glowing embers in the hearth, grabbed a fresh pen, and wrote it down.

Over the next few weeks, as the last of the summer vanished into a chill autumn, Maryn stayed in her bed every night. In the mornings he would linger in their chamber. They would sit in the sun if there was any or near the fire if there wasn't, and she would tell him what she'd discovered about the dun's history. Her serving women began to remark upon how happy she looked, and she had to admit that they were right. Others noticed the change in her as well.

'Well, your highness,' Nevyn remarked one afternoon, 'you seem a good bit more cheerful these days.'

'I am, truly,' Bellyra said. 'And I owe you my thanks for the idea of writing in a book again.'

'You're most welcome.'

They were sitting by a window in the women's hall on a day warm enough to leave the opening uncovered for the light. It was a pleasant enough view, Bellyra thought, when the sun gilded the dark towers. Down below in the ward servants were trotting to and fro on various errands, and as she watched, part of the Cerrmor warband returned from exercising their horses. From this height the clatter of hooves on cobbles and the jingle of tack sounded like a cacophony of bells.

'It's not just the book,' Bellyra said. 'Maryn's been much – well, warmer toward me in the past few weeks. He finds me interesting again, I suppose.'

'That's splendid! And it sounds as if you and Maddyn have ferreted out quite a bit of lore, all of it of some importance.'

'I find it so, certainly. I'm never sure if poor Maddo is just being patient because he can't get out of guarding me.'

'Naught of the sort. He told me that he finds it quite interesting.'

'Oh, good! But it's going to be an eccentric sort of lore book. All the other ones I've ever heard of were of herbs or the laws or suchlike.'

'True enough. But I'll wager the priests of Wmm will want copies anyway when you're done.'

'Truly?' Bellyra raised one eyebrow. 'It will be tainted, after all, because I'm a woman.'

'The priesthood of Wmm may not admit women, but it doesn't hold them in scorn, either, the way the priesthood of Bel does. Your book will be very welcome, I assure you.'

'That's gratifying. I was wondering if anyone else but me would ever care, you see.'

'Oh, I think your book will have a good many readers over the years. We'll get the scribes to make up several copies.' Nevyn paused, blinking as if at a sudden thought. 'You've been questioning the various servants, haven't you?'

'I have. They're ever so flattered, too, that someone will listen to them.'

'Well, I was wondering. Have you heard any tales of ghosts? In particular, a woman with blonde hair dressed in mourning – she speaks of a daughter that someone's stolen from her.'

Bellyra considered for a moment.

'I've not,' she said at last. 'I did hear that there used to be a haunted side tower attached to the royal broch. They had it torn down some eighty years ago to quiet the ghost in it.'

'What sort of ghost, did they say?'

'A young lad, a claimant to the throne, who was walled up alive in his chamber and allowed to starve to death.'

'Ych! Well, that's not what I was looking for.'

'Indeed? You mean you have a particular spirit in mind?'

'I do. If she appeared to the servants, they'd think her a ghost, but she's another sort of apparition entirely.'

'Ych, indeed!' Bellyra shuddered at a touch of cold on the back of her neck. 'Well, I've only talked with a few people so far. If I hear anything, I'll be sure to tell you.'

A bit of asking around did bring her several more ghost tales, but none fitted the description Nevyn had given her. She recorded them anyway, to add excitement should anyone want to read her histories.

Nevyn was having no more luck than the princess when it came to discovering the nature of the mysterious spirit who assumed Merodda's form. His books described nothing like her, his meditations told him nothing, and even the Lords of the Elements knew nothing of such as she. Once he saw her walking along the corridor that led to Merodda's old chambers, but at the sight of him she vanished. Finally, after some weeks of his futile investigations, Lilli saw her again.

'It was just as I was waking, my lord,' Lilli told him. 'I thought at first it was a dream about my mother. I do have them, now and again. But anyway, she was standing by the table in my chamber, and she looked just like my mother when she was angry. I asked her what she wanted, and she told me I was a cruel and ungrateful child. I started to cry, and she disappeared.'

'You're sure it wasn't a dream?' Nevyn said. 'It certainly sounds like one.'

'I could feel the wool blankets under my hands. And the tears were wet.'

'Ah. Well, then, you actually did see her. It's interesting that she knows you're Merodda's daughter. Most spirits have no understanding of kin and clan, but it seems to matter to her.' Nevyn paused, considering the idea that had just come to him. 'Tell me, how are you feeling? I've not heard you cough in a good long while.'

'I'm much stronger, my lord.'

'Do you think you're well enough for a bit of excitement? Hunting this spirit, say.'

Lilli's eyes went as wide as a doe's when she's ringed by dogs. 'I could be bait?'

'Only if you're willing.'

'Of course.'

'Of course?' Nevyn paused for a smile.

'Well, I'm frightened, but I want to know what she is. It's fascinating, a sort of ghastly grim fascination, but one nonetheless.'

'Very well, then. Let me tell you what to do.'

Merodda's old chambers still stood empty. In the reception room one of the hides had slipped from its window, and rain puddled under it on the floor. The smell of mildew hung so heavy that Nevyn hurried Lilli into what had once been the bedchamber.

'Lots of dust in here,' he said. 'Good. Now, you stand out of the way whilst I draw our trap.'

With the little broom of sticks he'd brought Nevyn swept a circle into the thick dust, then decorated it with five-pointed stars, one at each cardinal point.

'Or as close to the cardinals as matters,' he remarked cheerfully. 'Spirits rarely understand what north and south and so on mean anyway. Now, step carefully, Lilli, so you don't rub anything out, and go stand just there, in the centre.'

Lilli did as she was told. Nevyn raised his hands above his head and called upon the Light. A sheet of blue fire raced round the circle and formed a wall. When Lilli gasped aloud, he realized that it had manifested on the physical plane as well as the etheric.

'Does somewhat puzzle you?' Nevyn said.

'Not truly. It's much like the circle Brour made for a ritual. But he had to work so hard, my lord. He invoked things and broke out into such a sweat, while you – all at once the fire just sprang up.'

Nevyn laughed. 'Well, when I was an apprentice, I would have had to work much harder, too. Now, let me stand back in the curve of the wall here. Are you ready?'

Lilli nodded. In the dim light she looked pale, but she took a deep breath and steadied herself.

'Mother?' Lilli called out. 'Mother, are you here?'

Nevyn felt the hair on his neck prickle. Some entity was hovering close to them, quite close.

'Oh mother, mother,' Lilli continued. 'Where are you? Please forgive me.'

Across the circle from Nevyn she appeared, so like Merodda that Lilli sobbed aloud, just once.

'I cannot reach you,' the spirit said to Lilli. 'Rub out a bit of that circle, and I'll come to you.'

'I think not.' Nevyn stepped forward.

The spirit snarled and swung toward him, her mouth open like a beast's.

'Who are you?' Nevyn said.

'That I shall never tell you.'

'Why not? Let me help you find peace.'

'Naught will ever bring me peace but my daughter. Her father's hidden her from me.'

'And where has he hidden her?'

The spirit tipped her head to one side and looked him over.

'I'll not answer any more of your questions. You've stolen her daughter, and so no doubt you'll help him steal mine!'

With that she vanished, leaving Lilli shaking in the middle of the circle. With a wave of his hand, Nevyn banished the blue fire.

'Let's go back to my chamber,' he said. 'You need to get warm.'

Although Nevyn's chamber had no hearth – he'd sacrificed a fire to gain a view – his charcoal brazier put out an amazing lot of heat, thanks to the Wildfolk of Fire. He put the chair next to it for Lilli, then perched on the edge of his bed.

'That's better,' he said. 'You've stopped shivering.'

'I'm not sure I was truly cold,' Lilli said. 'It was more seeing the spirit.'

'Well, no doubt. I think it's time I taught you how to make a circle round yourself for protection. You're well enough now to try a simple ritual like that.'

'I'll be glad of it. It would take my mind off – well, uh, I do get bored of an afternoon.'

'Take your mind off what? The prince?'

Lilli nodded, suddenly miserable. 'He's not come to me in ever so long.'

'Oh here, child!' Nevyn said. 'I'm sorry.'

'Don't be. I always knew he'd tire of me sooner or later.' Bitterness cracked her voice. 'I don't want pity!'

'Very well, then. We'll let the matter drop.'

'My thanks.' Lilli wiped her eyes on her sleeve. 'I feel so hatefully greedy. After all, I have Branoic.'

'So you do.'

Nevyn waited for her to say more, but she merely looked across the chamber, her mouth set tight. With a sigh, he changed the subject.

Nevyn stayed awake late that night, sitting in his tower room with only a lantern for company while he thought about Prince Maryn and the dangerous misery he was bringing to the women around him. He had raised Maryn to be bold in war and to hold strong in defeat, but he had never considered that victory would bring its own snares and dangers. He realized then that despite the approval of the Great Ones and the desperate need of the kingdom, he had quite simply never believed that his grand plan would succeed. Never, when he was educating his prince, had he thought of educating him for peace.

On the morrow morning when he woke, Nevyn went to his window and leaned on the sill to look out. He could see over the brochs and sheds and general clutter of Dun Deverry all the way down the grassy hill to the outer walls. The grass glittered with frost, and the few trees left standing flamed with autumn colour. Soon enough the winter would shut them all in together, Maryn, Lilli, Bellyra, locked inside the grim stone walls of Dun Deverry with snow and storm for jailors.

'Little Lilli seems most unhappy these days,' Elyssa remarked.

'So she does,' Bellyra said. 'I suppose I should feel sorry for the poor child.'

'Why? Serves her right, I should think, for sleeping with your husband in the first place.'

'I'm afraid I've had thoughts that way myself. But she's dreadfully young, only a lass, really, and how many women have your strength of character?'

Elyssa shrugged the compliment away. Even some years after the incident it still amazed Bellyra that a woman existed who could resist Maryn. Elyssa had, in fact, sent him away with words so sharp that Maryn had ruefully repeated them to his wife. There will always be one woman I can trust, Bellyra thought. I suppose that's why he told me, so I'd know what a friend I have.

'Ah well,' Elyssa said at last. 'She'll live through it. She has her silver dagger, anyway.'

'So she does, and Maryn will make him a lord soon enough.'

The two women were sitting alone in the women's hall. Sunlight streamed in a nearby window and scattered gold across the newly-polished floor and the carpets. Bellyra rose and stood in the fugitive warmth.

'Summer's gone,' Bellyra said. 'I wonder how early it snows, this far north.'

'I wonder what real snow will be like. I gather it gets quite deep, not like the scatter we have back home.'

'Back home? Do you miss Cerrmor, Lyss?'

'I do. But it's certainly interesting, being here in Dun Deverry. You know, it's odd. All my life I've heard about it, but I never quite believed it actually existed. It seemed too unreachable, like the Blessed Isles or suchlike, to be real.'

'I used to feel that way, too.'

'At times you look happy enough to be in the Isles. It gladdens my heart to see.'

'My thanks. I am happy, I suppose.'

'You suppose?'

'Things change, Lyss. If I've learned one thing in my marriage, it's that.'

During the day she had her work upon the book, and at night she had Maryn's attentions again. Bellyra never allowed herself to think he loved her, not in any true sense. She amused him at those times when the kingdom gave him a little leisure – that was all. So long as she stayed mindful of this reality, she could take joy in his company and not ask too much of him or of her life, or so she told herself. The days passed, one after the other, in a calm as hushed as the silver moments before dawn. She refused to let anything break the calm, no matter what she had to ignore to keep it.

*   *   *

On a day when the frost lasted well into the morning despite the sun, messengers rode in from Yvrodur. Gwerbret Ammerwdd sent letters describing in some detail his meetings with the various members of the Council of Electors for the Cerrmor rhan. Prince Maryn summoned Nevyn and Oggyn to his council chamber to discuss them. The stone walls seemed to ooze cold despite the fire blazing in the hearth. Maryn had a servant pull a small table up to the fire and chairs for the three of them as well. Nevyn and Oggyn took turns in reading the letters aloud while Maryn slumped down in his chair and listened with grim intensity.

'So far so good, your highness,' Nevyn said at last. 'It appears that none of the electors truly objected to young Riddmar.'

'None of them jumped up and down in glee, either.' Maryn picked up one of the letters and waved it vaguely at his councillors. 'At least they understand the Eldidd situation.'

'They should,' Nevyn said. 'The wars would have been over fifty years ago if there'd only been two claimants for the kingship.'

Oggyn nodded his agreement. He was taking a second look at one letter and doing his best to mimic Nevyn's silent way of reading, a slow process for him, apparently. At last he tossed the letter back onto the table.

'If only, your highness,' Oggyn said, 'we could give them a good accounting of the Lughcarn rhan, I suspect that some of the objections would vanish. It's a rich prize by all accounts, and if we procure it by attainder, it will be yours alone to bestow.'

'True spoken,' Maryn said, 'but several of the electors for that rhan came over to me last summer, and I intend to give them a voice in the decision.'

Oggyn set his lips tight together.

'There are times,' Maryn went on, 'when generosity brings its own rewards. I want these men to stay loyal not just to me but to my heirs.'

'His highness is most far-seeing,' Oggyn said. 'And doubtless correct.'

'Which reminds me.' Maryn leaned back in his chair and considered Oggyn. 'I've had a complaint brought to me against you.'

'Indeed, my liege?' Oggyn turned white around the mouth. 'I trust it's no great matter.'

'It was to those who brought the complaint. The cook tells me that you had a talk with her.'

'My liege!' Oggyn tried to laugh, but his voice choked. 'How obnoxious of the vulgar little woman, to trouble you!'

'My wife brought her to me, actually.'

'Uh, well, then, of course it would be her right –'

'Hold your tongue,' Maryn snapped. 'Less flattery, more truth. She told me that you tried to extort coin and favours out of the servants for the leavings from my table.'

Oggyn went well and truly pale. Nevyn almost felt sorry for him, pinned by the prince's cold stare as he was.

'I'll not have any more of that,' Maryn said. 'Do you understand me?'

'I do, my liege.'

'The servants are welcome to eat what they wish after the noble-born have been served. That's how it was in Cerrmor, and that's how it shall be here. Is this clear?'

'It is, your highness.'

'Splendid!' All at once Maryn laughed. 'If you don't mend your grasping ways, Oggyn lad, I'll have Maddyn sing his little song about you to the entire great hall.'

Oggyn's pallor vanished in a flush of red. He tried to speak, failed, swallowed hard, and finally forced out the words. 'My liege, you know about that, then?'

'I do.' Maryn was grinning at him. 'My lady told me of it, and I had Maddyn play it for me, but in my private quarters. Don't look so wretched, Oggyn. Mend your ways, and I'll never mention a word of this again.'

'I assure you, your highness, I will. My word –' Oggyn

stopped, gulping, gasping, and at last sighing instead of speaking the more.

'Your assurance and your word are all I need.' Maryn rose, glancing Nevyn's way. 'I'll leave you now, good councillors. Don't rise on my account, and stay by the fire as long as you like.'

The prince strode out of the chamber. As soon as the door closed behind him, Oggyn dropped his face to his hands and wept.

'Here, here,' Nevyn said, as gently as he could manage. 'The prince will keep his word, you know. No one else will ever hear of this.'

Oggyn raised his head, snivelling. Nevyn fished in his brigga pocket, found a rag, and tossed it to him. Oggyn wiped his face and blew his nose, then crumpled the rag in one fat fist.

'It matters not,' Oggyn said. 'The prince has heard of it, and that's the worst thing of all. One of these days, I'll find a way to settle with that wretched bard. I know not how, but I will!'

He threw the rag into the fire. It caught and flared into a sheet of ash.

'Taking revenge on a silver dagger is a dangerous thing,' Nevyn said quietly. 'I think me you'd best be content with the prince's forgiveness and let the matter die.'

Oggyn turned and looked at him with eyes that revealed nothing. 'Perhaps you're right,' the councillor said. 'Indeed, no doubt you are right.'

Nevyn knew that he was lying, but he could do nothing one way or another but keep an eye on Oggyn and his scheming. He won't dare cross me, Nevyn thought, knowing what I know. Still, later that day he had a private word with Maddyn and warned him to be on his guard.

'Oh, I've never trusted Slimy Oggo,' Maddyn said, 'not from the day I met the man. But mayhap I'd best forget that flyting song. He may be a hound, but hounds can bite as hard as wolves.'

*   *   *

For some while Bellyra had been unusually tired. Life in Dun Deverry, she reminded herself, was a good bit more difficult than Dun Cerrmor. The autumn nights felt as cold as full winter did down by the sea. The dark stones and the vast disorder of stairways and towers, paths and unexpected walls, at times seemed half-alive, as if the very dun were a ghost, waiting for its chance to suck life from the living. No doubt she felt tired for all sorts of such reasons. She told herself that daily.

Yet the time inevitably came when she could no longer lie to herself. The first snow arrived on the north wind and fell hard all day, but the wind drove it off again by nightfall. From a window in the women's hall Bellyra looked up at the stars in an achingly clear sky and saw a fat slice of moon shining in its waxing quarter. *I should have had my bleeding before this – and it didn't come last month as well.* She stood gripping the windowsill with both hands and staring at the moon, while the cold night wind swirled around her.

'Your highness?' Degwa came hurrying over. 'Do come away from the window. You'll get chilled.'

Bellyra nodded and sat down in her chair by the fire, where Lilli and Elyssa sat waiting, Elyssa in her chair, Lilli on a cushion right at the hearth. Degwa hung the oxhide drape back over the window, then dragged a chair over to join them in the dancing light.

'Is somewhat wrong, your highness?' Lilli said.

'Oh, naught, naught. I'm a bit distracted, that's all. I was thinking about my book.'

They were all watching her, all three of her serving women, with such concern that she felt like screaming at them. She leaned her head against the high back of the chair and stared at the ceiling. Spider webs heavy with dust hung in a long fringe from the oak beams.

'My lady?' Elyssa said. 'Somewhat's wrong. Please tell us.'

'I think I'm with child again. Or wait, that's not true. I know

I'm with child. I can feel it, I've missed two bleedings, and ah Goddess! how I hate this.'

They all spoke at once in soft voices, reassurances and little flatteries. It would be better this time, they would all be there to help, her lord would be so happy at another heir –

'Please don't!' Bellyra snapped. 'Please don't lie to me!'

The voices stopped. The spider webs waved like grey plumes, back and forth. In her view Elyssa appeared, leaning over her chair.

'Well, of course it's going to be awful,' Elyssa said calmly. 'But this time we won't just stand around and hope for the best like half-wits. We'll be ready to ward it off.'

'The madness, I suppose you mean?'

'Just that. If it happens.'

Bellyra felt her cold hands start shaking. She rubbed them together and berated herself for demanding honesty.

'It might not, your highness,' Degwa said. 'Each time's different, or so they say.'

By the fire Lilli sat crouched on her cushion. Like a cat, Bellyra thought, a cat when she sees prey. She leaned forward in her chair.

'Maryn's going to run right back to you,' Bellyra said. 'I suppose you realize that.'

Lilli threw her head back and went stiff – more like the prey than the cat, all of a sudden. With one smooth motion Elyssa knelt beside Bellyra's chair and laid a hand on her arm.

'My lady,' Elyssa said. 'Please! Think well on your words.'

Bellyra knew that she was right, but Lilli looked so pretty, so young there on her cushion, all wide eyes and gold hair – no wonder Maryn's fascinated with her, Bellyra thought, her and her little slender waist!

'Is this what you've been hoping for?' Bellyra got up and took a step toward the girl. 'He'll desert my bed, you know. He did the last two times. And there you are, waiting for him. Well, aren't you?'

Lilli scrambled up, her mouth working, her face glistening

with tears. For a brief moment Bellyra felt as if the scene had turned to a painted design such as a scribe puts in the margin of a book. She could see them all clearly in the firelight: Elyssa kneeling beside her, one hand raised; Degwa with her hands clasped over her mouth; Lilli, weeping with the firelight bright on her face. Bellyra knew that she should apologize, go to the girl and clasp her hand, mutter some reassurance. It seemed that she had all the time in the world to decide, since Time had stopped around them. She felt her face crease in a smile, and some sharp thing deep in her mind goaded her.

'You little slut!' Bellyra snarled. 'I hope he does the same to you. I hope he gives you twins and the three of you die of him. Get out of here! Get out of my sight!'

Lilli sobbed aloud and ran for the door. She grabbed the bar and tried to raise it, but she struggled, wrestling with its weight. Bellyra grabbed a silver goblet from the nearest table and for a moment stood, listening to her mind scream at her to stop and sit down. Rage twitched her arm, and she threw the goblet as hard as she could, with more force, it seemed, than she'd ever summoned in her life. It struck Lilli full in the back just as the girl opened the door. She shrieked and ran, leaving the door swaying on its hinges behind her.

'Oh gods,' Bellyra whispered. 'What have I done?'

She sank into her chair and sobbed, rocking back and forth. She heard Elyssa mutter something to Degwa, then Elyssa threw her arms around her.

'Oh Lyrra, Lyrra,' Elyssa said, over and over. 'It will be all right this time. We'll make it all right this time.'

The tears stopped at last. Bellyra wiped her face on her sleeve and looked over Elyssa's shoulder. Degwa was gone and the door shut.

'I wanted to kill her,' Bellyra said. 'And it's not even her fault.'

'Isn't it?' Elyssa said. 'But truly, that was a bit much of a queenly gesture, heaving the royal silver at her, I mean.'

Elyssa smiled, trying to turn a jest, Bellyra supposed. In a few moments Elyssa let the smile fade and settled back on her knees. Bellyra leaned back in her chair and watched the dust plumes waving in the draughts. She still felt as if she viewed a picture of herself; she had merely turned the page in that hypothetical illuminated book.

'There are the herbs and suchlike,' Elyssa said at last. 'We've all heard the old women talking –'

'I know, but I can't do that.' Bellyra shuddered, shaking her head. 'Not to Maryn's child, I just can't.'

'They could kill you, too, anyway, those herbs, if they went the least wrong.'

'Oh, I'm mindful of that. Never fear.'

With a sigh Elyssa stood and stretched her back with her hands on her hips. In the fire a log burned through and dropped. Glowing coals flew onto the hearth stones. Elyssa hurried to the hearth and knelt, reaching for the poker. Bellyra watched her flicking the coals back into the fire.

'I'm really going to have to apologize to Lilli, I suppose,' Bellyra said at length. 'That goblet must have stung.'

'She's young.' Elyssa glanced over her shoulder. 'She'll survive. And you're the princess. She has no right to an apology from you.'

Bellyra was about to agree when her detachment deserted her. A wave of fear turned so cold that she nearly vomited.

'Oh ye gods,' Bellyra whispered. 'What if she tells Maryn?'

She could not talk, she could not sit upright, she curled over herself and twisted in the chair until she lay sideways in it like a child sore from a beating. The wood bit into her side and legs; she curled the tighter and wept.

'Goddess, help!' Elyssa came rushing over. 'Lyrra, don't, don't!'

She heard the door open, heard Degwa call out in alarum. She felt their hands on her arms, let them raise her up, let them help her stand, but still the tears came in long sobs.

'If she says one wrong word to your husband,' Degwa said,

'I'll beat her black and blue, and I'll wager she knows it, too. I gave her a good talking-to, I did.'

Tears and more tears – even in the midst of them Bellyra found herself thinking: so this is what shame feels like. No wonder the men would rather die than be shamed. With the thought, with the distancing it brought her, she could stop weeping at last. When Degwa brought her a rag dipped in cold water, she took it with a muttered 'my thanks' and wiped her face methodically, starting at the eyes and working outward in a spiral.

'Ah ye gods.' Bellyra handed the rag back. 'I suppose I'd best tell Maryn about the child straightaway. I'm such a rotten poor liar.'

Elyssa handed her a goblet of watered mead. Bellyra waved it away.

'I can't bear to be muddled now,' Bellyra said. 'I still don't know what came over me.'

'Righteous indignation, that's what,' Degwa said. 'She's still a Boarswoman, no matter what our Nevyn says. And we all know what *that* means!'

After Degwa left, Lilli sat for a long while on the edge of the bed and shivered in the winter cold of her chamber. Although a fire lay ready in the hearth, she had nothing to light it with. Normally she would have brought a candle or suchlike with her from the women's hall. She could fetch a splint from the great hall, she supposed, or find a servant there to do it for her, but she could not force herself to move. If she went to the great hall, she was sure that everyone would be able to read her shame from her face. They would know that she'd lost the princess's favour – doubtless forever – merely by looking at her.

When she could stand the cold no longer, she went to bed, fully dressed against the icy sheets. As her shivering eased, she fell asleep, but she dreamt of her mother, scolding her to eat more. You're too thin, Merodda kept saying, thin as

sticks, thin as sticks, and how will I find you a good husband now?

Lilli woke to grey dawn light and her misery. The bed had
finally got warm, and she curled up in her blankets, watching
the gleam of light from the shutters brighten on the walls. She
was remembering how generous Bellyra had been to her, an
exile without so much as a horse for a dowry. She took you in,
and you turned into a viper, Lilli told herself. Degwa's right,
I'm as bad as my wretched kin!

Lilli sat up, testing the air – so cold that her bruised back
cramped in pain. She lay down again and pulled the blankets
up as if she could stop her ears against the voice in her mind,
reproaching her for an ingrate and a fool both, to turn the dun's
women against her. What would Bevva think, if word of this
ever reached her in the Otherlands? Finally she managed to
drift off to sleep. When she woke, the sun had fully risen,
and Maryn was just shutting the door after letting himself
in to her chamber. He was wearing a cloak over a pair of
much-mended brigga and a shirt that hung sloppily over them;
he was unshaved, uncombed, and more beautiful than she had
ever seen him, or so it seemed to her.

'Good morrow,' he said. 'Will you forgive me my long absence,
my lady?'

Lilli shoved the blankets back and stood up, gathering words.
You must do this, she told herself. You can do this!

'I see naught to forgive, your highness. Men's affections
change.' She took a deep breath. 'So do women's.'

He stood blinking at her.

'I have my betrothed, your highness,' Lilli said. 'You have
your wife.'

Maryn laughed. He pulled off the cloak and tossed it onto
the floor.

'Beautifully put, my lady,' he said, grinning. 'But utter nonsense. Please, please, won't you take my apology? Truly, I know
I've treated you badly, and I deserve your haughtiness.'

'I'm not being haughty! I don't love you any more.'

'Of course not.' Maryn leaned over and caught her by the shoulders. 'I grovel at your feet, my lady, or I would if the floor weren't so blasted cold.'

When he kissed her, all her resolve disappeared. She slid her arms around his neck and kissed him open-mouthed in return. He laughed, picked her up, and laid her down on the bed in one strong swing of his arms.

Elyssa opened the door of the women's hall and let in Degwa, who was burdened with baskets of bread and cheese and a flagon of watered ale. Bellyra supposed that she had better eat something, but the very idea of food choked her.

'I met your husband upon the staircase, my lady,' Degwa said. 'He seemed troubled.'

'I told him about the child, that's why,' Bellyra said, 'when we first woke. You know, I have my reasons for being devoted to him. He apologized. He looked at me ever so sadly and said that he was sorry he'd done such a thing to me.'

Her serving women exchanged a glance that was anything but admiring. Had Degwa seen Maryn with Lilli? Bellyra wondered. She decided that she couldn't bear to ask. When Degwa walked over to the table near the princess's chair, Elyssa took the flagon from her, then helped her set down the baskets.

'Do eat somewhat, your highness,' Elyssa said.

'In a bit. I've got to get out for some fresh air first. I simply must.' Bellyra rose and waved a vague hand at them. 'But please, eat now. Don't wait for me.'

Bellyra sent a maidservant for her cloak and clogs, then summoned her pages and her bodyguard. As they were walking down the spiral stairs, it occurred to her that she might see Lilli in the great hall. The thought gave her an odd sensation: a cold, weak feeling that made her tremble before it mercifully passed on. She hesitated for a moment half-way down and looked out over the great hall, mobbed with riders and servants. At the table of honour Nevyn and Oggyn sat talking. She saw neither Maryn nor Lilli.

Outside the crisp air made her gasp. With Maddyn beside her, she walked slowly, gauging each step on the slick cobbles before she took it. Her pages ran on ahead to scoop up handfuls of the clean bright snow. She paused, watching them fling snowballs at one another and listening to them laugh. She found herself remembering the child she'd been at their age: a solemn little girl, not given to laughing at much of anything.

'Your highness?' Maddyn said. 'Are you unwell? I hope I don't speak above myself, but you're as pale as the wretched snow.'

'Am I? It's just the cold, truly. I'm not used to it.'

'Very well, then.' He was studying her face as if he could read truths upon it. 'I don't mean to presume.'

Bellyra turned away from his stare. She tipped her head back to look at the sky and saw the looming towers dance through tears.

'Oh, my lady,' Maddyn said, and his voice was as soft as a plucked harp. 'It aches my heart to see you sad.'

'Does it?' She turned around and wiped her face on a fold of her cloak. 'My thanks. I wish I were better at hiding it. I won't be much of a queen if I can't learn to lie.'

'Don't jest!' He reached out his hand, then jerked it back. 'Your highness, forgive me! I forget myself.'

'Do you, Maddo? Then I envy you.'

Before he could answer she turned and ran, slipping a little on the icy cobbles, ran all the way back to the broch with her pages haring after, yelling 'Your highness, wait!' over and over. At the door she stopped, took a deep breath, arranged a smile, and walked decorously inside.

'Lilli, has the cough returned?' Nevyn said.

'It hasn't, my lord. I'm just tired.'

Nevyn set his hands on his hips and studied her. In his tower room she was sitting in a spill of sunlight from the window. She slumped in the chair, and her pale face looked blotchy, as if perhaps she'd sat up late being sick.

'It's not good for an apprentice to lie to her master,' Nevyn said at last. 'Especially in our craft.'

'Well, in truth, I hurt my back.'

'Oh indeed? How?'

'I slipped on the stairs coming out of the women's hall.'

When Nevyn opened the dweomer sight, he saw that she'd hardened her aura around her till it looked like grey stone.

'Lilli, don't lie!'

'I'm sorry.' Lilli looked only at the floor while she spoke. 'It was rather awful, actually. I was in the women's hall, and the princess grew angry with me. Over Maryn, I mean, and she yelled at me and told me to get out.' Her voice shook badly. 'She called me a little slut. And so I started to leave, and she threw somewhat, I'm not sure what it was, but it hit me in the back. It still hurts, my lord, so I'd say it left a bruise.'

Nevyn was about to call her a worse liar than before – but her aura revealed her to be telling the truth.

'Lean forward,' he said. 'I want to see if there's a swelling.' When he ran his fingertips down her back, he could feel the contusion clearly even through her pair of dresses. 'I should make you up a poultice for that.'

'Will it make it heal more quickly? I don't want Maryn to see it. I'd better make up some story. He probably won't be able to tell if I'm lying.'

'I doubt it very much, truly.' Nevyn sat down on the edge of his narrow cot. 'I can see why you didn't want to tell me.'

'I feel so shamed,' Lilli whispered. 'I deserve a beating, no doubt, not just one blow.'

'Oh nonsense! Princess Bellyra's never acted so harshly before, and the gods all know that Maryn's given her plenty of reason to. I wonder what could have possibly set her off like that? I – wait. What about our wretched tablet?'

'Oh.' Lilli's eyes grew wide. 'Could the curse have touched her somehow?'

'It's but a guess, though it's quite possible. Not that the dweomer spell forced her to turn on you. It doesn't matter how powerful a dweomer you cast upon someone or some thing: you can never make them go against their own true nature. It's possible that the curse will bring out the worst parts of people's true natures.'

'I see. Do you think that Bellyra's been angry with me from the beginning, but she didn't let it out until the curse began working upon her?'

'Exactly. It takes dweomer to resist these things, and she has none.'

'Couldn't you make another talisman that's the opposite of this one? You know, it would make the good parts of everyone's nature sing out and maybe drown out the bad.'

'By the gods! That's a splendid idea.'

'But you won't need a dead thing to make it work, will you?'

'Of course not. We'll use a jewel of some sort instead, not a hard clear one, though.' Nevyn thought for a moment. 'We'll want a jewel with veins and depths for this job, an opal for instance, since it's meant to operate upon the hidden parts of the soul. It would be a long job, maybe the work of years, but still, a job worth doing.'

'I'd hoped you could make it quickly. To counter the curse tablet, I mean.'

'I only wish.' Nevyn smiled at her. 'Alas, that would take a dweomermaster with ten times my power – at least. But you've given me an idea. I've been afraid to destroy the tablet for fear the curse would redound upon our prince if I did, but to counter it might be another thing entirely. I might call down the Light per-haps and try to cleanse it somehow. It's not clear in my mind yet, but I'll meditate upon it. And then we'll see what we shall see.'

It was some while before Maddyn saw the princess again. A page told him that she'd left off working on her book, but the boy couldn't tell him why or when she might take it up again.

Every morning after breakfast, the usual time she would have summoned him, he lingered at the foot of the staircase in the great hall, just on the off-chance that she'd send him word of some sort. It never came, and neither did she.

Finally Maddyn cornered Elyssa when she appeared in the great hall to fetch bread. He knelt on one knee to block her path and caught the hem of her dress in his hands.

'What's all this?' Elyssa said, laughing. 'I've no bounty to dispense, bard, or boons to grant.'

'Oh, but you do,' Maddyn said. 'News of her highness. Is she ill or suchlike?'

'Not truly. A bit indisposed, I suppose one could call it.'

'I've been worried.' Maddyn found himself speaking with no power to stop himself. 'When last I saw her, she seemed so unhappy. I keep thinking there's somewhat wrong.'

'Oh.' Elyssa glanced around at the crowded hall, then lowered her voice. 'You truly are devoted to her, aren't you?'

Maddyn looked away. 'I suppose I am.'

'Do get up, will you?'

He stood, brushing the straw from the knees of his brigga, while she watched him with eyes that told him nothing of her thoughts.

'Can you tell me what's amiss?' he said at last.

'Why not?' Elyssa smiled in a twisted sort of way. 'She's had two babies in four years, and both of them were big. And now, oh ye gods! she's with child again, and little Prince Marro is what? Barely four turnings of the moon old. It sucks the life out of a woman. She's not a mare or a prize cow, you know, no matter what our prince thinks.'

Maddyn blushed and looked away.

'A bard without words,' Elyssa said. 'There's a rarity. Or are you angry that I've spoken ill of the prince?'

'Not in the least. I'd just not thought of things that way before.'

'No doubt, since you're a man like any other. Here – they

always say bards can speak freely, even to a prince. When you've got a moment, perhaps you might speak and mention that if his wife keeps on conceiving this way, it could kill her.'

'I'll do better than that. I'll have a word with old Nevyn and let him do the speaking. Maryn won't be listening to the likes of me.'

'You have my thanks. It's just a blessing that the prince has his little mistress. I hope to the gods he doesn't get her with child, too, and have no one to –' She paused, her mouth twisted tight, considering Maddyn. 'Oh never mind. Our princess has us – her women I mean – to see her through this, but Nevyn's aid would be a boon.'

'I'll get it for you.'

'Good. And I'll tell our lady about your concern.'

'If I can be of any further service, call upon me.' He bowed to her. 'My thanks, my lady, for this plain speaking.'

'You're welcome, I'm sure, but don't tell another soul but Nevyn. Our lady will be most distressed if you do.'

'Then tell her to fear not. There won't be one wrong word from me.'

Maddyn glanced around the great hall and saw a cluster of pages over by the honour hearth. He made his way through the welter of tables and joined them, asking them impartially if they knew where Councillor Nevyn might be.

'I do,' a lad piped up. 'Up in his tower room. He asked us to find his apprentice for him and send her there.'

'But we couldn't,' a second lad said. 'Find the Lady Lillorigga, I mean. If you see her, bard, could you tell her that her master needs her?'

'I will, at that. My thanks.'

The inside of the side broch felt no warmer than the ice-kissed air outside. As he panted up the stairs Maddyn was shivering inside his winter cloak. Heat, however, filled Nevyn's chamber like a memory of summer. Maddyn dumped his cloak on the floor and stood holding his hands out to the glowing brazier.

'It's splendidly warm in here, my lord,' Maddyn said. 'I'm surprised that the charcoal does so well.'

Nevyn raised an eyebrow and smiled.

'More fool me!' Maddyn said. 'I should have known it was dweomer.'

'After all these years, I should think so. What brings you to me, Maddo?'

'A message from Princess Bellyra's women. They need your help.'

'Indeed?' Nevyn's smile vanished. 'What's wrong?'

'The princess is with child again.'

Nevyn swore like a silver dagger.

'It was inevitable, of course,' the old man said at last. 'But it aches my heart that it comes so soon.'

'The princess doesn't want anyone else to know this but you.'

'Very well, then. I suppose she's had to tell the prince. Oh – by the gods! That's why Lilli been so hard to find, then. I've been wondering, this past few days, but she can be cursed sly when she wants to!'

For a moment Maddyn found it hard to speak. His rage broke over him and made him tremble.

'What's so wrong, Maddo?'

'I don't know, my lord. I – ye gods! It just gripes my soul, thinking of the prince with his mistress while – I mean, I know that's stupid of me. Why shouldn't he have as many women as he wants? He's the prince.'

'That's the usual way of thinking about these things,' Nevyn said drily. 'And there's naught we can do about it. I'll attend the princess straightaway, though. Just let me fetch my cloak.'

'It's not the birth itself I'm afraid of,' Bellyra said. 'It's the after.'

'I know that, your highness,' Nevyn said. 'Maybe things will be different this time.'

'That's what I thought last time. They weren't.'

'This time I'll be here.'

'You were there when Casyl was born. It didn't help. Oh, I'm sorry!' Bellyra looked on the edge of tears. 'I don't mean to be rude.'

'The last thing you need to worry about now is my feelings.'

Bellyra wiped her eyes on the sleeve of her dress.

In the women's hall they were sitting in front of the fire, which provided the only light as well as heat. The maidservants had covered the windows with several layers of hides, that morning, and the leather would remain up until the first signs of spring.

'I'm such a coward,' Bellyra said at last. 'I've gone to earth like a badger in her sett. I don't want to see anyone but my women or leave this hall.'

'You absolutely must! Do you want to let the black humour take you over now and ruin even more of your life?'

'I don't, truly. But –'

'There's no arguing with me, your highness. You need to get out into the open air.'

'That's the simple truth, isn't it? You'll not be argued with. I might as well give in, I suppose, and save us a squabble.'

'How sensible you are.'

Bellyra laughed.

'There's another thing, your highness,' Nevyn said. 'May I speak freely?'

'Whenever couldn't you?'

'Well, it's a delicate matter. About Lilli.'

Bellyra jerked her head to one side and stared into the fire.

'I've not seen your apprentice in some days.' Her voice sounded too high, too brisk. 'She doesn't come to the sewing in the afternoons.'

'She doesn't?' Nevyn said. 'She told me – well, no matter.'

'I think me we both know where she is at those times.'

'Imph. I take it you don't miss her.'

'I don't. But I feel like such a fool for being angry with her.'

'If you are, you'd be a greater fool to deny it.'

Bellyra shrugged. She had gone pale, he realized, and fine sweat beaded her upper lip. He waited, but she sat staring into the hearth in silence. The fire hissed as it covered a damp log with a curl of flame, and she tossed her head with a shudder.

'Your highness? Shall I leave you?'

'It would be best. But I promise you I'll take your advice.'

As Nevyn left the women's hall, he saw Lady Elyssa standing at the end of the corridor. She'd wrapped a shawl around her shoulders against the chill.

'Good morrow,' he called out. 'Are you waiting for –'

Elyssa held a warning finger to her lips. Nevyn said nothing more until he joined her on the landing.

'A word with you?' Elyssa said. 'Indeed, I was.' She paused to glance down the stairs, then spoke quietly. 'No one's about. Good. This guard our prince has given our lady, Maddyn his name is. You know him, don't you?'

'Quite well, actually,' Nevyn said. 'Why?'

'I was wondering what manner of man he was.'

'A good one, I'd say. If it weren't for these cursed wars, he might have been a first-rank bard.'

'That's not what I meant.' Elyssa pursed her lips briefly. 'His character. Is he reliable? Decent?'

'Most assuredly. Here! You don't suspect him of being slack in his duties or suchlike, do you?'

'Not in the least.' Elyssa paused for a bland smile. 'I merely want to ensure our lady's safety.'

'Well, naught's going to happen to her here in her husband's dun.'

'My dear Nevyn, there are dangers that can come upon a woman no matter where she is.'

'Well, that's true. You can trust Maddyn to deal with them.'

Elyssa dropped him a curtsy, then hurried back to the women's hall. *Now what was all that about, I wonder?* Nevyn thought. *No business of mine, most like.*

Lilli was in her chamber, reading over the dweomer passage Nevyn had set her to study, when Branoic called her name and knocked on the door. She went stone-still, wondering if she should pretend to be gone. The knock came again, and she rose.

'Do come in, Branno!'

He opened the door and stepped in, shut it again and leaned back against it, his hands behind him, as if he were pinning them against the wood to keep them under control. For a long moment he looked her over with eyes so cold that she began to tremble.

'I just had a bit of a chat with the prince,' Branoic said at last. 'He warned me off you.'

'He did what?'

'Told me to leave you alone. That's not the bargain I thought we had, you and I.'

'It's not! He's got his gall. Branno, you don't think I agreed to that, do you?'

All at once he smiled. He straightened up and walked into the chamber.

'My apologies,' Branoic said. 'The way he put it, I thought you knew, you see.'

'Naught of the sort! He promised me we could marry, and I never thought he'd go back on his word.'

'Oh, he talked about the marriage, all right. He's found a grand demesne to settle upon us, says he. The one that guards the bolt-hole. He'll rebuild the dun next summer, says he, in grand style, and we'll have it for the winter.'

'I don't understand.'

'Don't you? I did. Until we marry he wants you to himself.

After that –' Branoic paused, his mouth twisted, as if he'd bitten into spoiled food. 'Well, we'll be on our lands, and he'll be here, but I'll wager he visits now and again.'

Lilli sat back down with a long sigh. Branoic stayed standing and shoved his hands into the pockets of his brigga.

'I don't know what to do,' she said.

'Naught, I should think. Whatever else, he's still the prince. There's many a great lord who wouldn't be so generous to the man who stole his mistress's heart.' Branoic was staring at the floor. 'You've never weaselled around behind my back, Lilli. And when you come right down to it, the prince never has either.'

'Well and good, then. But I'm sorry.'

'Are you?' He looked up. 'So am I.'

Branoic turned and strode out, slamming the heavy door hard behind him. Lilli rose, half-minded to run after him, but, she realized, he was right. There was naught more she could say or do to ease their situation or his feelings. Unless, of course, she gave Maryn up.

'Don't be a fool,' she said aloud. 'You don't need dweomer to know that he'll not let you go until he doesn't want you any more.'

She sat down and wondered why she felt so weary.

So much of the troop had gone with Owaen to the Pyrdon border that the silver daggers' barracks stood mostly empty. Those remaining, Maddyn and Branoic among them, had taken the bunks closest to the hearth at the far end of the long narrow room. When someone was missing, the rest were bound to notice, and conversely they noticed as well when Branoic returned to sleeping in the barracks.

'And what's so wrong?' Red-Haired Trevyr said to him. 'Your lady turn cold to you?'

Branoic never moved, never spoke, merely looked at Trevyr in something of the way he might eye a joint of meat waiting to be carved. Maddyn stepped in front of him and turned to Trevyr.

'Hold your tongue,' Maddyn snapped, 'before Branno makes you bite it off with my blessing.'

'Here! Just a bit of a jest! I –' Trevyr caught himself. 'My apologies, Branno. I can be a dolt at times.'

'No offence taken.' Branoic turned away. 'I could do with a tankard of dark about now. Think I'll go to the great hall.'

Branoic strode off. No one spoke until the door had slammed behind him. Trevyr sat down on the edge of his bunk and massaged his twisted hand with the good one. A smack with the flat of a sword had broken most of the bones in his shield hand, and not even Nevyn had been able to set it straight again.

'My apologies to you, too, Maddo. I didn't mean to cause trouble.'

'I don't suppose you did, truly. But it's a hard tune Branoic's trying to whistle. He doesn't need anyone else to make it harder.'

'Poor bastard.'

'Is he? There's more than one husband of a royal mistress who's been rewarded with land and favours.'

'You're right enough about that. But still: poor bastard!'

'Well, so he is. Now let's go eat. I'm hungry.'

As they stepped outside cold wind slapped them, and the sky hung close and grey over the dun. In the ward dirty snow lay over the cobbles and the frozen mud. With their feet wrapped in rags servants hurried past them with armloads of firewood or buckets of water from the wells. Maddyn almost envied them – they at least had work to keep them busy, whereas he would spend another tedious day brooding about Bellyra from his distance. Yet, when they walked into the great hall, a page came running to meet him.

'The princess sent me for you, bard. She wants you to guard her like you usually do.'

'Well and good, then.' Maddyn steadied his voice to a fine

indifference, but he felt like shouting in joy. 'Will her highness mind if I just get a bit of bread or suchlike first?'

'Of course not. She'll be down in a bit, she said.'

The page trotted off. Maddyn got himself a chunk of bread and a tankard of watered ale, then sat with Trevyr at a table near the foot of the massive stone staircase that spiralled up one side of the great hall. They ate fast, without ceremony or conversation, leaving Maddyn free to watch the stairs. He was just finishing when Bellyra appeared, bundled in a red cloak, walking down slowly with her pages behind her. He was surprised at how good it felt to see her and to know that for this small space of time her company would be his.

'There's our lady,' Maddyn said. 'A silver dagger's work is never done, eh?'

'Better you than me,' Trevyr said, 'tramping around in this cold.'

'Lucky dog! Well, I'll join you at the fire soon enough.'

Maddyn grabbed his cloak and put it on, then hurried to the foot of the stairs. When Bellyra reached the great hall, he knelt, but she laughed and waved a hand at him.

'Do get up, Maddo! That straw's too mucky to kneel in.'

Smiling, he rose and bowed to her. 'Her highness is too kind.'

'Not truly.'

Her voice held an odd note, a hesitance perhaps. When he looked at her he saw something new in her expression, an ill ease of a sort he couldn't place. In all their other times together she had shown nothing but the graciousness of a great lady to a trusted servant. With the pages so close by, he could say nothing, but when they walked out into the ward the lads ran on ahead, as Bellyra generally allowed them to do.

'Have I displeased your highness?' Maddyn said.

'What? Not in the least!' Bellyra laughed a few brittle notes. 'What makes you say that?'

'I don't know, my lady. Forgive me.'

In silence they crossed the ward. The pages would dart ahead like dogs, then run back to circle the princess before they rushed off again. Bellyra hesitated, looking downhill through the jumble of buildings and walls, then pointed off to her right.

'Let's go through that gate,' she said. 'Someone told me there's a dedication stone from an old tower that's been used in another wall. I think they meant down in there somewhere.'

They went through the gate, hurried past pigsties shaped like beehives, followed a broken wall downhill, found another gate, and came out into a squarish little ward, defined by the stone walls of storage buildings. Bellyra stood looking around her. On the far side stood a long barn.

'There!' Bellyra pointed up toward its eaves. 'Just under the thatch. Look, you can see writing on that big stone.' She trotted over to the base of the wall and stood staring up, frowning a little. 'It's too high for me to read.' She turned to the waiting pages. 'Do you either of you know letters?'

'I don't, my lady.'

'Nor I either, my lady.'

'What a nuisance! Here, I know! You two lads run back to the royal broch. I saw some empty ale barrels standing by the servants' door. You roll one of them down here so I can stand on it.'

'Your highness!' Maddyn said. 'You can't go clambering about on ale barrels.'

'Can you read, Maddo?'

'I can't.'

'Well, then, there's no use in your doing the clambering for me, is there now?'

Maddyn glowered. Bellyra sent the two pages off, then moved a few steps away from him and watched them go. The hood of her cloak had slipped back to reveal her golden hair, caught back in a silver clasp, but in the cold light both seemed as dull as lead.

'Elyssa said she had a bit of a chat with you,' Bellyra said abruptly.

'She did, my lady. Your secret's safe with me.'

'Thank you.' She turned to face him. 'I never doubted it. But she also told me –' She broke off, staring up at him as if she were trying to read his thoughts through his eyes.

Maddyn realized that he could remember nothing more about that talk with her serving woman at the same moment as he realized he desperately needed to.

'Forgive me, my lady,' he said, 'for being such a dolt, but have I done somewhat to distress you?'

'Not in the least. Rather the opposite, actually.'

'Well, that's a relief.'

'I suppose it is.' Bellyra hesitated for a moment. 'Maddo, are you in love with me?'

Maddyn felt his face burn beyond the power of the winter wind to cool it. He groped for words, found none, could only stare at her helplessly while she studied him with all the fierce concentration she brought to her beloved stones and inscriptions.

'Oh dear goddess!' Bellyra said. 'You are. I didn't really believe – oh Maddo, I'm so sorry I blurted like that.'

Words – bard or no, he could think of not one. He should babble long apologies that he had presumed so far above him, he knew, but something deep in his soul refused to grovel and apologize. To belittle his feeling for her would be to kill part of his manhood. With that thought he found his tongue at last.

'Is it a wrong thing to love a woman like you? The true wondering would be at a man who didn't.'

'Like my husband, do you mean?'

'Him as well.' Maddyn turned, glancing around them, glancing up. No windows overlooked this sheltered space, but in a crowded dun like this one, privacy was more precious than gold, and who knew if they might be overheard or not? 'Shall I find you another guard?'

For a long moment she stayed silent.

'Please don't,' she said at last. 'Or am I being horribly unfair to you?'

'I don't care.' He turned back. 'I don't care if you are or not. It would be worse, never seeing you.'

'Very well, then. We'll leave things as they are.'

'Are you angry with me? You're as far above me as any woman could be.'

'Not in the least. If anything, I'm –' She hesitated briefly. 'I'm grateful to you.'

If the prince had appeared at that moment, Maddyn would have slapped him across the face, royalty or no. He took a deep breath and calmed himself.

'My lady,' he said, 'you'll never hear a wrong word from me again. I promise you that.'

'That would be best, wouldn't it?' She looked as if she might cry. 'Ah ye gods, there are times when I wish I were a farmwife! I could please myself without worrying about the wretched kingdom.'

The implication made him smile no matter how hard he tried to stifle it. She smiled in return, but at the same time it seemed she might weep. Maddyn risked – he risked everything, he felt, his life and happiness both with the simple gesture – risked raising a hand and touching her cheek with his fingertips, just once before he drew his hand away. Her smile steadied itself.

'I'm glad you still want to be my guard,' she said. 'But here come the pages back again.' All at once she laughed, her normal laugh, wicked with delight in life itself. 'I mostly sent them away to have a private word with you, but you know, Maddo, I truly do want to read that inscription.'

The pages had had the sense to bring a barrel short enough for the princess to climb upon it with some dignity. Maddyn twined his fingers together as if he were helping her mount a horse and gave her a boost up while the lads steadied the barrel. She read the inscription aloud, while he leaned back against the barn wall and listened to his heart, pounding as if he'd been running. He had never been so happy, he had never been so frightened. He could make no sense of his feelings and, finally, gave up trying.

With her inscription read and memorized, the princess jumped down on her own before he could stop her.

'I need to return to the women's hall,' she said, 'to write this down before I forget it.'

Side by side they walked together through the random maze of Dun Deverry while the pages followed at a respectful distance. Bellyra said nothing, and Maddyn refused to break the comfortable silence between them. He had been given more, he felt, than he could ever have hoped for. He would have to be content with it, too – he told himself that sharply, several times. They were walking uphill toward the main ward when they heard shouting and the jingling chime of bridle rings.

'Sounds like a lot of men, my lady,' Maddyn said. 'What – oh here, I'll wager it's your husband's brother and his escort.'

Maddyn was proved right when they reached the main ward. An orderly mass of dismounted men and horses filled every inch of it, it seemed, whilst over them tossed the ship banners of Cerrmor, the red wyvern of Dun Deverry, and the rearing stallion of Pyrdon.

'I can't see anything over this mob, my lady,' Maddyn said. 'But from the banners I'd say it must be Riddmar.'

'He comes at an ill-omened time,' Bellyra said. 'Tonight's Samaen.'

'Ye gods! So it is. But here! He's arrived now only by chance.'

'Chance?' Bellyra was watching the crowd with eyes that seemed focused elsewhere. 'I was born on Samaen, Maddo. Naught that happens on this day happens to me by chance.'

The quiet way she spoke turned him cold. He heard a voice like bells chiming deep in his mind, tolling out one of the prophecies that the gods give now and then to bards. Riddmar's coming was ill-omened indeed. The gods, however, refused to tell Maddyn why, and he kept his sudden fear to himself.

*   *   *

Nevyn felt the omen as well, though his trained mind could separate the possible threat from the boy himself, who would be blameless in any danger his presence might bring. What that danger might be lay beyond his knowing, at least for the nonce; he intended to do everything he could to find out.

Since he was standing just behind Prince Maryn in the doorway to the central broch, Nevyn got a good look at the boy. Riddmar, Second Prince of Pyrdon, was a lean child who shared his half-brother's blond hair, grey eyes and ready smile. When Owaen presented him to the prince, Riddmar pulled off his riding hat and knelt on the steps with a certain grace.

'You may rise,' Maryn said, smiling. 'Welcome to Dun Deverry, brother.'

'My thanks, your highness.' The boy got up, then bowed. 'It's awfully big, inn't?'

'Truly. And very confusing. Until you've been here for some while, don't go exploring by yourself. You could well get lost.' Maryn paused, looking this way and that among the crowd in the ward. 'I've no idea where my lady is. Nevyn?'

'I'll go look for her, my liege, if you'd like.' Nevyn stepped forward. 'I believe I heard that she'd gone outside to find lore for her book.'

'My thanks,' Maryn said. 'But first – Prince Riddmar, this is Lord Nevyn, one of my councillors.'

Nevyn bowed while the lad watched him wide-eyed.

'Are you the sorcerer?' Riddmar said. 'My father told me there was one. And he said I should never ever make you angry.'

'I am indeed,' Nevyn said gravely. 'But I assure you that I never turn anyone into frogs.'

Riddmar smiled in sincere relief. Nevyn glanced around, saw Lilli standing off to one side, and beckoned to her. With a nod to Prince Maryn, Nevyn walked down the steps while Lilli hurried after. Together they made their way through the mob of armed men and horses. The Wildfolk of Air darted ahead of them and led them so purposefully that he knew that they must have spotted Maddyn in the general confusion.

Sure enough, Nevyn found the silver dagger and the princess standing at a gate in the main wall. Behind them stood a pair of pages. Nevyn bowed to the princess. Lilli curtsied, but she stayed well back, and Bellyra never looked her way.

'Your highness?' Nevyn said. 'Your husband requests you join him.'

'Gladly.' Bellyra waved at the crowd. 'Once I can get through.'

'The grooms are beginning to take the horses to the stables, so you won't have long to wait.'

'Won't you come with me, Nevyn?' Bellyra said. 'There will have to be some sort of official meal or suchlike.'

'Which is precisely what I'd prefer to avoid, my lady, if you'll release me.'

'Oh very well. There's no use in my making you suffer.'

'My thanks, your highness. My apprentice and I have a working on hand.'

By circling the long way round by a devious little path between sheds and huts, they managed to avoid the mob in the main ward. Lilli walked with her head bent, looking only at the cobbles and the mud.

'If you want to regain the princess's favour,' Nevyn said at last, 'you might consider giving up her husband.'

Lilli looked up with tear-filled eyes. 'I did try.' Her voice barely rose above a whisper. 'Twice, in truth.'

'Indeed? What did he do?'

'The first time he just laughed. Yesterday he grabbed me and told me he'd never let me renounce him.'

'Ye gods! Did he hurt you?'

'He didn't, but he did frighten me. I keep thinking, my lord, of what you said to me so long ago. Do you remember? You told me that because I kept refusing him it was a kind of ensorcelment.'

Nevyn growled under his breath. 'I do remember, and now you're trapped good and proper, aren't you? Well, mayhap in time things will change.'

'I know that he'll tire of me –'

'That's not what I meant. In time Bellyra's good sense will reassert itself, and she'll forgive you.'

'I hope so, my lord. She was so good to me, and now she hates me.'

'Well, I'm hoping that will pass, too. She's terrified, Lilli, because she's with child, and she's sure the same old madness will come over her. Her fear colours everything.'

'Will it happen again, the madness, I mean?'

'I don't know.'

'Well, I'll pray it doesn't.'

'That's all any of us can do, alas.'

When they reached his chamber, Lilli hung her cloak on a peg in the wall, then took Nevyn's and hung it next to hers while he heaped charcoal into the brazier. When he snapped his fingers, Wildfolk of Fire appeared and strewed flame over the black sticks. Lilli smiled and stretched out her hands to the warmth.

'Will I ever be able to summon the salamanders like you do, my lord?'

'Some day, if you do your lessons well. There's many a long walk up that particular mountain, however, before you reach the top.'

While Lilli cleared off his table and stacked the clutter on the floor, Nevyn opened the big canvas pack of herbs where he kept the wooden box housing the curse tablet. He'd buried it deep inside, for fear a servant might find the thing, in the midst of cloth bags of herbs and roots. He fished it out and weighed it in both hands. He could have sworn the thing seemed heavier than it had before.

In the centre of the table he set the box down. With a stick of charcoal he drew a circle round it deosil; at each cardinal point, he physically drew a pentagram upon the table. When he called down the etheric light, it clung to the lines of the diagram and glowed silvery-blue. Only then, with the pentagrams radiating power, did Nevyn open the box and remove the lead tablet.

In the midst of blue fire it glowed with a light of its own, poison green and oily, somehow, just as Lilli had described it earlier. That he could see it so clearly troubled him. Nevyn shut the wooden box and set the tablet upon it in the midst of the sigils drawn upon the lid.

'Gods, it's ghastly!' Lilli said.

'It is that. Now, you take the chair and go sit by the door. Your part in this is simple. I'm going to try to banish the evil by driving it out and scattering it. I want you to watch the tablet and tell me if it appears to change.'

Lilli did as he'd told her. Once she was safely at a distance, Nevyn raised his hands high over his head. He took a deep breath, and as he let it out he called upon the One True Light that shines beyond the gods. He could feel his voice as much as hear it, booming and vibrating through his chamber. When he shut his eyes, he saw the Light with the inner vision as a river of pure brilliance, circling the earth and flowing among the stars. Into his outstretched hands Its power fell from the stars in a cascade of glowing white light. He felt it run down his arms, felt it pierce him like a spear and carry him away. His chamber disappeared into the blaze of white.

With a wordless cry Nevyn flung his arms out to the side, so that it seemed he hung on a brilliant cross of light. Upon it he floated over the edge of the waterfall. The tumbling light roared in his ears and carried him down from the stars. Slowly the brilliance faded and he could see once again. He stood in his chamber, but the light, turned silver, trembled within him, no longer cold like water, but burning like fire. Although he heard Lilli cry out in awe, her voice seemed to come from a thousand miles away, and he bent his concentration to the tablet lying amidst the sigils.

The strip of lead appeared shrunken, its poison light dimmed, while the pentagrams drawn on the table seemed to float free of the wood, as if they were made of shiny black metal instead of charcoal. Nevyn raised his arms and brought his hands together over his head. He saw the light as a spear, rising up from deep within him, rising up through his arms and out of his hands until it seemed he held a spear of blinding white. He could feel its weight, feel the warmth of the fire blazing at the tip.

'In the name of the Great Ones!'

Nevyn swung his arms down and thrust the spear of light deep into the talisman. It shrieked like a live thing, or so he heard it, and twisted round the point. White light drowned it and boiled; it seemed he could see red steam rise and hear it hiss. He could feel the light flow down his arms, flow through him and out of his fingertips while the tablet writhed. It might have melted, had only Nevyn possessed another spear of light, but all the power he had gathered, he had already spent.

Nevyn staggered back, let his arms fall to his sides, and caught himself just before he collapsed onto the floor. He could summon no more power, could physically bear to channel no more light than what he had already gathered, but still the tablet sat on the table-top, a dull grey strip, gleaming with oily light.

'Blast it!' Nevyn whispered. 'Wretched thing!'

Lilli grabbed his arm and guided him to the chair. He sank gratefully onto it and listened to his breathing, hard and ragged in his chest.

'The curse is weakened,' Lilli said. 'But it's not gone.'

'I know.'

'For a moment you were winning.' She sounded on the edge of tears. 'The light – it was so beautiful, I thought it had to win, and the lead seemed to be melting, just for a moment.'

'Win? That's an odd word to use, but truly, I suppose it was a battle of sorts.' Nevyn glanced around the chamber, which still glowed and shifted like flames to his dweomer-touched eyes. 'Get me some water, child.'

Drinking the water, icy cold from a metal flagon he'd set on the window sill earlier, brought him firmly back to his body and its normal perceptions. He banished the etheric fire from his magical diagram and scattered the grains of charcoal, returning the table to its normal self as well. The curse tablet went back into its box, and the box back into its hiding place.

'I wonder what went wrong?' Nevyn said. 'It felt as if I simply weren't strong enough, and that may be, but when the power of the Light came upon me, I thought it was potent enough to wipe away all manner of evil things.'

'Just so.' Lilli frowned in thought. 'When you fashioned the spear, my lord? I had the oddest feeling. It was rather like you'd missed your mark, but that didn't make sense, because the white light covered the whole tablet.'

'So I thought at the time. But, here, that's an interesting thought. Would you say I'd not found the heart of the tablet?'

'Somewhat like that. It's so hard to find words for this kind of thing.'

'It is, indeed. Huh.' Nevyn fell silent, remembering as best he could the downpouring of the light and its rush through his mortal flesh. 'There's somewhat about this wretched tablet that I've overlooked, perhaps. I've simply never had much affinity for it. That's been a problem from the very first.'

'But I do.'

'True spoken, but you've not had the training to do this sort of work. Don't you even think of trying such a working! Do you understand me?'

'I do, my lord.' Lilli managed a faint smile. 'I'm just as glad, to be honest. I know that I'm but an apprentice.'

'Good. Some day, perhaps, if you work hard, you'll be able to channel the light through your blood and bone, but that's years away. And I sincerely hope we've destroyed this wretched thing before then.'

'Will you try again, my lord? Is there some other spell you can cast?'

'I doubt it, unfortunately. I've spent many a long night thinking about it, and this was the best I could come up with. But we can change the conditions around the working. Perhaps it's the astral tides that are wrong. They run so low this time of year. Perhaps in the spring they'll be stronger and me with them.'

But even as he spoke, he doubted it.

The first snow melted quickly, and the weather turned dry if achingly cold. Princess Bellyra bundled herself up in two cloaks and started a new part of her researches, a catalogue of the various towers and outbuildings scattered around the main broch complex. It struck Maddyn as an odd thing to do, but since it made her happy, he was willing to follow her around.

'I'd really like to draw some sort of picture of the dun,' Bellyra remarked one morning. 'A map, I suppose I mean. I don't have the slightest idea of how to go about it.'

'No more would I, your highness,' Maddyn said. 'But Otho might. He seems to know a fair lot of odd lore.'

'That's true, and it's a good idea.'

They had left the main ward behind by then and gone round to the back of the broch complex to one of the odd little spaces marked off by the walls and rubble of buildings long gone. Pale sunlight fell on the dark stones with no power to warm them and cast black shadows onto the muddy ground. As usual the pages had run on ahead, this time to climb up a pile of old cobble-stones that looked dangerously unstable.

'Shall I go fetch them, your highness?' Maddyn said.

'In a moment. They won't kill themselves straightaway, or so we can hope. I've got a thing I want to give you.'

Bellyra took a small twist of cloth out of her kirtle and handed it to him. When he opened it, he found a silver ring, a flat band engraved with roses. He turned it between thumb and forefinger to admire the blooms, so tiny yet so perfectly drawn that it seemed he should be able to smell their scent.

'Well, see if it fits you,' Bellyra said impatiently.

'It's a lovely thing,' Maddyn said, 'but truly, do you think I should take a gift from you?'

'Of course! Why would I have Otho make it if I didn't want you to have it?'

'I'm worrying what others might think. Gossips, I mean.'

'I've given lots of other people little trinkets over the years.' She was smiling at him. 'And in fact, I asked Maryn if I should reward you for being so patient. He said indeed I should. So just don't go bragging about it, and no one will think twice.'

Maddyn laughed and slipped the ring over the middle finger of his right hand. He had to squeeze it over his knuckle, but it fitted snugly but comfortably once he had it seated.

'Otho's got a good eye,' Bellyra said. 'I thought he'd have to take it back and size it, but it's meant to be yours, sure enough.'

'You have my humble thanks, my lady. It's a splendid thing, and I'm honoured that you'd think of me.'

'Are you really?'

'I am. A gift from you is worth half the earth to me.'

Bellyra smiled in a way he particularly liked, glancing away as if she were a young lass and still shy. He would have given the other half of the earth to kiss that smile, but always he was aware of the dun looming over them, with a hundred windows like a hundred eyes.

'We'd best go in,' Bellyra said. 'I'm supposed to be teaching Riddmar about Cerrmor, as if the poor child will be able to remember all the things I've told him! And we'd better not let those pages break their necks.'

After he escorted the princess back to the women's hall, Maddyn decided to go back to the barracks before he joined the other men for the noon meal. He crossed the ward, thinking of very little, but at the stairs leading to his quarters he paused. Had someone called his name? All at once he knew he was being watched. He felt the hair on the back of his neck rising and spun around, his hand on his sword-hilt. Lady Merodda was standing about ten feet away, her hands decorously folded at her waist, and studying him with unblinking eyes. In the sunlight her yellow hair gleamed as if it had been oiled.

'That ring,' she whispered. 'It binds my heart. It chokes me.'

Without thinking he raised his hand.

'It bodes evil to me,' Merodda went on. 'But a worse evil to you, silver dagger.' She tossed back her head and laughed. 'But a far far worse evil to you.'

The laughter died in mid-peal. She had vanished.

Maddyn felt himself tremble, and cold sweat sheeted down his back. He sat down on the stairs rather than risk climbing them and tried to think. Was he ill? Had he imagined the whole thing? If the apparition actually had been a ghost, had she spoken true about his ring? He looked down at his hand and the silver roses. How could he give up the token his lady had given him, when it would cause her hurt to see him without it? He would do anything to spare her pain, even if it should mean his death.

Nevyn happened to notice the rose ring a few nights later, when Maddyn came to his tower room with a note from the princess. As he handed it over, the silver gleamed in the candlelight.

'That's a pretty thing,' Nevyn said. 'Where did you get that?'

'Our lady gave it to me,' Maddyn said. 'The prince suggested she reward my patience, not that it needed rewarding.'

'Ah, I see.'

Nevyn looked up and found Maddyn troubled. He raised an inquisitive eyebrow.

'Well, someone else noticed it, too,' Maddyn said. 'Lady Merodda's ghost.'

'What?'

'It was a blasted strange thing, my lord. She appeared in broad daylight and told me the ring would cause her harm, but it was a greater evil to me. I was fair troubled by it.'

'No doubt! Here, let me see it for a moment.'

Maddyn slipped the ring off and handed it over. Nevyn clasped it in his palm and stared off across the room. He could feel the ring emanating – something.

'It's odd,' Nevyn said. 'There's dweomer on this ring, sure enough, but I'd not call it evil, exactly. All dweomer is dangerous if you don't understand it, and that's the sort of danger I feel.'

When Nevyn gave the ring back, Maddyn put it on without a heartbeat's hesitation. He's accepted the dweomer, then, Nevyn thought. With the thought came the dweomer cold, racing down his spine, and grim knowledge. Within its silver circle the ring bound many a Wyrd within it: himself, Bellyra, Maryn, and Lilli as well, but no one would know the truth and the working of it for many years hence. At the centre of the circle of Wyrd, however, would stand Maddyn, down the long years and in the lives ahead of them all.

EPILOGUE

Spring, 1118

When a man wishes to study sorcery, the art drives him a hard bargain, to wit, that it will trade its secrets only for sacrifice and lonely toil. Should he try to clutch at common human happiness, he will find that he might as well pour wine into his hands. The sorcerer's art will allow him to drink no more of life's wine than the few drops he can lick from his fingers.

The Pseudo-Iamblichus Scroll

Without any effort on Evandar's part, spring came to his country. Formerly, a hundred years and more could pass in the lands of men and elves while a single afternoon crept by in his. Now spring burst upon him while he mourned his people, so quickly that he knew it must have fallen upon the physical world as well. He stood on the hilltop and watched, dazed, as the snow melted into rivulets that poured into the river below. Spring, however, came only where it wanted to come. He picked his way downhill across brown mud, flecked here and there with dead stone. Once the river had run silver, but now it oozed, a dark grey like lead. The water reeds along its banks stood dead and brown.

For a moment Evandar stared into the river, which in the past had shown him many a vision. He saw nothing. He turned away and set off upstream, walking slowly, listening for voices in the wind – none. As he walked, the dead terrain around him changed. First he spotted a few blades of grass, then some small saplings, more grass, and then trees until he found himself far from the river in a meadow of spring grass, dotted with white flowers. Still, even in the midst of this burgeoning life, he heard no voices, and he saw no visions.

For the seeming-space of an afternoon, Evandar walked his lands to see how they'd changed. All the images of cities had vanished, and the rose gardens, the arbours, the cloth of gold pavilions where his people had once feasted had disappeared with them. Much to his surprise the green hills remained, dusted with yellow buttercups and little daisies now instead of roses. Tall trees stood unpruned; straggly saplings grew amid tangles of weeds and shrubs. Now and then a flock of birds flew overhead, and he could hear bees among the clover. Once, when he passed a tangle of hazel withes near a stream, he saw a little pointed face and two bright eyes. He took a step closer, but with a noiseless slide into the stream, the water rat swam away. Above in the tangled thicket, a red squirrel chattered at him.

Where did they come from? he wondered. I never created any such. He found himself remembering other bestial faces, these snarling and dark, in the strange country just beyond his lands, where the old man sat endlessly peeling his apple and bringing life down from wherever it was that life sprang. The old man had redeemed those creatures, perhaps, and sent them off to live in the green fields.

'The wild things will endure,' Evandar said aloud. 'That soothes my heart.'

Perhaps the land had lost its voice simply because it had returned to the wild. Yet as he walked in the eerie silence another reason suggested itself to him. Perhaps he had no future for the omens to reveal. Perhaps it was time for him to die, whatever 'die' might mean to such as him. He found himself thinking of Jill, who had spent her life like a coin to ransom Cengarn from Alshandra. Must he do the same to stop his brother's meddling?

'I'd best make some other provision for Salamander, then, if that's true.'

On a sunny hilltop Evandar stood waiting. No voice spoke, no answer came to him from the future or from the green hills.

'Fade away and die!' He shouted it out. 'Is that what will happen to me? Fade away and die?'

Not even an echo floated back on the wind. Finally with a shrug he turned away. So this, then, was what fear felt like, a bitterness in the mouth, an empty coldness at the heart.

In winter, dragons tend to their dreams. Even on short summer nights dragons are great dreamers; when they wake they consider their dreams well, then lay them up in memory for the cold time. Once winter comes they can brood them properly, as they drowse deep within their fire mountain lairs. The old dreams hatch new ones, long elaborate visions and tales that often take several nights to complete.

All that winter Arzosah found the man she called Rori Dragonfriend woven into her dreams. At times she would relive the moment when he'd held up the rose ring and enslaved her with name-dweomer. From those dreams she woke shivering and hissing in fear. She would leap to her feet and stretch out her wings for flight until she remembered that she was awake and safe in her beloved home. She would lie back down on the stone ledge, and from her perch, high up in an enormous cavern, she would contemplate the steam rising from the hot springs far below until at last she felt soothed, ready to sleep and dream again.

At other times she would dream of the battles of the summer past: the stench of blood like perfume and Rori's berserk laughter ringing over the slaughter. From those she woke smug, yawning and stretching her claws at the memory of dead horses. The remembered taste of those feasts would drive her out of her lair if the day were clear. She would soar over the snow, seeking out the valleys where she could find deer. In the deep snow they floundered, easy prey. Once she'd gorged herself, she'd return to her home mountain and the warmth of its gutted interior.

Slowly the year turned toward spring. When Arzosah flew she felt warmer air and saw the snow growing thin. Eventually the rains came, and the world turned to brown mud. On a day when the trees were putting out buds, Arzosah returned from one of these hunts to find an unwelcome guest. She entered her home cavern through a fissure high up on the side of a cliff, and as soon as she started crawling down the tunnel inside, she smelled dweomer. To her all things magical smelled like the air immediately after a strike of lightning – sharp and clean, tingling with power – a scent so strong that it could mask the accustomed stink of brimstone and old burning within the cavern. She backed out of the tunnel, clung precariously to the little ledge below the fissure, and considered what to do.

The dweomer smell attracted her, but she remembered how she'd been mastered by dweomer in this very cavern.

'Once of that is enough,' Arzosah muttered – in Elvish. With a possible enemy so near, she refused to speak in Dragonish, a tongue the great wyrms keep to themselves.

She let go of the ledge and spread her wings with a slap of the air that boomed like a drum, but rather than fly away, she glided down to the valley below to perch on an outcrop of grey granite. Arzosah folded her wings, sat back on her haunches, and contemplated the mouth of the fissure, far above her.

'A clumsy trick like that isn't going to fool me.' His voice came first; then Evandar materialized in front of her. 'I heard you fly away.'

Hissing like a thousand cats the dragon leapt to her feet. Evandar laughed and stepped back, raising one hand as if to ask for peace. He had taken the form of an elf, dressed in a green tunic and tight deerskin trousers, but to her dragonish sight his body wavered and glowed. He smelled so strongly of dweomer that she longed to eat him. Unfortunately, he only looked like meat, she knew, rather than being made of it.

'So!' Arzosah snarled. 'I thought I smelled trouble, and trouble you are.'

'None other,' Evandar said, grinning. 'Arzosah Sothey Lorohaz, remember that I bound you by the power of your true name! I control and command you.'

'I keep trying to forget, but I can't, so there we are, you nasty bit of etheric slime! What do you want with me now?'

'A number of things. First of all, spring is here.'

'So it is, not that it's any of your doing.'

'You made Rhodry Maelwaedd a promise, that you'd return to him in the spring. Do you intend to keep it?'

'What's it to you if I do or not?'

'Ah, you don't, then. I thought not. You wyrms are faithless, aren't you? A promise is naught to you. Nasty and faithless both.'

Arzosah growled at him, but Evandar laughed, waggling a finger at her like a schoolmaster.

'I caught you out there, didn't I?' Evandar said.

'You did not! I never told you if I meant to go or not.'

'If you'd planned to keep that promise, you wouldn't have been so coy.'

'Coy?' Arzosah hissed again. 'How dare you call me coy? If you didn't have name-dweomer, I'd kill you.'

'But I do have it. The second thing I want is an errand. Rhodry Maelwaedd's brother lives in far-off Bardek, and he's gone mad. I promised I'd bring him home, but I find that I've got too many other important matters to attend to.'

'Hold your tongue! Do you expect me to fly across the Southern Sea and fetch him back?'

'I don't merely expect you to. I intend to demand it and bind you with your name to ensure you do it.'

'But I can't. The ocean's far too wide, days and days of flying. I can't fly forever without food and sleep. And how would I carry him home? In my claws? And what would he eat and drink, anyway?'

'Ah.' Evandar hesitated briefly. 'I hate to admit this, but you're right. It wasn't much of a plan, was it?'

'Why not send a ship for him? That's what ships are for, carrying things back and forth over the water. Dragons aren't.'

Evandar nodded, staring down at the ground with narrow eyes, as if he were thinking things through. Arzosah sat back down and considered just how much she hated him. He'd tricked her into revealing her name, he'd given the rose ring to Rhodry to enslave her, and now apparently he thought of her as some sort of servant, to run and fetch at his bidding.

'The third thing,' Evandar said at last. 'I have need of a vision, wyrm. It's one thing to say I'll return Salamander to Deverry. Where exactly in Deverry is another thing entirely. My heart is too troubled for me to see clearly.'

'Are you saying you want me to scry for you?'

'Exactly that.'

'No.'

'You can't say no. I have your name.'

Arzosah tipped back her head and roared her rage to the sky.

'Whine all you want,' Evandar said. 'But you'll do as I say.'

'Whine? Whine, is it?' Words failed her, and she snarled, tossing her head back and forth.

'The sooner you scry for me,' Evandar said, 'the sooner I'll leave you alone.'

'Oh very well, scry I will, but I've never met Rhodry's brother, so how can I scry him out?'

'It's the future I want to see. I know where he is now.'

'There's something else you need to know. You're a wretched nuisance. Come into my lair.'

Evandar vanished. Arzosah flew to the cliff-side, scrabbled her way into the fissure, and paused to breathe deeply. The dweomer-smell lay over everything, hot and exciting. She crawled down the tunnel and, when she emerged onto her sleeping ledge, she found Evandar there before her, sitting on the rock and staring down into the cavern. Far below them steam roiled and curled from the hot springs deep within the fire mountain's heart.

'How will you scry?' Evandar said.

'Into the mists.' Arzosah lay down on the ledge and tucked her front paws under her chest. 'That's the dragonish way. Tell me of this brother and his madness.'

While Evandar talked, Arzosah stared into the steaming mist below her. Shapes formed, mere illusions of the sort that anyone can see in clouds, then drifted into nothingness. In her mind she began to picture this Ebañy, began to see his wife as well and the children, playing among the tents of their travelling show. She saw in her mind Bardek, green with spring, and the white cities on their sea-cliffs. In the mists other images began to appear, fragments only and short-lived, until at last the scrying took her over.

'I see the ocean,' Arzosah began. 'The ocean pounding on

great rocks beneath a high slender tower. Night is falling. I see the tower again, and lo! a fire is burning at the top of the tower. Down below lies a dun, and beyond that, a little town.'

'Cannobaen!' Evandar whispered. 'Go on.'

'Strange ships are sailing into the harbour, ships with prows carved into the shape of dragons. On the deck stands a blond man with a child in his arms, a wild child with brown hair that's all matted and curly.'

'Salamander and his son Zandro. Go on.'

'There is naught more but mist.'

'Don't lie to me!'

'I'm not lying.' Arzosah swung her head his way and hissed. 'That's all I can see.'

'Well, it's enough,' Evandar said. 'Strange things, indeed, and things of great moment. To Cannobaen in ships in the elven fashion, is it? Strange and twice strange.'

Abruptly he was gone. She had no perception of his vanishing; he simply ceased to be there.

'Good riddance!' Arzosah muttered. 'The gall of him! Faithless and nasty, are we?'

She tipped back her head and roared out a dweomer command in the secret language of wyrmkind. Her answer came as a rumble and a hiss and spew of steam. Again she roared out the spell-word, and this time the mountain answered with a leap of fire deep in its heart. All round the peak, the land trembled in fear.

'I've looked everywhere,' Marka said. 'I can't find him.'

'I saw him just a little while ago,' Keeta said. 'He was walking toward Vinto's tent.'

'He's not there now. I've already asked Vinto.'

'Ye gods. He could have gone anywhere.'

The two women were standing at the edge of the public caravanserai on the outskirts of Myleton. Behind them the travelling show was still setting up camp. About half the tents stood, and all the animals had been watered. When she glanced back Marka saw that the acrobats were beginning to unload bedrolls and cushions from the wagons.

'Where are the children?' Keeta said.

'Kwinto's watching them,' Marka said. 'He hasn't seen his father since we pulled in, he told me.'

'He could have gone into the city to buy a permit.'

'Maybe. But something's wrong. I can just feel it. Come with me, will you?'

'Of course. Let's take the Myleton road. We've got a couple of hours till sunset.'

Side by side they walked down the archon's road. The winter rains had turned Bardek green, and on either side of the road, set back behind low stone walls, fields of hay bowed and rippled in the warm wind. In the ditches twixt wall and road wild flowers bloomed in scented tangles, red poppies, white alyssum, dark violets. It was in a ditch that they found their first hint of the trouble ahead: one of Ebañy's sandals, lying among the flowers. Keeta picked it up and inspected it.

'It's his, all right. Well, he can't have gone far, limping along on one shoe.'

The second sandal turned up about a hundred paces on, lying right out in the road. Keeta retrieved it, started to speak, then merely shrugged. They walked on in silence. Another hundred paces or so, and they saw something white flapping among the flowers: his linen tunic. Keeta wrapped his sandals in it, and they hurried on, walking faster. Ebañy's floppy-brimmed riding hat showed up next, lying off to one side of the road, and not too far on, the strip of white linen that he used for a breechclout.

'Ye gods!' Keeta snapped. 'He's wandering around stark naked.'

'It certainly looks that way.' Marka felt so suddenly, impossibly weary that sitting down in the middle of the road and weeping seemed like an excellent idea. Instead she took the bundle of clothes from Keeta. 'Maybe if you stood on top of the wall and looked around for him?'

'Good idea.'

Keeta climbed the nearest stretch of stone wall and shaded her eyes with her hand while Marka watched, hoping against hope that Ebañy hadn't got far. Keeta turned this way and that, peered into the distance on all sides.

'Hah!' Keeta pointed off into the hay field. 'Something's moving out there. Doesn't look like a dog.'

Keeta jumped down into the field. Marka trotted over and handed her the clothing. Scrambling over the wall, even with Keeta's help, took her a few moments, and she begrudged every one of them, fearing that Ebañy would run off again. The green hay, all sweet-scented and rustling, closed round her like water up to her shoulders. With her height, however, Keeta could easily see over it. She shaded her eyes with her hand and peered.

'Someone or some thing is rolling on the ground,' Keeta said. 'I hope he's not having a fit.'

'I hope this farmer doesn't see us trampling his hay.'

'We'll buy him off if he does. Don't worry about that now.'

With the hay murmuring around them they strode across the field. Marka could hear someone singing under his breath, harmonizing with the wind, it seemed at first. The song grew louder, burst into full voice – Ebañy, singing in the language of his far-off homeland. Marka wept in a brief scatter of tears. Keeta turned to her in concern.

'It's just relief,' Marka said, smiling. 'I was so afraid that he'd wandered into Myleton like this.'

The song stopped. Ebañy suddenly appeared, rising from the hay around him some twenty paces away, and waved.

'Well, there you are, my love,' he called out in Bardekian. 'I was just searching for prophecies.'

Marka nearly wept again, but she managed to force out a smile. Keeta sighed and shook her head.

'I see you've found my clothes,' Ebañy went on. 'I thought

I'd become a wild man and go live in the forest. They live among the trees like beasts, you see, and the lesser gods come to them and give them prophecies.'

'There isn't any forest near here.'

'I know.' Ebañy smiled brightly. 'That's what made me give up the idea.'

They got him dressed and led him back to the road, but getting him back to the camp took a long struggle. He would walk a few steps, then fancy himself a wild man again and try to disrobe. Each time Marka would have to talk him out of it while Keeta held him pinned in a strong grip. By the time they returned to the caravanserai, the sun was setting, gilding the tents. Cooking fires bloomed among them, and the rich smell of grilling meat and griddle breads baking beckoned them home.

'I'm hungry,' Ebañy said. 'Do wild men eat roast meats?'

'Of course they do,' Keeta said firmly. 'Look, there are your children.'

At the sight of them, running to meet him, Ebañy burst out sobbing.

'I'd forgotten,' he said between sobs. 'I can't leave for the forest.'

'No, you can't,' Marka said, and she hoped she sounded cheerful and strong. 'We love you, and we'd miss you.'

After he'd eaten, Ebañy seemed to return to himself. He discussed the coming show with Vinto, told the children several stories, and laughed and joked with other members of the troupe. But that night Marka was afraid to sleep. She kept waking to make sure that he hadn't run off into the night. Will we have to chain him? she thought. You hear of that happening to madmen. Toward dawn she lay awake for a long time, thinking about Evandar and the help he'd promised, months ago now. Would he return soon, now that it was spring? Perhaps his ship had never reached Deverry, what with the autumn storms and the pirates. Perhaps the healer he'd told them about wouldn't return with him.

There were too many doubts for her to have much hope. As she lay exhausted on their blankets, watching the canvas walls of the tent brighten with the dawn, she found herself thinking a traitor's thought, that perhaps if he should run off somewhere it would be better for them all.

Up by the plaza on Citadel stood a public well, which drew water from a spring sweeter than the lake. Every morning Niffa would carry two wooden buckets on a shoulder yoke to fetch the day's drinking water. With the coming spring in the air, the task gave her a certain domestic pleasure. The sky itself seemed lighter, as if the gods had spread a prettier blue upon it. From the plaza she could look down to the town and beyond the walls to the surrounding meadows, dark brown with mud, streaked here and there with dirty snow. At the well itself stood other townsfolk, gossiping while they waited their turn to draw.

On a day that was undeniably warm, Niffa trudged up the hill to the well. Councilman Verrarc's blond young servant, Harl, had just filled his buckets. He saw Niffa, smiled, and hurried over. 'Good morrow,' Harl said. 'And how do you and yours fare?'

'Well enough, my thanks,' Niffa said. 'And your household?'

'Fine, fine, though the master's woman still be sickly, like.'

One of the women at the well screamed. Niffa spun around just as two others began to shriek and point at the sky. Niffa looked up and saw a dragon flying toward Citadel.

In the pale sun the beast glittered like obsidian. Huge – Niffa could not judge how large, but at least the size of two wagons, and the wings spread out in vast sweeps of greenish black. She could hear each wingstroke beat the air like the pound of an enormous heart as the dragon dropped down, swooping in a soundless glide, then banking one wing to circle lazily over the plaza. Niffa could see the enormous copper-tinged head bend down as if it were looking them over. She nearly screamed herself, thinking it would land.

The dragon spoke in a huge rumble, but although Niffa could tell the sounds meant words, it spoke a language she didn't know. All she could think to do was raise a hand in the sign of peace. With one beat of its wings, it sheared off and flew, gaining height as it headed south and east.

Everyone at the well started gabbling at once. Niffa walked a few steps away and watched the dragon until it turned into a tiny speck against the morning.

'Niffa, Niffa!' Harl came running. 'What did the beast say?'

'I know not. Here! Think you I ken Dragonish or suchlike?'

'Well, truly, not.' Harl had the grace to look embarrassed. 'It be only that you – well, you do see things most folk can't see, and so mayhap, I thought, you heard hidden things as well.'

She realized that the other women had walked over to stand behind him. They were nodding their agreement.

'The only one round here who do ken secrets be Werda,' Niffa said. 'And I'd best be telling her about this wyrm.'

Werda, however, had heard and seen the beast herself. Wrapped in her white cloak she came striding across the plaza. When everyone started talking at once, she hushed them and beckoned to Niffa.

'Come walk with me a bit,' Werda said. 'I saw the beast speak to you.'

Niffa left her buckets at the well. As she and the Spirit Talker walked away, she looked back to see the townsfolk gathering to discuss the omen among themselves. At the edge of the plaza, where worked stone met the huge boulders of the hill, Werda stopped and turned to look out across the broad view. Citadel fell away before them down to the ring of Cerr Cawnen. Beyond the city walls the earth stretched out dark to the horizon.

'So,' Werda said. 'The dragon did mark you out, did she?'

'I know not. She spoke, but in some strange tongue, although I did think I heard our Jahdo's name.'

'Ah.' Werda turned and leaned against a boulder before she

continued. 'The lore of the gods do I ken, where each lives and what does please them. The witchlore I ken not. It be your road, not mine, young Niffa. I wonder if the spirits did take your Demet because you did love him so, more than you do love them and their lore.'

'Then I hate them all! They be fools, if they do think I'd follow those that did slay my love.'

'Nah, nah, nah!' Werda raised a hand in warding. 'Never curse the spirits! They'll be taking yet another fee, if you should spurn them. Wish you to lose your mother, say, or have some other death come upon you?' She lowered her hand. 'This be a harsh saying, I do know that. But the witch road is a long one and harsh as well.'

'And why should I walk it then?'

Werda smiled.

'Because the spirits will never let you rest till you do take up your Wyrd. When I was a lass, I wanted naught more than a farm and a good man to work it with me. I dreamt of that farm and what I would plant in its fields. But the gods called me to their lore. I did whine and beg and plead, but not for me the life of a farm wife with her butter and eggs. Not for me the daughters and strong sons I did covet. One winter I took ill with fever, and in the fever visions came to me. I could serve the gods or I could die. Those two were the only roads they would let me walk. And so I chose life and the lore. And here be a secret: once I did set my feet upon the road, then did I feel a joy beyond any the farm would have brought me.'

Niffa felt her eyes fill with tears.

'Why do you weep?' Werda said.

'Because in my soul I know the truth of what you say.' Niffa rubbed an angry hand across her eyes. 'But if you ken not the lore, where shall I learn it? It aches my heart to think of leaving my home and kin.'

'Where indeed? I know not. I think me though that if you do vigil, the gods will show you where you may go to set your feet upon the road.'

Niffa went back to the well to find that Harl had drawn water for her. She murmured a thanks, picked up her buckets, and started for home. The silver lady in my dreams, she was thinking. She must ken the witchlore, or she'd not be speaking to me there. At that moment she saw her life open out as if like the dragon she'd taken wing to see the future spread out below, a vast landscape wreathed in mist.

APPENDICES

A NOTE ON DEVERRY DATING

Deverry dating begins at the founding of the Holy City, approximately year 76 C.E. The reader should remember that the old Celtic New Year falls on the day we call November 1, so that winter is the first season of a new year.

A NOTE ON THE PRONUNCIATION OF DEVERRY WORDS

The language spoken in Deverry is a member of the P-Celtic family. Although closely related to Welsh, Cornish, and Breton, it is by no means identical to any of these actual languages and should never be taken as such.

Vowels are divided by Deverry scribes into two classes: noble and common. Nobles have two pronunciations; commons, one.

A as in *father* when long; a shorter version of the same sound, as in *far*, when short.

O as in *bone* when long; as in *pot* when short.

W as the *oo* in spook when long; as in *roof* when short.

Y as the *i* in *machine* when long; as the *e* in *butter* when short.

E as in *pen*.

I as in *pin*.

U as in *pun*.

Vowels are generally long in stressed syllables; short in unstressed. Y is the primary exception to this rule. When it appears as the last letter of a word, it is always long whether that syllable is stressed or not.

Diphthongs generally have one consistent pronunciation.

AE as the *a* in *mane*.

AI as in *aisle*.

AU as the *ow* in *how*.

EO as a combination of *eh* and *oh*.

EW as in Welsh, a combination of *eh* and *oo*.

IE as in *pier*.

OE as the *oy* in *boy*.

UI as the North Welsh *wy*, a combination of *oo* and *ee*.

Note that OI is never a diphthong, but is two distinct sounds, as in *carnoic*, (KAR-noh-ik).

Consonants are mostly the same as in English, with these exceptions:

C is always hard as in *cat*.

G is always hard as in *get*.

DD is the voiced *th* as in *thin* or *breathe*, but the voicing is more pronounced than in English. It is opposed to TH, the unvoiced sound as in *th* or *breath*. (This is the sound that the Greeks called the Celtic tau.)

R is heavily rolled.

RH is a voiceless R, approximately pronounced as if it were spelled *hr* in Deverry proper. In Eldidd, the sound is fast becoming indistinguishable from R.

DW, GW, and TW are single sounds, as in *Gwendolen* or *twit*.

Y is never a consonant.

I before a vowel at the beginning of a word is consonantal, as it is in the plural ending *-ion*, pronounced *yawn*.

Doubled consonants are both sounded clearly, unlike in English. Note, however, that DD is a *single letter*, not a doubled consonant.

Accent is generally on the penultimate syllable, but compound words and place names are often an exception to this rule.

I have used this system of transcription for the Bardekian and Elvish alphabets as well as the Deverrian, which is, of course, based on the Greek rather than the Roman model. On the whole, it works quite well for the Bardekian, at least. As for Elvish, in a work of this sort it would be ridiculous to resort to the elaborate apparatus by which scholars attempt to transcribe that most subtle and nuanced of tongues. Since the human ear cannot even distinguish between such sound-pairings as B> and <B, I see no reason to confuse the human eye with them. I do owe many thanks to the various elven native speakers who have suggested which consonant to choose in confusing cases and who have laboured, alas often in vain, to refine my ear to the elven vowel system.

GLOSSARY

Aber (Deverrian) A river mouth, an estuary.

Astral The plane of existence directly "above" or "within" the etheric (q.v.). In other systems of magic, often referred to as the Akashic Record or the Treasure House of Images.

Aura The field of electromagnetic energy that permeates and emanates from every living being.

Aver (Dev.) A river.

Bel (Dev.) The chief god of the Deverry pantheon.

Blue Light Another name for the etheric plane (q.v.).

Body of Light An artificial thought-form (q.v.) constructed by a dweomer-master to allow him or her to travel through the inner planes of existence.

Brigga (Dev.) Loose wool trousers worn by men and boys.

Broch (Dev.) A squat tower in which people live. Originally, in the homeland, these towers had one big fireplace in the centre of the ground floor and a number of booths or tiny roomlets up the sides, but by the time of our narrative, this ancient style has given way to regular floors with hearths and chimneys on either side of the structure.

Cadvridoc (Dev.) A war leader. Not a general in the modern sense, the cadvridoc is supposed to take the advice and counsel of the noble-born lords under him, but his is the right of final decision.

Captain (trans. of the Dev. *pendaely.*) The second in command, after the lord himself, of a noble's warband. An interesting point is that the word *taely* (the root or unmutated form of *-daely*,) can mean either a warband or a family depending on context.

Dun (Dev.) A fort.

Dweomer (trans. of Dev. *dwunddaevad*.) In its strict sense, a system of magic aimed at personal enlightenment through harmony with the natural universe in all its planes and manifestations; in the popular sense, magic, sorcery.

Ensorcel To produce an effect similar to hypnosis by direct manipulation of a person's aura. (True hypnosis manipulates the victim's consciousness only and thus is more easily resisted.)

Etheric The plane of existence directly "above" the physical. With its magnetic substance and currents, it holds physical matter in an invisible matrix and is the true source of what we call "life".

Etheric Double The true being of a person, the electromagnetic structure that holds the body together and that is the actual seat of consciousness.

Geis A taboo, usually a prohibition against doing something. Breaking geis results in ritual pollution and the disfavour if not active enmity of the gods. In societies that truly believe in geis, a person who breaks it usually dies fairly quickly, either of morbid depression or some unconsciously self-inflicted "accident", unless he or she makes ritual amends.

Great Ones Spirits, once human but now disincarnate, who exist on an unknowably high plane of existence and who have dedicated themselves to the eventual enlightenment of all sentient beings. They are also known to the Buddhists as Boddhisattvas.

Gwerbret (Dev. The name derives from the Gaulish *vergobretes*.) The highest rank of nobility below the royal family itself. Gwerbrets (Dev. *gwerbretion*) function as the chief magistrates of their regions, and even kings hesitate to override their decisions because of their many ancient prerogatives.

Hiraedd (Dev.) A peculiarly Celtic form of depression, marked by a deep, tormented longing for some unobtainable things; also and in particular, homesickness to the third power.

Javelin (trans. of Dev. *picecl*.) Since the weapon in question is only about three feet long, another possible translation would be "war dart". The reader should not think of it as a proper spear or as one of those enormous javelins used in the modern Olympic Games.

Lwdd (Dev.) A blood-price; differs from wergild in that the amount of lwdd is negotiable in some circumstances, rather than being irrevocably set by law.

Malover (Dev.) A full, formal court of law with both a priest of Bel and either a gwerbret or a tieryn in attendance.

Mor (Dev.) A sea, ocean.

Pecl (Dev.) Far, distant.

Rhan (Dev.) A political unit of land; thus, gwerbretrhyn, tierynrhyn, the area under the control of a given gwerbret or tieryn. The size of the various rhans (Dev. rhannau) varies widely, depending on the vagaries of inheritance and the fortunes of war rather than some legal definition.

Scrying The art of seeing distant people and places by magic.

Sigil An abstract magical figure, usually representing either a particular spirit or a particular kind of energy or power. These figures, which look a lot like geometrical scribbles, are derived by various rules from secret magical diagrams.

Taer (Dev.) Land, country.

Tieryn (Dev.) An intermediate rank of the noble-born, below a gwerbret but above an ordinary lord (Dev. *arcloedd*).

Wyrd (trans. of Dev. *tingedd*.) Fate, destiny; the inescapable problems carried over from a sentient being's last incarnation.

Ynis (Dev.) An island.